FIRST WALTZ

"My dance, I believe." Montagu's tone was warmer than she had heard it before.

"It is." Eleanor placed her hand on his arm.

"I have been waiting all evening for this." The look in his blue-green eyes caused her breath to stop.

"As have I. My partner for an earlier waltz was not nearly as skilled as you are."

The frissons that started when he placed his hand on her waist were even stronger than before. That was a surprise. She had come to the conclusion that the only reason she had had a reaction to Montagu before was because it was her first waltz with someone she had not known most of her life. The first waltz with the other gentleman had caused no feelings at all, except the desire to take care of her toes. Obviously, that was not the case. Carefully, she touched his waist, and almost jerked her hand back.

"Is anything wrong?" He appeared concerned.

"Nothing." Steeling herself, she took his hand. It was firm and warm.

John gazed at Eleanor's tightly pressed together lips quiver in suppressed mirth and wanted to kiss them. He had not particularly wanted a love match. Yet, he had the distinct feeling that if he wanted Eleanor, that was what it would take. . . .

Books by Ella Quinn

The Marriage Game
THE SEDUCTION OF LADY PHOEBE
THE SECRET LIFE OF MISS ANNA MARSH
THE TEMPTATION OF LADY SERENA
DESIRING LADY CARO
ENTICING MISS EUGENIE VILLARET
A KISS FOR LADY MARY
LADY BERESFORD'S LOVER
MISS FEATHERTON'S CHRISTMAS PRINCE
THE MARQUIS SHE'S BEEN WAITING FOR

The Worthingtons
THREE WEEKS TO WED
WHEN A MARQUIS CHOOSES A BRIDE
IT STARTED WITH A KISS
THE MARQUIS AND I
YOU NEVER FORGET YOUR FIRST EARL
BELIEVE IN ME
THE MARRIAGE LIST

The Lords of London
THE MOST ELIGIBLE LORD IN LONDON
THE MOST ELIGIBLE VISCOUNT IN LONDON
THE MOST ELIGIBLE BRIDE IN LONDON

Novellas
MADELEINE'S CHRISTMAS WISH
THE SECOND TIME AROUND
I'LL ALWAYS LOVE YOU
THE EARL'S CHRISTMAS BRIDE

Published by Kensington Publishing Corp.

The MARRIAGE LIST

THE WORTHINGTONS

ELLA QUINN

ZEBRA BOOKS
Kensington Publishing Corp.
www.kensingtonbooks.com

ZEBRA BOOKS are published by

Kensington Publishing Corp.
119 West 40th Street
New York, NY 10018

All Kensington titles, imprints, and distributed lines are available at special quantity discounts for bulk purchases for sales promotion, premiums, fund-raising, and educational or institutional use.

Special book excerpts or customized printings can also be created to fit specific needs. For details, write or phone the office of the Kensington Sales Manager: Kensington Publishing Corp., 119 West 40th Street, New York, NY 10018. Attn. Sales Department. Phone: 1-800-221-2647.

ZEBRA BOOKS and the Z logo Reg. U.S. Pat. & TM Off.

First Printing: January 2023
ISBN-13: 978-1-4201-5446-7
ISBN-13: 978-1-4201-5447-4 (eBook)

10 9 8 7 6 5 4 3 2 1

Printed in the United States of America

*This book is for everyone trying to find
the perfect match for them.
Albeit the list Eleanor, Alice, and Madeline wrote
is a bit old-fashioned for today, the concept is
sound. When we were dating some forty years ago,
I told my husband any man I married had to be
able to cook, clean, and take care of babies.
The baby is grown, but he still cooks and cleans.*

ACKNOWLEDGMENTS

Anyone involved in the publishing process knows it takes a team effort to get a book from that inkling in an author's head to the printed or digital page. I'd like to thank my beta readers, Jenna, Doreen, and Margaret for their comments and suggestions. To my agents, Deidre Knight and Janna Bonikowski, and my wonderful editor, John Scognamilgio, for helping me think through parts of this book and for their advice.

Again for John, who loves my books enough to contract them for Kensington. To the Kensington team, Vida, Jane, and Lauren, who do such a tremendous job of publicity. And to the copyeditors who find all the niggling mistakes I never am able to see.

As sad as it was, I had to add two new Great Danes due to the death of Duke and Daisy. As they always do, members of my readers' group, The Worthingtons, came through. Thank you to Michael Ransom and Chasity Parrish, who thought of the perfect Zeus and Posey respectively.

Last, but certainly not least, to my readers. Without you, none of this would be worth it. Thank you from the bottom of my heart for loving my stories!

I love to hear from my readers, so feel free to contact me on my website or on Facebook if you have questions. Those links and my newsletter link can be found at:

www.ellaquinnauthor.com.

On to the next book!

Ella

CHAPTER ONE

February 1821, near Birmingham, England

Lady Eleanor Carpenter gazed out at the ice-covered hedgerows and pulled her fur-lined cloak tighter around herself. The day was bright but bitterly cold. She was returning from a visit to her elder sister, Charlotte, the Marchioness of Kenilworth. Across from Eleanor, Mrs. Parks was knitting. One of the Kenilworth neighbors, she had been glad of the invitation to accompany Charlotte on her journey back to Worthington Place, her home.

Eleanor's view of the hedgerows was suddenly interrupted. She pounded on the roof. "Stop the coach!"

"My lady, what is it?" Mrs. Parks's voice was a mix of worry and astonishment.

Eleanor glanced over her shoulder as she opened the door. "Small children on the side of the road. Here in the middle of nowhere."

Families of all sorts were experiencing horrible conditions, but who would leave children on the side of a road?

"You cannot be meaning to—"

The carriage had barely stopped when Eleanor jumped down. She strode to the children, who were standing in front a woman lying on the ground. "Good day." She lowered herself so she was at eye level with them. "Is there anything I can do to help?"

A boy, who appeared to be the oldest because of his height, shook his head. But one of the two girls gazed up at her as if she had seen a savior and nodded. "Our mum can't walk."

In fact, the woman looked as if she might be dead. "I can take care of her. If you tell me where you live, I will take you there."

"Got no home," the lad muttered. "Mum said we had to go."

"Your da?" Eleanor thought she knew the answer but had to ask.

Two fat tears rolled down the little girl's thin face. "They kilt him."

She would have to discover the whole story later. Right now, she needed to get them all warm. "In that case, there is really only one thing to do. You and your mother will come with me." She signaled to her footman. "Turner, please carry their mother to the second coach. I'll bring the children."

"Is she still alive?" He looked at the body on the ground and whispered.

"I hope so." She slid a quick glance at the woman. "We will find out soon."

The mother lay limp in his arms and made no sound as he carried her to the carriage.

"Lady Eleanor." Mrs. Parks stood in the carriage doorway. "I must protest. Your sister and Lord Kenilworth would never forgive me if something happened to you."

How could anyone not help these people? Eleanor gave her companion what she hoped was a reassuring smile. She was certain everyone in her family would agree with her decision. "Everything is perfectly fine. We will be on our way momentarily."

As she approached the second coach, the door opened. "Jobert, I need your help. Turner is bringing their mother. She is unconscious."

"Yes, my lady." The maid began clearing off the backward-facing seat. "He can put her here. The seat is large enough to hold the children too."

Eleanor became increasingly worried about the mother. Her skin was almost blue. "Get her warm. If I am not mistaken, we will come to the Wheelwright Inn in about an hour, maybe a little longer. We can order a hot bath for her and fetch a doctor."

"That's a good idea, my lady." Jobert helped settle the children with blankets as Turner handed them up.

Eleanor waited until they were ready before going back to her carriage. Thank God Matt, her brother-in-law, had insisted she take the large servants' coach. The second footman assisted her into her carriage.

"You ready to go, my lady?" the head coachman asked.

"I am. We will need to stop at an inn. I think the woman might require a doctor."

"Leave it to me, my lady." A second later, they were moving again.

Mrs. Parks wrung her hands. "I do not know what your sister and his lordship will say—"

There were times when Eleanor forgot that not all people were interested in helping others. She stifled the urge to lecture the older lady. "Mrs. Parks, I appreciate your concern. But I know they will say that I did the right thing." Eleanor picked up the book she had brought with her. "We will be able to refresh the bricks when we stop."

An hour or so later, she was still staring at the book, but hadn't read a page. The only thing she could think about was the plight of the poor mother and her children. What if she had not happened by? Would they have been left to freeze to death? Eleanor glanced surreptitiously at Mrs. Parks. She would not have stopped. Even her maid had sniffed and failed to assist Turner and Jobert in making their guests comfortable. And what had happened to them that they were out in this sort of weather? Eleanor closed her book. Surely they would be at the inn soon. She looked out the window. A light snow had started earlier, and now it was coming down much more heavily. That probably meant an unscheduled stop for the night. She blew out a breath. It would be fine. If she was capable enough to wed, she was capable enough to deal with this situation.

Sometime later, they drove into the well-kept yard, and Eleanor glanced out the window. The familiar sign in the shape of a carriage wheel swung from the arm of a large white inn.

One of the outriders rode up. "My lady, Lord Kenilworth made arrangements for us to stop here if we ran into weather. I'll go in and notify them we have arrived." He glanced at the other carriage. "What do you want done with the family?"

"Arrange a room, baths, and food for them. They will not want to be separated."

The outrider bowed. "Of course, my lady. I'll explain the matter to the landlord."

And be told no. "Get Jobert. Mrs. Parks"—Eleanor waited for the woman to acknowledge her—"you shall accompany me."

Her companion gathered her knitting into a bag. "I have been thinking about what you did, my lady. You were right. Your sister would have done the same thing."

Eleanor gave Mrs. Parks a genuine smile. "I know. But now we will probably have to deal with a recalcitrant innkeeper."

"I have no doubt in my mind that you are equal to the task." Mrs. Parks smiled back.

"Ah, here is my maid and footman. Let us make an impression." Eleanor gathered her dignity around her like a shield as Turner helped her down the coach stairs. Another footman assisted her companion, and the head outrider ran to the door and opened it, bowing as she strode in.

A tall, thin man of middling years with a shock of brown hair mixed with gray waiting next to a desk bowed.

Behind her, Turner said, "Lady Eleanor Carpenter. Sister to the Marquis and Marchioness of Kenilworth."

"Name's Claiborne." The landlord bowed again. "I received a letter from his lordship asking us to set aside rooms for you."

She inclined her head and gave him a polite smile. "We will require one additional room for a family. A mother and three children had some trouble, and I have taken them up."

A shadow passed across the landlord's face as he looked in the direction of what must have been the common room, and for a moment he hesitated. "Yes, my lady."

"Good." Resisting the pull to glance in the same direction, she raised her chin slightly. "They will require baths, meals, and a doctor. Mr. Whitmer"—she indicated the outrider with her hand—"will assist you if need be."

"Thank you, my lady." Mr. Claiborne gathered several keys and slid a look toward the common room again. "If you will follow me, I'll take you to your chambers."

"Turner," Eleanor whispered. "Something is wrong. Get the family and take them around to the back."

"Straightaway, my lady."

"I'll have Whitmer wait for you."

Turner nodded and backed toward the main door. Eleanor's brain whirled with the possibility of danger. She had heard about the things that had happened to her sisters and Dotty, but Eleanor had never really expected to experience them herself. She followed the landlord up the stairs. The first thing she must do is assess from where the problem was coming. That should be relatively simple. Someone was obviously in the common room looking for a family. He was not the woman's husband. Who was he, and why did he pose a danger? Her footman would be happy to attempt to find out, but Whitmer wasn't wearing livery and Turner was.

The landlord showed Eleanor her rooms. Jobert, who was carrying a satchel, immediately entered.

"I have beds for your coachmen over the stables," Mr. Claiborne said.

Eleanor nodded. "Our ladies' maids will sleep in Mrs. Parks's and my respective chambers. I trust you have trundle beds for them?"

"We do, my lady." Between their rooms and the backstairs, he unlocked the door to another chamber. "Here is one big enough for a family."

Eleanor surveyed the area. There was one very large bed, a table, and a few chairs. "This should do. I would like a hot bath delivered as soon as possible. I want my footman on this floor if you have an empty chamber."

"Right next door. I'll have to get the key." Obviously, the man was not happy with her request, yet he dare not refuse. Kenilworth's family gave the inn a fair amount of custom.

"Thank you." Eleanor gave him a gracious smile. Once the landlord left, she turned to Whitmer. "Turner should be at the back door with the family. Please show him to this chamber. After that, could you see who is in the common room?"

"I'd like the other outriders to go with me," Whitmer said. "I saw the look on the landlord's face too."

"Very well." This might be a more interesting night than she had thought it would be.

Eleanor changed from her traveling gown to a walking gown. While she had been washing her face and hands, she had heard the children speaking softly. "Jobert, I am going to assist our guests. I should like you to come with me."

"Of course, my lady." The maid collected some scented soap and two of the towels they traveled with, as well as one of her nightgowns. "I'm glad I packed extras."

Eleanor did not know how her maid felt about giving a nightgown to a stranger. "You may give her one of mine, if you like."

"No, my lady. I'll wager she will feel more comfortable in this one."

Because it did not have all the ruffles? "I will replace it."

"As you wish, my lady." Jobert bustled out of the room, and Eleanor followed.

A fire had been lit in the chamber, warming it nicely. The children were huddled around their mother. Jobert was assisting the barely awake woman when a knock came on the door.

"The bath you ordered," a maid said.

Eleanor opened the door to find two young men with the servant. "Please, enter."

The woman bobbed a curtsey, and the men bowed. They brought in a bathtub and started filling it.

Once they left, Eleanor helped Jobert get the mother into the tub, then turned to the children. They were all painfully thin. "I am Lady Eleanor Carpenter. May I know your names and that of your mother?"

The boy gazed up at her. "I'm Billy. This here"—he put his hand on his taller sister's shoulder—"is Sally, and the youngest is Lizzy." He took a breath. "Our ma is Lottie."

Short for Charlotte. Eleanor's sister's name. "What is your surname?"

"Ward."

Eleanor took his rather grimy hand in hers and shook it. "It is nice to meet you." A moan sounded from the tub, and the children turned as one. "I hope that means your mother is coming around."

"We do too," Sally said.

Once Mrs. Ward had finished bathing, she was dressed in the nightgown and put in bed. A knock sounded on the door. "Who is it?"

"Mr. Patterson. I'm the doctor."

She opened the door and was pleased to see that he was relatively young. Probably not much older than Matt. "Please come in. I sent for you out of caution. Mrs. Ward was half frozen when we found her and the children."

Eleanor stood back while he examined Mrs. Ward. A few minutes later, he glanced at the children. "When was the last time you ate?"

Billy shrugged. "Yesterday or the day 'afor?"

"Feed them all broth and bread. Nothing heavier until tomorrow. How long are you here?"

She looked at her maid, who went to the door. "We will go to my home in the morning."

"Try to keep Mrs. Ward as warm as possible. If you had not found her when you did, she could have died. You should also know that she is with child."

"I understand." A thought occurred to Eleanor. "You do not seem surprised by any of this."

The expression on his face was grim. "You might not have heard about the miner uprising in the area. Several men were killed, and their families as well as those of some of the organizers have been left to the mercy of the mine operators. I am not surprised. I wish there were more people like you to help them."

Con Kenilworth, her brother-in-law, got all the news-sheets; this could not have occurred more than a few days before. "Thank you for coming. How much do I owe you?" The doctor appeared uncomfortable with her question. "Perhaps you would like to send the bill to Worthington Place, near Kettering."

"Thank you," he said in a relieved tone. "I must admit, I have never taken money from a lady."

Jobert slipped back into the room, followed by a servant carrying a large tray with bowls of soup, bread, and a pot of butter. When the doctor left, she whispered, "Whitmer said to tell you there's a man in the common room looking for a family by the name of Ward. He said they belonged to him."

Belonged to him? "There is no slavery in England."

She nodded. "That's what he told the man. He said he and the other outriders will take turns sleeping by the door, inside if the family didn't mind."

"Does he think the landlord might tell this man they are here?" Jobert shook her head and shrugged. "Let the landlord know I will match what that scoundrel is paying him and tell Lord Kenilworth how he helped us."

A rare grin appeared on her face. "That should do it, my lady."

That was what Eleanor had thought. "I still think we should take precautions."

"Yes, my lady." The maid left the room again.

Eleanor turned to find the children eating greedily. "Slow down or you will be sick." All three looked mournfully at the bowls. "I did not say you could not eat your soup. You just need to eat more slowly."

"Yes, my lady," the two older ones chorused.

She waited until one of the outriders knocked and entered the room. "I shall see you later."

Mrs. Parks chose to dine in her room. Eleanor ate a very good dinner of roasted chicken with several removes of vegetables, followed by a slice of warm apple pie and a glass of claret. When tea was served, she asked that Whitmer join her.

He entered the parlor a few minutes later. "My lady."

"What is the name of the man who is searching for the family and how much danger are they in?"

"Dobbins, my lady. I'd say he's a bad one. I wouldn't want him to get his hands on them."

She sipped her tea as she considered what the outrider said. "We will leave as soon as it is light enough to travel."

"Yes, my lady. I'll tell the coachman."

The next morning, her party broke their fast while it was still dark. The children did not look as worried, and Mrs. Ward's cheeks were more pink than blue. Eleanor was glad her guest was on the mend. As she watched the family settle themselves in the coach, she felt the hairs rise on the back of her neck and turned around. A man bearing a strong resemblance to a weasel stood across the road, tapping his hand with the broad side of a knife.

That must be Dobbins.

Eleanor met his glare with one of her own until he glanced away. She would not allow Mrs. Ward or her children to be harmed. "Turner, tell everyone to keep an eye out." Climbing in the coach, she tapped on the roof. "Let us be off."

April 1821, Worth Market Town

"Eleanor." Her twin sister nudged her arm. "You will miss the entire service day dreaming."

"I was thinking about the day I found her." She glanced at the woman standing before the altar—Mrs. Ward, soon to be Mrs. Johnson—and another image came to Eleanor. One of a sharp-faced man tapping his knife on her hand, trying to stare her down. *Dobbins*. The children and their mother had been afraid of him. She gave herself a shake. All was well now.

"I knew that." Alice grinned. "I *am* your twin."

As much as they had included Madeline Vivers, their sister-in-law, in all things, the bond Eleanor shared with Alice was closer and more profound and probably always would be. "You are."

"Pay attention."

"I now pronounce you man and wife." The vicar beamed at the newly married couple. "May God bless you with a fruitful marriage."

Everyone in the church laughed at that. The new Mrs. Johnson was round with a child from her late husband, who had been murdered at Cinderloo in a mine protest. Mr. Johnson, a well-off gentleman farmer, took her arm with one hand and ruffled the hair on his new son's head with the other, smiling at the little girls.

"They will be happy." Eleanor sent up a prayer of thanks she had been there to help the family and that her family had supported her decision, and the housekeeper had played matchmaker for Mrs. Ward and Mr. Johnson.

CHAPTER TWO

It'd taken Dobbins weeks to find the woman, and he wasn't about to give her up. He'd left last night on the stagecoach and hired the wagon to carry her and her brats back. At least the oldest could be put to work. He drove into the yard of the Worthington Arms and came to a stop.

"Do ye want me to unhitch 'em?" a lad asked.

"Ain't plan'in on being here long." Dobbins climbed down from the wagon. "I'm look'in for a Mrs. Ward."

The boy looked away. "Don't think she'll see ye today. She's pretty busy."

He followed the lad's gaze, where a large group of people were standing outside of the church. Others were setting up tables on the green. "Got a something go'in on over there?"

"Ye might say that." The boy grinned. "She's get'in married. We're hav'in a cel-ebra-tion."

Married? What the hell was he supposed to do now? Ever since he'd seen her, he'd wanted her bad. He'd even made sure her husband was killed during the mine protest. Dobbins was sure he'd have his chance after that. She'd need someone to take care of her and her brats. Then she'd run off. He'd found her at an inn, but some young mort took her up. He'd finally found her again and now this.

"Lady Eleanor planned it all right and proper."

Who the hell was that? "Lady Eleanor?"

The boy pointed to a group of young morts across the street. "Lady Eleanor Carpenter. She's Lady Worthington's sister. They're go'in to Lundun soon."

Dobbins peered at the women. One of them turned and laughed. That was the same mort who'd got in his way before. He'd come all this way for noth'in.

Meddling bitch. If there was a way to get revenge on her without get'in hanged, he'd do it.

Just then the mort who'd spoiled his plans glanced over. Her eyes narrowed, and she signaled to a footman. He had to get out of there quick.

On the way back, he stopped at the inn he'd planned to take Mrs. Ward to. Noth'in fancy. He couldn't afford that, but it was clean and the ale was good.

Dobbins had just sat down to dinner when another man took the chair across from him. "I ain't seen you in a long time."

He smiled at his childhood friend and waved to the barkeep for another ale. "Mitchell, it's good to see you."

"You look like you got somethin' sour on your mind."

The pint of ale arrived, and Dobbins told his friend about the trouble he'd had with the Ward woman, leaving out how he helped her dead husband to his grave. "Just when ye think yer going to get what ye want, someone comes along and ruins it."

"Damn grandlings." Mitchell scowled. "Think they own the world. I'd stay around and help put a scare in her, but I got ta get back ta Lundun."

"Lundun?" Dobbins stared at his friend. "Is that where you're liv'in now?"

Mitchell puffed out his chest. "Fer the past two years. Got a good job there."

"That's where Lady Eleanor's go'in to be."

14   *Ella Quinn*

"Well, now." He took a long drink of ale. "It looks like I can help ye after all. Been in Lundun for a few years now and got no love for those aristocrats. We ought to have us our own revolution. Like the Frenchies did."

It was too much of a risk to do real damage to the woman, but . . . "Scare her real good. So she's always looking around her."

"Easy enough to do. It's a busy city. Anythin' can happen." His friend grinned. "It'll be a real pleasure helpin' ye get back at her."

Early morning, Hyde Park, London

Lady Eleanor Carpenter rode to the left of her sister, Madeline, with Alice on the right. Six years ago, Madeline's brother, the Earl of Worthington, married Eleanor and Alice's eldest sister, Lady Grace Carpenter, thus combining all eleven of the brothers and sisters into one family. Early on, all of them had decided they would refer to each other as brothers and sisters without regard to last names or blood ties. Without any discussion needed, Eleanor and Alice had decided they and Madeline would be triplets and included her in everything they did. Still, Eleanor's bond with her twin never lessened. Shortly thereafter, Charlotte, Dotty, her closest friend, and Louisa, Madeline's eldest sister, wed.

Breathing in the early spring air, Eleanor spotted bulbs sprouting from the edges of the Park. The forsythias had already bloomed, showing off their bright yellow flowers. "I cannot believe we are finally here."

"We have been here for years." Alice used the dry tone she had been perfecting in preparation for their Season, along with a regal demeanor. It was all a hum. Granted, they were not nearly as silly as they had been in the schoolroom, but none of them were grandes dames . . . yet.

Madeline rolled her eyes. "You know what she means. We are finally making our come outs. It seems as if we have been waiting for years."

"We have been waiting for years." Eleanor grinned. "So have Matt and Grace."

Alice gave her a doubtful look. "You mean they have been dreading it for years."

That was probably true. Eleanor met Alice's gaze and knew they were both thinking how things would change for them.

"At least we will not be without assistance," Madeline commented brightly. "For a very long time, Matt has been saying that it is 'all hands on deck.'"

She had mimicked his stern command so perfectly, Eleanor and Alice chuckled.

Indeed, the past week had seen a steady stream of their older married sisters and family friends arriving in Town. The only ones missing were their sister Augusta, now Lady Phineas Carter-Woods, her husband, Phinn, and their older brother Charlie, Earl of Stanwood.

Eleanor guided Adela, her Cleveland mare, to the right, knowing the other two horses would go the same way. They all had Cleveland mares from the same breeder who were trained together. It was not only the mares that had trained together. Eleanor and her sisters had, for the past six years, done everything from getting into trouble, to studying Latin, French, and German, to learning what they would need to know to be married ladies together. It was odd to think that after this Season they might not live in the same house any longer.

Madeline glanced around. "Why are we turning?"

"I am hungry." Eleanor's stomach growled, adding emphasis to her statement. "By the time we are home, we will have just enough time to wash before going to breakfast." She glanced quickly toward the gate and saw two men entering. For some reason, the one on the black horse caught her interest. "I wonder who they are."

"Where?" Madeline peered around Eleanor.

Alice leaned forward and looked as well.

"Do not stare. They could see us." When the other two straightened, Eleanor said, "There were two gentlemen riding just off to the side. They were galloping."

Madeline leaned forward to see. "What did they look like?"

"They both had reddish hair, but of different hues. Well dressed. One rode a black horse and the other horse was gray."

"I wonder if they are the type of gentlemen who will be introduced to us," Madeline mused.

"Only time will tell." Eleanor took the lead through the gate. They had discovered early on that once the carts, wagons, and drays were out, they could not ride three abreast.

They made their way toward Berkeley Square, where Worthington House was located. It seemed strange that by the end of the Season it would no longer be her London home. Nor would Worthington Place be her home. She had never thought it would bother her to leave home. None of their older sisters had minded having their own houses and estates. Still, the thoughts kept popping into her mind.

Suddenly, a boy ran out into the street, waving his hat and shouting at something. Eleanor's mare shied, but she was able to maintain control. What in God's name had that been about?

"Eleanor, are you all right?" Her twin was at her side, and the boy was nowhere to be seen.

"I am fine." A small tremor shook Eleanor's hands.

Alice's brows drew together and Eleanor shook her head. There was nothing they could do without questioning the lad.

Jemmy, her groom, rode up. "That weren't no accident, my lady. He was standing quiet until he saw you."

"Thank you, Jemmy. You have confirmed my thoughts. Come, Adela, let's go home."

The horses' hooves clattered to a stop outside the house, and their grooms came forward to take the mares.

"Good morning."

Eleanor glanced around to see their sisters, Charlotte, Marchioness of Kenilworth, and Louisa, Duchess of Rothwell, strolling toward the house holding their children's hands. Charlotte, Louisa, and Grace all had children in the five-year-old range.

"You must be joining us for breakfast." Eleanor leaned down for kisses from the children.

"We're going to spend the day with Gideon and Elizabeth," Constance, Charlotte's daughter, informed them.

"I still think they should be our cousins and not our aunt and uncle," Hugh, Constance's twin grumbled.

"You are just being silly," Louisa's daughter, Alexandria, opined. "It doesn't matter. We are all friends."

"I agree," Madeline said, taking Alexandria's hand. "Let us break our fast."

"I am not sure where Grace is," Eleanor said as the children raced up the stairs to the nursery. "Or the dogs."

"Her ladyship and the Danes are with the twins in the babies' room," Thorton, their brother's butler, informed them.

"We will go to her," Louisa said. "Alexandria loves Posy." Sadly, Duke and Daisy, their old Great Danes, had died three and two years ago respectively. Pets never lived long enough.

Now they had Zeus and Posy who were wonderful Danes with their own personalities.

"We will see you in the breakfast room." Eleanor followed Alice and Madeline to the back of the house, where they had separate bedchambers as well as their own parlor.

Jobert was waiting for her when she entered her room. "We are going to have a full table this morning."

"So Mrs. Thorton, the housekeeper, said." The maid had already laid out Eleanor's clothing for the morning.

She heard her dresser moving around the room as she washed off the horse smell. "It will be almost like when we first came to Town." Matt and Grace had met within days of them arriving and had married three weeks later. But even before they had wed, the whole family began breakfasting together. "I wish the boys and Augusta were here."

"Mrs. Thorton said Masters Walter and Phillip would be here for Easter."

"Augusta had better arrive soon," Eleanor muttered to herself. Her sister had been off traveling for the last three years but had promised to return for their Season.

Jobert helped Eleanor don a pretty sprigged muslin day gown in light yellow with purple flowers. Footsteps clattered down from the nursery floor. "I must hurry."

She met her sisters in the corridor. Suddenly, squeals of delight filtered up from below. "Something is going on."

Alice and Madeline nodded, as the three of them tried to walk sedately down the stairs, but they gave up at the first landing. Augusta, Phinn, and Charlie were being mobbed by everyone in the house who could walk on their own. Their sisters, Theo, now fourteen, and Mary, eleven, were taking turns hugging the new arrivals.

It was not until Mary broke from Charlie and embraced

a Great Dane that Eleanor realized it was there. "Whose dog is that and what is its name?"

"This is Minerva." Augusta pointed to a box on the floor. "Etienne is in there. We found them in Vienna. Minerva's original owner died, and Phinn bought Etienne for me."

"It was one of my attempts to get her to marry me." Phinn grinned.

"We are very happy to have you all back home." Grace exchanged a glance with Matt, who was smiling broadly.

"And in good time too," he added, leading them toward the breakfast room. "Will you stay with us, or have you made other arrangements?"

Augusta tucked her hand in the crook of her husband's arm. "Charlie has asked us to reside with him for the Season."

"How did you all manage to arrive at the same time?" Eleanor asked.

Charlie took his usual seat at the table on Grace's right. "I was in Spain when I ran into them on their way home. I decided it was time for me to return as well."

"What happened to your bear-leader?" Matt asked.

"He wanted to explore Europe for a while longer," Charlie said, accepting a cup of tea from Grace. "I was with family members, so we agreed to part ways."

"I am glad everything worked out so well." Eleanor accepted a baked egg from one of the footmen. "Albeit knowing Augusta, that does not surprise me at all."

"Oh, no. I cannot take credit." Augusta cut a piece of toast in half. "Cousin Prudence and Mr. Boman, Phinn's secretary, usually make the arrangements."

"They married not long after we did. They'll be visiting their families for a month or so," Phinn added.

Charlie took a slice of rare beef from a platter. "Speaking

of secretaries, I must find one. I must also take my seat in the Lords."

"Well, then." Matt nodded thoughtfully. "I am happy to help you with both things."

Augusta glanced at Eleanor, Madeline, and Alice. "I suppose your first event is Lady Bellamny's soirée for young ladies."

"Almost," Eleanor said. "Lady Exeter's sister-in-law, Penelope, is coming out as well. We have been invited to tea with her and two of her friends."

"I would like to accompany you." Augusta's eyes smiled over the rim of her teacup. "I would love to see Dorie Exeter again. We have written to each other over the years, and she knows I'll be here soon."

"Or now," Madeline commented.

Eleanor and Alice covered their mouths but could not stifle their laughter. Eleanor glanced at Charlotte and Louisa, who were silently laughing as well.

"Yes, now," Augusta agreed good-naturedly. "While we have you all here, Phinn and I have an announcement. We are expecting a baby in September."

The noise level rose as everyone congratulated their sister and brother-in-law. Alice caught Eleanor's eye and noticed Madeline was looking at her as well. They all knew that if they married this Season, it could soon be them having babies. But the first thing they had to do was find gentlemen they wished to wed.

CHAPTER THREE

John, the Marquis of Montagu, had noticed the three young ladies headed for the gate, and his gaze lingered on the one riding closest to him. She had a fine seat. Perhaps he should add that to his requirements for a wife. Since he'd arrived in Town, he had found himself distracted by the problems at home. Fortunately, it was still early, and the Season had not yet begun. He *had* to find a wife. His mother and sister would nag him until he did. And it was his duty. If only there was an easy way to go about it. Perhaps he'd meet some gentlemen who were looking for likely husbands for their daughters and John could arrange a match. Of course, the lady would have to agree. He didn't want a wife who didn't want him.

"We need to discover a way to meet them," Giffard, the recently elevated Marquis of St. Albans, heir to the Duke of Cleveland, said.

"If they're making their come outs, we will not be able to avoid it." John had already decided what he wanted in a spouse. Someone who was not interested in politics, or causes, or charities. A lady who would not bother him about what he should do. He'd be happy if she read nothing but novels and knew only polite conversation. In other words, someone the exact opposite of his mother and his twin sister. An arranged match was looking better and better.

"I need a lady who will be acceptable to my father." Giff scowled. "Excellent bloodlines are important. She must also be intelligent and not afraid to stand up to him. He detests cowards."

"I'm surprised he did not make a match for you." John's mother had tried that with his sister to no avail and had suggested she provide him a list of names. Of course Aurelia's godmother had helped her stand her ground until she'd found Lytton and married him. John had been lucky that the lady his father had wanted him to wed eloped with another man before they married. But that was four years ago. He'd been the head of the family for over three years, and it was time to take a wife.

Take a wife. It was his mantra until he completed his task.

"Wouldn't have worked." Giff shook his head. "Any lady who would do what her father or mother said wouldn't have enough strength of character to be a daughter of his."

"I don't envy you your search." Meeting the type of lady John wanted had to be much easier. After all, his sister had given up finding a husband because they all wanted a docile lady without much intelligence.

"I'll find her," Giff said. "And when I do, I'll do everything in my power to make sure she marries me."

John didn't want to know to what ends his friend would go. With the type of lady Giff wanted, anything other than her full agreement would get him in trouble. "I daresay it will not be that hard for either of us. We're titled, not bad-looking, and wealthy."

"Speak for yourself," Giff grumbled. "Until I don a leg-shackle, I have only what my father gives me. To be fair, he did increase my allowance when he gave me the marquis courtesy title. I just hope I meet someone who doesn't care about a love match. Messy things, those."

"I agree." Actually, John didn't see the point in them. His parents rubbed along extremely well, and theirs had been an arranged match. "My sister didn't care to have one, but they seem to get on well enough." Although she *had* chosen Lytton. John knew how his friend felt about money. He'd been on a strict allowance. Yet, the restraint he'd learned had served him well. When he'd had to take over the marquisate, he knew how to manage his money and take care of his holdings. Too many peers and other aristocrats wasted what they had. "Did you say your parents were in Town?"

"They arrive tomorrow." Giff had a heavy frown on his face. "Your mother and sister?"

"Got here yesterday. M'sister's at her town house, but Mama is staying with me."

"That will be helpful. If you decide you do like a lady, she will be able to arrange a party for the theater or some other event." His tone became a little lighter.

"I hadn't thought of that, but you're right." John just hoped that neither his mother nor sister would interrogate his prospective wife, whoever she might be. He was sure they wouldn't like the lady. She would be the opposite of them.

"They can also tell you which events to attend," Giff added thoughtfully. "I don't have a clue which entertainments have the most eligible ladies."

That was also true. John didn't either. "In that case, I will rely on her." Mama would be thrilled to hear him admit he required her assistance. "As long as she doesn't try to matchmake."

Giff pulled a face. "I'm not sure mothers know how *not* to matchmake. Mine certainly doesn't."

"This is going to be a long few months." The sooner John found a wife, the better. He turned his horse back to the gate. "I'm hungry. Would you like to break your fast with me? I've instructed my cook I shall eat early, even in Town."

"Thank you." Giff brought his gray gelding up beside John. "There won't be anything but toast to eat at my house for another two hours."

John had been lucky that his father enjoyed an early morning ride before breaking his fast. His mother usually had breakfast served in her parlor. He hadn't decided where he'd like his wife to break her fast. Though he'd wager that the three ladies who were out here this early didn't wait another two hours to eat. "In that case, you're welcome to take your potluck with me anytime you wish."

"Thank you." His friend smiled with relief. "I'll take you up on your offer."

When they entered the breakfast room in Montagu House, John grimaced at the dark green walls. He hated the color, but he didn't know what he'd like better. That was another reason for a wife. She would be able to decorate his home. With his approval, of course. He needed to be in control of his life. After selecting his food from the sideboard, he sat at the head of the table, where he found two cards to early entertainments and a note. He popped open the seals and perused them. Unfortunately, they were not the types of event to which young ladies were invited. If it hadn't been for Parliament, he never would have come to Town so early. The letter was from the Earl of Worthington, inviting John to meet with a group of other like-minded peers for luncheon at Brooks's. Once Worthington and his circle discovered John's political leanings, they had taken him in. He would pen his acceptance after Giff left.

His butler entered the room holding a note. "My lord, this is from Lady Lytton."

"Thank you, Lumner." John opened the seal and scanned

the short missive. "I've been invited to m'sister's to join them for dinner. If you like, I'll ask if you can come as well."

Giff swallowed what he'd been chewing. "Do you think she'll know some eligible ladies?"

"If she doesn't, she'll be happy to help." That might keep her off John's back. "I'll send a note around asking." It was actually a shame Aurelia, his twin, would not approve of the type of lady he wanted. Until their father had died, they'd agreed on almost everything or could understand the other's point of view. Still, she could also help select events for him to attend. He thought back to the three ladies he'd seen earlier. Perhaps one of them would meet his qualifications. Hopefully the one he'd particularly noticed.

The next morning, John met with St. Albans to go riding again. Perhaps today he would arrive when the ladies he'd seen the other day did. "It is too bad you cannot attend Parliament."

St. Albans gave John a confused look. "Why do you say that?"

"I was at a meeting at Worthington House yesterday. Several gentlemen I met have wives who will hold social events this Season. Of course, you know Turley. I believe even Littleton is supposed to be in Town this year. But I also met Exeter, who is a friend of Turley's, and, of course, Worthington as well as some other peers." John had been relieved they felt the same way about the Corn Laws, and the horrible event they now called Cinderloo, where miners protesting a cut in their wages had been massacred. "If you were a member, you would come to know the gentlemen more easily."

"Ah." St Albans stared off into the distance for a second. "For some reason, I hadn't thought of our friends' spouses holding entertainments. Silly of me, really. Of course they would. They are part of the *ton*, and this is the Season, after all." They had ridden to the Serpentine before he said, "I hope not to become a peer for a number of years yet. As much as m'father irritates me at times, I do not wish him dead."

"There is that." John had not wanted his father to die either. "I hope you get your wish."

They rode through the gate and saw the same three ladies they'd seen yesterday turning their horses in his direction. They were obviously leaving. It was a shame they had not yet been introduced. Although where that would have occurred he had no idea. But today he got a better look at them. Two were blond and one had dark hair. The one he'd especially noticed before was one of the blond-haired ladies. He liked fair hair, and hers was particularly lovely. It was as if it had been gilded. She smiled as she chatted with her companions. That must denote a pleasant demeanor. One of the qualities he wanted in a wife. "I wonder who they are."

"We're bound to find out at some point," St. Albans replied. "But it occurred to me late yesterday that if you want a lady who is a bit dim, you might want to appear the same yourself. Otherwise she could be wary of you."

John had not even considered that. It would be natural for a lady of just average intelligence to be cowed by a gentleman who possessed a great deal more intellect than she did. Still, now that he thought about it, the idea made sense. He would not want to scare off a lady by appearing to be knowledgeable. All he had to do was look at his friend Fitz Littleton and his lady. They were very much in accord in their wish to lead a quiet life. Like begat like. "That is exactly what I will do. Thank you for the hint."

"Anything to help a friend." St. Albans spurred his horse forward into a gallop and John did the same.

With any luck, they could help each other. John guided his friend to his house, where St. Albans was taken to a room to wash his face and hands before breakfast. Soon they were partaking of ham from Littleton's pigs, eggs, fresh toast, and tea.

"Littleton was right. This ham is excellent." John cut another piece.

"Did he tell you what he feeds them?" St. Albans asked.

John swallowed. "Chestnuts."

"I'll have to suggest it to m'father." His friend bit into his fourth piece of toast. If this was to continue, he'd have to tell his cook to increase the portions at breakfast. "Have you visited Weston yet?"

"No. He has my measurements. My valet sent over my requirements. You?"

"I have an appointment later this morning. I like to go myself. It gives me something to do."

Again, John thought it was a shame his friend was at such loose ends. "Will your father not give you any responsibility at all?"

"Not until I'm wed." St. Albans finished the rest of his tea. "I must be off. By the time I bathe and change, I will have to be at Weston's."

"Of course." John wondered what it would be like to have the time to go to Weston's. "I'll see you out."

Later that day, John's mother entered his study without even knocking. "Good day, Montagu." She held up a piece of foolscap. "I have been making a list of the qualities you will require in a wife and a list of potential names."

He was tempted to either order her out of his sanctuary

or sink his head into his hands. Instead, he rang for tea. "Please have a seat."

She looked at him suspiciously. "You *are* going to look for a wife this Season, are you not?"

"Yes. Yes, I am." It was time. His father had died four years ago, and the closest heir was a distant cousin. "I said I would." However, he'd be much happier if his mother and Aurelia, who'd been with them over Christmas with her husband and child, would stop trying to interfere with this wife-finding business. He was old enough and capable enough to find one on his own.

His butler arrived with the tea tray in a very short period of time, and his mother poured, then settled more firmly into the chair. "Now then"—she peered down at the paper— "Naturally, she must be a strong-minded young lady."

"Naturally." He wanted someone with whom it was easy to live, not who was strong-minded.

"She must have all the necessary social accomplishments."

"That goes without saying." Were there any ladies attending the Season who had not been trained for their place in the *ton*? Perhaps a lady who was a bit shy might be nice.

"She must be able to run the estates when you are busy with your parliamentary duties."

That he had not considered. Most likely because he wanted to be there and not in Town. "I suppose you have a point."

"You will want a lady who can act as a political hostess and gather support for legislation you support."

He inclined his head, pretending to agree with her. He'd rather have a lady who made his home comfortable and was not overly interested in politics. "Is there anything else?"

"It would be helpful if she came from a large family," Mama said rather cryptically.

He had to ponder that for a second. Ah, yes. Breeding capabilities. "I believe I follow your line of thinking."

"If you would like to hear the names I have—"

"No." He infused his tone with a firmness he rarely used with his mother. "The requirements are quite enough."

Mama frowned at him. "Would you like me to rewrite the list leaving off the names?"

"No, thank you. I am capable of remembering them." Although his sister never seemed to believe he could remember anything these days.

"Very well. In that case, I shall keep them with me in the event you need to look at them."

"Thank you. I appreciate your offer." Perdition! He'd find his own damn wife.

CHAPTER FOUR

Eleanor and her sisters were in a room known as the "Young Ladies' Parlor" when several packages arrived. The parlor, situated close to all their bedchambers, was large enough for them to be comfortable and contained a writing desk, three chairs, a small sofa, and a square cherry wood table with four chairs. The walls were painted pale yellow and there were light green curtains. She unknotted the twine around the brown paper that had just come from Madame Lisette. The modiste had had the family's custom since her older sisters' first Season.

Holding up the rich, cream silk evening gown covered with the same color netting embroidered with leaves in Pomona green that covered the silk, Eleanor was amazed at how beautiful it was. "I never believed this would turn out so well."

"I do not know why." Madeline lifted up a white gown that was embroidered in blue. "You selected the colors, and Madame agreed they would be perfect for you." She grinned at Alice, who held a gown of buttery yellow. The bodice had been embroidered with vines and purple brilliants. "As we all did."

Hurried footsteps sounded on the floor above. "Quickly.

My room." Eleanor gathered up the gown and packaging. "We need to put these someplace safe. We are about to be invaded."

They had just laid the gowns on her bed and got back into their parlor when Posy bounded into the room and to Alice, the first person the dog saw.

"Yes, yes, I love you too," Alice said as Posy wiggled against her.

Zeus, only a little less exuberant at two years old, knocked Madeline onto the small sofa and sat on her lap. "I will never understand why Danes think they are lapdogs."

Their nephew and niece, Gideon, five, and Elizabeth, four, ran through the door after the dogs.

"They got away from us," Elizabeth panted.

"I seem to remember that happening to Mary"—the youngest of the brothers and sisters—"when she was your age."

"With Daisy?" Gideon asked.

"Yes." It was amazing how one forgot what puppies were like after the Great Danes became adults.

"I remember Duke knocking Theo down when he was young," Madeline added.

"Did he hurt her?" Elizabeth cast a worried look at Zeus.

Madeline patted the cushion next to her and Elizabeth crawled up on it. "No, he just wanted to chase a squirrel and she happened to be holding his lead."

Gideon gave his sister a superior, older brother look. "That's why Papa says that either he or one of the footmen have to hold Zeus and Posy when we go walking."

"I knooow." Elizabeth rolled her eyes at him.

"There you are." Nurse, an older woman who had been with the Vivers part of the family since before Madeline was born, bustled into the room "You are supposed to be outside taking the air."

Elizabeth jumped off the sofa. "Zeus, Posy, come. It's time to play."

Madeline rose and shook out her skirts. "We know who those Danes belong to."

Eleanor laughed. "I suppose it is only fair. We had Duke and Daisy."

"And we will have our own dogs," Alice added. "That reminds me. We should make a list of what we want in our husbands."

Eleanor shot a smile at her twin. That was exactly what she had been thinking.

"What an excellent idea." Madeline went to the desk and drew out a piece of cut foolscap while Alice and Eleanor took chairs from the round cherry table and moved them to the writing desk as Madeline dipped a pen in the standish. "I think he should be intelligent."

"Yes." Eleanor wouldn't want a dim husband, but there was something even more important. "He should be kind."

"Oh, indeed." Alice nodded. "I agree."

"I as well." Madeline wrote down the first two qualities. "He must like animals."

"House animals," Alice insisted. "Most men like horses and hunting dogs."

"And children." Having been raised in a family where the children were never confined to the nursery, Eleanor believed allowing young children around was important.

"Like children more than just the getting of them," Madeline wrote.

"Make us laugh," Alice added. "It is not good enough that he has a sense of humor. Most people do to some extent, but the gentlemen we wed must be able to make *us* laugh."

"And think that we are funny as well." Eleanor was glad her twin thought of doing this.

"He must be interested in the plight of the poor and unfortunate," Madeline added. "Ever since Dotty and Grace started the charities, the rest of our sisters and their husbands have added to them. I wish to do the same, and my husband must support me."

"I agree," Alice said.

"I do as well." That was another good idea. Eleanor would not be happy with a man who did not care about others.

"Good-looking?" Madeline asked scrunching up her face.

Eleanor leaned back in her chair. "Well, I do not want to cringe when I gaze upon him. But his character is more important. Think of Byron and how handsome he is said to be, and he is a complete cad."

Madeline nodded. "I shall write 'passable-looking.'"

"That will do," Alice agreed.

"He must allow me to be myself. I will not have anyone trying to control me." Eleanor could not think of a worse fate.

"Indeed," Alice and Madeline said at the same time, then laughed.

Madeline set down her pen. "It would be nice if we were not too far apart."

"That would be ideal," Eleanor said. "Yet none of our sisters or their friends live at all close to one another, but they all seem to know everything that is going on, and we do get together every summer and every other Christmas."

"Very well." Madeline picked up the pen. "I will leave that off the list. What else can you think of?"

Alice raised a brow. "He does not have to be as wealthy

as Golden Ball, but he does need to be able to support a family."

"Agreed." Madeline dipped her pen into the ink. "No falling in love with a fortune hunter or pauper."

Eleanor quickly stayed her sister's hand. "Do not write that. It will be tempting fate."

Madeline's eyes widened. "Oh, you are right. I will just say 'must be able to support a family.'"

"Anything else?" Alice asked.

The three of them looked at one another and shook their heads.

"This does not have to be the end of the list," Eleanor pointed out. "We can always add to it."

"Very true." Alice nodded.

"We can watch our sisters and their friends with their husbands," Madeline said. "That might give us other ideas."

Eleanor remembered some of the fraught beginnings they had. "But do not forget, not all of them had an easy time falling in love and getting married."

Alice frowned. "Did any of them have an easy time?"

"You know"—Madeline tilted her head to one side—"I do not believe they did."

Eleanor thought back to what they knew of the courtships and caught herself frowning. "Perhaps it will be better for us. Although, that brings up something we forgot to write down. Any gentleman I marry must love me as I love him."

Madeline turned back to the desk. "How could we have forgotten that?"

"We probably simply assumed it," Alice said.

As Madeline wrote down the last point, a knock sounded on the door.

"Come," Eleanor called.

Charlotte, their eldest sister, entered the parlor. "I am glad you are all here."

Madeline looked around the room. "Where are the children?"

"Playing with Gideon and Elizabeth. Mr. Winters agreed to begin their Latin instruction while we are in Town and help us find a tutor before we go home."

Madeline pulled a face. "I remember how hard I found it to catch up when we all started living together. But Mr. Winters made it seem easy."

"He is very good at explaining things," Alice agreed.

Eleanor realized that her sister was still standing at the door. "What are we thinking? Please come in. Would you like tea?"

Laughter danced in Charlotte's eyes, the same sky-blue as Eleanor and Alice's. "No, thank you. I came to ask if you would be interested in joining Louisa, Dotty, me, and some of our friends in a charity meeting. We must hold several fundraisers for the orphans and families while we are here. Because Easter is so late, we decided to hold the first one before the Season begins."

Eleanor glanced at Alice and Madeline, who nodded. "We would love to. We just started our list of attributes any future husbands must have, and not interfering in our charitable work is on it."

Charlotte's lips twitched and Eleanor could see that her sister was having a hard time trying not to laugh.

She narrowed her eyes. "What is it?"

"Louisa, Dotty, and I made a list as well." Charlotte heaved a sigh. "All of our husbands do have the qualities we wanted, but it was not immediately apparent when we first met them, or even became betrothed."

"Merton." Madeline gave their older sister a knowing look.

"Him certainly." Charlotte smiled. "But the same was true

for Con and Rothwell too. My only advice is not to decide too quickly. It might take some time before you know who they really are. Gentlemen wear as many masks as ladies do." She opened her reticule, took out a folded piece of paper, and handed it to Madeline, who was the closest. "Here is the date, time, and place of the meeting. I will come fetch you a half hour before it begins."

"Thank you," Eleanor said. They truly were being treated like adults instead of children. Coming out was a wonderful thing.

John was in the morning room, the only room in the house that wasn't covered with dark colors, sketching a drawing of a horse, when his sister strode through the door. He quickly closed the sketchbook and stood. "What are you doing here?"

"Is that any way to greet your twin?" Aurelia bussed his cheek. She was right. They had been at odds recently, and he missed their closeness. If only he could think how to mend the breach. "I am here to fetch Mama for Lady Bellamny's soirée."

Even he knew her ladyship was one of the major hostesses. "There's an entertainment this evening?" Why had he not heard of it? He'd received dozens of invitations. "I thought nothing of import would be held until after Easter."

"This is an event she holds every year so that the young ladies making their come outs can meet one another. No gentlemen are allowed until the end of the evening, when they may come to take the ladies home." He frowned and knew his sister was hard-pressed not to smirk. He'd have done the same if their positions were reversed. "It was always an extremely popular entertainment, but it became even more so when the Earl of Worthington arrived to fetch his sister and stepmother and immediately fell in love with Lady Grace Carpenter. They wed quite quickly. I believe it was no more than three weeks."

John hoped that didn't happen to him. Marrying so quickly did not give one a chance to get to know the lady better. Still, it was a good opportunity to look over the new crop of young ladies without having to ask one to dance or even be introduced to them. "Excellent. I shall come for you and Mama, then."

"Hmm." Aurelia gave him a curious look, and it was one of the rare times he had no idea what his twin was thinking. "Very well. Lytton is coming for me, but of course you can take Mama home."

"Take me home from where?" Mama said from the door.

Aurelia gave their mother an affectionate hug. "I just told John about Lord and Lady Worthington meeting at Lady Bellamny's soirée several years ago. He has offered to bring you home."

"Ah, I understand." Mama would probably be on the lookout for eligible ladies for him. "Very well. I shall see you at eleven o'clock."

He executed a short bow. "It will be my pleasure."

Laughing, Aurelia linked her arm with their mother's. "Come, let us see what is in store for us this evening. I understand that Lord and Lady Worthington have three sisters making their come outs."

His mother and sister strolled out the door. "Where did you hear that?"

John moved closer to the corridor to listen as they strolled up the corridor. "From Lytton. Worthington has made it very clear that no ineligible gentlemen need come near his sisters."

"I am glad he is taking his duties seriously," Mama said. "More gentlemen should do so."

They must have reached the hall because John could no longer hear them. That was interesting. Worthington hadn't mentioned his sisters during their meeting the other morning. Yet that had been all business. John glanced down at his clothing and found a smudge of charcoal on his cravat. He'd have to change before fetching his mother. Perhaps he would see the lady he'd seen at the Park this evening and discover her name. St. Albans would enjoy a peek at the ladies as well. Was it allowed to bring a friend? John shook his head. He had better not try. Lady Bellamny was a stickler for her rules. Aside from that, the Season started next week. There would be plenty of time to meet any lady he wished. He looked at his pocket watch. It was only eight thirty. He still had time to work on this sketch.

He went to the bell-pull and tugged. A few moments later, his butler came in. "My lord?"

"Please inform Pickerell that I must change into fresh evening wear. I am to go bring her ladyship home shortly before eleven."

His butler bowed. "Yes, my lord."

Now John could draw without fear of being late. His valet would send someone for him in time to change. He opened the book and was relieved to see the charcoal hadn't smudged. He finished the horse and kept sketching. Soon a skirt appeared draped over the horse, and the figure of a woman emerged, including a curl that had escaped from its confinement.

Strange.

He did not think he had seen a curl, yet it had come out from his subconscious mind. A clock chimed as he studied the drawing. He *had* noticed her seat and was certain that he would recognize her even off a horse. There was a way she held her shoulders that stood out to him, and the way her swanlike neck curved when she turned her head toward her friends. He had trouble capturing her hands. Perhaps it was the gloves. The bodice of her habit was short and the neckline was high, ending with a ruff beneath her chin. Yet that did nothing to hide what promised to be generous breasts. She seemed so natural and at ease, but she was also alluring. He would like to see her in an evening gown. Perhaps he would tonight.

"My lord." Lumner bowed. "Mr. Pickerell said that if you are not to be late you must come at once."

"Thank you." John put the drawing book in a cabinet, where his mother would not find it. She knew he drew, but this was one sketch he did not want her to see.

Shortly before eleven he arrived at Lady Bellamny's house in Upper Brook Street and joined the long line of carriages. John hoped he had not missed most of the ladies leaving. He knocked on the roof. "I'll get down here and walk."

"Very good, my lord," his coachman said. "I will try to get closer."

"Keep an eye out for me if you do." Although the line did not appear to be moving at all. He strode to the house and up the stairs to be met by a butler. "I am Lord Montagu here to collect my mother."

The servant bowed. "You will find the ladies at supper." The butler signaled for a footman. "He will take you there."

"Thank you."

The supper room was filled with small round tables that were filled by ladies and some gentlemen. He spotted his mother with three other ladies, but she was deep in a conversation. Glancing around, he saw Worthington in a group where the tables had been put together to accommodate the size. Exeter was there, next to two blond ladies, but neither was John's blond lady. Then he saw her sitting across the table with the ladies with whom she had ridden.

Instead of going immediately to his mother, he made his way to Worthington's group and bowed. "Good evening, my lords."

"And to you. Who are you fetching?" Worthington asked.

"My mother." John glanced her way, and she saluted him. He inclined his head before turning back to Worthington.

"I may as well make you known to those of my family you do not know. I believe you have met the gentlemen. . . ." He caught the attention of the lady John wanted to meet, as well as the other two. "Eleanor, Madeline, Alice, may I present Lord Montagu? My sisters, Lady Eleanor Carpenter, Lady Madeline Vivers, and Lady Alice Carpenter."

Her name was Lady Eleanor. She looked very much like Lady Alice, but John could see the difference. He'd been right that she was even more beautiful, more compelling in an evening gown. She lifted her champagne glass, and John was finally able to see her long, elegant fingers. He bowed again. "My ladies, it is a pleasure."

All three inclined their heads, but Lady Eleanor stared at him for a long moment. "Are you the gentleman who rides a black horse in the Park most mornings?"

He tried not to puff out his chest that she'd recognized him. "I am."

The corners of her deep pink lips rose, making him want to see if they felt as soft as they looked. He hoped her smile was for him, but it could have been because she had excellent manners. "Perhaps you will join us some morning." Lady Eleanor's forehead puckered adorably. "If you get up earlier, that is."

"I am certain I can manage that, my lady." He felt someone at his elbow and turned. "Mama, Aurelia."

"Thank you for agreeing to come for me," his mother said, as if he had not been the one to suggest it.

"It was easily done."

Mama turned to the other ladies. "I have enjoyed meeting all of you this evening." The ladies seemed to speak at once, agreeing that they had liked meeting her as well. Then she took his arm. "I hope to see you again soon. We must not keep the horses waiting."

"There you are, my dear." Lytton came up to them. "There were so many ladies here that I was in despair of finding you."

Aurelia tucked her hand in the crook of his arm and the smile she gave him was much warmer than John had expected it to be. "You always find me."

"Yes. I am lucky that way." He gave her the same type of smile in return.

Had they fallen in love? Why had John not known? They used to be able to just know what the other was thinking. Yet that was the only reason he could see for the amount of affection they were showing, and in public at that!

Worthington rose. "We should be off as well." He glanced at his sisters. "Ladies?"

Before John could ask if he could escort Lady Eleanor, his mother practically dragged him off. "What are you doing?"

"Keeping you from making a cake of yourself. You will see her at church on Sunday, and at several entertainments next week."

"Oh." He hadn't thought of that. He supposed that singling her out in this crowd would be rash. "Thank you."

"That is what mothers are for," Mama said smugly. "Now come along."

He would have to get up earlier tomorrow morning. John just hoped she would meet his requirements.

CHAPTER FIVE

"That was interesting," Madeline whispered in Eleanor's ear.

"What?" Eleanor and her sisters were following Matt and Grace out of the supper room.

"The way Lord Montagu looked at you," Alice said.

Eleanor glanced at her twin. "How did you hear her?"

"I did not." Her sister shrugged. "I knew what she was going to say because I thought the same thing."

"I will be very surprised if he can tell us apart. A great many people will not be able to do so."

"It is a shame we are past the age of pretending to be each other," Alice mused.

"But if he can." Madeline's tone was insistent as she looped her arm with Eleanor's. "It means that he sees you. That you are not just some young lady."

"Perhaps." Eleanor was not sure about that. "We shall see. Remember, neither Louisa nor Charlotte married the first gentlemen they met."

"Very true." Alice took Eleanor's other arm, putting them out of order. "But simply because they did not does not mean you will not."

"As I said, we shall see." The only thing Eleanor knew

about the man was that he rode a lovely horse, he had an excellent seat, and he was very handsome. His blue-green eyes had almost tempted her to stare at him. Almost. But there had to be much more to his lordship than a good seat and a handsome countenance.

"He must have the funds to support a family," Madeline added. "Otherwise Matt would not have introduced him."

Right then, he was sufficiently wealthy. "I am not falling in love at first sight. He has many more qualities to meet."

"So it begins." Ahead of them, Matt groaned.

Grace patted his arm. "They have become shrewd ladies."

Eleanor exchanged glances with Alice and Madeline. It was nice to have Grace's approval, but poor Matt.

He helped them all into the coach and took the seat next to Grace. "What did Lady Bellamny say? I remember Louisa telling us she thought she'd look at her teeth."

"Not much," Madeline said. "Grace introduced us. We curtseyed and greeted her."

Alice picked up the story. "Then she stared at us for what seemed like an eternity, but none of us let her see we were nervous."

"At that point," Eleanor chimed in, "she said we would do, and told Grace she had done an excellent job, and she supposed the gentlemen would make up some silly name for us."

Across from them, Eleanor could see Grace in the coach light. "I think it was a matter of like recognizing like. I was very proud of the way the girls held their own under that gaze. Most of the young ladies would have started weeping."

"One of them did have tears in her eyes," Alice said. "What was her name? She and her friend want to marry gentlemen who live close to each other so that they will not have to be parted."

For a moment, Eleanor thought Grace would roll her eyes. "Either Miss Tice or Miss Martindale. Their older sisters wanted the same thing."

That was interesting. "Were they successful?"

"As it happens, yes, they were," Grace said. "You should ask Henrietta about them. One set of Martindale-Tices came out when she did."

"We haven't seen her since last summer," Alice complained.

"Dotty has invited us to Easter dinner," Grace said. "You will see her then."

That was good news. Yet Eleanor was certain Henrietta would be at the charitable meeting as well. She and her husband, Nate, Lord Fotherby, had met rescuing a child. "I shall look forward to it. It's nice to have so many people in Town we already know."

"It is," Madeline said. "Even if they are not coming out at the same time."

Eleanor tried to stifle a yawn. "I do not know how I will stay awake during the entertainments."

Grace chuckled. "You will have so much to do during them that you will not be tired until you get home."

"Just remember, we leave after supper," Matt added. "That worked well with your sisters, and now we have even younger children in the house."

Eleanor hoped that she and her sisters would not be too tired to ride in the morning. And not because she was interested in learning more about Lord Montagu, but because she wanted the exercise. Still, it was exciting to have a gentleman interested in her. Yet, she would not get her hopes up. After all, even if he met all the other criteria, they might not fall in love.

* * *

The ride home was quiet. Too quiet. John was surprised his mother said nothing about Lady Eleanor. "Why did you attend a function for young ladies?"

"My dear, it is not only for young ladies. It gives us older ladies a chance to spend time together in person or to see those with whom we are not in regular correspondence. You would not have noticed, but the Patronesses of Almack's were there. Naturally, some of us have received our vouchers, but for others, the soirée gives them an opportunity to see how the young ladies behave in public. Not that I think any lady making her come out whom Lady Bellamny invited would be denied a voucher." His mother shrugged. "It also allows those of us with sons to meet the younger ladies."

"I see." He'd not known how important the event was. But was he being obtuse? His father had warned him the ladies controlled Polite Society. They decided who was invited and who was not. Even dukes required a lady to sponsor any events they wanted to hold when respectable ladies were invited. "Were you impressed by any of the young ladies?" If she was, he knew to stay away from them.

"I did not have a chance to speak to many of them. They were meant to mingle with one another. There were one or two who were not quite up to snuff. Very gigglish, if you take my meaning. Their mothers should have waited another year to bring them out."

As much as John did not want a wife with strong opinions or one who was managing, he also did not want a spouse who was still a child. "That would be irritating to live with."

"So I think." His mother fell silent again.

It might be a good omen Mama had not mentioned Lady Eleanor as someone she liked. He wanted to come to know the lady himself. The coach pulled to a stop, and a footman opened the door and put down the steps. John jumped out and assisted his mother from the carriage.

"I am for my couch," she said as they entered the house.

"I'll wish you a good night. There are a few things I want to finish before I retire." Now that John had seen Lady Eleanor's hands, he had to draw them.

His mother looked up at him. "You have become the man your father and I always thought you would be." Tears glazed her eyes when she mentioned Father. She must still miss him. It occurred to him that even if their marriage hadn't begun with love, they must have grown into the emotion. What was it like to love someone so much? "Good night."

John waited until she had reached the first landing before heading back to the morning room and his sketch. Now that he had been much closer to Lady Eleanor, he could refine her other features, as well as her hands. By the time he'd finished, he was having trouble keeping his eyes open, but he was proud of the result. He had captured her. At least what he knew of her now.

John crawled into bed, knowing he'd dream of Lady Eleanor.

"My lord, do you plan to ride this morning?"

Pickerell's voice interrupted John's dream of Lady Eleanor, or what they were doing. Really, it was unlike him to be so interested in a lady. "Yes. What time is it?"

"Past seven. Lord St. Albans just arrived."

Damn. John had forgotten he'd wanted to wake up early enough to ride with the ladies. "Tell him I'll be right down."

His valet stepped to the door, said something to someone, probably a footman, in the corridor, and began to lay out John's riding kit. He splashed water on his face and cleaned his teeth. His cravat was not a masterpiece, but it would do for a ride.

He hurried downstairs to a small parlor off the hall. "Sorry I'm running late. I had meant to send a note around to you so that we could go earlier."

"Earlier? Why?" St. Albans strode to meet John.

"Let's get our horses and I'll tell you all about it." John's gelding, Aramus, was just being brought around. St. Albans's gray was being walked by a groom. They mounted and made their way toward the Park.

"Well, then. What did you want to write to me about?" St. Albans asked.

"Last evening Lady Bellamny held a soirée for the young ladies making their come outs. But they are not the only ones who attended. Many matrons did as well. My mother and sister went. M'sister let it slip that although gentlemen were not invited, they were allowed in during the last part of supper to fetch the ladies."

His friend frowned. "Why do they have to be fetched?"

"I have no idea. It's just what they do." That was a good question. John had not even thought to ask. "In any event, I saw Worthington, and he was there with his sisters, who are the three ladies we have seen riding."

St. Albans suddenly looked interested. Was he attracted to Lady Eleanor as well? That would not do. If he was, John would have to warn the man off. "I take it you were able to gain an introduction?"

"I was." But John wasn't at all sure he wanted to make his friend known to *her*.

"Good." St. Albans tilted his head in the direction of three riders, followed, as always, by three grooms. "You may now beg an introduction for me."

Well, damn. John trotted toward the ladies. "Good morning, my lady."

Lady Eleanor smiled, and even the cloudy day seemed brighter. "Good morning, my lord."

Ladies Madeline and Alice greeted him as well.

"I meant to awaken earlier, but I had a great deal of work to do last night." Ladies Madeline and Alice exchanged glances that seemed to indicate they didn't believe him.

But Lady Eleanor said, "Sometimes duties cannot be put off."

At least she believed him. St. Albans cleared his throat rather loudly. "Allow me to introduce my friend, Lord St. Albans. St. Albans, Lady Eleanor, Lady Madeline, and Lady Alice."

The rogue bowed gracefully from his horse. "Ladies, good morning. It is my absolute pleasure to finally meet you."

Fortunately, Lady Eleanor did not appear to be impressed. "Indeed, my lord. We have wondered who was riding the gray. Now we know."

Lady Alice cast her eyes to the sky and gave her head a small shake. "Good morning, sir. It is very nice to meet you as well."

Lady Madeline's lips twitched. "I shall add my greetings, my lord. It is a pleasure."

Before St. Albans could continue, John said, "Must you return home now, or do you have time to ride some more?"

"I am afraid we are required to be back in time for breakfast with our family," Lady Eleanor said. "However, perhaps you will not have to work so late this evening and will be able to join us tomorrow morning."

"Yes. I will arrange that." He gave her his most charming smile. "Until tomorrow."

John was about to ride to the other side of the Park when St. Albans said, "The least we can do is to escort you to the gate."

Damn the man. John had never realized how irksome

St. Albans could be at times. "Yes, of course, we are at your command."

St. Albans glanced at John and raised a brow, but he fell in beside Lady Alice when John beat him to Lady Eleanor's side. Fortunately, she did not seem to notice their antics.

"How are you enjoying Town?" It was such an insipid question, but it was the only thing he could think of at the moment.

Once again, his gaze was drawn to her mouth. Her lips tilted up at the ends even when she wasn't actually smiling. "We always enjoy our time in the metropolis. Our brother must attend to his duties in the Lords and we come as a family to be with him."

She had probably spent more time here than he had. "I have heard that you have a great many members in your family."

"There are, indeed, and the number continues to grow," she said in a softer tone. "My three elder sisters—the Duchess of Rothwell, Lady Kenilworth, and Lady Phinn Carter-Woods—are married and either have children or will have them. Matt and Grace have three little ones. Our cousins, Lord and Lady Merton, also have children. Lady Merton's family lives near my brother Stanwood's estate, and we know them well." She caught his gaze. "Do you have a large family?"

He'd had no idea how well-connected she was. Although, if he had given the matter any consideration, it would have come to him. "Er. No. In my immediate family there is only my twin sister and me."

"Are you close?" Eleanor did not know why she asked, except it was clear they no longer lived together.

"We used to be much closer; even when I was at school there was a tie between us. We drifted apart after our father died." Something he was not going to discuss with Lady Eleanor. "Still, there is a special bond."

"I understand that." Her tone was low and melodic. "What other family do you have?"

"There are some relatives on my mother's side, but they live in the North, and we don't see them often." He smiled at her again. "I am more than happy for you to talk about your family. It must be fascinating to have so many children about."

She glanced at the gate. "Thank you for your escort. Perhaps I will see you tomorrow."

"I shall make it happen." He made his bow as elegantly as he could. "Until then, my lady."

Lady Eleanor inclined her head. "My lord."

John waited until they were through the gate before he turned back. He might have to revise what he wanted in a wife. He'd not realized how important graciousness was in a woman, or dedication to family.

"So, that's the way the wind's blowing, is it?" St. Albans said as he came up next to John. "I must admit, I'm quite taken with Lady Alice. She is very sharp-witted."

"It is much too soon for me to make any sort of decision, but Lady Eleanor appears to meet all my qualifications." Still, it was a little strange the twins could be so different.

"You should have warned me off," St. Albans said good-naturedly. "I have no wish to poach."

"I–I wasn't quite sure what to do." John frowned to himself. His behavior toward Lady Eleanor was not like him at all. "I've never been this attracted to a lady before."

"Nothing odd in that." His friend started his horse to a trot. "They are all very lovely women. There will be a great many gentlemen vying for their hands."

"Yes." Perhaps that was it. Some competitive part of him must have known he should be the first to impress her.

But had he? John was trying to appear to be a man who was happy with small talk. Although now that he'd experienced it, he found it frustrating. If only he'd been on the Town when he was younger, he might have developed the knack. On the other hand, they had just met. No one would expect anything but simple conversation at this point. John gave himself a shake. He was worried about nothing.

CHAPTER SIX

"Dear me," Madeline said teasingly as they came to a halt in front of Worthington House. "You two already have gentlemen interested in you and there is no one for me."

"I am not sure about that," Alice said, sliding down from her mare. "I think Lord St. Albans is a bit too, too"—her brows drew together as she thought—"I cannot find the right word. Worldly? That might be it. He seems too experienced in capturing a lady's attention."

Madeline glanced at Eleanor. "What do you think of Lord Montagu?"

What did she think of him? "He is very nice. He asked about our family and told me his is quite small. I think I would like to speak with someone who knows him. It is very easy for anyone to pretend to be something they are not."

"What do you not like about him?" Madeline asked.

"It is silly of me to expect him to mention political interests at this point." If he had them. His comment about having children around being fascinating was strange. Busy, yes. Maddening at times, naturally. But fascinating? Eleanor did not think that word applied. If he wanted a wife who was solely interested in her family, she was not the lady for him. It sounded almost as if he was saying something he thought she might like to hear. Yet perhaps she was being too hard on him. After all, she was not in the habit of conversing with gentlemen she did not know well. She and her sisters had practiced on their brothers-in-law, but they certainly were not trying to impress them, and they were not in the habit of saying silly things. That was what it was. He sounded silly.

Eleanor started up the stairs. "We should hurry. Breakfast will be served soon."

About three quarters of an hour later, when she strolled into the breakfast room, she was surprised to see Rothwell and Con had accompanied Louisa and Charlotte. Eleanor was almost sorry for Rothwell. He had been delighted when Grace and Matt had named their boy Gideon, only to discover it was not after him. Gideon was also the name of their grandfather. Not only that, they all called Kenilworth Con, but never called Rothwell Gideon. "Good morning. What brings the two of you here this early?"

"Lords," Con said, taking another piece of toast. "We have an early vote. If I wanted to break my fast with my wife, it had to be here."

"The same." Rothwell drained his cup of tea and poured another one.

Matt sat at the head of the table with Gideon and Grace sat at the foot with Elizabeth. Eleanor took her regular seat in the middle of the long table. "Do either of you know Lord Montagu?"

Con shook his head and swallowed. "Not well. He's much closer to Turley and Fotherby."

That was good news. Fotherby had married Henrietta, and he was in Town. They would be at the Easter dinner. Eleanor took baked eggs from a platter one of the footmen brought, as well as a piece of rare roast beef. A rack of fresh toast was set before her, as well as a pot of tea. Theo and Mary dashed into the room ahead of Madeline and Alice, and more toast and tea were brought, as well as what each of them liked to eat.

"When will the boys be back?" Mary asked about their brothers at school.

"Walter arrives today," Grace said. "He has a meeting at the Foreign Office right after Easter. And Phillip arrives to-morrow."

Eleanor glanced around the table. They would have to add another leaf if Rothwell and Con dined with them again. His five-year-old twins waved at her, but Hugh forgot he had food on his fork and it flew to the middle of the table.

He gave his father a contrite look. "Oops."

Con scooped up the piece of scrambled egg from the table. "I must believe he will eventually learn to empty his utensils before waving them around."

Eleanor struggled not to laugh.

Beside her, Madeline held a serviette to her mouth.

Constance, Hugh's twin, sighed heavily. "I will teach him."

That was apparently too much for Mary, who dropped her face in her hands to hide her laughter.

"Come along." Matt stood and took Gideon's hand. "Hugh, Constance, Alexandria, Elizabeth, it's time to clean up for your lessons."

They waited for the door to close before breaking out into laughter.

"That was so funny," Theo said, then glanced at Mary. "You are not supposed to laugh. It will only encourage them."

"I know." Mary went off into a peal of giggles. "I couldn't help myself. The way he looked at Con and said 'oops' was so droll."

"It was Constance that set me off," Louisa said. "She is so serious."

Mary and Theo ate quickly. What had made them late?

"We must be off as well." Theo rose and Mary followed.

Con looked at Rothwell. "Ladies, we should take our leave." He leaned down and kissed Charlotte. "I'll see you sometime today."

Rothwell kissed Louisa. "I hope to be home before dinner."

Once they left, the rest of them glanced around at one another.

"The table looks much larger with them all gone," Alice commented.

They all nodded.

"Grace," Charlotte said. "Are you joining us this afternoon?"

"I shall. Matt and I were discussing the problems that brought on Cinderloo, and I have some ideas."

"Cinderloo?" Madeline asked.

"You must remember," Eleanor said. "It was the killing of miners protesting their wages being reduced." How could her sister have forgotten? "It is the reason I brought Mrs. Johnson and her family home with me from Charlotte's, and it was in the newspapers."

Her sister's face cleared. "I remember the events. Somehow I missed that Cinderloo was the name."

Charlotte put her serviette on the table. "Louisa and I must be running along as well. We promised Dotty we would help her with the meeting, and we have modiste appointments."

"We will see you later." Eleanor poured another cup of tea. There might be time to speak with Henrietta about Montagu today. Eleanor wondered if she would like what she discovered. But if she did not, there were other gentlemen. He was merely the first one she had met.

* * *

By the time John and St. Albans arrived at Montagu House to break their fast, Aurelia and their mother had already finished one cup of tea each. The look of shock on John's face when he saw them almost set her into whoops. He must think she had moved in without him knowing about it.

He took a plate, filled it from the sideboard, then took his place at the head of the short table. "Good morning. Did Lytton decide not to join you?"

Something or someone had him distracted. She wished they had not had such a falling out. He was her twin. It was like losing part of herself. "He had an early meeting at the Lords. There is a vote today. Are you not planning to be there as well?"

"I completely forgot." He looked longingly at his plate. "You'll have to excuse me. I must change. Please stay and enjoy your meal."

"Thank you, I will." Still standing, St. Albans smiled and bowed before taking a seat.

"Well, then, I'm off." John strode quickly out of the room.

When she ceased to hear his steps, Aurelia focused her attention on St. Albans. "Good morning. I trust you had a good ride."

"Good morning." St. Albans's glance included her mother in his greeting. "We had an excellent ride."

She wondered how hard it was going to be to pry the information she wanted from him. "I understand Lady Eleanor and her sisters are early riders as well. Did you happen to see them?"

"We did indeed. They were on their way out of the Park as we were arriving. Montagu took the opportunity to introduce me to the ladies." He sipped the cup of tea her mother had poured for him and took a piece of toast. "They are all lovely."

Well, he definitely was not going to volunteer information. Maybe she could somehow give him permission to talk about John's interest in Lady Eleanor. "My brother seemed taken by Lady Eleanor when he met her last evening."

"That was the impression I got this morning." St. Albans took a mouthful of scrambled eggs. Aurelia supposed he must be hungry after the morning exercise, but she had the information she wanted from him. "I am not one to betray a trust, but I believe Montagu is making a mistake."

That was a surprise. "In being attracted to Lady Eleanor?"

"No." He raised a brow. "In thinking he wants a wife of only moderate intelligence. He believes it will be calming. I think he'd be bored within a month, if that long."

"I completely agree." What in God's name was her brother thinking? Then it struck her. "He wants a lady who is not like me."

"I believe he did say something to that effect." St. Albans quickly took a drink of tea.

"That does make a certain amount of sense, my dear," Mama said. "We were all affected when your father died, but John most of all. You *were* rather hard on him."

Aurelia had taken it upon herself to keep her twin from falling into melancholia. "Someone had to be. He needed to take up his duties. You and I could only do so much without his approval." She turned her attention back to St. Albans. "Did you tell him what you thought?"

"Not I. There is no point in telling a gentleman something he must discover on his own." An almost evil smile appeared on his face. "I did suggest that if he wanted a stupid woman, he must make sure not to show his own intelligence or it might frighten her away."

That was the most ridiculous thing Aurelia had ever

heard. She was about to say just that when her mother started to laugh.

"Oh my," Mama said after a few moments. "This I cannot wait to see."

It suddenly dawned on Aurelia the ramifications that might occur when it came to Lady Eleanor. "Oh dear. I have a feeling Lady Eleanor is not at all stupid, or of even moderate intelligence."

"The look she gave him when he told her he thought the size of her family was fascinating was interesting," St. Albans said. "Granted, I was speaking with Ladies Alice and Madeline, but I caught that part of the conversation, and her profile. I could be wrong."

"I do not believe you are." How could John say something so inane. Aurelia knew him as well as she knew herself. He would detest an unintelligent wife. "If it was not unkind to the lady, I would introduce him to a truly dim female."

"We mustn't do that. Expectations might be raised before he discovered his mistake," Mama said. "I believe we should see how this unfolds."

"I would not be averse to taking a slight hand in giving them an opportunity to spend more time together. A ball, I think. Or something less formal."

"A theater party?" St. Albans asked. "Or a party to Vauxhall?"

Aurelia looked at him. "And would you like to be included, my lord?"

"If you wouldn't mind, I would be delighted to be invited to make up your numbers." His countenance had held an amused air for most of the conversation. It was now absolutely serious. "I am looking for a wife, and she must be intelligent and have great strength of character. I get the feeling you would be the one to help me find such a lady."

She inclined her head in assent. "That would give me a great deal of pleasure." Unbeknownst to him, he might have already met the lady. "Mama and I are attending a meeting today that many ladies of that ilk will also attend. I would not be surprised to find a few young ladies there as well."

Mama gave him a hard look. "Would this have anything to do with your father?"

To Aurelia's surprise, he ran a finger under his collar. "Partially. I do want to spend my life with a woman of intelligence, but she must be able to stand up to my father. I will be able to aid her only so much."

Her mother nodded, as if she already knew the answer. "As I thought."

If she was going to help him, she had to know the problem with the duke. "Is he cruel?"

"Not in the sense you most likely mean. He is not a brute. In fact, I can only remember him spanking me twice, and both times I had put my life in danger." St. Albans tilted his head back for a few moments. "He can be difficult. If he thinks he can get the better of you, he will. When he tells someone to do something one ought not do or really does not want to do, one fares much better by standing up to him and telling him no, rather than to meekly do what he wants. It is hard to explain."

"Your mother's garden," Mama said suddenly.

Aurelia glanced at her mother. "You know them?"

"Of course I do. I came out the same year the duchess did. Now, let me tell you the story. St. Albans's father told his mother he was going to tear out her garden to build a tennis court. She refused. When he pressed the issue, she had the gamekeeper arm his helpers and the gardeners with hunting guns and refused to allow the men he had hired to enter her garden. She even held one of the muskets herself."

"He gave up the scheme when she told him that he'd have

a difficult time using a tennis court with a ball in his arm," St Albans added. "She would have done it. M'mother doesn't make idle threats."

"Hmm, I see what you mean." Aurelia glanced at her watch pin. "I shall give it some thought. As for now, I should be going. I have things I must accomplish before this afternoon."

"I will stay and keep you company until you finish eating," Mama said. "We can discuss the forms of events suitable for young ladies."

Aurelia bussed her mother's cheek. "Have an enjoyable time."

She gathered her coat, bonnet, and gloves from the butler, then strolled to the pavement toward home. If the Worthington ladies were at the meeting—and she had no doubt they would be—Aurelia would find the time to get to know more about Lady Eleanor. Something must be done about John's latest start.

CHAPTER SEVEN

Eleanor and her sisters—even Augusta—arrived at Dotty's house as some of the other ladies were entering as well. The rooms were already filling up. Dotty had ended up making three large drawing rooms into one room by opening the pocket doors.

"How is this going to work?" Eleanor had envisioned a raised platform at one end and rows of chairs. There were plenty of places to sit, but it was not set up as a lecture would be.

"We all mingle, tell each other what we've been doing, and discuss other things we might do or want to do." Dotty embraced Eleanor.

Eleanor grabbed Henrietta's arm as she hurried past. "What is—Oh, Eleanor, it has been an age since I've seen you." Henrietta enveloped Eleanor in a hug. "I was hurrying because I had a glimpse of Madeline and, I thought, Alice too."

"They are both here." The three of them had separated after arriving. "I would like to speak with you about something."

"Of course." A footman came around with lemonade and chilled white wine. Henrietta took two glasses of lemonade and handed one to Eleanor. "Come to the window seat. We can be private there." Once they had settled in on the cushion, she asked, "What do you wish to talk about?"

There was no point in beating around the bush with Henrietta. "I want to know more about Lord Montagu."

"Hmm." Her forehead wrinkled. "I do not know him very well personally. I can tell you that since taking his seat in the Lords, he has been extremely active."

"Is he a Whig?" Eleanor thought he must be if he was friends with Turley and Fotherby, but one never knew.

"Yes. On the liberal side." Her friend grinned. "Not as radical as my father, but close."

Henrietta and Dotty's father had been a vicar before inheriting his brother's baronetcy and was known to espouse doing away with the peerage, even though both of his older daughters had married into it. "That is good to know. Has he introduced any bills?"

"Not to my knowledge. He just took his seat. His father died a few years ago; I do not know why it took him so long. I can ask Nate if it matters."

"No. I met him, and he is a possibility, but nothing more than that." Eleanor would simply have to see for herself.

"His mother and sister are expected to be here. When I see them, I shall introduce you." Henrietta searched the room. "There they are. Come along."

Eleanor laughed. "That is what you used to say when we were children."

"I had forgotten." Henrietta smiled. She led Eleanor in a winding path around groups of ladies to the two women. Both of them had the same dark auburn hair and the blue-green eye color as his lordship. "My ladies," Henrietta said, getting their attention. "I would like to introduce you to a close friend of my family, Lady Eleanor Carpenter. Eleanor, Lady Montagu and Lady Lytton."

The ladies inclined their heads and Eleanor curtseyed.

"How lovely to meet you," Lady Lytton said, holding out her hand. "We are acquainted with your older sisters and friends of your family."

"I hope we will see quite a bit of you this Season," Lady Montagu said. "I remember my come out fondly."

"I expect it will be exhausting but a great deal of fun," Eleanor responded. She could not ask them about Lord Montagu, but she could discover more about the family and the ladies' pursuits. "In which charities are you interested?"

"We have donated to Lady Merton's charities, naturally," Lady Lytton said. "I have thought about starting one of my own, but I am not quite sure where to begin."

"My sister, Lady Worthington, helped Lady Merton form the one to which we all donate. She started a school for the children on the Worthington estates and villages."

"I have begun a school project on my husband's estates," Lady Lytton said.

"I did for the Montagu estates as well," Lady Montagu commented. "I do wish they were better attended."

"Yes, that is the difficulty." Eleanor scanned the room for Adeline Littleton, whose husband had solved the problem. It was always better to speak to the person who had first-hand knowledge, but Eleanor could not find her. "I do not see the person you should talk to, but I can tell you what her husband did. He paid the families for any work the children missed due to attending school and then had a cart come around to pick them up in the mornings."

"What a brilliant idea," Lady Lytton said. "I do not know why neither of us thought of it."

A lady Eleanor thought she remembered joined them. "Good day. I am Serena Beaumont, a friend of your sister Grace." The woman, who had a light, lyrical Scottish accent, smiled at Eleanor. "I have not seen you in years. That is what comes of living in Yorkshire and all of us being so busy with our families."

Eleanor remembered her the first year they were in Town. When Matt and Grace wed. "It has been a long time. I am glad to see you again."

"I am happy to meet you again." Lady Beaumont smiled with her eyes. "Aside from that, I heard you were interested in what you could do about the people suffering due to the Cinderloo killings."

"I am. Very interested." Eleanor glanced at Lord Montagu's mother and sister. "I hope you do not mind this discussion. I wish to find a way to help them."

"Not at all." Lady Lytton indicated her mother with a hand motion. "We would like to know more as well."

"Thank you." Eleanor moved so that her back was not to any of them. "I know there is a group that is raising funds and other things, but what I would like to do is raise enough to buy a mine and run it humanely. The work will never be easy or particularly safe, but surely there is a way to manage the enterprise so that the workers are sufficiently paid."

"My husband acquired a mine in Yorkshire," Lady Beaumont said slowly. "He has complained about the managers. They are, apparently, always trying to find a method of enriching themselves and can be more than a bit brutal."

"What if one hired a mineworker to run the day-to-day business?" There had to be a way to make that work. "They know what has to happen to make the mines safer and what a sufficient wage would be."

"My understanding is that they are uneducated and cannot read or write," Lady Montagu said.

There had to be a way to make up for that lack. "The simplest thing would be to teach them, but that takes time." Eleanor hoped they did not laugh at what she was about to say. "If an accountant or bookkeeper was hired—naturally, he would have to be trustworthy—to take care of the books and read any correspondence while the miner was learning those skills, that would resolve the problem. There should also be someone to assist the miners in reading their contracts. I assume they have them. Even our scullery maid has a contract."

All three older ladies appeared thoughtful. Finally Lady Beaumont said, "Let me put it to my husband. He has been searching for a way to change things but has not yet found it."

Eleanor let out the breath she had been holding. "Thank you."

"I find your idea to be inspired," Lady Lytton said.

"Yes, indeed." Lady Montagu agreed. "I would be willing to donate to the mine fund."

Bubbles of happiness rose through Eleanor, making her a bit light-headed. "Thank you, my lady."

"Let me know when you begin the project," Lady Lytton added. "Parliament might not take action, but we certainly can."

That had been exactly what Eleanor had decided. It was nice to be around other ladies with like ideas.

"I trust you will be at Almack's on Wednesday evening?" Lady Montagu asked.

"Yes." Eleanor had almost forgotten that the Season began in only four more days.

"We will see you then." Lady Lytton smiled. "It was a great pleasure to make your acquaintance."

Eleanor watched as the two ladies strolled off. They were both so nice. She could tell they were serious about helping. No matter what happened with Lord Montagu, his mother and sister were bound to become friends and supporters of Eleanor's mine project.

* * *

John opened his eyes and wondered why his valet hadn't woken him. Then the clock chimed, and Pickerell entered the bedchamber. "My lord. You wished to rise early this morning."

"Thank you." John threw off the covers and swung his legs over the side of the bed. This morning would be the first chance he had to speak with Lady Eleanor for longer than a few seconds. He strode to the washbasin and peered into the looking glass hanging on the screen. A lightly bristled visage stared back at him. If he shaved, he'd be late. He'd do it later. At the moment, he needed to see if his supposition about the time she rode was correct. John finished his ablutions and dressed, tying his cravat in a Mathematical before shrugging into a riding jacket. "Please tell Cook that I will want to break my fast a bit earlier this morning."

"It has already been done, my lord."

"Good man." John took his hat and gloves from Pickerell and strode out the door.

St. Albans was approaching the house as John mounted Aramus.

"I do hope we have timed this right." His friend yawned, and John noticed St Albans had shaved. He hoped Lady Eleanor didn't mind his shabbier state of dress. "I could have used another hour or two of sleep."

"As could I." They made their way toward the Park. Not far from the gate, he saw the ladies riding abreast on the mostly empty street.

"Let's catch up to them." St. Albans brought his horse to a trot and John followed suit.

"I'm going to ask Lady Alice to stand up with me at Almack's on Wednesday," St. Albans said.

"That is an excellent idea." John would ask Lady Eleanor. He didn't know much about the place other than that it was famous, and his sister had attended the assemblies and hated them. How did St. Albans know the ladies would be there? John shrugged. He would ask if Lady Eleanor would be attending.

"Good morning," he called, hoping Lady Eleanor would be happy to see him.

"Good morning," the three ladies said at the same time.

They were in the same order as they had been before, allowing him to ride to Lady Eleanor's side. "As you see, I am able to rise earlier."

She smiled politely. "When you are not working too late."

He thought she was teasing him, but the expression on her face told him nothing. "Yes." He glanced up at the sky, as if he'd not noticed it before. "It promises to be a lovely day."

"It does." They walked the horses through the gate. "The later spring flowers and shrubs are beginning to make an appearance."

John hadn't particularly noticed. He should have, if he was going to talk about flowers and the weather. "Are they?"

"Yes." She nodded. "The lilac in our garden is starting to bloom. It *is* almost the end of April."

"Eleanor," Lady Madeline said. "I am for a good run. What about you?"

Lady Eleanor glanced at him. "We come early so that we can gallop. You may join us if you wish."

As she spoke, the mares were already increasing their speed. He had not even answered when the horses began to canter. Damn, she had an excellent seat. He urged Aramus faster. "Come on, boy. You don't want to be beaten by a mare."

"Blast it, they're fast," St. Albans said.

John's gelding broke into a gallop. He'd almost caught up to them when the ladies reined in next to a giant chestnut tree, all of them smiling broadly. He wanted to be the one to make Lady Eleanor smile that way. He thought about telling her she rode well, but that might sound even more stupid than he wanted her to think he was. She had to know she was an excellent rider. "That was exhilarating."

St. Albans had gone to Lady Alice and said something that made her laugh. John needed to think of something witty to say. Once again, he wished he'd spent time on the Town. But he hadn't wanted to leave his father as Papa's health declined. "Are you up to another gallop?"

"Yes." Finally she gave him a real smile. "I'd like that. To the willow." She took off again, fluidly moving as one with her horse.

"Drat the woman," he muttered to himself as he rushed to catch up with her again. This was going to be a lot more work than he thought it would be.

She pulled up to the tree and her eyes widened as he arrived on her tail. "Back again? I must take advantage of the fact that few people are in the Park. At some point my sisters and I will have to come earlier."

John patted Aramus's neck. "I hadn't thought of it, but I daresay you are correct." Even he knew that ladies were not supposed to gallop when Polite Society was present. But he was becoming tired of being left in her wake. "On the count of three?"

"Very well." She settled more securely on her horse. "One, two, three."

This time he was ready, and Aramus kept pace with her mare until they reached the chestnut tree again, but the others were not there. "Where did they go?"

"The Serpentine." Lady Eleanor pointed toward the river. "Here they come now. We frequently ride that way as well."

He wondered if she preferred the country to Town. "You must ride a great deal when in the country."

"We ride every day." She appeared a little wistful. "That

is one of the things I miss when we're in Town. Yet there are many things we can do here that we cannot do there."

She probably meant shopping. According to both his sister and mother, the shopping in London was far superior to any other city in England. "Such as shopping?"

"That is always fun." Her rosy lips tilted at the corners. "I especially like the bazaars. There are so many different vendors. It is almost like a fair but inside and always there." She tilted her head slightly and regarded him. "Aside from that, there are museums, theaters, and, of course, book-stores. What do you like to do when in Town?"

"I haven't been here for a few years." John was not going to discuss his father with her. Not yet. "I too needed to do a bit of shopping. And I remember visiting the theaters and the British Museum and Hatchards when I was younger. But now I have duties in the Lords to which I must attend."

"My brother and brothers-in-law do as well." Lady Eleanor gave him a look he couldn't interpret. "They seem to derive a great deal of pleasure from it."

If he told her he too was finding taking an active part in the Lords interesting, what would she think of that? He decided to err on the side of caution. "I can understand how that might be."

A small line formed across her forehead. Fortunately, the rest of their group had reached them. "Has the Serpentine changed at all?"

"Nary a bit," St. Albans said. "However, I am indebted to the ladies for giving me bread for the ducks. They are an avaricious group."

"We saved his boots." Lady Alice's tone was both droll and slightly smug.

Lady Eleanor opened a watch hanging from her brooch. "We must be going."

John fell in next to her as they walked their horses toward

the gate. "Do you plan to attend Almack's on Wednesday night?"

"We do." She grinned. "We have heard so much about it over the years, I am looking forward to seeing it for myself."

"Our sister, Louisa, said she felt ill the first time she went," Lady Madeline said.

"Are you sure it was Louisa?" Lady Eleanor frowned. "I cannot imagine that."

Lady Madeline shrugged. "Perhaps it was someone else. But I do know that someone we know felt ill."

"That I can well imagine," Lady Eleanor said. "I am determined not to be frightened. After all, our sisters and their friends all lived through it."

John wondered if gentlemen had the same reaction to the place. "This will be my first time as well."

"Truly?" Lady Eleanor's brows rose as she focused on him as if she found that odd.

"Yes." Now what was he supposed to say? That many gentlemen avoided Almack's until they wished to wed? "I never got around to it. My mother expects me to accompany her."

"Ah," Lady Eleanor commented knowingly. "You do not actually wish to attend."

He absolutely could not tell her that the only reason he intended to go at all was to search for a wife. "I am interested to see it as well. May I beg a set from you and your sisters?"

"I would be delighted." She gave him a smile that matched the promise of the sun rising in the morning sky.

"I would as well," Lady Madeline said, then turned to her other sister. "Alice, Lord Montagu has asked us all for a set."

"Oh." She looked surprised. "That would be nice. Lord St. Albans has just requested a dance."

He leaned forward and glanced at Ladies Eleanor and Madeline. "I would like to request sets from the two of you as well."

"Delighted." Lady Eleanor inclined her head.

"A pleasure," Lady Madeline said.

They had reached the gate and bid the ladies adieu. "Until tomorrow."

That had gone well. John merely had to convince his mother to accompany him to Almack's.

CHAPTER EIGHT

For a second or two, Eleanor watched Lord Montagu ride away. He seemed nice, but an inner voice told her something was not quite right.

"Do you like him any better after today?" Alice asked.

"I hardly know. We spoke about the weather, flowers, and what we liked about Town, in no great detail, I might add." He was very handsome but either reticent to talk about himself very much or not very intelligent. Was a lack of intelligence what she had sensed? "What do you think of Lord St. Albans?"

"Hmm." Alice pursed her lips. "I am wondering if he is actually a rake."

"Do you think we ought not know him? It is not as if someone in our family introduced him." Madeline appeared bothered by the thought. "My mother is arriving today. She would be upset if we had made the acquaintance of a rake."

That was true. Matt's stepmother, now Lady Wolverton, could be a stickler. None of them had realized how much of one until Augusta announced that rather than attending the Season and finding a gentleman to wed, she planned to attend the university in Bologna, Italy. That had caused quite a muddle. Lady Wolverton even threatened to have her new husband gain guardianship over Matt's sisters. Fortunately, Grace had fixed everything by arranging for Augusta to travel to the Continent with Cousin Jane and her husband and their little boy. It all turned out well in the end. Augusta married, and when the university refused to allow her to attend, Phinn made them give her the final examination, and she earned her diploma. Still, no one wanted that type of trouble again.

"We will ask Matt." Eleanor was certain he would know which gentlemen were ineligible.

Her sisters nodded their agreement.

Eleanor took the rear of their column as they passed several maids carrying baskets and started single file around a milk wagon. Her sisters had just passed the conveyance when she heard another vehicle. A coal dray was coming directly at her. "Go!"

Adele jumped forward and the dray swerved just before it would have hit her. Eleanor turned her head to see Jemmy had the dray's leader and was yelling at the driver.

"We have to tell Matt." Alice's voice was hard and flat.

"I agree. But not when the rest of the family is around." Eleanor thanked the Lord no one had mistaken her twin for her. But that meant someone had taken the time to recognize her apart from Alice. Otherwise how would they know which horse was hers?

Less than an hour later, Eleanor and her sisters entered the breakfast room, but her brother was not there. In fact, the room was almost empty. "Where is Matt?"

"He is with Walter." Grace picked up a teapot, set it down, and glanced at their butler. "They should be here soon."

"Is something wrong with Walter?" Eleanor took her seat and took a piece of toast.

"Not at all." Fresh pots of tea were placed on the table in front of them all. "Walter has been offered a post in Spain and he wanted Matt's opinion. Augusta, Phinn, and Charlie are with them as well."

That made sense. Her sister, brother-in-law, and brother had all been to Spain and knew something of the embassy and consulates. "I am happy for him. How long will it be before he has to leave?"

"I have no idea." Grace poured a cup of tea. "Not too soon, I hope. I feel as if I barely see him anymore."

So many things were changing all at once. Yet Grace was right. As Walter got older, he tended to go on walking tours with other young gentlemen rather than coming home during school holidays. It had begun when he was at Eton and continued when he attended Oxford.

A few minutes later, Walter and the others strolled into the breakfast room, still talking. Grace glanced at him. "What did you decide?"

"I'm going to take the offer," he said. "I'm not expected there until September. Augusta is going to work with me on my Spanish."

That made sense, Eleanor thought. Augusta spoke almost every language there was, even so-called dead ones. Eleanor let Matt pour a cup of tea and take a sip before asking her question. "What do you know about Lord St. Albans?"

Madeline gave her a *really?* look and glanced at Matt. "Is he a rake?"

His dark brows raised, then lowered, forming a crease above his nose. "Not that I have heard, and I've made a point of discovering who should not be made known to you." He took another a sip of tea. "How did you meet him?"

Eleanor glanced at her sisters. Apparently, she was to answer this question. "Lord Montagu saw us in the Park and Lord St. Albans was with him. He seems to be rather worldly."

"So he might." Matt took a piece of toast. "He's been on the Town for several years."

"He has asked us all to stand up with him at Almack's," Alice added.

"Lord Montagu has as well," Eleanor said. There now, they knew everything. She looked at Augusta. "How did you like Almack's?"

Phinn, who had just taken a drink of tea, quickly covered his mouth with a serviette and swallowed. "She thought it was a dead bore until she met me." He grinned at his wife. "She was sick to death of talking about the weather."

"I know the feeling, and the Season has not even officially begun." Eleanor groaned at the thought of having to have the same conversations over and over and over again. Suddenly, what Phinn did not say prompted a question. "That means you were the only gentleman who would talk about something that mattered. What did you discuss?"

He flashed Augusta a smile and she returned it. "Do remember about whom you are speaking. We discussed Aztec architecture in Nahuatl."

Naturally, they did. Languages were her sister's passion. "And to think I have been afraid to bring up anything other than the weather." Was that the reason Lord Montagu did not speak about anything important? It might be the time to take her conversations with the gentleman in hand. "You have given me an idea."

"Did Louisa become sick at Almack's?" Madeline asked

"No. It was Lucinda, her sister-in-law." Augusta gave her sister a dubious look. "I cannot imagine Louisa being afraid of anything."

"She and Charlotte were a little nervous, but nothing to speak of," Grace said. "You will all be fine as well."

Madeline glanced at Grace. "Will Mama be accompanying us?"

"She and Richard will join us there," Matt responded. "I agree with Grace. You will all do well. Do not get into a state about attending." He rose. "Unfortunately, I must leave. I will see you at dinner."

Drat. Eleanor would have to speak with him later. Still, his advice was good. She had not been at all worried before, but now she felt a twinge of anxiety. She would simply decide not to be nervous. The worst thing that could happen was that no one asked her to dance, but she already had two sets spoken for.

"Walter and I will be there as well," Charlie said, giving her, Madeline, and Alice an encouraging look. "Remember. All hands on deck."

"That's right." Walter grinned. "You have nothing about which to be concerned."

Next to her, Madeline blinked rapidly. "I am very glad you are my brothers."

"I am too," Alice said.

Phinn whispered something to Augusta, and she nodded. "Augusta and I will be there as well."

"Yes." Eleanor reached under the table for Madeline's hand and gave it a squeeze. "We are very, very lucky."

Almack's would not be the problem. Whether Lord Montagu could actually talk about something substantial might be. Eleanor would simply have to find out.

John and St. Albans were just finishing breakfast when his mother entered the room.

They both rose and greeted her.

"Good morning." She inclined her head graciously. "Please take your seats. You do not want your tea to become cold."

"You should ask her ladyship if she has vouchers for Almack's." St. Albans's tone was so low only John would be able to hear it.

Vouchers? Why the devil would John need a voucher? He asked in a hushed voice, "What for?"

St. Albans rolled his eyes. "You can't get in without them."

Normally John did not rely on his rank, but he was a marquis. "My rank should be enough."

"Well, it's not." His friend sounded exasperated. "Ask her or you won't be dancing with Lady Eleanor."

"What are the two of you whispering about?" Plate in hand, Mama took her seat, and a footman placed a pot of tea at her elbow.

"Almack's." John practically choked out the word. "St. Albans said we need vouchers. How does one obtain a voucher if it is required?"

His mother gave St. Albans a beatific smile. "His lordship is correct. Vouchers are required. Fortunately for you, I obtained them from Lady Jersey." She dipped her spoon into a coddled egg cup. "I have been meaning to ask if you would attend. I suppose this means you would like to."

"Yes." John felt a little bit like a child again. "I would. I have asked Lady Eleanor and her sisters if they would like to stand up with me." He glanced at his friend. "So has St. Albans."

"How aforehand of you." Mama gave them an approving look. "Will you ask any of them to waltz?"

When John had thought about dancing with Lady Eleanor it was always a waltz. "Of course."

"Hmm." His mother picked up her cup and gazed at him over the rim. "You do know that in order to waltz with a young lady who is just out, you must be recommended by one of the Patronesses?"

Ask one of those gorgons? He wouldn't do it. From the corner of his eye, he could see the smirk on his friend's face. John just managed to resist running a finger under his collar. "Er, no. I was not aware of that requirement." But if he didn't ask, he wouldn't be able to waltz with Lady Eleanor and some other gentleman would. He'd be stuck with a country dance or something.

Mama set her cup down. "I will help you if you wish."

Bloody hellhounds. He swallowed, hard. "Yes, if you would not mind. I appreciate the offer."

"It is no problem at all." She gave her hand an airy wave.

It occurred to him that for his conversations with Lady Eleanor he needed to know more about flowers. "Can you tell me when lilacs bloom and if we have one?"

Next to him, St. Albans scoffed. "Is that what you discussed with Lady Eleanor?"

"Naturally." What else would John speak to her about? "You are the one who told me to appear to be innocuous."

"Ah, yes." St. Albans's tone was as dry as John had ever heard it. "Such scintillating conversation one has when one is pretending to be dull."

He decided to ignore his friend and looked down the table at his mother. "Lilacs?"

She had a strange glint in her eyes but merely said, "Yes, we have two of them. They are just budding."

"Thank you."

St. Albans pushed his chair back and stood. "Thank you for breakfast. I believe I am to attend my mother this morning and afternoon." He looked at John. "Shall we meet again tomorrow morning?"

"Yes. I have estate work I must do today. Running the properties from here is deuced troublesome."

"You do have a steward, my dear," Mama pointed out.

"I always follow Father's advice to keep track of everything. One never knows when a lack of vigilance will cause problems."

She seemed to accept his answer. "Before you go, I have

some things I would like to discuss with you, if you have the time."

"I'll see St. Albans out and come straight back." As they strolled up the corridor, John asked, "Would you like to join me for luncheon at Brooks's?"

"Unfortunately, I will not be able to." He pulled a face. "M'mother is taking me on morning visits this afternoon."

Thank God Mama had not suggested that. "I wish you well."

"I'll let you know how it goes." A footman opened the door.

"I'll be interested in what happens." That, though, begged the question of whether it was a good idea or not to go on morning visits. John could ask his mother her opinion, he supposed.

St. Albans left, and John strode back to the breakfast room, taking a chair next to his mother's. "What did you wish to discuss with me?"

"It occurred to me that by not having been on the Town, as it were, in some respects you are at a disadvantage."

He knew that he didn't have the amount of Town bronze his friends had, but he would not necessarily call that a hindrance. He could quickly learn what he needed to know. "How so?"

"For example, I will assist you in gaining a waltz with Lady Eleanor, but you must be the one to ask Lady Jersey if you can be presented to her as a suitable partner for the waltz."

He had no idea it was that formal a request. "I see. Very well. I'll do what I must."

Mama's eyes focused on his riding jacket. "Your older clothing is fine for morning rides, but you must be better dressed when you attend the Grand Strut."

John had heard about the afternoon horde of the *ton* at the Park. Why would he want to put himself through that? "I had not considered attending."

"My dear boy." She took a breath. "When you find the lady you wish to court or make an impression upon, you must invite her for a carriage ride in the Park."

"Oh." That was unexpected. However, if it was accepted behavior, he would do it. "I must see what we have for a sporting carriage."

Hi mother gave him a satisfied look. "Once I knew you were coming to Town, I took the liberty of ordering one. I received a note yesterday that it is ready to be painted. You must choose the colors. The only thing I selected was the dark brown leather for the seats."

"What kind of carriage is it?" He had seen the new Tilbury Gig and did not like them.

"It is a curricle."

"That is a good choice." John had one at home and was used to driving it.

His mother's smile looked like one of relief. "I am glad you approve."

"It has occurred to me that I did not give this visit to Town the amount of consideration I should have. Again, I appreciate your assistance." He was not used to relying on others to know how to get on. "Is there anything else?"

"You must wear evening breeches at Almack's. Now that trousers have become fashionable, some gentlemen, most famously Wellington, have tried to enter without the proper attire and have been denied entrance."

"Are trousers worn during the evening?" They were not in the country. Although he knew the metropolis was more advanced.

Mama sighed. "They are starting to become acceptable."

"I must think about that." He was in no way a dandy, but he did not want to be unfashionable while in Town. He'd already had an appointment with Weston. Between Weston and his valet, John could rely on them for advice. "Is there anything else?"

"Not at the moment." She rose. "I will let you attend to your business."

"Thank you." He bussed her cheek. "I'm glad you looked into all of this." And had gone ahead and taken the initiative to order the carriage. He was not certain he would have ordered one. "Will you write down the address of the carriage maker? I will visit them today."

"I had Lumner put it on your desk."

He caught a whiff of horse as he rose. "And thank you for not complaining about breaking your fast with the smell of the stable." She laughed; he was glad to see it. "I shall see you at luncheon if you are at home."

He started upstairs to wash and change, but if he had to go out again, he might as well visit the coach maker now. He made his way to his study, found the paper his mother left, and went out the back of the house to the stables. A gig required horses. He must see if the coach horses would do. After all, if he was going to have a fashionable carriage, he should have a handsome pair. John wondered if Lady Eleanor cared about such things. As well as she rode, he supposed she must. Most ladies only seemed to be concerned about whether the horses looked well or not. The type of lady he wanted to wed would care about the build and action of the horse as well as flowers and fashion. Once married, the house and, eventually, children would keep her busy.

CHAPTER NINE

Dobbins didn't like paying for the letter, but even if it didn't have a return address on it, the note was postmarked from Lundun. It had to be from Mitchell. Dobbins had been wonder'in if his friend'd had any luck scaring the bitch.

It's started. Soon she'll be afraid of her shadow.

Smiling to himself, he tore up the paper and tossed it into the stove. If only he could be there to see it.

Eleanor finished balancing the estate accounts, which were sent weekly from Worthington Place. She, Madeline, and Alice took turns with those, the household accounts, and the Stanwood accounts. Alice was across the square going over the Stanwood accounts with Charlie. Eleanor closed the book and put it on the shelf of the account room. She had been able to speak with Matt the afternoon of the last incident. He had decided to add another groom and an additional footman when she went out. But since then, nothing had occurred. She wanted to think the events had been accidents but could not make herself believe it. Alice had said she had a bad feeling about the whole thing, and Eleanor agreed.

She walked down the corridor to Grace's study, knocked, and waited to be called in.

"Come."

"I finished the books and I wanted to discuss something with you."

"Have a seat. I shall ring for tea."

"Thank you." Eleanor had forgotten to have a tea tray brought to her when she was working. "I am a bit parched."

She waited for Grace to finish what she was writing. The tea, along with some biscuits, arrived as she finished sealing the letter. Eleanor poured cups for them both.

"Now, then." Her sister focused on her. "What would you like to talk about?"

"Mines." She had originally thought to raise enough money to buy a mine, but then she remembered something she had been told, almost in passing, when she was younger.

Grace's brow puckered. "What about mines?"

"I want to purchase one so that I can prove it is possible to run a mine humanely. I just remembered that several years ago I was told that I had an inheritance from Aunt Margaret. Is Matt the trustee for the inheritance?"

"No. Uncle Herndon is the trustee for that property. Aunt Margaret died while Mama was still alive. I am not sure it ever came up after Matt and I wed. Although he must have been aware of it by now, as it is part of your dowry." She took a sip of tea and frowned. "In fact, the subject has not come up in years. I am not even sure if it is money, or property, or both." Grace tapped one finger on her desk. "You will have to speak with Uncle Herndon about it. But I think you should talk with Matt first. Uncle Herndon is fairly staid, and it is possible he will not approve of you managing any part of your inheritance. Yet, if Matt thinks it's a good idea, he might be talked around."

Excitement welled inside Eleanor. "Do you think Matt will approve?"

Her sister raised one brow and grinned. "He has been letting you keep the main estate books. Granted, he reviews them, but he has been impressed with how well you, all of you, are doing. I think he will give you a fair hearing."

That was all she could hope for. "Is he here?"

"I do not know. He had to go out this morning, but he might be back. The Lords aren't in session today." Grace reached over and tugged the bell-pull.

A few moments later the door opened, and Thorton bowed. "My lady?"

"Has his lordship returned?" Grace asked.

The butler appeared to think about it for a few seconds. "I believe he has. Shall I send for him?"

"Yes." Grace glanced at Eleanor. "Please ask him to attend me."

"Certainly, my lady." The butler bowed again.

Eleanor drank her tea and ate two lemon biscuits before Matt strode into the room. He immediately went around the desk to Grace and kissed her cheek. "What is so urgent?"

"I did not say it was *urgent*." She shook her head. "Eleanor has something she wishes to discuss with you. But first, did you know that she has an inheritance from a great-aunt?"

"Yes. Before we traveled to Town, Herndon wrote to me giving me a brief sketch of Eleanor and Alice's property. I should receive the full details soon." He glanced at Eleanor, then came back around the desk and took the other chair in front of it. "You have an inheritance from an aunt, and Alice has one from an uncle." He frowned. "Is something amiss?"

"Not of which we are aware." Eleanor sat a little straighter.

"I want to perform a sort of experiment, and I remembered the inheritance." She took a breath. "Do you know if it is enough to purchase a mine?"

Matt leaned back against the chair cushions and seemed to study her for several moments. "A mine?"

She nodded.

"What do you wish to do with it?"

Eleanor tried not to wring her hands. She was more nervous than she thought she would be when the idea came to her. "I want to prove that a mine can pay fair wages and be run with the health of the workers in mind and still make a profit."

"Well." He glanced briefly at Grace. "They are definitely getting more ambitious as they grow older."

Grace's eyes sparkled as she chuckled. "She is not attempting to attend university in Italy."

"That's true." He turned back to Eleanor. "Do not get excited, this is in no way finished. Herndon will make the final decision. But I have a recollection that your property includes a mine. If I'm right, and you do what you plan to do, there will be a great deal of resistance from whoever is running it. In fact, Merton recently discovered, to his chagrin, that he must wait for the contract to be renewed before he can have more control over the mines on his properties."

I have a mine!

Or she might have a mine. Eleanor wanted to bounce in her seat. Then what Matt said about Merton sank in. "What is our next step?"

"We talk to Herndon." Matt glanced at Grace again. "Do you have any idea if they are in Town yet?"

She tapped her desk again. "Aunt Herndon has not called on us. I'll send a note around, asking them to join us the day after tomorrow for tea. We will soon know if the knocker is up yet or not."

Surely it could be faster than that. Now that there might be a way forward, Eleanor wanted to act on it. "Why not today or tomorrow?"

"No. It is too late for today, and tomorrow everyone will be preparing for Almack's." Grace gave Eleanor her I-am-sorry-you-cannot-do-this-now smile. "The day after tomorrow is for the best."

That was the end of the conversation. Eleanor would have to accept her sister's decision. "Very well." At least they were both on her side. She rose from her chair. "Thank you for your help."

"You're welcome. Before you go, I should tell you I am attempting to discover at which mine the man Dobbins works. Unfortunately, Mr. Johnson took his wife and children on a holiday to celebrate them being a family."

That was unfortunate. "Thank you again. I am sure you will hear from him when they return."

Until then, Eleanor would have to be watchful.

She ambled to the hall as her twin and Madeline came down the stairs as quickly as was proper. "What is going on?"

"Dotty is here, and she brought her brother, Henry," Alice said. "We have not seen him in years."

Had it been that long? He had missed the Easter dinner. "Was he not home for Christmas last year?"

"Only for a day, and we did not see him," Alice reminded her.

She might be right. He had been at school, then university, and then in Bristol, working as a barrister. "What is he doing in Town?"

"That is what we are going to find out," Madeline said. "I think I have only met him once and for a very short time."

Eleanor glanced at the parlors off the hall. Both were empty. "Where are they?"

"In the morning room," Alice said over her shoulder.

Madeline and Eleanor hurried after her. Until they had been twelve, when Matt married Grace, Eleanor and Alice had grown up not far from Dotty and her family, and she and Charlotte were the best of friends. Charlotte had been responsible for Dotty being able to make her come out with her.

Harry rose as they entered the room and smiled. "You grew up."

Alice gave him a haughty look. "And, apparently, you did not."

"She has you there." Dotty laughed. "This is the problem with knowing someone since he or she was a child."

"Yes indeed." Harry bowed. "Please forgive me, my lady."

Very much on her dignity, Alice curtseyed. "It is good to see you again."

"It is good to see you too." He glanced at Eleanor. "How have you been?"

Unconstrained by her dignity, she hugged him. "We are all fine." She waved her hand for Madeline to come forward. "Do you remember our sister, Lady Madeline Vivers?"

He seemed to study her for a moment, then shook his head and smiled. "I remember a dark-haired girl who was always sheltered between you and Alice." Harry bowed. "My lady, it is a pleasure to meet you again."

Madeline laughed lightly and curtseyed. "I am pleased to meet you again."

She, Alice, and Eleanor hugged Dotty and took seats. Eleanor turned her attention to Harry. "What are you doing in Town? As I recall, you were always too busy to bother coming."

His eyes started to sparkle and he grinned widely. "Meet the newest member of Parliament from Bittleborough."

"Excellent!" Eleanor knew it was what he had wanted,

but there had been a problem with his uncle, the Duke of Bristol. "How did it happen?"

"Grandmamma spoke with Uncle and convinced him that even if he had not liked Mama and Papa's marriage, he should not hold me back. She reminded him of the success I'd had." Harry slid a look at his sister. "Dotty also spoke with him." He grinned again. "She, you know, is in his good graces for having married to fit her station." He shrugged. "When the seat came open, he supported me for it."

"Papa, as you also know, does not support the idea of peers selecting candidates for Parliament," Dotty said. "But he does believe that Harry was the best man for the position and was prepared to campaign for him if our uncle had not supported him."

Madeline titled her head to one side. "Will you do as the duke tells you to do?"

Harry's smile dimmed. "Only when I believe it is the right thing to do. Merton has invited me to his circle's next luncheon so that I may discuss with them which ideas that group has been supporting."

"But until then," Dotty said, "he has come to ask you three to stand up with him at Almack's."

"Excellent." Eleanor exchanged glances with her sisters. "That makes three sets for which we have partners."

Almack's was beginning to look like it would be more fun than she had thought it would be. The only question was if she or any of her sisters would be allowed to waltz. Perhaps Lord Montagu would brave one of the Lady Patronesses and ask to be recommended to her.

CHAPTER TEN

John affixed a jade tie-pin to his cravat. He had dressed with care for this evening. After all, this was his first time at the famous Almack's, and he wanted to make a good impression on Lady Jersey when he asked to waltz with Lady Eleanor.

"My lord," his valet said. "Your sister and his lordship have arrived."

"I'd better be off, then." He picked up his chapeau-bras and gloves and strolled out of his chambers.

He entered the drawing room as one footman was lighting the last candles and another was closing the dark blue brocade curtains. Why did all the rooms in this house have to be so damn dark?

"Ah." Aurelia said. "You are just in time to pour us all a glass of wine."

Bringing his attention to her, he strode forward, bowed to her, and shook his brother-in-law's hand. "My pleasure. I suppose Mama will be down soon."

"Yes." She took the proffered goblet. "Lumner said she is being told we are here."

He gave Lytton a glass. "Why is it we are all going together?"

"I remembered how nerve-racking my first time at Almack's was and I wanted to support you."

Lytton took a sip of claret. "Other gentlemen might not worry about attending, but I too recall that I was not completely sanguine about my first evening there."

"St. Albans said there was nothing to be concerned about, but he has attended the assemblies many times before." John supposed it must get better. Having his family with him would help. "Thank you. I'm glad you decided we would all go together." His mother entered the parlor. "Would you care for some wine?"

"Please." She held out her hand for the glass he'd already poured. "I am looking forward to seeing some old friends this evening."

"Indeed," Aurelia said. "That will be fun."

"Did you go last year?" John asked.

She glanced at Lytton and smiled. "We did. It was my first time in ages. I think the older ladies were shocked that I had finally wed."

That John did not doubt at all. She had been enormously hard to please. But once she met Lytton she had wasted no time marrying him and presenting him with an heir. He had once asked Lytton why he wed her, and he told John it was because she was a lady of great good sense. Since he'd been in Town he'd noticed that many of the gentlemen he knew had praised their wives for that same trait. But was good sense really necessary in a wife?

A short while later they made their way out to the larger Montagu town coach. After his mother and sister were seated, he and his brother-in-law took the backward-facing seat across from them. He folded his chapeau-bras. "I gather there will be someone to take this hat. One cannot dance with it."

"It will go with our cloaks," Aurelia said. "I do not know why they are required. No one sees them."

"For the same reason breeches are still required," Lytton

said drily. "Because the Lady Patronesses treat Almack's like their own fiefdom."

They settled in for the short ride and joined the line of carriages when they arrived. After making their way up the steps, they relinquished their cloaks and hats to a footman before approaching a man dressed as a butler and handing him their vouchers and tickets.

The man bowed. "Welcome, my lady, my lord."

Mama inclined her head. "Good evening."

John quickly followed suit. When they were a few steps past the man, he whispered, "Who is he?"

"The gatekeeper," his mother said. "No one is allowed in without the proper dress, a voucher, and a ticket."

John knew that, but he hadn't thought about there being someone whose sole purpose was to enforce the rules. "Interesting."

They entered the large assembly room. Long, curtained windows were spaced along the walls and a small balcony with an orchestra jutted into the room from above. As far as he could see, there were no hidden alcoves to encourage private conversation. Everything here took place in full view of all the guests. He surveyed the crowd, hoping he'd see Lady Eleanor.

"Come with me." His mother tugged his arm. "I want to make you known to Lady Jersey before it becomes too crowded."

He couldn't believe even more people would squeeze into the rather large ballroom. There were quite enough people already. Still, he went along. Waltzing with Lady Eleanor was his primary purpose in attending, and for that he must meet at least one of the Patronesses.

"Sally, Emily, good evening." Mama greeted a slender, dark-haired lady standing with another matron. "It is good to see you again."

"You as well," the lady called Sally said. The other lady smiled politely and inclined her head. They glanced at him.

"May I present my son, Montagu? Montagu, Lady Jersey and Lady Cowper."

He bowed and they curtseyed "My ladies, it is a pleasure to meet you."

"We are glad you have finally decided to come to the metropolis, my lord." Lady Cowper raised a brow of enquiry. "Is there anything with which we can assist you this evening?"

John cleared his throat. "As a matter of fact, there is. I would like to be recommended to Lady Eleanor Carpenter for the waltz."

The ladies glanced at each other and nodded. "I will be happy to perform the task," Lady Cowper said. "I see that Lord and Lady Worthington are just now arriving." He turned in the direction Lady Cowper was looking and there *she* was, wearing a cream evening gown with green dotted all over it. "The only trick will be to tell her apart from her twin."

"I know which one is Lady Eleanor." Even from across the room, he knew her. "Her gown has green on it."

St Albans strode up to them, nodded at him, then turned his attention to the two Patronesses. "My ladies." He bowed. "It is wonderful to see you again."

"St. Albans, I trust your parents are well," Lady Jersey said.

"They are. My mother has accompanied me this evening."

One of Lady Cowper's mobile brows rose again. "And is there someone who has interested you?"

"Yes. Lady Alice Carpenter. I would like to waltz with her."

Her ladyship's lips seemed to twitch. "And are you able to recognize the lady apart from her twin?"

St. Albans searched the room, then stopped. "Yes. She is

wearing a butter-colored gown with purple on it. Why do you ask?"

"We would not wish to recommend you to the wrong lady," Lady Jersey said. "I will perform the duty. Find me at the end of the second set."

John watched as several gentlemen headed toward the Worthington group. One gentleman bowed to either Lady Eleanor or her sisters. He would not like it if someone else got there first. "Is it possible to be recommended earlier?"

Lady Jersey must have seen the same thing he did for she said, "I do believe we are going to have one of those Seasons."

Lady Cowper nodded. "I think you are correct." She glanced at John. "Accompany me, my lord."

St. Albans gave a frustrated sigh, and Lady Jersey took pity on him. "Very well, my lord, you may come with me."

John tried to keep a polite smile on his face, but he was failing. By the time he got to Lady Eleanor, he was afraid he would be smiling widely. Lady Cowper glanced at him, and he straightened his lips. He could see Lady Eleanor clearly now. This was really going to happen. He was going to be able to waltz with her. Be able to hold her in his arms. Perhaps brush his lips against her hair. Speaking of which, her golden tresses seemed to glow more brightly in candle-light. Her pearl necklace barely touched the top of the plump mounds rising from the neckline of her bodice. What he wouldn't give to be able to carry her off. But a waltz would have to do. For now.

"Lady Cowper is approaching with Lord Montagu," Grace said.

Eleanor wondered what Lord Montagu was doing with one of the Patronesses. She and her sisters had renewed their acquaintances with the other Patronesses at Lady Bellamny's soirée, but Lady Cowper had not yet arrived in Town.

"My lady, how good to see you again." Grace inclined her head.

"It is nice to see you as well." Lady Cowper also inclined her head. "I see you are again bringing out three ladies this Season."

"I am indeed." Grace smiled politely. "Of course you already know Ladies Eleanor Carpenter, Madeline Vivers, and Alice Carpenter."

Eleanor, Madeline, and Alice curtseyed.

"What a difference just a year has made. I always knew they were very beautiful. Yet you have exceeded my expectations. I wish I had been able to attend Lady Bellamny's event." With an elegant motion of her hand, her ladyship called their attention to Lord Montagu. "Ladies, allow me to present Lord Montagu."

They again made their greetings, and her ladyship then said, "Lady Eleanor, I recommend Lord Montagu as a suitable partner for the waltz."

Eleanor made sure to put a polite smile on her face, keeping her much wider one to herself. "Thank you, my lady, my lord."

He bowed as if he did not know quite what else to do. "Well, then, I will see you for the third set."

She had always thought he was good-looking, but tonight he was extremely handsome. As with most of the gentlemen in her family, his jacket fitted perfectly over a set of broad shoulders that his riding jacket had disguised. The blue of his jacket and breeches brought out the red in his hair and the jade tie-pin almost matched his eyes. Eleanor had also not realized how tall he was.

Then again, the only time she had seen him standing was at Lady Bellamny's event. "I look forward to it."

Grace glanced toward the crowd again. "I believe we have another request for a waltz coming."

"At least one," Matt said. "Dotty is walking this way, and she has her brother and Mrs. Drummond-Burrell in hand."

Over the years, Eleanor and her sisters had met all of the Lady Patronesses and had renewed their acquaintances during the soirée. Once again greetings were made, but Lord St. Albans and Harry had apparently informed Lady Jersey and Mrs. Drummond-Burrell that they had already met the sisters. Lady Jersey recommended Lord St. Albans to Alice for the waltz, and Mrs. Drummond-Burrell recommended Harry to Madeline for the same purpose.

Before the three Patronesses left, Lady Sefton, another of the Patronesses, approached accompanied by a gentleman who reminded Eleanor of a blond Byron, he was so magnificently handsome.

"Oh dear," Lady Sefton said with a small pout. "I fear you are out of luck, my lord." She smiled at them. "Lord Lancelot wished to be recommended for the waltz, but unless I am vastly mistaken, the other ladies have already recommended these gentlemen to you."

Eleanor's opinion of the man sank. Handsome was as handsome did. And she and her sisters had already heard of Lord Lancelot. Augusta's husband, Phinn, had been the cause of the gentleman leaving Town three years before because he had practically run her down being stupid on his horse. Eleanor hoped he had grown up since then.

Lord Lancelot bowed gracefully. "Ah, my dear Lady Sefton, that only means that they may now waltz." The music for the first set started, and he bowed to Alice. "May I have this dance, my lady?"

Probably remembering what she had heard, Alice stiffened slightly. Nevertheless, she knew she could not deny him the set. But Harry, who was closest to her, said, "I am sorry, my lord, but Lady Alice has done me the honor of promising her first set to me."

Before his lordship could ask either Eleanor or Madeline, Lord St. Albans had made the same claim about dancing with Eleanor and Lord Montagu said that Madeline was dancing with him.

"Their first three sets are taken," Matt said, looking none too kindly at the gentleman. "We will leave after supper."

Well, that was the end of that. Eleanor wondered if her brother knew something the rest of them did not.

Lord Lancelot bowed and sauntered away. By then, the rest of their sisters and their husbands had joined them.

"Good Lord," Phinn said. "Not him again."

Augusta frowned at the man. "He looks to be improved. At least he is not wearing a spotted kerchief as a neckcloth."

"But is he?" Matt raised his quizzing glass at his lordship's retreating form. "I will make inquiries."

"It would be a shame not to be able to stand up with someone that gorgeous," Alice mused.

"If you like peacocks," Lord St. Albans drawled scornfully. "He reminds me of a Gainsborough painting I once saw of a young boy in a light blue suit."

Eleanor wondered what caused that reaction. "Do you know him?"

"Not so much know him as know of him. I went to school with one of his brothers. Lord Lancelot is said to be as spoiled as his name might suggest. He fancies himself a poet."

Charlie shook his head. "I was in school with him. He was

a dead bore. Perhaps it will be easier if I have a conversation with him to see if he has changed."

"I, for one, will stand up with him if he asks," Madeline said. "Then we will soon know if he has improved or not."

Matt rubbed his forehead as if it ached. "He will not be allowed an introduction until I have determined he is the type of gentleman you should know."

Yet, speaking of boring conversation, Eleanor wondered if Lord Montagu would improve. If not, she would have to look to another gentleman.

St. Albans led her out for the quadrille. Her sisters and their partners, along with one other couple, joined them in the circle. It was easy to carry on a conversation during the quadrille, as two couples danced at the same time while the other two couples waited until it was their turn to dance.

Eleanor and Lord St. Albans took their places, she curt-seyed and he bowed. "Lady Alice said that the only thing different about being in Town this year was that she was finally making her come out."

Eleanor could easily imagine her sister saying that. "We have been coming to Town during the Season for several years. However, I do think she will change her mind. After all, we have never before been to balls and other entertainments. This is the first year we are allowed to go riding in the mornings without Matt or one of our brothers with us."

"I hope you are right. I would hate for her to be bored." He had used his habitual drawl, but the mirth in his eyes betrayed him.

The other two couples returned to their places and it was time for them to begin. She and her sisters had practiced dancing for years and had even gone to a few local assemblies and dances last winter in preparation for their come outs, but this seemed completely different. It was as if they were doing it for real now.

She danced the next set, a country dance, with Harry. It was much like dancing with one of her brothers. Finally, it was time for the waltz.

CHAPTER ELEVEN

Lord Montagu led her to the dance floor and bowed as she curtseyed. He took one of her hands, and despite their gloves she felt the warmth of his touch. But when his palm touched her waist, Eleanor had to stop herself from moving closer to him. It did not help that she had to place her hand on his waist as well. She was expecting the layers of his clothing to be a barrier to the flames darting through her body, but they were not. Apparently, the mere fact that she was touching him was enough to strengthen the sensations she was experiencing. This was nothing like waltzing with any other gentleman. She tried to quell the urge to shiver.

"Are you all right?" He gazed at her with concern.

"Perfectly." She smiled at him as if nothing had happened. "I just felt a bit of a breeze." Although how that was to have happened with the long windows in the room closed, she did not know. The music began, and for a few moments she reveled in the feeling of dancing on air. "You dance very well."

"Thank you." Lord Montagu grinned. "I was just about to say the same thing to you. With you the steps are effortless."

Before she had taken those types of compliments as

nothing special, but with him it was different. They did dance well together. It was effortless. "Thank you."

He looked at her as if he wanted to know something, and she was about to tell him to just say it when he did. "When I stood up with Lady Alice she said that all three of you are involved in a particular charity."

Oh good. They were not going to talk about the weather or how she was enjoying her Season. "We are. Lady Merton and our sister, Grace, started it, but we, my other sisters, all became involved. We rescue children and provide homes for war widows and their families if needed. My brothers-in-law all make a point to hire former soldiers and train them as grooms and footmen, or whatever profession they decide to learn." Eleanor could not tell him about her sisters and friends taking more active roles that had put their lives at risk. "Lord and Lady Littleton"—Eleanor frowned to herself—"do you know them?"

"Yes." Lord Montagu nodded. "I met them a few years ago."

"Well, it turns out that he, or it might have been his father or mother, started a program to train local youths to be in service."

He appeared struck by the idea. "That is interesting. I have often thought individuals could make a large difference, but I had no idea where to start."

This was encouraging. Although he must not have much of an imagination if he could not work out how to begin helping his own tenants. His mother and sister had mentioned schools. "Do you have schools on your estates?"

"I believe there has been an attempt to open a school." His tone held a great deal of discomfort over the scheme.

She decided not to pursue the topic of his possible schools and instead tell him about her latest venture. "We are now discussing other training programs and more advanced schools for those who wish to attend university."

Lord Montagu's dark brows came together as he gave her a curious look. "Who would attend the advanced schools?"

"Anyone with the interest and ability to do the work." They raised their arms for the next twirl, and she was distracted by his breath softly brushing her neck. "The only difficulty of which I can think is with the parents. Some of them do not understand how important an education is, even a basic education."

Eleanor surreptitiously studied him in order to gauge his reaction. If he was to be eligible for her, he had to be interested in helping others. Unfortunately, the lull in their conversation only served to remind her how heavy his hand felt on her waist. As if it would leave a permanent brand, and how firm his back was under her palm. Her older sisters had mentioned *sensations*. And she wondered if these were the sensations they meant. She gave herself an inner shake. Surely it was much too soon.

His eyes widened, as if he realized what she was thinking. "You have given me a great deal to consider."

But was that good or bad? "I have always found engaging with the charities to be rewarding."

"I can see how that can be." They lifted their arms for another twirl.

This discussion was frustrating. Eleanor wanted to be able to help him plan his charitable programs. Someone must. Why should it not be her? She disliked inaction when action was clearly required. Still, she supposed that not a lot could be done during a waltz. At least she had given him some ideas. Aside from that, the dance was ending, and she still had not discovered what she wanted to about him. Was he unable to work things out for himself, or was he merely adhering to the *ton*'s form of politeness when speaking with an unmarried lady? Eleanor completely understood Augusta's aggravation with gentlemen.

Lord Montagu brought them to a halt and bowed. "My lady, I can safely say I have never enjoyed a dance so much. I feel as if I have had nothing more substantial than a feather in my arms."

In his arms.

Heat rose into Eleanor's neck and cheeks as she curtseyed. "I greatly enjoyed it as well, my lord." Knowing the tingling she would probably feel, she lightly placed her hand on his arm. "Thank you for arranging to waltz with me."

"It was my pleasure." They strolled to where Matt and Grace stood chatting with the others in their group who had not danced. "Why do you depart after supper?"

Eleanor almost laughed when she remembered Matt's derision at Almack's version of the meal. "Because of the children." Lord Montagu had a confused expression. "When Matt and Grace first married, Mary was only five, and Theodora and Phillip were eight. None of them were able to adjust to Town hours." Eleanor was not going to admit that she, Alice, and Madeline had not done well with them either. "Grace insisted that everyone take breakfast and dinner together. Ergo, they had to retire earlier."

"It's unusual, but it makes a certain sort of sense." His lordship's tone was considering.

What had his childhood been like? "What did your family do when in Town?"

"My sister and I remained in the country. My father was not fond of the metropolis and believed the air was bad for us. The few bolts to Town we made were short and devoted to visiting the museums and other educational pursuits. When my sister came out, she was up very late most evenings.

Then again, we did not have younger brothers or sisters, nor were we allowed to dine with our parents until after I had gone to school."

From what Eleanor had heard, that was the normal way of things. "The only time we do not take meals together is when Matt and Grace have a formal dinner."

Eleanor opened her mouth to expand on the conversation and shut it again. She would not tell Lord Montagu about the time Con had invited himself to breakfast in order to court Charlotte simply because he wanted to show her he was good with children.

"Do they have many formal dinners?"

His voice shook her out of her reverie. "No. Not at all. Most of our large dinners are due to the whole family being together." The question came to her. Would Lord Montagu do the same if he was interested in her? "They have the formal dinners before balls, and there are only one or two of those entertainments during a Season. They are much more likely to have events where politics are discussed."

He suddenly grinned. "This is all becoming clearer. I can understand why anyone still in the schoolroom would not be allowed during a dinner before a ball."

A scene with the children attempting to eat with everyone dressed in evening wear and Hugo flinging food around appeared in her mind, and she laughed.

He was still grinning as they approached her family. "I see you have the same vision of that as I did."

"Yes. But my vision is probably more vivid. I dine with the children most of the time."

"I would be interested in seeing how that worked." He sounded as if he was thinking of it as some sort of experiment.

"I am sure Grace would be happy to invite you." She was always happy to add another place setting to the table.

"Hmm. I must think of a way to obtain an invitation." He glanced at Eleanor with a glint in his eyes. "Do you think that if I tell her I have never dined with children she would feel it her duty to ask me to join you? Merely to broaden my experience."

Eleanor thought it was very possible. It would also cause a great deal of hilarity among the rest of her relatives. She ruthlessly suppressed the burble of laughter attempting to escape and composed her features to display only an inno-cent mien. "You could try."

"I believe I will."

They had reached her group and she started to remove her hand from his arm but remembered it was time for supper. Then the realization that she had not wanted to lose the heat of his arm made her wonder why that was.

"Let's get this over with," Matt grumbled.

Lord Montagu dipped his head so that his lips were close to her ear, and again she shivered as his breath caressed her neck. "Is something wrong?"

"Did no one tell you that the only thing served at supper is dry cake and tea?"

He made a face. "No."

"Indeed. My sister will have ordered a repast to be served when we arrive home."

"Remind me why it is so important to come here." His lordship's tone was so disgusted she wanted to go into whoops.

"Because it is extremely select. There are even some dukes and other members of the peerage who are not allowed vouchers. It is all based on bloodlines and connections."

As they followed her elder brothers and sisters down

to supper, Eleanor considered how and how soon Lord Montagu would attempt to secure an invitation to a meal. Or if he really cared to do so. He could have been making polite conversation, but she did not think he was. He had not appeared a great deal more intelligent this evening, yet he had appeared more interested in the topics she had discussed. And she had had a wonderful time dancing with him.

John could not for the life of himself decide if he had made any progress with Lady Eleanor or not. He didn't know how or when he had determined that she was the lady for him. He simply had. And the waltz he'd danced with her seemed to solidify the idea. He might not have spent much time in Town, but he had attended numerous local assemblies and other entertainments. He'd never felt the way he did around her with any other lady. It was as if they were made for each other. Not only that, but when he had indicated that he had not thought of schools for his tenants and the like, she had not pushed him to immediately come up with a plan, as his sister would have done. Lady Eleanor had been happy to plant the seed, as it were. St. Albans had been right; John wouldn't be happy with a dim lady. Yet he still wanted a wife who'd let him take the lead and not drag him behind her. He'd always thought that was what Aurelia did with Lytton, but seeing them together this Season, John wondered if he was correct. She appeared to defer to him as much as he did to her. Perhaps having a home of her own and a child had tempered his sister's need to be in charge. If only he could test his hypothesis. Yet he couldn't do it with a currently unmarried lady. He'd have to find a lady who had a reputation of being managing before she wed and compare her behavior after she married. But how would he do that?

Drat it all.

If only he'd spent more time in Town. On the other hand, his mother might know. He glanced around and didn't see her. Then again, there were a great many people here. Lady Eleanor's group easily exceeded fifteen people, and almost all of them were related in some form or fashion.

Exeter approached Worthington and said something to which the other man nodded. Was there to be another meeting? John would have to ask about it. When they took their seats, he found himself next to Lady Worthington.

She gave him a polite smile. "I understand this is your first time at Almack's."

"It is." He noticed that the other gentlemen had gone to a long table. "Am I correct that I am to fetch the cake from the table?" He had been to all sorts of suppers, some where everyone sat at a dining table. Those were the smaller ones and others where the gentlemen served the ladies.

Her lips tilted at the corners like those of Lady Eleanor's. "You are correct. The footmen will bring around lemonade and tea."

"Excuse me." He stood and bowed to Lady Worthington. "I will be back directly."

He was halfway to the long table when St. Albans handed John two plates. "I thought you might not know."

"Thank you." He accompanied his friend back to the ladies. "Is this typical of an evening at Almack's?"

"Yes." His friend seemed focused on their table. "Albeit it is more interesting to be in the Worthingtons' group. They are all quite remarkable."

"I've been thinking about what you said about dull ladies. I told you I did not want a lady like my sister, but recently I have noticed that my sister seems to have changed a bit since she wed." How was he to phrase his question?

But this was St. Albans. John did not have to worry so much with him. "Do you know of a lady who was managing before her marriage and is not quite so much afterward?"

He thought he saw a brief smirk on his friend's face but couldn't be certain. "From what I have heard, Lady Exeter and Lady Fotherby sound like they meet your definition."

John knew Exeter better than Fotherby. But how would he go about asking the question?

"Montagu," Worthington said. "If you're interested, we are meeting at my house again tomorrow after luncheon."

"I am interested. Are we meeting at Brooks's beforehand?" John hoped they'd continue their discussion about aiding the miners.

"The others might. I have something else to which I must attend."

Exeter joined them. "I'll go with you to Brooks's for luncheon. My wife has to take my sister around."

"Excellent." John was happy that he had met Exeter before this Season. It had smoothed his way in the Lords.

They made their way back to the ladies, who had managed to secure tea. John took his seat between Lady Eleanor and her sister. After placing the plate of cake in front of her, he took a sip of tea. "I do not think I have ever had tea this weak. Perhaps I should try the lemonade."

"It is worse than the tea." Her nose wrinkled adorably. "I had a taste. It was horribly sour."

He'd order sustenance when he arrived home. "Will you ride in the morning?"

"Of course." She nibbled a piece of cake and swallowed. "I will not be up late enough to miss riding."

John remembered what she had said once about not being late for breakfast. They must break their fast even earlier than he did. "Am I correct that you breakfast after riding?"

"Yes." She took a sip of tea. "Although soon, with more people arriving to ride when the Park is empty, we will have to go even earlier than we do now."

If only there was a way to invite her to break her fast with him. His mother was in residence, but a niggling voice told him inviting only Lady Eleanor would not be proper. He would have to arrange for a group to attend the breakfast. But that would defeat his purpose of trying to spend time with her alone. "Then what will you do?"

"She will do what her sisters have done before her." Lady Worthington had apparently turned her attention to John and Lady Eleanor's conversation. He wondered if her ladyship had known which direction his mind had taken. "She will have toast and tea before she goes out and after riding she will join the family for breakfast." Lady Worthington gave him a considering look. "My lord, you are welcome to break your fast with us if you wish. It is no trouble at all."

"Early breakfast?" St. Albans piped up, as if he had not been eating with John but starving instead.

Lady Worthington laughed lightly. "You may join us as well."

John wondered if she was used to taking in strays.

"Thank you, my lady." St. Albans smiled broadly, but Lady Alice did not look as pleased as he obviously was.

A quick glance at Lady Eleanor told John nothing. Well, in for a penny, in for a pound. "I am happy to accept your invitation, my lady. Would tomorrow be too soon?"

She picked up her cup and looked at him over the rim. "Not at all."

Lady Alice raised one brow at Lady Eleanor, who gave an imperceptible shrug. Did she not care at all if he spent more time with her? He had thought that after their waltz she would feel the same way he did, but perhaps not. Still,

John would stay with his decision. What was the saying, nothing ventured, nothing gained? Lord, he hadn't thought of so many clichés at once since he was a child and trying to make a point.

CHAPTER TWELVE

Lady Worthington rose, and the rest of them did as well. "It has been a very pleasant evening. However, we must depart." She inclined her head to him and St. Albans. "Gentlemen, I shall see you in the morning after your ride."

He bent his head so that only Lady Eleanor could hear him. "I would be happy to escort you out."

"Thank you." Her finely arched brows drew together slightly, causing a line to form between her eyes. "Are you sure you do not wish to remain?"

There was no reason to stay if she was gone. From the corner of his eye, he saw that his mother and sister had risen as well. Lytton would escort them down. "I am positive. My mother and sister are ready to depart."

"In that case, let us be gone." She laid her fingers on his arm, and he felt her touch heat his whole body. Even when he'd been younger and randy, he'd never had that reaction to a female before.

They followed the family out of the room. Fortunately, the entrance was not far. After Worthington called for their coaches, John did the same. He finally had a chance to actually count the number of people who were with them and they were twelve. All the gentlemen except two were with their ladies. The two single men approached them. Both of them sharply resembled Ladies Eleanor and Alice, and John recognized the older one as Lord Stanwood.

She smiled at them before turning to John. "My lord, have you met my brothers, Mr. Walter Carpenter and Stanwood?"

"My lord." John inclined his head to Stanwood. "We met recently at the Lords. Mr. Carpenter, I'm happy to make your acquaintance."

The younger brother bowed. "It is good to meet you as well." He grinned. "I hear you are to join us for Morning Mayhem."

"Morning Mayhem?" John wasn't certain to what her brother was referring.

Lady Eleanor glanced at the ceiling. "That is what he and our younger brother, Phillip, have taken to calling breakfast."

His mother, sister, and brother-in-law joined them before he could inquire further. They greeted the rest of the group. He was a little surprised they all knew each other.

Mama turned to him. "Did you have a good evening?"

Aurelia chuckled under her breath. "Perhaps you should ask if it was as bad as he thought it would be."

His mother gave a slight shake of her head, and he noticed that other people were starting to leave the supper room. It would not do to be heard criticizing Almack's. Fortunately, he didn't have to lie. "I had an excellent evening."

"The coaches are here," one of the gentlemen said.

He followed Lady Eleanor's brother-in-law and sisters to a large town coach and assisted her in, then stepped back and bowed. "I hope to see you in the Park tomorrow."

"Until then." She gave a little wave before the coach started forward.

John watched the carriage leave before joining his family in their town coach. Again, he sat on the backward-facing seat with Lytton.

The only sound was the horses' hooves on the cobblestone as they made their way to Montagu House. John was glad his mother and sister didn't want to interrogate him. Although everything that occurred had happened where everyone could see it. When they arrived home he was relieved to see his mother had ordered a light meal. Did everyone do that because of the truly inferior offerings at the assembly? Ah well. It really didn't matter. What was important was that he'd been able to dance with Lady Eleanor. When he held her in his arms he knew she belonged there. But if she did not feel the same, he would need to find a way to convince her. And John had the sneaking feeling that gaining her whole family's approval would be necessary. He blew out a breath. Morning Mayhem it was. How disruptive could breakfast with a few children be?

Eleanor and her sisters rode home with Matt and Grace. Both the inner and outer lanterns had been lit, allowing them to see one another.

Grace settled her skirts before glancing at them. "What did you think of Almack's?"

"It was not as oppressive as I thought it would be," Madeline said. "Yet that might have been because I was surrounded by my family and friends."

"I was happy to be able to waltz." Eleanor had never enjoyed a waltz so much. But she needed time to work out the physical feelings she had experienced.

"It was fine." Alice's tone clearly conveyed that she was not happy about something. "I suppose we will have to go back next week."

Grace gave her a sympathetic look. "We will. But there are many other entertainments to which to look forward."

"We were supposed to attend Lady Castlereagh's—no,

Lady Londonderry's ball tomorrow, but they are now in mourning." Eleanor wondered what the major event would be now that the ball had been canceled.

"Is there anything else to attend?" Madeline asked

"Lady Markham has arranged a ball to take its place," Grace replied.

"The following night is Lady Harrington's ball." The lady and her husband had returned from Paris last year after she had given birth to a boy. Eleanor would have to remember to ask her which city she liked the most.

"You will not have to worry about being well entertained." Matt's tone was so dour they all chuckled.

"We will not give you any trouble at all," Alice assured him.

He raised both brows and pinned her with a stern look. "I've heard that before."

"It was not Dotty's fault those ladies mistook what she and Dom were doing," Madeline said, taking up the defense. "Or that Charlotte was kidnapped. Or that Louisa announced her marriage a bit too soon. Or that Augusta wanted to attend university."

Matt dragged a hand down his face. "Be that as it may, I would like to get through this Season without any of those things occurring again."

Honestly, Eleanor could not conceive of anything like that happening to them. On the other hand, she could understand her brother-in-law's concern. She would have said something if it would have done any good. They would simply have to show him that they could get through the Season unscathed.

She was not surprised when her sisters, brothers-in-law, and cousins joined them at Worthington House for a far more substantial supper. Her twin did surprise her.

"Grace, did you have to invite St. Albans to breakfast?"

Alice took a glass of wine from Thorton. "I am not at all certain I want him there."

"She did not have much of a choice," Matt pointed out. "He was rather like a hungry puppy."

"I suppose so." She sat down next to Charlotte and Con on one of the two large sofas in the drawing room.

If their family kept growing, they might have to rearrange this room to add a third sofa. Eleanor just realized that Harry Stern was with them as well. She would have to ask Madeline what she thought of him later.

"Are you upset about Lord Montagu coming to break his fast with us?" Matt was staring at her.

"No. No. Not at all." She did not know why, but she actually wanted to see how he would do around all the children. "In fact, I think that everyone should bring the four-and five-year-olds."

Louisa suddenly broke out into laughter. "She is setting a test for him."

Next to her, Rothwell groaned. "He's in for it now." He glanced at Eleanor. "If you are sure that is what you want, we'll bring them."

"I, for one, think it is a very good idea," Dotty said. "After all, if he cannot deal with the whole family, what good is he?"

Eleanor glanced at Charlie, who appeared thoughtful. After a second or two he nodded. "I agree. We are an extremely close family. As evidenced"—he grinned—"by the extra trunk I had to purchase to hold all the letters I received from you."

"One does not marry the person but the family." Rothwell grimaced slightly. "As I have reason to know."

"It was not that bad." Louisa took his hand and held it.

He glanced at Matt. "It did teach me to listen to more experienced heads."

Eleanor did not quite know what had happened, only that Grace and Matt had gone to Rothwell's estate to assist Louisa.

"It's settled, then." Kenilworth tossed off his glass of wine and stood. "Any potential spouse must get on with the whole family." He helped Charlotte up. "If we are going to participate in Morning Mayhem, we must be off."

"Not you too!" Eleanor meant to use a sterner tone, but she barely held back a giggle. "Morning Mayhem indeed." Yet she received no support at all. Everyone seemed to think it was an excellent description.

"You must admit"—Grace finally stopped laughing—"it does fit. Marquises picking egg from the table—"

"And dukes wiping eggs from faces," Dotty added. "The *ton* would be in shock."

And that was the least of it. Eleanor had to admit that they did have a point. And once she and her sisters wed, the table would only grow larger. "I'm for my bed as well. Morning comes earlier and earlier. Good night."

"I'll join you." Alice rose and glanced at Madeline.

"Yes, I'm coming as well." She said something to Harry, and he nodded. What was that about? "Good night."

The three of them followed Con and Charlotte out of the drawing room to the hall. After the couple left, Eleanor and her sisters headed up the stairs to their bedchambers. Normally they would have gathered in the parlor to discuss the evening, but tonight they all seemed to need to keep their own counsel. Or, Eleanor thought, consider their next steps. Her body still tingled when she thought about Lord Montagu's hands on her waist and the nearness of him. Her older sisters had mentioned something of the sort happening with their husbands. Ergo it must be a good sign. Eleanor was glad Con and Charlie had said what they had and she was pleased that Lord Montagu wanted to come to breakfast, even after he had been warned. It *was* a test of sorts. The only other thing she must discover is if he possessed more than merely moderate intelligence. And if he cared about doing something concerning the plight of the poor in Britain. The question was how to do that? If only they were attending a political event. She would ask Grace if it could be arranged. In the meantime, Matt was to discover if Uncle Herndon was in Town and if he was make an appointment with him so that she could discuss her plan.

CHAPTER THIRTEEN

John woke early the next morning. He'd already left word for Cook that he would not be home for breakfast. Even though the prospect of breaking his fast with children still in the schoolroom was a bit daunting, he was inordinately excited about it. He had wondered what it would be like ever since Eleanor mentioned it. Drat it all, he must remember to call her Lady Eleanor. If he kept this up, he was going to slip, and it would be at the worst possible moment. That was always the way those things worked. John hoped he would be given a chance to at least wash his hands after riding. Smelling like a horse in a dining room of any sort did not appeal to him.

Making the final adjustment to his cravat, he shrugged on his jacket. As usual, St. Albans rode up just as John reached the pavement. "Good morning." He swung onto his horse. "Are you looking forward to breakfast as much as I am?"

"Good morning." St. Albans inclined his head. "At least as much. I have decided Lady Alice is the right lady to be my wife."

"That narrows down your hunt." John did wonder what the lady would think about that. If her expression at supper last evening was anything to judge by, she might not be happy about the prospect. But it wasn't Eleanor's happiness at stake. Ergo, it was no bread and butter of his. At least not yet. It suddenly dawned on him that he seemed to have a protective streak when it came to Eleanor. Would that extend to the other members of her family? It certainly seemed that it did for her brothers-in-law. He hadn't realized it until he was getting ready for bed last night, but all of them had kept an eye on all three sisters. It was conceivable it would happen to him as well.

John had just turned the corner onto Park Lane as Eleanor and her sisters were riding toward the gate and him. She looked glorious. The small, feathered hat she wore allowed her golden hair to reflect the early morning sun. And her Pomona green habit was different from the ones he'd seen lately. Instead of a short jacket, she wore one that hugged her form to her waist, causing him to remember how she felt when he'd waltzed with her last evening.

He urged his horse to her side. "Good morning."

"Good morning." Her smile made something inside him warm. "Are you ready for a good gallop?"

"Both Aramus and I are." As John spoke, the horse snorted.

Eleanor's laugh was like a light tinkling of chimes. "In that case, we'll go to the large willow by the Serpentine."

"On the count of three." The second he said "three," she was off. Eleanor and her mare moved as one being, but he was ready for her. It wasn't long before he had drawn even with her. It occurred to him that if he did marry Eleanor, he might spend the rest of his life trying to keep up with her. John gave himself a shake. That was probably only on horseback. In every other way she was a typical young lady.

She reined in her horse. "You caught up quickly."

"It did not take me long to realize that you waste no time starting. What is your mare's name?"

"Adela." Eleanor motioned to his gelding. "You said your horse's name is Aramus?"

John patted the gelding's neck. "Yes."

"I like it." Her gaze moved over his horse. "Aramus is a much better name than Brutus or some of the others I have heard."

"Adela is pretty." He wanted to say *just like her rider*, but that would be too forward. "Just like she is."

Eleanor laughed again, this time from deeper inside her. "It is a much better name than the one I had for my first horse."

He thought of the names he and his sister had for their first horses. "I believe better names come with age."

She leaned down and patted her mare's neck. "My first horse's name was Butterfly. What was yours?"

"Blacky. Naturally because he was black." They turned to walk along the Serpentine. "Why Butterfly?"

"Because she was pretty, and my sister had already named hers Pretty Lady."

John laughed. "That's what my sister named her first horse."

"I think there must be a great many horses with that appellation." Eleanor smiled and shook her head. "Did your sister want you to name your horse Galahad? We tried to convince our younger brother to do that."

"No, Lancelot. He was, apparently, a much more romantic figure."

She lifted a light brown brow. "I am of the firm belief that Lancelot is a fine name for an animal, but not for a person. Phinn told us that Lord Lancelot almost ran down my sister, Augusta, on his horse to express his undying love."

"Good Lord." John always knew Lord Lancelot was an idiot, but he hadn't known how much of one. "The man must have been mad."

Eleanor gave a firm nod. "Phinn sent him home with a groom and was preparing to speak with his father, but someone else did it before he could, and Lord Lancelot was sent home."

"At least Worthington did not allow any of you to stand up with him." John must try to make the time to find out if the man had changed at all. "Does that mean that you do not have to accept an offer to dance with him?"

She nodded. "Matt said he would not allow it until he was convinced that his lordship had reformed."

"That's good." There was a ball this evening. "Are you attending the Markham ball?"

"Oh, yes." She looked excited about it. "My family is close to Lady Harrington, who is Lady Markham's daughter-in-law. It will be nice to see her again." Eleanor glanced at him and tilted her head as if she'd forgotten something. "Did you know that Lord and Lady Harrington were in Paris with the embassy?"

"I believe my mother mentioned it. She knows Lady Markham." John really should have made a point of coming to Town sooner. "May I have the supper dance if you still have it free?"

"Yes. You may." Eleanor smiled at him. "I imagine this will be much more fun than Almack's was."

"It was rather stuffy there." Her family had left much earlier than any of the others. The early supper made it seem even more so. "I expect the food and drink will be far superior to what was offered at Almack's."

She went off into a peal of laughter. "It was truly horrible. I am so glad sustenance was ready when we got home."

"My mother ordered a small supper for us as well." It said a great deal about the power the Lady Patronesses had over the *ton* that they could thrive, as they offered horrible food and drink. "The cake was not too bad."

"No, that was the best thing about it, though." She glanced around. "We have lost my sisters."

Behind them, the groom cleared his throat. John had forgotten the servant was there. "They went to the old oak tree, my lady."

"Thank you, Jemmy." Eleanor looked at John. "We should find them. We will have to go home soon."

"Very well." He'd soon discover if Walter Carpenter was exaggerating about breakfast or not. "Gallop?"

She tilted her head again for a moment. "Canter."

"As you wish." It was strange that he suddenly wanted to make a courtly bow to her, as if they were in a story of some sort. They urged their horses into canters and headed for the giant oak tree where her sisters, St. Albans, and Harry Stern were talking.

"Good morning, Stern," John said as they came to a halt.

"Good morning to you as well." Stern inclined his head.

Ladies Alice and Madeline glanced at Eleanor, and all three of them made imperceptible nods. He wished he could read their minds.

"Well, gentlemen," Lady Alice said. "Whoever is joining us for breakfast, come along. We must be going back."

"Excellent," Stern said. "I'm famished."

John stared at the other man for a moment. When had he been invited? Then he remembered that his sister and her husband were cousins of Lord Worthington. As long as

Harry Stern didn't turn his eye toward Eleanor, he could do as he pleased. Their coterie rode toward the gate, then on to Worthington House in Berkeley Square.

As one would expect, the butler greeted them. "Gentlemen, please follow James"—the butler indicated a footman—"he will show you where you may wash."

By the time they started up the stairs, the only thing he could see of the ladies was a flash of green as Eleanor turned a corner. "I wonder how many people there will be at breakfast."

St. Albans shrugged. "Couldn't say."

Harry Stern was quiet, but the corner of his lip twitched. They entered a room that had been set up for them with three washbasins. John was wiping his face dry when he heard what sounded like stampeding horses on the stairs. "What in God's name was that?"

Instead of answering, James said, "Gentlemen, breakfast is being served."

The footman led them to the hall, then to a large, bright room where it seemed like a dozen children were claiming chairs. John counted eight who were clearly in the schoolroom, but five of them were quite young. Not a dozen. But more than enough.

"The babies and toddlers are in the nursery," Eleanor said, taking his arm. "You will sit next to Grace."

He noticed St. Albans was on Lady Worthington's other side. Everyone who'd attended Almack's in the Worthington party was present this morning. He glanced around the room looking for a sideboard but found none.

"The footmen will serve us," Lady Worthington said. "It is much easier with the children."

Trays of various meats, different styles of eggs, and fish

were brought by footmen. All the adults received their own racks of toast and pots of tea.

"Hugh, what have I told you? Put your fork down when there is food on it," Kenilworth's little daughter said in a very stern tone. She glanced at John, who was across the table from her. "The last time we were here for breakfast he threw his eggs on the table. Papa had to clean it up."

Despite the admonishment, scrambled eggs went flying to the center of the table. "Sorry, Constance, I forgot."

"You *always* forget." John looked to his left as the little girl glared at her brother. He knew just how the boy felt. She raised her small chin. "You will have to stay in the nursery with the babies if you cannot behave."

"No, I won't." He raised his eyes to his father.

Around the table, napkins covered mouths while eyes couldn't hide the laughter, the older members appeared determined not to show their mirth.

"Do not laugh," Lady Worthington whispered.

"You will," Lady Kenilworth said as her husband cleaned up the mess his son had made. "I suggest you put your fork in your mouth before you wave it around."

The girl sitting next to Rothwell leaned over her plate. "Hugh, you are behaving like a baby."

With each admonishment, his look became more mulish. "Am not."

"You are," the boy next to Worthington said. "You are the only one of us making a mess. Elizabeth is a year younger, and she has better table manners."

The incipient laughter died as the older members of the family glanced at one another, including two girls and a boy who were older but obviously still in the schoolroom.

Hugh let out a large sigh and addressed himself to the rest of his food.

"What are all of you doing today?" Lady Worthington asked.

"Lords," John and the other peers at the table said in unison.

"We have some shopping to do," Lady Madeline said.

Worthington gave Eleanor a pointed look. "Don't forget, we have an appointment when I return."

"I will be here." Her eyes shone with happiness, and John wondered what the meeting was about.

"I have a meeting at the Foreign Office," Walter Carpenter said.

Her Grace of Rothwell glanced at Lady Worthington. "Are we still taking the babies out this afternoon?"

"We are. The older children are going to the Tower today."

"The Tower?" Hugh's attention was immediately diverted from his plate.

"Only if we behave," his sister said.

"And after we take our exercise," Rothwell's daughter added.

A girl who resembled Worthington dabbed her lips with a serviette. "After our dancing lessons, Mary and I are going riding with our grooms."

John studied the younger children for a few seconds and finally saw the resemblance they all had to each other in one form or another. He recalled Walter Carpenter saying something about a bunch of five-year-olds. "Are you all five?"

There were nods around the table, but it was Rothwell's daughter who had her mother and uncle's bright green eyes, who answered. "We are all within a few months of one another except for Elizabeth, who is four." On the other side of Worthington a little girl smiled. "Gideon is the eldest"—the boy next to Worthington inclined his head—

"Vivienne is next"—the little girl seated beside Merton grinned at John—"I am next, then Hugh and Constance; they are twins."

John had never felt the need for a large family, but what would it have been like to be part of a group of cousins all the same age or close to it? If he did marry Eleanor, he'd be a member of this family, and if her sisters wed this Season, his children would have cousins close to their age.

The clock chimed the time, and the children rose and began to file out of the room.

"School," Hugh muttered as he passed John. "I must be good."

A few seconds after the door closed behind them, everyone started to laugh. "I take it that poor Hugh has difficulties behaving?"

"Very much like his father," Worthington drawled.

Kenilworth shrugged. "He will eventually grow out of it."

"When he's over thirty," Worthington agreed amiably.

"It didn't take me quite that long." Kenilworth appeared a bit pensive. "Close, but not quite. Aside from that, he has his sister and cousins to help him along."

John had a feeling Kenilworth was right. That was another benefit of having a large family. "Not that I have been around many children before, but they seemed very well behaved."

"That is because you and St. Albans are here," Walter Carpenter pointed out. "And they have been promised an outing if they behave."

Eleanor shook her head. "I think they are not as bad as you believe they are." She wrinkled her nose. "But they are usually much louder." She glanced at John. "Generally they hold their own conversations without regard to what other conversations are going on. If they confined it to the one nearest to them, it would not be so loud."

He could imagine them, especially Hugh, shouting across the table to get someone's attention. John decided he'd like to get to know the children better. He glanced at the clock and stood. "I regret to say I must take my leave if I am not to be late for the vote today." He bowed to Lady Worthington. "Thank you for inviting me."

"It was my pleasure."

"I must be going as well." St. Albans rose.

Worthington pushed back his chair and stood. "I'll walk you to the door."

Once John and St. Albans had mounted their horses and were heading out of the square, John said, "That was enjoyable."

"I'm glad you think so." St. Albans frowned. "Breaking my fast with the infantry is not my style."

Yet John though it might be *his* style. Which was a good thing if he wished to wed Eleanor. The possibility was becoming more and more likely. He could already see her at his breakfast table presiding over a group of children. It was the first time he'd been able to actually conceive of a lady breaking her fast with him. Before, he had always imagined his wife, whoever she was, would breakfast in her chambers. He wished he'd been seated closer to her.

"I suppose you are going to the Lords." St. Albans's disgruntled words broke into John's thoughts. He was beginning to think his friend didn't have enough to keep him occupied.

"I am." He must also perform the service to which he'd committed himself directly after that. "Then I am going to hunt down Lord Lancelot."

"Good God, man. Why would you do that?" St. Albans looked so appalled, John almost laughed.

"I promised myself I would find out if he is still an idiot." He looked up and found he'd almost missed his street. "I'll see you later."

"This evening." St. Alban's nodded.

John would also see Eleanor this evening, and sit with her at supper, where he'd have a chance to talk to her. Learning more about her had never felt so urgent.

CHAPTER FOURTEEN

The rest of the gentlemen left the breakfast room shortly after Lord Montagu did, and Eleanor pondered whether her opinion of him had changed in any way. She had been glad that he had been interested in the children. Any gentleman she decided to wed must love children and want to have them around. He seemed particularly sympathetic to Hugh.

"Eleanor." She glanced at Dotty. "What do you think about Lord Montagu?"

That was the question. Eleanor was not quite sure. "He seems to have liked the children, but he did not talk much." Why was he so quiet? "I had expected him to engage in conversation with Con or Grace. They were the two adults closest to him, and he knows almost everyone else."

"There are different kinds of knowing one," Grace said. "We are all used to each other, and our husbands knew one another, in some cases for years before joining us for breakfast and, eventually, joining the family. It is not surprising to me that he was a little quiet."

"That is true." Eleanor just wished she could discover more about how he thought. Or if he thought. "I suppose breakfast was not the place to discover everything I wish to know about him."

"At least you now know that he can tolerate a lot of small

children at one time." Charlotte grinned. "Even naughty ones."

That made Eleanor smile as well. "I wonder what his childhood was like."

"There is only one way to find out," Grace said. "Ask him. As long as you do not ask anything shocking, there is no reason for you to be reticent."

That was an excellent point. "I will." Tonight at the ball, Eleanor would get him to talk about himself. "He has asked me for the supper dance."

"That will be a waltz," Charlotte said. "Elizabeth Harrington stopped by yesterday and told me the order of the sets."

"How does she like being back in England?" Eleanor had been wondering if Elizabeth missed Paris. And ever since Walter had announced he would be going to Spain, Eleanor had been thinking about what it would be like to live on the Continent instead of merely passing through places. From what Augusta and Phinn had told them, traveling seemed like a fascinating thing to do.

"She has mixed feelings. She loved Paris and France, but now that her brother has started a family and hers is increasing, she likes the idea of all the children growing up together. She and Harrington still plan to visit Paris regularly."

Madeline had placed her elbows on the table and cradled her face in her hands. "I want to visit the Continent. It is a shame that ladies cannot do a Grand Tour as part of their education."

"Perhaps someday." If only Cousin Jane and Hector were back home, Eleanor could probably talk Grace into letting them go for a few months, but Madeline's mother would no doubt argue against the trip. "We will have daughters one day. We could make it part of their education." Eleanor looked up and found Dotty staring at her. "Do I have a spot on my gown?"

"No. You have just given me an excellent idea. There is no reason I can see why young ladies should not be able to travel before marrying and starting a family."

In Eleanor's mind she could hear at least one of her brothers-in-law groaning. But she knew they would go along with the scheme. Any gentleman she married must as well. "This is the nineteenth century, after all."

They pushed back their chairs and rose as if by silent consent. She would definitely have to start putting Lord Montagu through his paces this evening. If he was not going to meet her requirements, there was no point wasting time with him. It would be better to move on to another gentleman who would.

Alice was smiling broadly as she, Madeline, and Eleanor walked up the stairs. "You are happy this morning."

Her twin glanced at her. Alice's eyes were twinkling as well. "You obviously did not see how disgruntled Lord St. Albans was by having to share his breakfast with the children. I do not believe he approved at all."

"You think this will convince him to look elsewhere for a lady?" Eleanor was not quite sure he would.

"I certainly hope he does." Alice reached the landing first and waited. "He must see that he does not fit in with the lives we have."

Alice started down the corridor ahead of Madeline and Eleanor. Madeline sighed and shook her head. "This might prove to be interesting."

Eleanor stopped at her bedchamber door. "What do you think of Lord St. Albans?"

"I am not sure yet." Madeline raised her brows. "However,

I do not think he is one to give up easily. He might just see Alice as a challenge."

"Oh dear. I cannot see her liking that at all."

"That was exactly what I thought." Madeline smiled and went to the next door down. "We shall see."

Eleanor walked into her room. They would indeed see how things turned out. But for now, not only did she have Lord Montagu about whom to make a decision, but she had her own charity to form. Something must be done about the miners and their families. With wages being reduced, there was less money for food and clothing. Matt had reminded her that they planned to meet today, and she wondered what he would propose. In the meantime, there were last-minute items to collect and purchase before the ball and Hatchards to visit. There must be some sort of tome on running mines. It behooved her to become more familiar with the business.

Less than an hour later, Eleanor and her sisters set out with their footmen to the corner of Old Bond Street and Piccadilly to the Burlington Arcade, where they could find gloves, fans, and hairpins.

"It is a shame the Pantheon Bazaar has become so shabby," Alice said. "It used to be fun going there."

"And so inexpensive," Madeline mused.

Eleanor had to agree. "But the Burlington Arcade is much nicer now." She entered a store with fans and other items. "I need a fan for this evening." She scanned the selection offered and found one with a scene painted in emerald green, deep pink, cream, and yellow. Eleanor turned to her sisters. "What do you think?"

"You are wearing your yellow and cream gown?" Alice asked.

Eleanor nodded. "Yes."

Her twin nodded. "It will brighten it up."

"Ooo. Look what I found." Madeline pointed to a pair of garnet combs displayed in a glass case.

"They are beautiful." Eleanor could image them in her sister's dark chestnut hair. "They will sparkle in the candle-light."

"What are you wearing in your hair?" Alice asked Eleanor. "I was going to have my maid use pearls, but now I think I would like the hairpins."

There were rows upon rows of different hairpins. Eleanor agreed pins were very nice. The pearls could wait for their come out ball. "Our gowns must be of pale colors, but nothing else does. What do you think of the emerald-colored ones?"

"Yes." Alice nodded. "They would be perfect. I like the purple hairpins."

Eleanor brought up an image of her sister's ball gown with the lavender-blue embroidery. "I agree. The purple will go well with your gown."

They took their purchases with them and made the short walk to Hatchards. Eleanor had planned to ask the clerk where she might find books on mining, but when they strolled through the door there were two ladies at the counter and two others waiting. She turned to her sisters. "Where do you think the books on mining might be?"

"Around the same area as agriculture," Madeline said.

Alice nodded. "We can begin there."

Having been encouraged to read books on farming and the like, they started up the stairs to that section and started their search to no avail.

Eleanor looked around. "They are not in this section. Minerals?"

"It is worth a try," Alice said.

A few minutes later, Eleanor pulled out a heavy volume from the shelf. "*Mineralogia Cornubiensis; a Treatise on*

Minerals, Mines and Mining by William Pryce. It is a place to start."

"Good," Madeline said. "Now let us find some novels we actually want to read."

"I do want to read this." Or at least Eleanor wanted the knowledge. She might have to ask Matt if he knew of some other sources of information.

By the time they left the bookstore, it was almost time for luncheon. Her stomach growled as she walked through the Worthington House door. "I am famished."

Thorton bowed. "Luncheon is being set out."

Eleanor smiled. "Thank you, Thorton. Have you seen his lordship?"

"Yes, my lady. He and Lord Stanwood arrived not long ago."

They would most likely be in the small dining room, where they had luncheon. "Thank you."

She caught up with her sisters on the stairs. "I need to speak with Matt. Charlie might be able to help as well."

"Do not wait for us, then," Alice said. "We will be down shortly."

"Thank you." Eleanor rushed to her chambers, removed her bonnet, gloves, put her house slippers on, and grabbed the book she had just purchased before going back downstairs to the dining room. Matt and Charlie had just put their plates on the table and were getting ready to sit when she walked into the room. She picked up a plate as well. "Good afternoon. How did the vote go?"

Charlie straightened. "Good day. It passed, but not by much."

"Please sit. I will not be a moment." Luncheon was, as usual, a cold collation accompanied by soup. A footman stood next to the tureen. "I will have a bowl please." Eleanor then selected some chicken, cheese, bread, and an apple.

She placed her plate on the table and sat. "What was it about?"

"It is the first reading of a bill that would prohibit bribery for votes. There has been a documented problem in two of the boroughs."

"That sounds serious." She had not given much thought to voting before. After all, as things stood now, she would never be able to vote.

"We believe it is," Matt said. "However, one member stated that it was an overblown charge." He peered at the book. "What is that?"

"*Mineralogia Cornubiensis; a Treatise on Minerals, Mines, and Mining* by William Pryce." Eleanor dipped her spoon into the soup. "I wanted to begin reading about mines and their management."

"There is a book that will be published in July," Charlie said. "It will be more modern, but I doubt it will help you very much. The owners and men studying mines have little to no care for the workers." He pointed to the tome. "That will tell you what they think is the best way to extract the minerals."

She swallowed her soup. "Are they not the best ways?"

"Not for the workers." He took a bite of the sandwich he had made, chewed, and swallowed. "I visited a few mines in Germany and Austria. They are so eager to get the minerals out that almost no safety for the workers is taken into consideration."

"In that case, safety is what I must focus on." She took a few more spoonfuls of soup. Today it was a very tasty chicken with vegetables.

Matt glanced up at her. "I received a note from Herndon. They are back in Town."

Butterflies suddenly fluttered madly in Eleanor's stomach

and she put her spoon down. "Have you asked him for an appointment yet?"

"No. I thought it might be better if I met with him first and brought Charlie along with me. We will explain what it is you want to do and tell him you will require more information about the mine before you can draw up a plan."

"I know you wanted to speak with Uncle first," Charlie said. "But remember that he is a little old-fashioned. You will have to impress him with your scheme before he'll agree to it. Having Matt and me on your side will help."

The fluttering in her stomach vanished and she buttered bread to make a sandwich. "Yes, of course." She knew the scheme would not be as easy as she had wished it to be. "What do you suggest I read if this book will not help?"

"I've been giving that some thought," Matt said. "There have been some local pieces written in support of the miners. I have sent to one of the publishers to see if he will provide me copies."

"That makes sense. I suppose I should read what the other side is saying as well." She started to wave her hand around, but it still held the knife with butter on it. Perhaps poor Hugh had not inherited that habit from his father's side of the family. Eleanor put the utensil down. "Although I cannot understand how anyone can justify lowering wages and allowing unsafe working conditions."

"Ellie"—Charlie called her by the name he used when she was a very small girl—"It is worse than what you might think. Women and children are made to work in the mines as well."

Mrs. Johnson had told her the same thing. But the prior knowledge did nothing for Eleanor's appetite. The bread and chicken turned to dust in her mouth, and she had a hard time swallowing. "Just like in the factories."

Her brother nodded. "And worse. Their health appears to be permanently damaged."

"Well, then, we must do something to help them." At the very least, she would do whatever was in her power.

Charlie grinned. "When I next write to Sir Henry, I'll tell him we have another radical in the family."

"Yes, do." She smiled thinking about his reaction. "He might have some ideas about how to go about this."

Matt cocked a brow. "He probably already has contacts that are writing about the issue. I'm surprised I didn't think of him when you first mentioned your plan."

"None of us did, but it is an excellent idea." Eleanor liked that she would have others to help and advise her, especially her family.

"I'm proud of you, Ellie." Charlie reached over and patted her back. "You really did grow up while I was gone."

"I should hope I did." She was glad he was home. "I am eighteen, after all."

"Have we given you enough time?" Alice rushed to their brother and hugged him when he rose. "Charlie! I'm so glad you are here."

"We do not see you enough." Madeline embraced him as well. "Did you come to help Eleanor?"

"Yes. Matt thought the two of us working on this was better than one." He seemed to stand straighter. "I am the head of the family, after all."

"You are indeed." Alice motioned with her hand. "Do sit and finish your luncheon."

Charlie always stood when any of the sisters entered a room. It was something Matt had insisted upon, and Eleanor appreciated the courtesy. "Thank you, but I am going to get a bit more food."

Next, Walter and Grace strolled into the dining room in

deep discussion about something. Her face lit when she looked at Matt. "Good afternoon."

He came around and kissed her cheek. "Good afternoon to you as well, my love. Will you serve yourself or shall I do it for you?"

"I will do it." She glanced at his plate. "You should finish eating."

Eleanor cut her apple into quarters as she watched how Matt behaved with Grace. It had been six years since they had wed, but he still treated her like he had before they married.

As the talk swirled around Eleanor, Charlie leaned over. "It is a fine example. You might not remember, but Mama and Papa were the same way with each other. It is what we should all aspire to in our marriages."

Tears pricked Eleanor's eyes. She had only been seven when their father died, and a year later they lost their mother. Grace had taken over after that. It was a miracle she had been able to keep them all together. "I agree." Eleanor took out a handkerchief and blew her nose. "Are you thinking about marrying anytime soon?"

"I will give myself another two or three years." Charlie glanced around the table, then back at her. "No longer than that."

Although he had always seemed mature for his age, she could see it more clearly now. "We have all grown up."

And soon they would all be married and having babies. That brought her back around to Lord Montagu. Hopefully she would make a decision about him soon.

CHAPTER FIFTEEN

John strolled into the small dining room, expecting to be able to enjoy his luncheon in peace and prepare for the meeting he and some other gentlemen were having at Merton House concerning the reading of a bill that had been approved that morning. And about another bill they were only just starting to look at regarding mines in Britain.

"Good afternoon, dear." Mama smiled quickly, hiding the expression of dismay she'd worn when he entered the room. "I did not expect you home so soon."

He had not even seen his mother sitting at the table with his sister. They both had plates of food, and there were several papers laid out in front of them.

"Good afternoon." He couldn't very well ask them what they were doing there. He went to the sideboard. "What are you working on?"

His mother smiled. "How was your breakfast this morning? Was it as commotive as you thought it might be?"

"Not at all." John picked up a plate. "The children were all very well behaved." He grinned to himself. "They had apparently been told that if they were on their best behavior, they would have an outing to the Tower this afternoon."

"That was an inspired idea," his sister said.

He finished filling his plate and ambled over to the table, stretching his neck slightly to see what the papers were. "What are you two doing?"

His sister efficiently stacked the newssheets and pamphlets together. "We are gathering information to assist a friend in a—a project she wishes to undertake."

Aurelia wasn't normally so evasive. A footman pulled out his chair for him. That was one thing that had not happened at breakfast this morning. Everyone seemed much less interested in the formalities. He set down his plate and took his seat. "What kind of project?"

His mother and sister shared a look that seemed like more of a communication. Mama smiled. "Nothing in which you would be interested."

"I might be." What the devil were the two of them up to? His mother handed him a cup of tea. "Thank you. You won't know if I'm interested unless you tell me." John decided to try prodding his sister. "Unless it is about clothing or some such thing."

"It is not." Her tone was almost chilly.

That hadn't worked. "Very well, keep it to yourselves."

"Thank you. We shall." Documents in hand and now bound by a string, Aurelia rose. "Mama, I will make sure she receives this information."

"That is kind of you, my dear." Their mother turned her cheek for the expected kiss. "Would you like to join me when I go out for morning visits?"

His sister glanced at the thin bundle. "Yes. That would be nice. Come fetch me when you are ready." Aurelia flashed him a bright smile. "It was good seeing you. Perhaps you would like to join Lytton and me at the theater or come to dinner sometime. After all, there is no need for us to stand on formality."

No need at all, except that she and Mama were hiding

something from him. Still, his sister's invitation would give him an opportunity to discover if they had fallen in love. "Yes, I would enjoy spending time with you."

Aurelia swept out of the room and Mama rose. "I should get ready for my visits. Have a good day."

"You as well." He slowly chewed a piece of beef. They had never been so secretive before. And why would they not want him to know what they were doing? John swallowed and glanced at the footman. "Get Lumner for me, please."

"Yes, my lord."

Seconds later, John's butler entered and bowed. "How may I help you, my lord?"

"When my sister arrived today, did you happen to see what kinds of papers she had with her?"

"I did not, my lord. But Spindle might know. He held them as I assisted her ladyship with her mantle. Shall I send for him?"

"Yes, please." John hoped the footman had been curious enough to at least have glanced at the bundle.

A few moments later Spindle entered the dining room and bowed. "My lord, you wished to see me?"

"I was told you held the documents Lady Lytton brought with her today. Did you happen to notice what they were?"

"I am afraid I did, my lord." The man colored slightly, as if caught doing something he should not have done. "The one on top got my attention because my eldest sister lives in York, and the writing was about a mining accident in the area."

Mining? Why would his sister and mother be interested in mining? "Was it a newssheet?"

"Er, no, sir. Not the sort like the *Morning Chronicle*"— the newssheet John and most other Whigs read—"it was more like one of those reformer newssheets."

This was starting to make more sense. The Cinderloo

massacre obviously was concerning the ladies as well. "Thank you, Spindle. That will be all."

"Very good, my lord." He strode out of the room.

"Is that what you wanted to know, my lord?" Lumner asked.

"It is. Thank you. Tell me when her ladyship departs."

"Of course, my lord." The butler bowed and left.

If John could bring himself to believe that his sister, and his mother too, he supposed, could limit themselves to raising funds or clothing for displaced families, he wouldn't be concerned. But would they take a more active role? One that had the potential of putting them in danger. He must speak with Lytton. And he might as well do it while the ladies were making their morning visits. He took his time finishing luncheon. But the more he thought about the papers, the more he considered how useful the information might be. He couldn't ask his sister for the information, but he could obtain his own copies.

It was almost an hour later when Lumner returned. "Her ladyship has departed, my lord."

"Thank you. Tell Pickerell I require him." John rose and went to his rooms. His valet was there when he arrived. "My gloves, and hat, and my cane as well."

Pickerell also refilled John's card case and handed it to him. "I'll be back before dinner."

He left his home and was halfway to Lytton House when he remembered something his sister had said.

I will make sure she receives this information.

She.

Did that mean his mother and sister were only passing on information? In that case, he needn't worry about them. But why his sister and mother? Then he recalled that Lytton's estate was in Yorkshire. Naturally Aurelia would have the wherewithal to obtain information another female might not. John changed his direction and headed toward Brooks's. There was no need to bother his brother-in-law with it if Aurelia was only gathering information.

The day had brightened after a cloudy morning and the weather was becoming warmer. It was at times like this he missed the country. A long walk across the meadows would do him good. He'd been inside too much of late. Then again, he had been quite busy with the Lords, and letters from his estates, and social obligations. Speaking of which, he should send flowers to Eleanor. He'd meant to do it earlier.

He turned onto Piccadilly Street and turned left until he reached Coventry Street, which took him to Covent Garden. He was relieved to see that the flower sellers were still out.

"Sweet violets, a penny a bunch," one young girl called out.

"A penny a bunch for lavender," another girl said at his heels.

"Peony, one for a penny," a third child said.

Stopping, he looked at them. All three were very young and too thin. The "bunches" were not that large. "I'll take all of them." His housekeeper could help him make a bouquet for Eleanor. He took out the coins, being careful that no one was close enough to pick his pocket. "Here you are."

"I can take 'em fer ye," a boy almost as young as the girls and just as skinny stopped about a foot away from John.

"Montagu House on Grosvenor Street." He handed the child a coin and the flowers. "Tell my butler I said to match that."

The lad tugged his cap and ran off toward Coventry Street. At least he was going in the correct direction. He scanned the square that, at first, appeared to be in complete chaos. For the most part, the houses lining the area were in need of repair. But the vendors had managed to sort themselves into some semblance of order. Glancing at his watch, he remembered that he was due at Merton House. If he

walked quickly, he'd just make it in time for the meeting.
But first he had to go by his house and hope the flowers
were there. They must be sent to Eleanor as soon as possible. Even though she had not danced with many gentlemen,
several had been introduced to her. It would not surprise
John at all if numerous bouquets had already been delivered
to Worthington House.

Eleanor and her sisters were in the hall waiting for Grace
when a knock sounded on the door.

Thorton opened it, and a footman in a livery she had not
seen before handed the butler a slender sheaf of papers.
"These are for Lady Eleanor Carpenter, compliments of
Lady Lytton."

The butler handed the footman a vail. "I will see she gets
them." Once the door closed, he turned to her. "My lady,
would you like me to have them taken to your chambers?"

"First, what are they?" She was not expecting to receive
anything. Thorton handed them to her. "Oh my."

"What are they?" Alice asked.

"Information on mines in York. At least this one is."
Eleanor handed the papers back to The butler. "Please have
them taken to my rooms."

The front door opened and one of their footmen came in
and bowed. "The coach is ready, my ladies."

"Where is Grace?" Madeline asked.

"Here I am." Grace came from the corridor to her study.
"I had to finish a letter. Shall we go?"

Eleanor followed her sister out of the house. Fortunately,
morning visits were something they had already experienced. The three of them had accompanied Grace on a few

of them last Season, and they did the same in the country as well.

Once in the coach, Eleanor settled her skirts. "Where are we going first?"

"I thought we would see Lady Thornhill. She was a great friend of Mama's." Grace glanced at Madeline. "She is also a friend of your mother's. You will all want to attend at least one of her salons."

They had all heard of Lady Thornhill and her salons but had not been permitted to attend one before. "That will be interesting."

Alice and Madeline nodded, and Madeline said, "I am interested in the philosophic discussions."

"You will find several of them going on at once," Grace said. "There is usually everything from the rights of women to politics, and discussions concerning Aristotle and other more modern philosophers."

"Augusta said that many foreigners attend," Alice added.

"It reminds them of the salons held on the Continent," Grace said. "The French especially miss those sorts of events."

Eleanor wondered if the people and conversations were only during the salons, or if any of them attended the morning visits. "I am looking forward to going to a salon."

"Everyone in our family looks forward to them." Grace chucked lightly. "After Lady Thornhill, we will visit Lady Bellamny. As you know, she is also a longtime family friend."

Lady Thornhill greeted them as they entered her good-sized drawing room. Eleanor was happy to see Lady Lytton and her mother already seated and drinking tea. It was nice to know some of the other ladies. After Lady Thornhill exclaimed over how much Eleanor and her sisters had matured, she introduced them to the other ladies and one gentleman who had accompanied his mother, Lord St. Albans. From behind her, Alice emitted a low groan.

"Your grace." Lady Thornhill smiled at Eleanor and her sisters. "Allow me to introduce to you Lady Eleanor Carpenter, Lady Alice Carpenter, and Lady Madeline Vivers." They curtseyed. "Ladies, the Duchess of Cleveland."

"It is very nice to meet you." The duchess had a faint Scottish accent. "May I present my son, the Earl of St. Albans?"

They curtseyed, and Alice's eyes narrowed slightly. "We already know his lordship."

Brows raised, the duchess glanced at her son. "Indeed?"

That was interesting. Obviously, he had not been keeping his mother informed. Alice put her hand over her mouth, hiding her smirk.

"Yes, ma'am." He cleared his throat and bowed. "We were introduced by Lord Montagu one morning when the ladies were riding, and again at Almack's."

Lady Lytton moved over on the couch upon which she was sitting and patted the space next to her. Eleanor smiled at the duchess. "If you will excuse me."

As soon as she settled on the cushion, her ladyship whispered, "Did you receive the pamphlets I sent?"

"I did, but they came just as we were leaving. I will be able to read them when we return home." If they were not too late. Eleanor did have a ball to attend that evening.

"Perfect." Lady Lytton smiled. "I had a friend send them. They discuss the most common accidents in the mines and have some recommendations to increase the safety as well as some other matters."

"Recommendations made by miners themselves?" Eleanor was sure her ladyship would have remembered their conversation at Merton House.

"Yes. There are even one or two names mentioned." Lady

Lytton took a sip of tea and swallowed. "When the time comes, and if you are interested, I can arrange for you to correspond with them." She glanced at Grace. "If your sister agrees, of course. I do not wish to be accused of encouraging you to do anything you should not."

Eleanor nibbled the inside of her lip. "I do not think that will be a problem. Both my brother-in-law and my eldest brother, Stanwood, have agreed to assist me."

"Excellent." Her ladyship's eyes lit up. "I look forward to hearing from you after you have had a chance to digest the material." Her mother rose. "I shall see you this evening."

St. Albans scowled after failing to capture Alice's attention. Did he think she would want him because he was the heir to a dukedom?

That was one thing about Lord Montagu Eleanor liked. He did not seem to believe a lady should want to marry him because of his title.

CHAPTER SIXTEEN

John arrived at Merton House just as the meeting was getting underway. "Sorry I'm late."

"The only thing you missed was Stanwood telling us he was being admitted to the Lords tomorrow." Merton inclined his head to the gentleman. "Our ranks are growing."

"Congratulations." John found an empty seat. "Who is sponsoring you?"

"Worthington and Endicott." Stanwood accepted a cup of tea. "We were waiting for him to arrive in Town."

"Excellent." John had only heard of Earl Endicott and was looking forward to meeting him.

Merton sat behind his desk and stared at a sheet of paper for a few seconds. "I have a note here that suggests we discuss nongovernmental ways to mining reform."

"Interesting and probably necessary," Kenilworth muttered.

The rest of the gentlemen frowned but appeared to agree. The chances of getting mine reform through Parliament with the Tories in the majority were slim. Then he recalled the papers his sister had that addressed the issue. "I believe in some areas of the country there is already interest in the subject."

Merton tapped his forefinger on the desk. "To do it without government reform would take owners agreeing to the changes."

That meant finding the owners. Something they'd discussed previously. "There must be a list of mines and their owners."

Rothwell grunted. "It will be at the Home Office. I'll request the information."

"You do know that the only ones interested in reform will be fellow Whigs," Exeter pointed out.

John agreed. "Very true, but there is no harm in starting with the members of our party first. In fact, it might be to our benefit to do so, considering the violence we've seen against reformers from those resisting change."

"Very well." Merton nodded. "That is where we'll begin."

"I advise we keep our plan to ourselves for the time being," Kenilworth commented. "Any change at all has the potential of being forcefully challenged."

The back of John's neck prickled. If his sister and mother were not going to do anything about the mines, who was the information for? Could it still put them in danger? He didn't believe either their status or their sex would protect them if the wrong people discovered their plan. He needed to get to the bottom of whatever they were doing. He glanced around the room, wondering if he should mention it, but what would he say? He didn't even know to whom the papers were to be delivered.

The door opened. Merton's daughter, Lady Vivienne, closed it softly, curtseyed to them, and flashed her father a sly smile before walking across to the door to the garden, and taking off at a run. Everyone's attention was riveted on the door.

Several moments later, Worthington's son, Gideon, dashed through, glanced around, and huffed. "Why is it ladies never stay where you think they are?"

"If you work that out," Kenilworth drawled, "let the rest of us know."

Gideon gave his uncle a look of disdain. "She must be in the garden." And rushed through the door.

"At least he's learning early," Rothwell commented as the rest of the men chuckled.

They were all peers with responsibilities they took seriously. Had none of them wanted a wife who would be quiet and soothing? John glanced at Merton. "Do you not think she should be taught to be more accommodating? Did you not want that in a wife?"

"I did," Merton drawled. "And I'm very glad that is not what I got. I would have been bored silly." He gave John a knowing look. "I fully expect my daughter to lead whomever she weds on a merry dance."

Kenilworth nodded. "I hadn't given marriage much thought, but when I did it was always to a nondescript sort of lady who wouldn't bother me. I'd much rather the wife I have." He grinned. "Constance will be right with Vivienne and Alexandria, causing problems for gentlemen."

Rothwell shook his head slowly back and forth. "I don't know what I would do without Louisa. Her ability to manage makes my life so much easier." He pursed his lips together. "It also means I can't control her, but what would be the point?"

"It's the same with Dorie." Exeter looked at Stanwood. "What will you be looking for in a wife when the time comes?"

"I've been fortunate enough to be the beneficiary of strong women." Stanwood glanced at John. "If it wasn't for my eldest sister, all of us would have been scattered around to different relatives. Grace wouldn't allow that to happen. I will look for someone like her, my sisters, and my mother."

"Interesting." John greatly respected all these gentlemen, and the married ones appeared to have excellent marriages. Perhaps he was incorrect about what it took to be a peer's spouse. Still, he could not get Eleanor out of his mind. And he was certain she was exactly what he had been looking for in a wife. Then again, Stanwood said that he'd look for someone like his sisters. Surely he meant his older sisters. They were clearly forces to be reckoned with. On the other hand, he wouldn't have to worry about what Eleanor was getting up to as he did with his sister and mother. He doubted she knew anything about mines, other than what she had read in the newssheets, that was.

"I think that is all for now." Merton rose. "Rothwell, we'll wait to hear from you."

The duke inclined his head. "I'll have a letter sent by tomorrow. And I will see you this evening."

John wondered if they were all going to Lady Markham's ball. They probably were. It was the primary event of the evening, and that was where Eleanor and her sisters would be.

They filed out of the study, and he saw a bit of white cloth whisk around a corner. Her father was right. When the time came, she would lead the gentleman on a merry dance. A vision came to him of a young girl with golden hair playing hide-and-seek in the same way as Lady Vivienne did. Every gentleman here had spirited children. And John liked them all. He hadn't wanted his life to be complicated, but it appeared it might have to be if he wanted the future he was beginning to think he did.

Aurelia settled back against the soft velvet swabs of her town coach and smiled. "That went well."

"Do you mean the part with Montagu or the part with Lady Eleanor?"

"Both." There had been many times Aurelia had been grateful she had married Marc. This was especially so when he entered into her schemes. "Lytton told me John has joined a group of gentlemen who are working on mine reform." Thankfully, that had dovetailed nicely with Lady Eleanor's interest. "For the most part, the gentlemen are also known to have familial connections to Lord and Lady Worthington, and to have wives who are forces to be reckoned with in their own right."

"It is certainly true Lady Eleanor appears to fit that mold." A line formed across Mama's still-smooth forehead. "The real difficulty is to make Montagu realize that he wants the same type of lady."

"I agree. However, having met a few of them, it is safe to say that the gentlemen dote on their wives. I think that example might cause a seed to take root in my brother's mind."

Mama sighed. "I do hope you are right, my dear. I would greatly dislike having a stupid daughter-in-law."

"Or sister-in-law." Aurelia thought it was a pity that John had not been on the Town or in enough of the right company to see the benefits of having an intelligent and capable mate. "I have never understood the idiocy of gentlemen thinking they want a docile wife, or of parents trying to make young ladies hide their gifts."

"Sadly, I do not believe that will change anytime soon." Her mother's tone held the disgust Aurelia felt. Unfortunately, it was not the opinion her mother held when she was a young lady.

"Be that as it may, I and others like me do not have to raise daughters or sons to behave conventionally."

"No, you do not." Her mother glanced at her. "Do you

have a plan that reveals to Montagu and Lady Eleanor that they have a similar interest in the mines?"

"Not yet. I am sure something will come to me." On the other hand, it might be better if they discovered it on their own. "I do wonder if one of us should tell John that we do not think Lady Eleanor is the right lady for him."

"Hmm. That might not be a bad idea." A devious smile appeared on her mother's lips. "We would have to be subtle about it."

"Yes, of course." After all, her brother was not stupid. He merely had some stupid ideas at times.

Dobbins broke the seal on the letter. He'd been wondering what was going on and hadn't even minded paying for the news.

We had to stop for a while. The mort's got more fart catchers around her. I'll give them a week or two of doin' nothing, and she'll be easy to get to again.

He tossed the paper in the fireplace. She must be good and scared to have more footmen going around with her. Mitchell was right. After a week or so, they'd think it was nothing but her imagination.

Several hours later, John entered the Markham House ballroom after the receiving line had ended. He had begged off escorting his mother and sister so that he could arrive before the supper dance, but not early enough to be forced to dance with other young ladies. Despite the crowded room, his gaze was immediately drawn to Eleanor. She turned to smile at someone, and his breath left him as if

Jackson had landed a punch. My God, she was beautiful. She seemed to sparkle from the top of her head to the bottom of her gown. Little puffed sleeves showed off the small bit he could see of her arms above her gloves. Yet even the long kid gloves couldn't hide the perfection of her arms. A few curls danced around her elegant neck. And her bosoms rose temptingly from her bodice. He almost wished she would wrap her shawl around her shoulders, but the room was too warm for that. He'd simply stand by her side until the supper dance. Bolingbroke led her out to the dance floor for a country dance, and John wanted to go up to them and demand she stand up with him. The feeling was so strong, he grabbed onto a potted plant to stop himself from walking forward.

"Dancing with trees?" St. Albans held up his quizzer.

"I wanted to see how sturdy it was."

John's almost former friend lowered the glass. "It had nothing at all to do with Lady Eleanor standing up with Bolingbroke, I suppose."

"Nothing at all," John lied.

"Of course not." St. Albans took out a handkerchief and polished his quizzing glass. "That would indicate some sort of jealousy. One doesn't experience that emotion unless one is falling in love."

John noticed St. Albans staring at the dance floor right where Lady Alice was dancing with a gentleman he didn't recognize. "I would think gazing at a lady standing up with another gentleman is the same thing."

"I'm sorry, did you say something?" The insouciant look on St. Albans's face didn't fool John for a second. St. Albans cared more for Eleanor's sister than he wanted to let on.

"Nothing." John barely kept his lips from twitching. "Nothing at all."

"Your mother, sister, and Lytton arrived quite a while ago. What made you decide to come later?"

He was not going to admit it was to avoid dancing with other ladies. "I had some business to finish."

"Lord St. Albans," a handsome lady in her middle years said. "Please make your friend known to me."

That was forward. Did John need to warn her off?

"My lady, allow me to present Lord Montagu. Montagu, Lady Markham."

John quickly bowed. "Good evening, my lady. I trust my mother told you I would be a bit late."

"She did." Her ladyship smiled at him. "Now that you are here, I shall introduce you to a young lady who is in need of a dance partner." She raised a brow at St. Albans. "You may come along as well, my lord."

John stifled a groan. This was exactly what he had not wanted to happen. Miss Battersley had very large, blue-gray eyes and blond hair and seemed very young. He bowed. "Miss Battersley, a pleasure."

She curtseyed. "It is very nice to meet you, my lord."

"Miss Battersley is making her come out. Her father, Sir Cecil, is in the diplomatic corps in Belgium."

Perhaps she would be more interesting than he had originally thought. "Will you do me the honor of standing up with me?"

A pretty blush appeared on her cheeks. Then again, she was a pretty girl. "I would like that very much."

She placed her hand on his arm. "How do you like Belgium?"

"Oh, I have never lived there. I attended school here. My aunt, Lady Kirkwall, is sponsoring me." She glanced up at him. "The weather has been quite nice recently."

"Yes, it has. I hope it will continue." Suddenly he was tired of talking about the weather.

"As do I. My aunt wants to hold an al fresco luncheon and rain would spoil her plan." Miss Battersley smiled politely. Or appropriately. Not too wide. Not too anything.

"Ah, yes. Rain would certainly put paid to that idea. Are you enjoying your Season?"

"I should not admit it, but I am rather." She peeped at him from beneath her blond lashes.

Someone had told him that ladies were supposed to show a proper ennui. Eleanor never did that. Everything she did, she did with purpose and honest emotion. "Excellent. What do you like most thus far?"

"The shopping and carriage rides." Miss Battersley appeared to think for a moment. "And the morning visits. They are very nice." Her forehead puckered. "As long as it does not rain."

Fortunately, as she did not seem to be able to discuss much beyond the weather, the set was a country dance that didn't allow for much conversation. The thought stopped him, and he had to remember to continue dancing. She was exactly what he had thought he wanted. Except that even in this short time, Miss Battersley bored him. John didn't know why that should be. Eleanor discussed the weather and he didn't find it boring. Then it occurred to him that whenever Eleanor mentioned the topic, he'd been the one to bring it up in the first place. Was she as weary with him as he was with this young lady? If so, her manners had never allowed her to show it. Perhaps it was time to take a different approach.

The set ended and he returned the young lady to her aunt.

"I had a lovely time dancing with you, my lord." Miss Battersley curtseyed.

"I enjoyed it as well." John bowed. "Please excuse me." He made his escape and glanced around to locate Eleanor's circle again but saw his sister instead.

Devil it. There was nothing to do but greet her before finding Eleanor. "Mama, thank you for making my excuses to Lady Markham. Aurelia, Lytton, good evening."

Lytton inclined his head.

"You are most welcome, my dear." Mama smiled. "Did you enjoy your dance?"

"She was a very pretty girl," Aurelia said. "Who is she?"

"Miss Battersley. Her father is with the Foreign Office overseas. Her aunt is sponsoring her."

"Has she been with her parents?" Aurelia's interest was genuine. She had always wanted to travel.

"No, she was sent to school here." John thought that was a shame.

"That makes sense." He did not understand why his mother would say that.

"In what way?"

"She would need to be raised to be a proper wife. That is much harder if she is constantly traveling around." As matter-of-fact as his mother's tone was, had he caught a hint of disapproval? That didn't make sense. She was the one who had disliked Aurelia being different.

"If you will excuse me, there is someone with whom I must speak." He gave a short bow and hastened his steps to reach Eleanor's circle before her next partner claimed his dance.

CHAPTER SEVENTEEN

Eleanor felt the second Lord Montagu entered the ballroom. It was as if there was some invisible thread between them. When she turned he was speaking to Lady Markham, giving Eleanor an opportunity to take in his form. If there was one thing Montagu was, it was very good-looking. Tonight he was dressed in unrelieved black and white, with what looked like gold embroidery on his waistcoat.

"I see he has finally arrived." Alice was very punctual and expected everyone else to be on time as well.

"I am certain there is a reason he is late." Although Eleanor could not conceive of one, she had a feeling he would tell her. Lady Markham took him to a group of matrons and young ladies.

Eleanor's dance partner arrived, and they repaired to the dance floor for a country dance. Only one more set before the supper waltz. She and Madeline were escorted back to their circle at the same time.

"He is coming this way," Madeline whispered.

"Good evening." Montagu bowed to Eleanor, her sisters, and to Matt and Grace. "Ladies, my lord, my lady."

"Good evening." Eleanor curtseyed. "I wondered if you were coming. I saw your sister and mother earlier."

"I, er, was held up by some estate business." She was not quite sure she believed him and could not think why she would not. "I could not miss my waltz with you."

"Thank you." Heat rose into her face. Why was she blushing? She was supposed to remain unaffected by him until she had made up her mind. "I received your flowers. They were lovely."

"They reminded me of you." That was unfortunately trite, but she supposed she should be flattered. He cleared his throat. "They are lovely, as you are." He met her gaze. "That is the truth. But the rest of it is that I found I was unable to say no to the flower girls." He gave her an almost pleading look. "They were so small and thin."

Lord Montagu sounded so contrite, Eleanor wanted to hug him. He had gone to Covent Garden to purchase the flowers himself instead of sending a servant. That was unexpected. "How many flowers did you buy?"

"Everything they had left." He had a sheepish expression that appeared at odds with his strong, aristocratic features. "I haven't a clue how to arrange flowers, so my housekeeper did it for me. I really do hope you liked them."

"I did indeed." She liked even more that he was being honest with her, and that he could not but try to help the children. "I do not have any experience with the flower girls, but I have heard about them."

Lord Harrington strolled up to them, bowed, and glanced at Lord Montagu. "Lady Eleanor, this is my dance, if I am not mistaken."

"It is, my lord." She looked at Lord Montagu. "My lord, allow me to introduce Lord Harrington, Lord and Lady Markham's son. He and his wife recently returned from several years in Paris."

Montagu bowed. "My pleasure. I believe you are related to a friend of mine, Gavin Turley."

"Yes." Harrington smiled. "He's my brother-in-law." He glanced around. "He and his wife are here somewhere." The beginning notes of the set sounded. "Lady Eleanor, do you wish to dance or would you rather converse with his lordship?"

Elizabeth Harrington was being escorted to the dance floor and Eleanor would be spending the next hour and a half with Montagu . . . Lord Montagu. "I would like to dance. This is, after all, my first ball. I will have time to talk with Lord Montagu after this set."

Harrington made a slight bow and held out his arm. "It is my pleasure."

"And that is what several years in Paris will do for you. One cares less about convention," Phinn teased. "Augusta, my love, shall we?"

Eleanor felt a little sorry for Montagu. . . . Drat it all. Lord Montagu. He did not have a partner for this set, and she had left him with her elder sister and brother-in-law. She supposed he would find something to say to them. She did like him much better after his story about the flowers. The flowers had been a pretty but unusual arrangement, two peonies interspersed with lilacs and surrounded by violets. It was almost like seeing them in a garden.

They took their places for the cotillion. "Do you like being back in England?"

"We will get used to it." Lord Harrington seemed resigned to his fate. "My wife is adjusting a bit better than I am. On the other hand, I am used to being busy with diplomatic affairs. I must now find another occupation."

"I would think they could find something for you to do at the Foreign Office here."

"If I were a career diplomat they would. But I am destined to take over the marquisate." Then he grinned. "It is not a bad thing, you know. That said, I hope it is not for many, many years. I fear I am more like my mother. She was quite depressed when they had to return from Paris."

"I hear it is beautiful." Eleanor would visit the city. Sooner rather than later, she hoped.

"It is. But we knew our time would end. There is an estate reserved for the heir. I will take over the responsibilities for that when the Season ends."

"What an excellent idea." Perhaps if all peers did that, there would not be so many heirs doing nothing.

The movements of the dance separated them, and she started to think about the duties of a peer. If their estates were to prosper, they could not be gone for long periods of time. That reminded her of what Montagu had said about business to which he had to attend. Which meant he did care about his estates and dependents, even if it made him late to an entertainment, unlike some gentlemen, who came late and left early only to draw attention to themselves or to avoid dancing with young ladies. Eleanor had seen him stand up with a young lady she had met at Lady Bellamny's soirée, a Miss Battersley. A thread of, oh, not unhappiness, had wound its way through Eleanor, but there was something she had not liked about seeing them together. She gave herself a shrug. One of her goals this evening was to discover more about him.

The set ended and the next one was the supper dance. Montagu was speaking with her older sisters and brothers-in-law when Lord Harrington returned her to her circle. Harry Stern, Dotty, and Merton had also joined them. As usual, St. Albans was there as well. Augusta and Phinn had drawn in their group of friends. How much larger would their circle be once Eleanor and her sisters married? And, eventually, her brothers too. It was comforting knowing so many people for her first Season.

"My dance, I believe." Montagu's tone was warmer than she had heard it before.

"It is." Eleanor placed her hand on his arm. "I have been waiting all evening for this." The look in his blue-green eyes caused her breath to stop.

He was absolutely serious. "As have I. My partner for an earlier waltz was not nearly as skilled are you are."

The frissons that started when he placed his hand on her waist were even stronger than before. That was a surprise. She had come to the conclusion that the only reason she had had a reaction to Montagu before was because it was her first waltz with someone she had not known most of her life. The first waltz with the other gentleman had caused no feelings at all, except the desire to take care of her toes. Obviously, that was not the case. Carefully, she touched his waist, and almost jerked her hand back.

"Is anything wrong?" He appeared concerned.

"Nothing." Steeling herself, she took his hand. It was firm and warm. Her heart was beating as if she had been running.

Stop it! You are acting like a peagoose.

The dance began, and she decided talking was a good way to get rid of these unwanted sensations. "Did you make a Grand Tour?"

"No. My father was ill for several years before he died and I stayed with him." Well, drat. She hoped she had not made him sad. "I understand your brother recently returned from his."

"Yes. So did my sister, Augusta. She and her husband were traveling for the past three years."

"Do you wish you could travel?" She tried to place his tone. It was somewhere between politeness and curiosity.

"I would like to visit Paris." They performed a twirl. "I do not think I would like to be gone for a long amount of time. Do you wish to travel?"

He did not answer straightaway; after a few seconds, he said, "Yes. I believe I would. Not for a long period of time. But I'd like to have an opportunity to see something of the world, even if it is only another city in another country."

"It would be difficult to be gone for more than a few months." She had her charitable duties and, with any luck, a mine to see to.

"I agree." They moved back into the starting position "Estates that run themselves do not do as well as ones who have more oversight."

"That is what Worthington says. Although he encouraged my brother to go do what he was unable to do." Eleanor had not realized until now just how selfless Matt had been. "Then again, he also watched over my brother's interests for him."

"I have to say that I greatly admire Worthington and your other brothers-in-law." Montagu's eyes caught hers and, as they twirled, her heart skipped a beat.

"Well." Eleanor could not but smile when she thought about her sisters' courtships. "They have become wonderful husbands and fathers, and good men."

"I sense stories behind that remark." He gave her a curious look. "Does it have something to do with what Worthington said at breakfast about Kenilworth?"

"That is part of it." He had been paying more attention than she had given him credit for. "They all have their tales."

"Perhaps it is like that with most couples. My sister and her husband have a short but interesting story as well."

"They seem devoted to each other." In love. Eleanor had noticed how they looked at each other.

Montagu seemed thoughtful. "I believe they are. I did not expect that from her."

"What do you mean? Did she not want a love match?" What in the Lord's name made her ask that question? This conversation was becoming much too personal.

"She never did." He smiled at her again. "But I'm beginning to think that is what she got."

Did that mean he had not wanted a love match but now thought he might? "Interesting."

"It is, rather," Montagu agreed. "One hears accountings of arranged matches that developed into love matches. Her match was not arranged." He frowned. "Or it was, but by her."

Eleanor was tempted to go into whoops. She could absolutely see Lady Lytton arranging her own match. Eleanor had to press her lips together to stop from laughing.

"It is funny." John gazed at Eleanor's tightly pressed-together lips quivering in suppressed mirth and wanted to kiss them. He had not particularly wanted a love match. Yet he had the distinct feeling that if he wanted Eleanor, that was what it would take. How would he even know if he was in love? He had lusted over women. He lusted over her. But love? Questions began to form in his head. Chief of which was how he would know if he was in love. Who could he ask?

The set came to an end and, once again, he realized that dancing with Eleanor was so easy he did not need to think about the steps at all. And he didn't want to let her go. He would have been perfectly happy to waltz with her all evening.

"We will be the last couple on the dance floor." Her soft voice made him drop his hands.

"I was thinking."

"I had a feeling that was what you were doing." She laid her hand on his arm. "Shall we go to supper?"

"Yes." He had to be quick enough to select her food for her. They reached her family as they were making their way down wide stairs. "Is there anything particular you would like?"

"Always lobster patties"—Eleanor smiled, as if she was savoring the taste—"and asparagus if they have it. No soup."

"I shall see what I can do." He led her to the table several footmen were putting together for their group. "Does everyone always sit together?"

"I do not know." She stared at the tables. "I think so. I recall hearing about it in previous years."

"Ah." He noticed Lady Worthington speaking with his mother, who shook her head. What was that about? "Let me find our seats." He picked two chairs in the middle of the tables. Hopefully, that would give him more time to talk with Eleanor. "Do these suit?"

"Yes." She sank gracefully onto the chair he held out for her. "Thank you."

"My pleasure. I will be right back." John was happy he was one of the first gentlemen to reach the table.

"How is it going?" St. Albans was at John's elbow.

"Well, I think." How would he even know? "You?"

"I'm not sure. There are times I think she is warming to me, then I think she wants me to go away. Far away." That was the first time he'd heard St. Albans doubt himself. Yet John had noticed Lady Alice's coolness to the man.

"Perhaps you are being too forward." Or arrogant. Lady Alice did not seem like the type to like arrogance.

"A faint heart never won a fair lady." His friend motioned to the footman serving the lobster patties.

John quickly indicated that he would like some patties as well. "This fair lady might have a different view."

"Nonsense. All ladies want the same thing." He raised a brow and his friend rolled his eyes. "Send them flowers, waltz with them, compliment them. Being wealthy and having a title is all part of it. She will see that being a future duchess is in her best interest."

He spotted the asparagus and held out the plate. Next was a selection of cheeses. He selected several, then the sweets and ices. Eleanor had not mentioned sweets. He knew that she liked ices. "Two lemon ices, please."

"Yes, sir. You might want to try the champagne ices as well," the footman suggested.

"Thank you, I will."

"There is no need to be so polite," St. Albans muttered.

"I believe there is." John's father had always said to treat everyone with dignity.

The servant signaled to another footman. "Help the gentleman."

He led the way to the table as St. Albans juggled his dishes. Apparently, he had not been offered any help. There was proof a little consideration went a long way. "My lady." John bowed. "I hope you like what I chose."

Eleanor's eyes widened at the assortment of dishes. "It looks perfect. Thank you."

The footman put the plate and ices on the table, and John gave him a few coins. "Please share them."

"I will, my lord. Thank you." The man went off with a jaunty step.

Eleanor seemed to study the selection as if trying to decide what to eat first. "Share with whom?"

"The footman who called him over to assist me." John

took his seat. "He was also the one who recommended the champagne ices in addition to the lemon."

"I have never tasted champagne ice." Another footman came around and set glasses of champagne and lemonade on the table.

"Neither have I." He held one up. "Shall we eat it first?"

Eleanor gave him a brilliant smile. "What an excellent idea."

The ices were perfect, as was his idea to sit in the middle of the tables. Now that he had decided he wanted an intelligent wife, even if she was a bit managing, he had to craft his questions to discover more about her. "You seem to be surrounded by gentlemen who are interested in politics. Is that an interest shared by your sisters?"

When she finished her ice, she had selected a lobster patty and now had to swallow the bite she'd taken. "Yes. We are all concerned by politics. I do not know if I want to be a great political hostess, but I am very attracted to the bills and gathering support for their passage."

For some reason, John's heart sped up. "That is the part I like as well. Are there any particular areas that concern you?"

"Almost anything to do with people's welfare," she answered quickly, as if she'd given the matter a lot of thought. Eleanor fixed him with a steady gaze. "All people. As a nation, we are responsible for the poor and unfortunate as well as the others."

"Again, I agree." Yes. This was what he wanted. She was what he wanted. Like him, Eleanor cared about the plight of the unfortunate or those who could not help themselves. She probably even gave part of her pin money to charity. She took a breath and her breasts rose, drawing his eyes to the soft mounds that barely showed above the neckline of her gown. Lord, how he wanted her. He wanted her in his bed and across from the breakfast table from him in the morning, and beside him as they journeyed through life together. As if he were watching a play in his head, he could see them with their children. John quickly dragged his eyes away from her bodice. The question was, did she or could she feel the same about him? And how to find out?

CHAPTER EIGHTEEN

"I have never been so frustrated in my life." Eleanor paced the floor of the parlor she shared with her sisters. "I told him I was determined to help those who are less fortunate than we are, and all he did was smile and agree with me. One would think he would have engaged in conversation about what he had done or planned to do, or legislation he might propose." Stopping, she faced her sisters. "I have a great fear that he might truly be a little slow."

Madeline gave Eleanor a sympathetic look. "You did say he was kind, and from what you said about your conversation, he would probably let you continue your charity work."

"Yes, but I want a husband who will work with me." Eleanor bit the inside of her lip. "The worst part of it all is that I got *those feelings* again when we were dancing."

"The ones our sisters and Dotty told us about?" Alice asked.

Eleanor nodded. She did not wish to *feel* things for him, not yet.

"Oh dear. That does complicate the matter." Madeline yawned.

"It does." If it were not for that, she would forget about Montagu and look for someone else. She stopped pacing.

No, she would not. This was just so aggravating. "How do I find out if he has more hair than brains?" She started pacing again. "Honestly, gentlemen should be required to submit their qualifications in writing. A *résumé*, if you will."

"He does have very nice hair." Madeline leaned back against the cushions of the love seat and closed her eyes.

"He does." Thick, curly, and such a lovely auburn color. And his eyes were a magnificent shade of blue-green. Eleanor gave herself a shake. "But he needs to have a brain as well."

Alice handed her a cup of tea. "I have an idea."

"Go ahead." Eleanor took a sip and waited for her sister to explain.

"Matt is meeting with several of our brothers-in-law and a few others about the mine legislation on which they are working. From what I heard, Lord Montagu is to be part of the group. Perhaps there is a way we can arrange for them to meet in Grace's study."

Madeline's eyes opened and she sat up straight. "The antechamber. We have not used that in a couple of years."

Not since Henrietta Stern, now Lady Fotherby, came to talk to Grace about her problems with Fotherby. "It will only work if we are very careful not to fall into the room again."

Alice nodded. "That would be mortifying."

Especially in front of Lord Montagu and any other gentlemen to whom they were not related. "It would be. When will they have this meeting?"

"Other than some afternoon this week, a time was not mentioned," Alice said. "But I'll wager that we can get one of the footmen to tell us when they arrive."

Madeline pulled a face and flopped back against the

cushions. "Yes, but if it is in the afternoon, we will be on morning visits."

"Charlie." Their brother would be there, Eleanor was sure. "I will ask him to tell me. Tomorrow I shall send a note around, telling him I need to speak with him." She set down her scarcely touched cup. She hoped they would be able to ride in the morning. She needed to work off some of her anxiety. Yet it was not promising. The clouds were already gathering when they left the ball. "Well, then. I'm off to bed."

That night, Eleanor dreamed about auburn-haired children with turquoise eyes and woke with a start when Posy climbed in bed with her, nudging her arm to be stroked. "What are you doing here?" One or both of the children must be having baths. Like all the Great Danes she knew, they thought water was only for drinking. "Did you try to save them from the water?"

Posy sighed and snuggled in closer. The dogs were usually taken on their walk when Edward and Gaia, her eighteen-month old nephew and niece, were being bathed. What had happened? Eleanor finally heard the sound of rain splattering on the windows. No riding this morning, but she still had to write a note to Charlie. She glanced down at the sleeping Dane and decided to get out of bed on the other side so as not to disturb her. The second she abandoned her pillow, Posy's head found it. Eleanor padded around to the side of the bed, stuck her feet in her slippers, then went to her writing table and drew out a sheet of pressed paper. She considered giving him a full explanation but decided to just tell him she must speak with him, and it was urgent. After sealing the missive, she reached for the bell-pull.

"I thought you would sleep in this morning," Jobert said.

"I probably would have, but"—Eleanor glanced at the bed—"I had company."

"There she is! They've been looking all over for her." Her maid smiled. "She took one look at the rain and ran back inside."

"That sounds like something she would do." Indeed, it was what any self-respecting Dane would do. Eleanor handed her maid the letter. "I need this to go to Stanwood House immediately. It is for my brother."

"I'll see it done." Jobert went to the door. "I'll be right back. If you start washing, I'll get your gown out."

"Thank you." With any luck, Charlie would join them for breakfast and they would be able to talk afterward. If there was not something pressing at the Lords today.

But there was. Charlie is taking his seat in the House of Lords today, and the family is to watch it from the gallery.

Perhaps this was not a good time. "I should not have bothered him with the letter this morning."

It was too late now. Eleanor washed and donned her chemise, stockings, and robe. Jobert had laid out a day gown. "Should I not dress to go out?"

"Her ladyship said you will all have time to change." Her ladyship was always Grace. "Very well." Perhaps he would have time to talk to her. From the bed, Posy sighed in her sleep. "I feel like I should cover her."

Jobert glanced at the bed and shook her head. "Rain or no, she is going to have to get up soon."

Eleanor was not so sure about that. Duke had once gone a whole day without going outside. She looked at the clock. It was still early, but the tea might be ready.

Elizabeth, her four-year-old niece, came into the bed-chamber walking on tiptoes and whispered, "I heard she was here." She had the Carpenter blond hair, but the Vivers lapis-blue eyes. She turned those eyes on Eleanor. "She is hiding."

"She must be if she is in my room." Duke and Daisy had

frequently been found in Eleanor, Alice, and Madeline's chambers. But Zeus and Posy spent the vast majority of their time with the younger children. Then again, Eleanor and her sisters had been younger back then. "We should let her sleep."

"Yes." Elizabeth nodded seriously. "She must be tired. Edward and Gaia wanted to play in the middle of the night."

What had got into the two of them? They usually slept well. "Did the rain wake them up?"

"I do not know," Elizabeth said. "Nurse sent their nurse-maids to bed this morning after hearing about it."

"Come." Eleanor held out her hand. "We shall go down to breakfast."

Her niece placed her tiny hand in hers. "Everyone is very busy here."

Elizabeth had only been two when Augusta came out and would not have remembered what a Season could be like. "Yes, we are. It is because Alice, Madeline, and I are making our come outs."

"I know," Elizabeth said in a serious tone. "Constance, Alexandra, Vivienne, and I have decided we will not make come outs. We would have to stay up too late."

Resolved not to laugh, Eleanor pressed her lips together. "That will make your papas very happy."

"Yes." Elizabeth nodded. "They like it when we go to bed on time." With that settled, she skipped along beside Eleanor as they made their way to the breakfast room.

She remembered how sad Grace had been at the thought of never marrying and having her own children, and Eleanor knew she wanted marriage and children as well. But why did she have to have *those feelings* when Montagu touched her? The only thing to do was to make sure her plan to discover if he was intelligent bore fruit.

They reached the hall as Charlie, Augusta, and Phinn

entered. All of them wore the waterproof coats they had gotten while traveling and boots.

"It is wet out there." Augusta handed a wide-brimmed hat to a footman. "Thank goodness we have the clothing for it."

"This reminds me of that deluge we were caught in in the Pyrénées." Phinn shrugged off his coat.

"When we went to visit the village that had some sort of old language Augusta had to learn." Charlie sat down and took the covering off his boots, then glanced at Eleanor and Elizabeth. "Never go traveling with Augusta. She will take you on journeys to the most remote places."

"Admit it," Augusta said. "You had much more fun with us than with that group you were with before."

"I definitely became fitter," Charlie retorted. "Ellie, let's speak now. Thorton said no one else is down yet."

Augusta held out her hand to Elizabeth. "Let's find some toast and tea, shall we?"

"What are the Pyrénées?" She took Augusta's hand.

They started walking down the corridor. "They are mountains in the north of Spain, but they do not really want to be part of Spain. . . ."

Phinn stared after them. "She will be an excellent mother. Everywhere we went children loved her."

"She'll have your children traveling the world." Charlie grinned.

"That is not such a bad thing." Phinn strode after his wife and niece.

"Do you think they will stay in England?" Eleanor asked as she walked toward one of the front parlors.

"I don't know." Charlie shrugged. "His brother has still not had an heir."

Phinn's brother, the Marquis of Dorchester, had a bevy of daughters but no sons. He was depending on Phinn and

Augusta to produce an heir. "That must be difficult for him and his wife."

"I suppose it is." Charlie closed the door. "Now, what can I do for you?"

"I need to know when the meeting about the mines will be, and if you can find a way to hold it in Grace's study."

"Tomorrow, and I can. May I ask why?"

As much as Eleanor loved her brother, she did not want to tell him everything. "There is something I must find out about Lord Montagu."

Charlie's brows drew together, and he studied her for a moment. "And you think you will discover whatever it is if we have the meeting in Grace's study?"

Well, Eleanor supposed she would have to tell him part of it. "There is an unused antechamber at the back of her study. One can hear conversations from there."

He closed his eyes and took a breath. "What exactly do you expect to learn?"

Well, drat. She would have to tell him after all. "I need to know if he is intelligent."

A light entered Charlie's face. "I see. You could, of course, ask someone you know, such as Matt or me, but I suppose it is always better to find out these sorts of things for oneself."

"You will do it?" She held her breath waiting for his answer.

"Yes. I'll do it." He grinned at her. "Mind you, don't get caught."

Eleanor huffed. "It would have been too much to expect that no one told you the stories."

"It would," he agreed with a grin. "Let's go to the breakfast room. I'm starving."

"I am too." Finally she would know what she needed

to about Montagu. That was a relief. Today was all about Charlie. "Are you glad to be taking your seat in the Lords?"

"I am. I've had my time to play. It's now time to take up my duties." He glanced at her. "Augusta thinks that young ladies should have an opportunity to travel before they marry." He stopped for a moment. "Although she combined the two."

"That would not be a bad way to do it." It would be nice to travel with someone you loved. "Sort of like an extended honeymoon."

"Yes, but most people cannot either afford to travel or cannot take the time from their duties," Charlie said. "I was fortunate that Matt encouraged me. Phinn is lucky that he has his own funds."

"What about Phillip and Walter?" It was strange that Eleanor had never thought of her other brothers' financial situation.

"They each have an easy competence, but as with Walter, Phillip will be encouraged to find a profession."

Life was so much easier for gentlemen. Eleanor and her sisters were fortunate, but other ladies either had to wed, find work they were allowed to do, or be at the beck and call of relatives. She wondered if it was possible to widen the areas of employment for ladies. First, she would work at improving the mines, then she would look at the other situation.

She took Charlie's arm. "We are lucky we have one another."

"That we are. All of us and the people we bring into the family." He gave her a significant look.

"Matt and Grace have made sure we all remain close." What would happen if one of them married someone who wanted to keep them from the family? Eleanor had a feeling it would not be allowed to happen. If she decided on Lord

Montagu, it was fortunate he already seemed to accept that the family stayed together.

She stepped into the pale yellow breakfast room and a rush of love for her brothers and sisters almost overpowered her. Her niece and nephew were there, as were Grace, Matt, Alice, Madeline, Theo, Walter, and Mary. Phillip would join them soon for Charlie's ceremony for the Lords. Tears pricked her eyes. If things went as expected, she and her sisters would be wed before the Season was done. They would have husbands, new homes, and then children. But every other Christmas and summer they would join with the rest of the family at Worthington Place. And every spring and autumn they would gather in Town. She could almost feel their arms wrapped around her. And no matter where she was, that feeling would never go away.

Eleanor found her chair as she blinked tears away, poured a cup of tea, and took a sip. "I am so glad we are a family. I love you all."

Then, to her horror, she burst into tears.

Madeline and Alice quickly hugged her and gave her a handkerchief.

"What on earth brought that on?" Matt asked.

"I think she has finally understood the magnitude of what this Season means," Charlie said.

"I knew it was a good idea Constance, Vivienne, Alexandria, and I decided not to have a come out," Elizabeth said.

"Did you?" Grace sounded like she was choking on her words.

Eleanor dabbed the last of her tears as Matt leaned back in his chair and crossed his arms over his chest. "I knew you were clever girls. You have made me and the other fathers very happy."

"That is what Aunt Eleanor said."

Theo swallowed a piece of toast. "Enjoy it while you can."

"It will not last," Mary opined.

"I don't understand," Gideon said. "Why is she sad?"

"You are too young to remember, but when one has a Season a lady marries, and then she has to move away and live in a different house," Mary explained. "Just like Charlotte, Louisa, Henrietta, and Dotty did."

Gideon's face puckered. "But I don't want them to move away. Papa, you must take us all home right now."

Matt dragged a hand down his face. "Can we please eat our breakfast and have this conversation later?"

Theo whispered something to a footman and rose. "Come along, Gideon. I will explain it to you. It is not as bad as you think it is."

She took him by the hand and left the room. A footman followed them with their breakfast plates.

"I am sorry." Eleanor placed the handkerchief on the table and picked up her cup of tea. Charlie was right. They had been planning for this for years, but she had just realized what it really meant.

"It is fine." Grace's gentle voice soothed Eleanor. "This was bound to happen sooner or later. You have been here his whole life."

"Better he gets it out now than at the wedding," Mary opined. "The hardest was seeing Charlotte get married and go away. Then I realized I just would not see her as much, but she was still my sister. And we all really like Con."

Eleanor had to agree with Mary. All their sisters had married good men. And she would too. Now that there was a scheme in place, she would know soon if that gentleman was Montagu or not.

CHAPTER NINETEEN

"She thinks I'm an idiot."

"Did you say something, sir?" Pickerell asked from the dressing room.

"Er, no." John went back to tying his cravat. That was the only thing it could be. At least he thought it was the only thing it could be. No. He was right. It had been in her eyes. But what in the hell had he done to give her that impression? He needed to talk with someone, but who? His valet helped him into his jacket. It had to be someone who had had problems with his future wife.

Pickerell handed John his gloves. Although from what he'd heard, that was practically every gentleman he knew, with the sole exception of his brother-in-law.

Lucky man.

He positioned his hat on his head at a bit of an angle, then picked up his cane. He had received an invitation to Stanwood House to celebrate Stanwood taking his seat in the Lords. John fully expected Eleanor to be there, and he had to speak to someone before then. "I will most likely be away until midafternoon."

"Yes, my lord."

He left his house and reached the pavement. The day

was overcast, but the early rainstorm had passed and the sun was trying to push through what was left of the clouds.

"Good morning, Montagu." Exeter's cane swung as he strolled toward John.

"Exeter." Exactly the person John should ask, and the walk to Westminster was sufficiently long to hold a conversation. "Good morning."

"My stable master said it will be a fine day." Exeter smiled as if he didn't have a care in the world.

"It looks like it will be." When John was young there was an old groom who knew just what the weather would be. He was never wrong. He opened his mouth to start the conversation about his difficulty with Eleanor and couldn't do it. Exeter was a friend, but not a longtime one. Blast it all. Who the devil was John to ask?

They turned right on Bond Street, and he saw Turley. "Good morning."

"Good morn to you." He inclined his head. "Exeter, good day. I'm glad the rain stopped in time to allow a stroll to Westminster."

John was as well. He'd missed riding this morning. He'd missed seeing Eleanor. "We are fortunate."

He glanced at Exeter and Turley. John knew Turley much better, and he knew that he'd had problems too. But he couldn't talk to him with Exeter present.

Someone grabbed his arm and pulled him to the side. "What the deuce—"

"Horse apples." Exeter indicated a pile in the street. "You need to watch where you're going."

"Thank you." John really did need to pay more attention. "I didn't see them."

His friends barked laughs, and Turley said, "That was obvious. I've never seen you so distracted."

Now was the time. What did it matter that Exeter knew? "I don't think I've ever been so at a loss about what to do."

"This wouldn't have anything to do with Lady Eleanor"— Turley raised a knowing brow—"would it?"

Hell and damnation. "How did you know?"

"Let me see." Turley tapped his cheek with one finger. "Could it be that since the Season began, you have been focused on her to the exclusion of every other lady?"

"That must be it," Exeter agreed. "Even the ones that have been attempting to catch your attention."

"I've been making a cake of myself." How lowering.

"You won't be the first gentleman to have done it and you won't be the last." Exeter's dry drawl spoke volumes about his own quest.

"Exeter, Littleton, and I assisted each other when we were courting. Littleton's not here yet, but Exeter and I will do what we can to help you." Turley gave John a sharp look. "Yet you must first tell us what the problem is."

John blew out a breath. "After last evening I am almost certain she thinks I am an idiot."

Exeter frowned. "Why would she believe that?"

"Because I took St. Albans's advice." Both men looked confused. "Let me start from the beginning." He told him how he thought he'd wanted a rather dim wife, and what St. Albans suggested, and that he'd thought he'd found what he wanted in Eleanor.

Exeter and Turley almost went into whoops. "I do not know what is so humorous."

Turley put his hand on John's shoulder. "Do you not know that this is the family who agreed to support one sister's desire to study at the University in Bologna, Italy?"

Surely John had not heard his friend correctly. He shook his head to clear it. "What did you say?"

Turley's eyes twinkled with humor. "Augusta, now Lady Phinn, was allowed to travel with her cousins to Europe. Phinn was determined to marry her and followed them. She was equally determined to complete university before marrying. To make a long story short, she and Phinn married, and she did indeed get a diploma stating that she had graduated from the University of Bologna."

"How many offers did she refuse?"

Turley rubbed his chin as if thinking about it. "At least twenty."

"Must have been something like that." Exeter nodded. "But we digress. No one in that family, certainly not the ladies, is at all dim, as you put it."

"Oh my Lord." John wiped a hand down his face and groaned. "She's right. I am an idiot."

Turley narrowed his eyes a bit. "Yet she is allowing you to dance attendance on her."

She was, wasn't she? "What does that mean?"

"Lady Eleanor has obviously found something else she likes about you," Exeter explained. "That said, it is high time you find a way to show her your wits aren't lacking."

"I did engage her in a discussion about her opinions on the less fortunate." And that had not worked at all.

Exeter frowned. "What did she say when you told her what you have done or the projects on which you are now working?"

"I didn't tell her. I listened to her." By the dumbfounded looks on his friends' faces, that had not been the right course to take. "I had changed my mind about my requirements for a wife and was attempting to ascertain if she was more intelligent than I had originally thought."

Turley heaved a sigh. "Ergo you gave her the impression you would happily stand back and allow her to do what she wished."

"Not that you would be an active partner"—Exeter held up one hand—"I am fully aware of how modern and radical I sound, but that is what my wife wanted."

Turley nodded. "Mine as well, and they are not the only ones."

John truly had made a mull of things. But perhaps it was not too late to change her mind about him being less than intelligent. If only he could just tell her that he wasn't really stupid. Although about her he might be. He'd have to show her. This afternoon would be the perfect time to begin his new campaign. "Thank you. I believe I know what I must do."

They reached Westminster and made their way to the Lords' chamber. Several ladies were already in the visitors' gallery, or the Strangers' Gallery, as it was officially called. John saw Eleanor speaking with an older lady he didn't know. He recognized most of the other ladies. Unsurprisingly, they were all related to Stanwood's family in one fashion or another, or friends of the family. Lady Mary, apparently the youngest member to be allowed to come, gave Stanwood a small wave. Next to her, Lady Theo regally inclined her head, then ruined the effect by smiling broadly. Yet John could see how they too would grow up to be formidable ladies. Thinking back to the breakfast, he had even seen it in the much younger members of the family. Clearly, they were being allowed—nay, encouraged—to develop their own talents, not be molded into what Polite Society thought a young lady should be. If his sister was any example, attempts to shape them into persons they were not would have failed in any event. How had he not understood that before? It wasn't as if he hadn't lived with the perfect example.

A hand landed on John's shoulder. "They are impressive, each in her own way." Kenilworth steered John to where the marquises sat. "When I first met Charlotte, I was completely fooled by her golden hair, her blue eyes, her beauty, and her youth into thinking she was simply another young, simpleminded young lady." His smile seemed to be more for himself than for John. "Did you know she picks locks?"

Dumbly, John shook his head. A lady picking locks? "I've never heard of such a thing."

"Neither had I. The strength and ingenuity she showed under extremely adverse conditions knocked me down a peg or two and made me rethink my opinions about the capabilities of ladies."

"Yes." John had been having similar thoughts. Not that he thought ladies were incapable, but that they should be there to comfort their husbands and not live for themselves as well. "I know what you mean."

"Good." Kenilworth slapped John's shoulder. "I'm glad you understand."

He wandered off to speak with Rothwell, who glanced at John and met his eyes.

I've just been warned. Intentionally and formally warned. If I don't want a strong, intelligent lady, I can take myself off immediately and not look back.

He should have expected it. He knew how protective the family was. Still, it was interesting that they all seemed to have come to the conclusion that he wanted someone less. It was either take the whole package or none of it. Fortunately for him, he had decided her intellect was what he wanted in a wife.

"What did Kenilworth say to you?" Exeter asked.

"Something along the lines of what you, Turley, and I had been discussing earlier." Just put in another way and with a far different meaning. John glanced around and saw the dukes beginning to sit. "I think we should take our seats."

The ceremony was very formal and rather dull, but the suppressed excitement from the gallery seemed to enliven the proceedings. Shortly after Stanwood was seated, his family left. John hoped he'd see Eleanor later at Stanwood House.

"Did you see him staring at you?" Mary had just settled into the large family town coach.

"I did." Rather, Eleanor had felt him staring at her. It was unnerving how her whole body had tingled in reaction.

"I think he is very handsome," Theo said.

Everyone thought he was handsome. "Handsome is as handsome does."

Madeline, Alice, Phillip, and Walter joined them.

"That is true," Mary said.

"What is true?" Phillip asked.

Mary turned to Phillip and related the short conversation. He nodded somberly. "That's what Grace says."

Madeline and Alice exchanged glances with Eleanor. She loved the redundant conversations when someone, or more than one person, was explaining to someone who had not been there what had occurred. It had started after she and Alice, and then Madeline, had complained at length that no one told them anything.

Walter looked at Eleanor. "Grace said we will have a small celebration with Charlie at Worthington House before he goes to the larger one at Stanwood House. That will allow the children to join us."

"That is a good idea." Eleanor had wondered if the reception at Stanwood House would be mostly peers. "We will most likely go on morning visits after that."

"We are staying home this evening. Tomorrow Lady Brownly is hosting a musical evening," Madeline said.

Good. That would give Eleanor time to work on her plans for the mine.

It was raining again the next morning. Eleanor pulled her covers up and rolled over. If she was in the country, she would dress warmly and take a walk, but this was not the country.

"Someone needs to ask William Coachman if this is going to continue all day," she muttered into her pillows. He was never wrong when it came to the weather. Eleanor turned over onto her back. "I wonder where Posy has got to this morning."

She stared out her window, praying in vain for the rain to stop, then sat up. Two knocks sounded on her door. "Come."

The door opened and Alice entered, followed by Madeline and Posy.

"Traitor." Eleanor glared at the dog. "Who was she with?"

"Me," Alice said as she sat on the bed. The mattress dipped as Posy got up with her.

Eleanor reached out and jiggled the Dane's soft ears. "I wonder if they are looking for her again."

"I do not have a clue." Madeline yawned. "I am very tired of this morning rain."

Alice stroked the dog's back. "It is supposed to do this for the next few days. Rain in the morning and dry in the afternoon."

The dog laid her head on Eleanor's stomach and looked at her with beseeching brown eyes. "I do not know what you want." She glanced at Alice. "Who told you about the rain?"

"My maid, who heard it from William Coachman." Alice lay down next to the dog. "At this rate they would all be yawning. "I am tired, but I am not, if that makes any sense at all."

"I think rain makes one tired," Madeline opined. "At least it always seems that way." She yawned. "When I think of a rainy day I think of reading a good book."

That sounded like a good idea. But Eleanor had work to do.

Alice turned her head toward Eleanor and Madeline. "If we did that every time it rained, we would never get anything done."

"This is where you all are," Jobert said. "My ladies, your maids are looking for you. Miss Posy, there is a footman who needs to take you out."

Madeline and Alice scrambled out of the bed, taking the Dane with them.

Eleanor sighed. It had been quite like old times, when they shared a room on the nursery floor. "I will see you at breakfast."

When she arrived in the breakfast room she was not surprised to find only the family who resided in the house at the table. Even Augusta and Phinn had not braved the weather. What Eleanor did need to do was try to discover when the meeting would be. She waited until Matt had poured a cup of tea. "Are you off to the Lords early today?"

"No. The session has been pushed back until this afternoon. I have a meeting with some of the gentlemen concerning mine legislation."

"That sounds interesting." She selected a baked egg and some chicken from the plates brought around and picked two pieces of toast from the rack. "I have been reading some pamphlets and handbills from those wanting mine reform. There are several interesting ideas."

Matt's attention focused more completely on her. "How is your scheme coming along?"

"I have yet to write anything down other than notes, but I have an idea what I want to do." If Uncle Herndon was going to allow her to take over the mine, Eleanor must have a coherent plan to present to him.

Matt took a sip of tea. "Let's arrange to discuss it at luncheon."

Depending upon how long it would take her to discover if Montagu was actually intelligent or as dim as he seemed, that would give her time to organize her notes. "Very well. I will have an outline ready."

"Are we going on morning visits?" Madeline asked Grace.

Grace had just taken a bite of toast and nodded, then swallowed. "Yes. According to William Coachman, the rain is supposed to stop by noon at the latest."

"About this musical evening"—Alice had a pained expression—"Are the young ladies expected to perform?"

Grace laughed lightly. "No. Lady Brownly prides herself on hiring the Season's most prominent singer to perform."

Alice blew out a breath in relief. They were all accomplished on the piano, but she did not like to play in public. "In that case, I shall look forward to it."

Elizabeth, who had just begun piano lessons, shot her mother a suspicious glance. "Is this like the player with a monkey? I should like the monkey, but I do not wish to play for strangers."

"Oh Heavens." Grace put her elbow on the table, cradling her chin in her palm as she regarded her eldest daughter. "No, sweetheart, it is not like the performer with the monkey." Elizabeth opened her mouth and Grace hurried on. "And we are not getting a monkey. Two dogs are enough."

Eleanor stifled a chuckle. "If you will excuse me, I shall see you later."

"I am finished as well." Alice rose.

"I will see you at luncheon." Madeline pushed her chair back.

They left the room and strode to the hall, before breaking out into whoops.

"A monkey!" Eleanor gasped, holding her sides.

"It never would have occurred to me that she would think of the fellow playing the pipe." Madeline's voice quivered.

"The things they come up with." Alice waved a hand in front of her face. "Who would have thought?"

Eleanor heard steps in the corridor. "That must be Matt. I need to get ready."

Her sisters sobered and they climbed the stairs.

"I do hope this turns out well." The doubt in Alice's voice almost made Eleanor hesitate.

"It will." Madeline smiled. "I have a good feeling about it."

"It has to." Eleanor prayed they did not fall out of the room as they had every other time they had listened at the antechamber door. "I have given him every chance. This must work."

CHAPTER TWENTY

Less than an hour later, a knock sounded on the Young Ladies' Parlor door, and Eleanor's heart started pounding so hard she was sure her sisters would hear it. "Come."

A footman opened the door. "Lord Stanwood said this is for Lady Eleanor."

"This" was a folded scrap of paper. "Thank you."

As soon as he had left, her sisters gathered on either side of her.

"Open it," Alice said.

"Yes." Oddly, Eleanor's hand trembled. She unfolded the note.

In five minutes.
       S

She glanced at the clock. This was going to be a long five minutes.

"Why do you think he wants us to wait?" Madeline asked.

Eleanor looked at the clock again. A very long five minutes. "They will spend time greeting each other before settling down to business."

No one spoke as the rain pattered against the windows. That and the loud ticking of the clock were the only sounds in the room.

"This is excruciating." Alice ran her hands down the sides of her skirts.

Madeline blew out a breath. "I loathe waiting."

Eleanor stared at the clock and finally the hand moved. "Let us go. Slowly and quietly down the servants' stairs."

When they reached the anteroom the door to Grace's study was cracked slightly, allowing Eleanor and her sisters to see the men sitting in a half circle in front of the large cherry desk. The corner of a wooden chair that had been placed in front of the door barely showed. Montagu sat in a position that gave her a good view of him. Next to him, Charlie was staring at the antechamber door. He must have seen her because he turned his attention to the group.

"What have we discovered, if anything?" Matt took out a sheet of paper.

Merton leaned back in his chair. "I have sent for information, but it has been slow in coming. What I do know is that my uncle, acting on my behalf, signed a long-term lease. My solicitor is still researching whether or not I will be able to make any changes until the lease is ready to be renewed."

Matt nodded. "That's what I'm hearing as well." He turned to Harry Stern. "Have you heard anything from your grandmother?"

"Not yet. However, my uncle Bristol has just arrived in Town. I have a meeting scheduled with him later this week." Harry pulled a face. "I don't expect much. He's a Tory. I did discover that the majority of the mines are owned by the Crown."

Montagu frowned as he listened to the accountings.

"That's an interesting piece of information. What about Littleton?"

Turley shook his head. "No holdings. He does have an interest in canals."

"That could be of benefit if he was willing to help us." Eleanor's excitement grew. She could practically hear Montagu formulating a plan.

"What are you thinking?" Merton asked.

"If we can't find any mine owners or operators to support our ideas, perhaps we could convince the canal owners to slow down shipments until changes are made." She wished she knew more about canals. "Our success will most likely depend on whether the canals are owned by one person or a consortium."

Eleanor felt a smile growing. Not only was he not stupid, Montagu appeared to be quite intelligent. She had the perfect way to help him and the others. She was also certain that between Mrs. Johnson and the pamphlets, she would be able to gather enough information to get the public behind safety legislation.

Turning to her sisters, she mouthed, *Let us go*.

As quietly as they entered the room, they left. It was not until they were on their floor that Eleanor dared speak. She opened the door to their parlor. "That was intriguing."

"I assume it answered your questions?" Madeline asked.

"It did." Eleanor thought about the information Lady Lytton had sent her. "I am going to go back over the documents I have, taking into account what we heard today. I do not want to have missed anything on long-term leases. I will see you at luncheon."

"What will you do about Montagu?" Alice asked.

"Continue discovering more about him." Eleanor must ensure they held the same beliefs, especially about family. Yesterday had been an epiphany of sorts, and she was more certain than ever that any gentleman she married must agree to abide by the family visiting schedule that had already been established. And she must be able to trust him enough to keep his word. Too many gentlemen promised ladies what they wanted to hear before marriage and reneged afterward. It was unfortunate that even though they said their word was their bond, they did not apply it to their wives. There was also the question of why he had hidden his intelligence. Eleanor had heard of ladies doing so— some were even advised to do it—but never gentlemen. She shrugged. First mines. They seemed to be much more straightforward than gentlemen. And she must not forget her meeting with Matt.

Right, then. Plan to present to her uncle first. Legislation later.

She went to the desk in her chamber and pulled out the drawer where she had put the documents and her draft scheme. First, she went over the complaints about mines and how they were run. There were indeed long-term leases, but it appeared that they did not necessarily stop a landowner from making changes. For her purposes, the most important being that the landowner could have the manager removed for certain reasons having to do with damage to the part of the property not managed by the mine owners. The problem was that she did not know exactly what would constitute the damage. That might be included in the individual contracts. Eleanor sat back in her chair. Before she could proceed with her ideas, she must be allowed to review the contract. She definitely did not want women and children working in the mines themselves. Although she supposed that women who wanted or needed to would be allowed to do work aboveground. One of the pamphlets had described the horrible deaths of young children. They ought not to be allowed to work in a mine, or anywhere else for that matter, at all. Children should be in school. Which, of course, meant she must establish a school for them to attend. The question would be at what age they could work in a mine. Factories were not allowed to employ children under ten years of age. But from what Dotty had said, the law was not enforced. Eleanor also knew that the average age of apprenticeship in general was around ten years. However, she could not accept that children that young should work in a mine. This would be a subject she should discuss with the person she hired to manage the mine. And that brought her to who she would hire to do that. He must have worked as a miner. He must also be a natural leader. There must also be regular safety inspections.

She put down her pen and looked at her list. That would do for her meeting with Matt.

A knock came on the door. "Come."

"My lady," Turner said. "His lordship said he is free to meet with you."

"Thank you." She glanced at the other correspondence waiting for her that would have to wait and gathered the plan and some of the pamphlets. Matt was sitting behind his desk when she walked in. "How did your meeting go?"

He raised one brow. "How do you think it went?"

Naturally he would have wondered why the door was slightly open and a chair had been placed against it. "I did not stay for the whole thing. I had to know if Lord Montagu was intelligent or not."

Matt looked at her as if he thought she had lost her mind, then shook his head. "Of course he is. Why would you think otherwise?"

She sank into one of the two chairs in front of his desk. "Because he seems to have gone out of his way to act like he is not."

Her brother-in-law's eyes narrowed as he stared at her. "I don't understand. Why the deuce would he do that?"

"I have absolutely no idea. Yet he did." She placed her papers on Matt's desk. "Perhaps one day I will ask him."

"Or I will," he muttered under his breath. "Let's see what you have."

She pushed the documents across the desk to him. "I was able to acquire some information written by those supporting mine reform that was very helpful."

He perused her list. "Short but succinct. I agree you must read the contract. I'll have my solicitor come to explain anything you do not understand." Matt glanced at her. "He has a way of explaining that makes a concept easily understood."

Eleanor was glad he had added that last part. For a second she had thought he did not believe her capable of understanding a contract. She did have some knowledge of them when it came to domestic and estate issues. "Yes, please do."

"I take it you know that women and young children are working in the mines because of your conversations with Mrs. Johnson."

Eleanor nodded. "She told me about it, and there was more information in the pamphlets. They covered a broader aspect."

Matt grunted. "I like your idea to have a miner run the mine." He glanced up. "Bringing people up and promoting them is what we do for almost everything else. Why it would not be done at a mine baffles me."

"It does not make any sense to me either. I did not even know they brought in other men until I read it in the information I received."

He sat back and looked at her with a steady gaze. "Where did you come by the pamphlets?"

Lady Lytton had been rather secretive about sending them to Eleanor. When she did mention the information, she had talked in a way that anyone listening would not know what they were. Her ladyship might not want others to know she had helped Eleanor. "I attended a gathering of ladies interested in increasing their charitable work with the possibility of developing legislation and met a lady who had heard about the problems and knew people in the area."

"It sounds as if she went out of her way to help you." He placed his elbows on the desk and steepled his fingers. "Would you allow me to read the pamphlets and anything else you received? I'm sure they would give me a better understanding of the situation."

"Yes, of course." She was extremely glad he had not demanded a name. "You can keep those. I will send down the rest." She glanced at the list. "When do you meet with Uncle Herndon?"

Matt looked at the clock. "In about an hour. If you do not object, I will first ask what he knows about the operation and ask for the contract and any other relevant documents."

"That is a good idea." She wished she could accompany Matt to her uncle's house, but he had a plan and they would stick to it. Eleanor rose. "If that is all, I should be going."

A light tap sounded on the door and Grace strolled in. "Good day. Eleanor, are you going riding with Lord Montagu this afternoon?"

Riding with Montagu? "I did not know he had asked me."

Grace pressed her lips together. "I knew I should have told you myself. He wrote yesterday. I read his invitation and put it in your correspondence."

Eleanor thought about the short stack of letters on her desk. "Do you think it is too late to send an answer?"

"Not if he really wants to spend time with you." Matt grinned. "And you want his company."

She smiled back. "A ride would be nice."

A short while later, she wrote to Montagu.

Dear Lord Montagu,
   I am sorry for this late response. I did not know you had written until my sister told me.
I would be happy to accompany you this afternoon.

Yours sincerely,
E. Carpenter

Eleanor read over the missive. It was good enough for now. She sanded and sealed it. She thought about sending it down but decided to have Turner take it. The response was already late enough.

She gave the bell-pull two tugs, and a few minutes later he arrived. "Please take this to Montagu House."

"Yes, my lady."

"Thank you."

This had been a productive day thus far. Eleanor was glad Matt had been as confused about Montagu's deception as she. It really was quite strange, and she hoped he had a satisfactory answer when she approached him about it. Until then, she would carry on with determining if he was the right gentleman for her.

CHAPTER TWENTY-ONE

John arrived home and went directly to his study. He shuffled through his correspondence, separating letters from his estate manager from social invitations, and threw the letters back on his desk. He should have heard from Eleanor by now. He'd written to her as soon as he'd received his curricle yesterday. He'd been very pleased with how it looked and was excited for her to join him on his maiden ride. She wouldn't have received his invitation directly. John knew from his sister's experience that either Worthington or his lady would review John's invitation before giving it to Eleanor. What if they had not had time to go through their letters? He pulled out his pocket watch and flipped open the cover. There was still time. If he did not go driving with Eleanor, he had nothing to do with the rest of his day. Although it would give him time to hunt down Lord Lancelot. John had wanted to be the one to speak with the man and hadn't yet had time.

"My lord." His butler stood in the open door. "A note for you just arrived."

He held out his hand, praying it was from her. The second he touched it, he knew it was the answer to his request. Her handwriting was as elegant and direct as the lady herself. He broke the seal, shook open the letter, and scanned it. "Lumner, I shall require my curricle this afternoon at five."

"Very good, my lord." Before the butler bowed, John thought he'd caught a faint, very faint smile on the servant's face.

Would his staff be happy if he wed? It wasn't something he'd thought about before. But, of course, marriage meant the next generation would carry on the title. It was security for them, even though it also meant the changes a new mistress would bring. Yet that was the way of the world.

John quickly sorted through the rest of his letters. Most of them were easily answered. However, the one from his steward required that he give the answer some thought. He took out his watch again. Only three o'clock. He could either mope around here or he could go find Lord Lancelot.

John rose from his desk and strolled to the hall. "I am going out for a bit." Lumner handed John his hat, gloves, and cane. "I shall be back well before five."

When he reached the pavement he decided to start his search at Lancelot's parents' house on Park Lane. John plied the knocker on the door and a footman opened it.

John handed the servant his card. "Is Lord Lancelot in residence? I am an old school friend."

"He has rooms on Jermyn Street, my lord."

As John turned to leave, Lord Cedric, the brother John had known at Eton, was strolling up the walk. He had the same fair hair as Lancelot, but his complexion was much browner. "Montagu, is that you?"

"In the flesh." He held out his hand. "You're looking well. How have you been keeping yourself?"

"Well." The man smiled. "Very well indeed. I'm home on leave. I've been with the East India Company for a few years." He squinted. "Who are you here to see?"

"Lord Lancelot."

Cedric's head snapped back. "Why in the devil would you want to see him? Does he owe you money?"

"No." John was glad he wasn't much of a gambler. "Is he in the habit of owing money?"

"I'll walk with you." Cedric had taken his hat off and donned it again. It wasn't until they reached the pavement that he spoke. "Why do you want to see him?"

"I'm making an inquiry about his character. He attempted to be made known to a young lady."

"Is she wealthy?" Cedric's tone was as dry as dust.

"Does he need a wealthy wife?" That was something John had not considered, but Worthington probably had. John had been more concerned about the man's character.

"I will tell you this: My father arranged a position for him at the Home Office. He lasted less than two weeks. Lance has an allowance that allows him to reside in his own rooms, but not enough to gamble or live extravagantly. Unfortunately, he is known for his excess. I know m'mother has covered some of his debts. Our father has refused to assist him further or help him publish his book of poems. As far as he is concerned, Lance needs to stop living in a fantasy land." Cedric slid John a look. "If he wants to continue being a poet, he must marry a female with money."

John wondered if the duke was merely aggravated by a son who wanted to write poetry or if Lancelot was not any good at it. "Have you read his poetry?"

"Even our mother thinks it's rubbish, and she reads a lot of poetry. But Lance was born after several babes died and she has always spoiled him." Cedric had a wry look on his face. "I can tell you, she never cosseted the rest of us."

John could understand how a woman who had lost several children would cling to the next one who was born. He supposed she was never able to have any more. "Thank you for telling me."

"I won't say it was a pleasure. It's not a good thing when one must speak badly of a family member. But I wouldn't want him to wed anyone I know."

"I understand." The only thing to do now was to warn Lord Lancelot off the Worthington ladies. "Thank you again."

"Perhaps I'll see you around. I'm here until the end of June." A smile cracked Cedric's sunbaked face. "I'm here to marry a lady I met in India."

"Congratulations. Will she be returning with you?"

"She will. It's a rather long story, but her family returned to England and, naturally, she had to go with them. Now that she's reached her majority, she has decided to become my wife and come back with me."

John sensed the lady's family was not in favor of the match but kept his thoughts to himself. "She sounds like an interesting lady. I hope to meet her before you depart."

"I'll see if I can arrange something." Cedric stopped walking. "I'd better head home. I must meet with my father about the settlement agreements."

"I look forward to seeing you again."

Cedric turned back toward Park Lane and John continued on to Jermyn Street. The only building with which he was familiar was 22 Jermyn Street. He arrived there only to be told his lordship was out and would not be back until it was time to change for the evening. Well, damn. He'd probably have to try one morning. Early. He grinned to himself. That wouldn't make Lancelot at all happy.

John arrived at Worthington House shortly before five o'clock. The door opened as he strolled up the short walk. "Good afternoon, my lord." The butler bowed. "Lady Eleanor will be down directly." He motioned with his hand to one of the rooms off the hall facing the square. "Would you like to wait in the parlor?"

"Thank you, no. I will remain here." Where he could watch her descend. Even though it had only been yesterday, he felt as if he hadn't seen her for days. Fortunately, he didn't have to wait long. His gaze was drawn upward by a slight noise from the staircase. Eleanor stood briefly on the landing before gracefully descending the stairs. She wore a buttery-yellow carriage gown with green, pink, and blue embroidery around the hem and the edges of her spencer. All of which he would like to see puddled on the floor at her naked feet. Her hat, decorated with a wide ribbon, hid the hair he wanted to take down and run his fingers through.

Stepping forward, he held out his hand. "My lady. It is a pleasure to see you."

She lightly gripped his fingers and smiled as if she was truly happy to see him. Was he finally making some progress with her? "I am glad to see you as well, my lord."

He placed her small, gloved hand on his arm and inclined his head as the butler bowed. "I hope five o'clock is a good time for the Promenade."

"That is the time we usually went when Grace took us." He liked how artless her answer was. They strolled out of the house, and she stopped. "What lovely colors. And the horses!" Eleanor glanced at him, her eyes shining. "How beautiful they are."

"I am glad you like them." He had chosen dark green with gold piping for the curricle body and found a matched pair of dark bays to pull the carriage. "They are sweet goers." He waved the footman away and assisted her into the curricle. The second he'd touched her hand he didn't want to let go. "Do you drive?"

"Yes, but at home. I have never driven in Town." She

settled her skirts. "Matt has ordered my sisters and me a high-perched phaeton. We will have to share it."

Why would Worthington have bought just one carriage for three young ladies? "How will that work?"

A line formed on her forehead and she shook her head. "We are not exactly certain. I suppose on days like today, when one of us is engaged, the other two could take it out."

He started the horses and kept them to a sedate trot on their way to the Park. "The weather is fine today."

The second the words were out of his mouth, he regretted them. He did not wish to talk about the weather with her. The problem was that he had no idea which topic to discuss.

He could feel her staring at him and glanced at her. Her beautiful eyes were slightly narrowed and one brow was raised. "Do you really wish to discuss the weather?"

"No. I would much rather talk about anything other than the weather. I can only think it has become automatic."

"Good." She sounded pleased. "I thought we might discuss something more interesting." Eleanor paused. "Mines, for example. I understand that you have an interest in mines and how they are run."

John's fingers tightened on the reins. When the horses jerked he made himself loosen his hold. His stomach clenched, giving him a sick feeling that he now knew to whom his sister gave the information. "How did you know?"

"My brother Worthington told me." Eleanor's reply was airy, and his stomach relaxed.

"Ah. Yes, I am part of a group of other peers looking at legislation to make the mine situations better."

"I rescued a family who lost their father during the Cinderloo massacre. They told me the conditions were dreadful."

"They are. I have been taking in families from Cinderloo as well." They had entered the Park, and he glanced at her only to find she was looking at him. "The influenza in my area was horrible last winter and, unfortunately, I lost many of my dependents. I am looking for ways to train those arriving in professions we need."

Her eyes widened, not in surprise but more in interest. "Are you indeed?"

He nodded, wondering what she was thinking.

"I may be able to help you. Fortunately, we were not much affected by the grippe. Consequently, we have older sons looking to go out on their own. Perhaps we could compare your needs with our people who would like to move to a new area."

John almost dropped his jaw. He was stunned. Nay. He was astonished. Yes, he knew she was intelligent, but he had no idea she was so . . . so . . . He couldn't find the word. Organized? Willing to immediately assist him? Rather, willing to assist others. His growing understanding of the wife he needed had been right. Lady Eleanor Carpenter was exactly the type of lady he wanted and needed. "Yes, I would like that very much. Should we speak with Worthington?"

She fluttered her hand. "There is no need. I know what must be done. Once the decision is made, I will tell him about it."

John knew enough about her brother to surmise he would not allow anyone to make those kinds of decisions unless they were well trained and knowledgeable. It suddenly dawned on him that there was much more to Eleanor than he could have imagined. "When would you like to discuss the matter?"

"I will make up a list, and you should do so as well. Then we will consult each other. I am certain my sister will allow us to use her study, or perhaps the morning room would be a better place. The desk there is set up for more than one person."

John prayed it would be soon. His steward was becoming more and more desperate. "Let me know when you are ready."

"I will." She smiled at him briefly, then her gaze was drawn away. "Oh, there is Lady Merton and my sisters Kenilworth and Rothwell. We must greet them."

Drat. Why couldn't she have continued to look only at him? He drew up to the Merton landau. "Good afternoon." The three ladies greeted him and Eleanor. That was when he noticed the four little girls as well. "Ladies Alexandra, Vivienne, Constance, and Elizabeth, I wish you a good day."

All four girls smiled and inclined their heads in exactly the same manner the older ladies had.

"We should go," Eleanor said. "We are holding up traffic."

Once they'd driven on, he turned to her. "Were you taken for carriage rides during the Grand Strut when you were young?"

She shook her head. "No. My parents died within a year of each other when I was around their age. Grace did start bringing us with her the year we came to Town for my sisters' and cousin's come outs. I believe those rides helped us become accustomed to Town. I suppose that is the reason the little girls are out today."

It would never have occurred to him, but, like many of the Worthington family ideas, it was forward-thinking and probably did help. He could ask his mother if she took his sister out for drives during the fashionable hour, but John had a feeling he already knew the answer.

The rest of the drive was passed greeting this person and that. Eleanor was extremely well-connected and, from what he could see, well liked. There were also those, mostly older ladies, who greeted Eleanor as if they had known her for years and studied the two of them with interest. Had they discerned his intent? If so, his mother would hear about it soon, and he wasn't certain if he was ready for that to happen.

After they made one circuit—which took over an hour—he drove her back to her house and jumped down before a footman could reach her. Once again he placed his hands on her waist and lifted her slowly down to the pavement. She sucked in a breath, and he had the same heated reaction to her now as when they danced. But this time it was stronger. He had to force himself not to slide his hands to her breasts. He had never had such a strong physical reaction to a female before. It must mean something more than mere lust.

He knew he wanted her. Yet did she want him? Would she even know what wanting was? "I greatly enjoyed myself."

"I did as well." She gazed into his eyes. "If it is not raining tomorrow, my sisters and I will ride. We start out when it gets light enough to see."

"If it is not raining, I will see you then." He placed her hand on his arm and escorted her to the door. "I hear Lady Brownly is holding a musical evening tonight. Might you consider sitting with me?"

"For part of the time, yes." Eleanor smiled again. "Until then."

John watched her until the door closed, then turned and went back to his carriage. "This has been an extraordinarily illuminating day."

"Did you say something, my lord?" the footman holding the horses asked.

"No." He flipped the man a coin. "Thank you."

"Thank you, my lord."

John felt as if he had just met the real Lady Eleanor Carpenter. She was an unexpected pleasure. He started the horses. Tonight would be even more fun than he had wished. But first, he had some serious thinking to do. She had completely upended him.

CHAPTER TWENTY-TWO

Eleanor strode into the small parlor off the hall and discreetly peeked out the window, watching as Montagu drove off. Then she rushed up to the Young Ladies' Parlor and was disappointed to find it empty. She went back into the corridor and found one of their maids. "Where have my sisters gone?"

The woman bobbed a curtsey. "They took the new phaeton out, my lady."

Why had she not seen them at the Park? "When did it arrive?"

"About ten past five." The maid glanced at Alice's dressing room door. "If you'll excuse me, I have to finish some work."

"Yes, of course. I am sorry to have held you up." Well, drat. Just when Eleanor had something important to tell them. She did not want to pace the parlor for however long it took them to come home, but she was too excited to do nothing. Perhaps Matt had received an answer from Uncle Herndon. She went back downstairs to his study and knocked on the door.

"Come."

She strode in. "What did Uncle have to say?"

Matt glanced up and smiled smugly. "It took some

convincing, but Charlie and I managed to bring him around."

Eleanor sank into one of the chairs in front of the desk. "I take it there will be stipulations."

"Not many. In fact, only two. You must consult us along the way and not"—he cocked a brow—"visit the mine without us."

"That is fair." She raised a brow of her own. It was truly amazing how much a raised brow could convey. "I am aware of how dangerous mines can be. And I really cannot travel all that way without a chaperone."

"It's not just the area, Eleanor. Those managing the mines have been known to become violent."

"I am aware of that as well. I understand they have—people—who make sure their orders are obeyed." She wondered if that was who was after the Johnson family. "I agree to the terms. When will he send over the contract?"

"There is something else. Your mine will be not only a model but has the potential to upset those who do not want change."

The incident with the man at the inn looking for Mrs. Johnson and her children came to mind. "Could I be in physical danger?"

"I wish I could tell you." Lines creased Matt's forehead. "Once you are able to institute your ideas, you must take care. I"—his lips formed a thin line—"as a matter of fact, I don't want your name involved. But I don't know if that is possible."

She knew that other members of her family had crossed those who did not like their actions on behalf of others, and the rogues had attempted to harm them. Even though she was never alone when she left the house, Eleanor knew she would have to be more aware of her surroundings. She nodded. "I understand. Now, about the contract?"

Matt's countenance cleared. "Herndon will have his solicitor send the document to my solicitor, who will, in turn, bring it to us."

"As you know, I would like to hire one of the miners to take the place of whoever is managing the mine now. There is usually a leader the workers look up to. He would be the best person. My only problem is discovering who that man is." Eleanor wished she could see the mine herself. "I also need to know what the conditions are."

Matt tapped his fingers in a tattoo on the desk. "I can send my steward to look it over." He glanced at her. "The only problem is, he knows nothing about mines."

She sat up straighter as an idea came to her. "He can speak with Mrs. Johnson. She must certainly have some knowledge about how mines work."

"That is an excellent idea." He smiled at her. "Is there anything else?"

"Yes." It was time to tell Matt her other plan. "Lord Montagu has taken in some refugees from the Cinderloo massacre. He also suffered the loss of many of his dependents from the influenza last winter. He is trying to train his new people, but he also needs farmers, for example. I thought of some of our families who have children who will not remain. I would like to make them offers of employment, as it were." Matt stared at her as if he did not know what to think. "Is anything wrong? I was certain you would agree."

He shook his head. "I was just wondering when you had matured so drastically. Somehow I missed it."

"Ah well." Eleanor grinned at him. "It was bound to happen sooner or later." Sounds filtered in from the hall. "I shall see you later."

His mien still had a stunned look when she strode out

of the study toward the hall, her mind turning to what she wanted to tell her sisters about her carriage ride with Montagu. Alice and Madeline were taking off their gloves when Eleanor reached the hall and went straight to one of the side windows next to the front door to see the phaeton, but it had already been taken off. "How did it drive?"

"Beautifully." Alice grinned.

"Yes." Madeline nodded. "And the pair is so well-behaved and easy to handle."

Eleanor really did not expect anything less. "Where did Matt find them?"

"Phoebe Evesham." Alice started toward the stairs. "She knows more about horses than almost anyone."

The Countess of Evesham was one of Grace's oldest and dearest friends. "She has that reputation."

"How was your ride with Lord Montagu?" Madeline asked.

"Better than I had hoped." Eleanor climbed up the stairs with her sisters. "I took a page out of Augusta's book and told him I thought we had discussed the weather enough and asked him what he thought about the situation with the mines."

Alice's jaw dropped for a second. "Good for you!"

"What made you decide to do that?" Madeline opened the door to their parlor.

"It had become clear that if I was to get what I wanted, I must take action instead of hoping it will come to me."

A footman with a tea tray followed them into the room, and Alice began to pour. "You are right. Hope is not a strategy."

Madeline took her cup of tea and sipped. "It is not, is it?"

Eleanor took the cup her sister handed to her but set it

down and went to the desk. "I need to look at our list." She pulled out the paper.

Like house animals

Like children

Make us laugh and think we are funny too

Be kind

At least moderate intelligence

Want to help those less fortunate and
     support our work in the same.

Passable looking

Good character

Allow us to be ourselves

Enough wealth to support a family

Love us

"I am adding one more thing. He must agree to the family gathering schedule." Eleanor added the requirement, then ambled back to the sofas.

"I had not thought of that." Madeline handed Eleanor her cup of tea. "This will get cold if you do not drink it."

Alice leaned forward. "How many of the requirements does Lord Montagu meet thus far?"

"Some of them, at least. I am not sure about his sense of humor, or if he would allow me to be who I am instead of some idea of who he would like me to be. And I do not know if he could fall in love."

"Are you in love with him?" Madeline asked.

"Not yet." In fact, Eleanor had not given that much thought. "But there are the *feelings*, and I believe I could fall in love with him." That reminded her of what she had to tell her sisters about the rest of her conversation with Montagu.

After she had finished, Madeline glanced at Eleanor. "Very promising."

She was glad her sister had the same idea she had. "I thought so. I am sitting with him this evening at Lady Brownly's musicale."

"Perhaps you can find out about his sense of humor. Musical evenings are usually good for that," Alice ventured.

"Yes, that is an excellent idea." With any luck at all, Eleanor could test more than his sense of humor. She took the list back to the desk. This evening ought to be interesting.

John had to force himself to pay attention to the traffic and other distractions as he drove home. Eleanor had stunned him. In a good way. He was actually glad she had taken the conversational reins, as it were, into her own small but clearly capable hands. Her brothers-in-law had been more correct than he could have imagined.

"Watch where ye're goin'!" A dray driver shook his fist at John.

He had to get home quickly. Not thinking about Eleanor was an impossibility. Fortunately, he was close to his street. A cat ran across the road, and he stopped his horses from shying just in time to avoid an accident with another carriage.

John had never been so happy to pull up in front of his house. Jumping down, he waited impatiently until one of the footmen had the horses' heads and a groom had been called. "Thank you."

"You're welcome, my lord."

Strolling up the walk, he went through the already open

door, not giving his actions much thought. She had turned him upside down. "Send tea. I'll be on the terrace."

His butler bowed. "As you wish, my lord."

"Have Pickerell call me when it's time to dress for dinner."

John didn't wait to hear his butler's reply as he ambled down the corridor to his study and out the French windows to the terrace. Someone had placed large potted plants along the sides, effectively providing him with a private terrace. A large, well-padded leather chair John had never seen before was there, next to a smaller version of the same chair. Small, square, plain walnut tables stood on either side of the chairs with one in between them. A large, rectangular table was in front of the chairs. Who had done this?

Lumner brought a tea tray. "My lord, is there anything wrong?"

"No." John's head was in a fog, but not from the tables and chairs. The tables and chairs were just as unexpected as Eleanor had been. "I have never seen this furniture before."

"It has not been out for a few years. His lordship, your father, liked to sit out here when the weather was nice."

"It looks to be a comfortable seating arrangement." One that was perfect for thinking about Eleanor.

"I am glad you approve." His butler put down the tea tray, then pointed to a bell on the table between the chairs. "A footman will be posted to listen for the bell."

John sat in the larger chair, poured a cup of tea, and picked up a lemon tartlet. He had begun the Season wanting a comfortable wife who was rather dim. Then he had changed his mind and wanted a more intelligent wife. Now, he had been introduced to a lady who exceeded any expectation he might have had. He bit into the tartlet, savoring the light taste. John did not doubt for a second that she would make a home comfortable, though slightly chaotic after there were children. And she herself would be involved not only in what he did but with her own projects as well. It was all too easy to picture little boys and girls running around with golden hair and summer-blue eyes. Perhaps one or two would look like him. She would also draw him into her much larger and growing family. Attending family gatherings would certainly be required. For the first time, he understood that with Eleanor, he would not be just marrying her but her family as well.

But will she wed me? What will it take to get her to agree to be my wife?

A vision of them riding in the morning and breaking their fast together came to him. He could see her alternately reading a newssheet and discussing important topics with him. That would be before the children, of course. And then there was how she appealed to him physically. Today, before she had bowled him over, all he'd been able to think about was how he would like to remove her spencer and her gown and discover the joys of her supple body. He had to stop thinking about her naked and in his bed. If he didn't, he'd be salivating when he arrived at Lady Brownly's house this evening. Not to mention having an erection that would be plain for anyone to see.

John drained his teacup and poured another. Yes. He wanted to marry her and have everything that came with Eleanor. The question was how to win her affections. He could not fool himself into thinking her offer to help him meant she had decided to wed him. She liked the flowers he'd sent. She liked riding and the carriage ride. She liked politics and helping others. He could give her all those things. Yet he must be able to become closer to her.

Dancing.

Especially waltzing. It enabled him to hold her, to touch her. Yet he was only allowed one waltz at a ball. He might have been able to make it two, but her family only took her to one major event in an evening. Where could he . . . That was it.

Vauxhall.

No one cared how many times a lady and gentleman danced there. He'd need to get up a party, but his mother would have to make those arrangements.

John rose and went to his study. Mama had sent down the invitations she had accepted on their behalf, and they were on his desk next to his diary. Once he entered the events, he would be able to see which date was the best. He glanced at the door leading to the secretary's office. Unfortunately, his father's secretary had retired, and John had not hired a replacement. Something else he had to do. Could Eleanor help him with that as well? Exeter had told John how he had become close to his wife when she assisted him. John could do the same thing with Eleanor. That would definitely give them more time together. The erection that had gone away was back. He really had to think of something other than her and the more physical aspects of having her as his wife. First, he had to marry her.

John quickly made the entries and studied his diary. There were two nights next week for which he had nothing planned. He tugged the bell-pull and a footman opened the door and bowed. "My lord?"

"Is my mother at home?"

"She returned about a half hour ago. A tea tray was taken to her parlor."

"Thank you. That's all."

The servant stepped back as John rose and made his way to his mother's sanctuary. He tapped on the door and opened it. "Mama?"

She glanced up from reading something. "Yes, dear?"

"I would like you to arrange an evening at Vauxhall and invite Lady Eleanor and anyone else you think proper."

She removed the specs she used for reading. "Vauxhall?"

"Yes. Next week, if that is not too soon." He stood waiting for her to nod or give him some indication she would honor his request.

"I must look to see what they have going on." She returned her lunettes to her nose.

That, apparently, was the best he could expect. "Thank you."

He left the room and went back downstairs. The only person about was a footman. "I will be on my terrace, but I do not wish to be disturbed."

"I will tell Mr. Lumner."

"Thank you."

John reached the terrace and settled once more into the large chair. Now he could think about Eleanor all he wished and make a plan to convince her to marry him.

CHAPTER TWENTY-THREE

They had a small family group attending Lady Brownly's musical evening. Eleanor and her sisters were accompanied only by Grace and Matt. Once they arrived, Eleanor found herself searching the large room for Montagu and immediately stopped. She would not wear her heart on her sleeve.

Heart on my sleeve?

Eleanor gave herself a shake. She was attracted to him, but not in love with him. Yet. The *ton* was littered with love matches that had gone wrong because the couple did not want the same things. By insisting a potential husband meet certain qualifications, her sisters and their friends had gone about it the right way, and so would she.

Footmen brought around champagne and lemonade. She took a glass of the latter and sipped. It was not too sweet and not too tart, with just the right amount of water. Something else had been added to it as well. She took another taste. Mint. "This is good."

Alice took a small drink. "Mint has been added. We should try that."

Eleanor could not imagine telling their French cook to do anything. "I would like to see you make that suggestion to Jacques."

Madeline cringed. "I do not want to be anywhere near when you do. I would also suggest you warn Grace."

"You have a point." Alice pulled a face. "Perhaps I shall wait until I have my own house to run."

She glanced at her twin. "That is probably a better idea."

The back of Eleanor's neck started to tingle. Surreptitiously, she glanced around. Montagu had arrived. Her heart began to beat faster and she fought to maintain an outwardly calm countenance. Unfortunately, a large part of her that did not wish to listen to reason wanted to turn to him and smile. Until she was sure how she felt and what she wanted to do about him, she must not be distracted by her physical reaction to the man.

Ignoring the warmth that had spread from her neck to her shoulders, she studied the room or, rather, rooms. Pocket doors had been pulled back to give the illusion of one large drawing room. A stage had been placed at the far end and rows of chairs set up. "Did we ever discover what kind of musical evening this was?"

Madeline shook her head. "I only know that *we* will not be performing."

"An opera singer has been engaged for the evening." Montagu's warm breath caressed Eleanor's bare neck.

Determined to pay no attention to the tiny bumps Eleanor was sure had risen on the back of her neck—she detested horripilation; next time she would wear a fichu to cover her neck—she turned toward him. "My lord, good evening."

Bowing, he took the hand she held out and actually kissed it! Not the air above her fingers, but the back of her glove. Thank the deities that it covered her arm almost to the small, puffed sleeves of her gown. She really would resemble a plucked goose when this was over.

Straightening, he caught her gaze with his own. "Good evening, my lady."

Eleanor had to remind herself to curtsey. This was not at all good. Where had all her training gone? Not only that but her mouth was dry. She quickly took a sip of lemonade. "Do you know which opera singer?"

"I do." He took a glass of champagne from a passing footman. "It is Giuditta Pasta. She is said to be excellent. Do you enjoy the opera?"

"Very much. My sister has been taking us for a few years now." Thankfully, the horripilation was starting to subside, at least for the moment, and Eleanor took a breath. "Having learned Italian helped."

"I imagine it would." The corners of his lips rose. "Perhaps I should learn the language."

How he had gotten so close to her, she did not have a clue, but if he took one step forward, her skirts would brush against his evening pumps. "To better understand the words?" He gave her a sheepish look. "Have you ever been to the opera?"

"I must confess I have not. As you know, my father was ill for a few years before he died." A shadow seemed to cross his eyes when he mentioned his father. "I did not come to the metropolis at all."

He had told her he had never been on the Town. "I hope you will enjoy the singer."

"If she is as good as my mother says she is, I am sure I will." He glanced around. "Would you like to stroll with me before the performance begins?"

"I would." She took the arm he held out. "I have heard that the opera in which she is performing this year was written expressly for her."

"In that case she must be excellent. I don't see the rest of your family."

"Not this evening." Eleanor tried not to pay attention to the guests glancing at them. Who knew a musical evening could be so fraught? "Although Augusta said she and Phinn might come. They have been to operas in Italy."

"I have always wanted to travel." Montagu glanced at her. "Not for years, but for a few months at a time."

This was the second time he had mentioned traveling. "To see Paris and other of the great European cities? I would like to do that."

"Yes. I cannot stay away too long." Montagu had a wishful expression.

Of course he could not. He took his duties seriously. He must not have been able to go on a Grand Tour because of his father's illness. "I think two, possibly, three months are long enough to be away."

John had not wanted to talk with her about his dependents, or lack thereof, but he was running out of conversation. And she was not the type of lady with whom one could simply make small talk. They were also not at the point where he could speak to her about the future. Yet it had become clear to him this afternoon that he did want her as his wife. No other lady would do. "Have you been able to give my estate problem any thought?"

She glanced at him and smiled. "I have. There are several possibilities. Have you written the list of positions for which you need people?"

"It is at home." He just stopped himself from dragging his hand down his face. "It's more extensive than I had originally thought it was."

She pressed her lips together and tilted her head to the

side. "If you wish, you could join us for tea tomorrow. That will give me time to look at what you have."

Thank God. He sent up a prayer to the deity. "Thank you. That would be perfect."

Lady Brownly, a woman in her middling years wearing a cherry-colored turban, clapped her hands and called the guests to order.

"If you will take your seats," she said. "I will introduce our special guest for the evening."

He bent his head to whisper in Eleanor's ear and saw her shudder slightly. Was that good or not? "Where would you like to sit?"

She glanced around. "All opera singers are used to projecting their voices. We could find chairs near the back if you wish."

That was fine with him. John really had not wanted to be in the middle of a group of people. Although from the look of it, he would not be alone with her no matter where they sat. He steered them toward the back of the room until he found seats not far from her family, but not too close to them either. The one thing he could not do was upset Worthington or his lady. John caught Lady Alice sending him a sharp look. Perhaps he should make that the whole family. He smiled at her, then guided Eleanor to the second chair in the row.

She flashed him a grin. "Now that I know who is to be performing, I am quite excited to hear her again."

"I heard Lady Madeline say she was glad it was not any of you."

"She does not like to play in front of anyone but family. Alice and I do not mind." Eleanor shrugged lightly. "We have practiced for it."

"My sister didn't like it either." He had been in Town to

provide her support during her first Season. "In fact, I believe I am safe in saying that she disliked almost everything about coming out. Except for the new clothing."

Laughter entered Eleanor's eyes. "Somehow I can see that. She does not appear to me to be the type who suffers fools easily."

When did she come to know his sister so well? "If memory serves, I believe she likened it to being a horse at auction."

A peal of light, tinkling laughter erupted from Eleanor and she quickly covered her mouth, but not before the sound caused others to stare. "Oh dear."

The words sounded choked, as if she could not stop laughing. He took a glass of champagne from a footman, her glass of lemonade having been finished during their stroll. "Drink this."

She took a sip, followed by a breath, and nodded. "There. Much better."

Her eyes were still sparkling, and somehow he knew if he even smiled, he'd set her off again. Fortunately, Lady Brownly had stepped back and a woman with dark hair piled elaborately on her head took her ladyship's place. She nodded to the quartet, which was obviously there to accompany her, and began to sing. Eleanor immediately became aware of the music and, from what he could make out, sat spellbound by the singer. He had hoped to be able to converse a bit. But that was clearly not going to happen. John settled himself back to listen to the performance as he watched Eleanor's enjoyment of it. The French he'd learned did not help him at all in understanding the words, but they were beautifully sung.

When Pasta brought the song to an end, Eleanor sighed. "She is wonderful." She turned to him. "What did you think?"

"I enjoyed it." He nodded to himself. "However, I do think I should learn Italian."

She graced him with a broad smile. "I am glad you liked it. Italian might take a little while."

He liked her. It occurred to him that she was a woman who could be a friend as well as a wife. He had never thought of that before. "You could explain it to me until I am sufficiently proficient."

She was still smiling as she tilted her head slightly. "I daresay I could, but not until intermission."

The room became quiet, and she put one finger to her beautiful, plump lips. For a second, all he could think about was kissing them. John had to blink before turning his attention to the singer as her voice soared through the drawing room. If attending the opera allowed him to be with Eleanor, he would learn to love it.

Thinking of love, it occurred to him that he might be falling in love with Eleanor. Discreetly, he glanced around. Lord and Lady Phinn had joined them at some point. They looked at each other, smiling. Her hands were in her lap and his hand covered them. Worthington had his arm across the back of his lady's chair and, even though John couldn't see his hand, he would wager it was on his wife's shoulder. It struck him forcefully that when he had seen her family at entertainments, all the gentlemen were affectionate with their wives, even Rothwell. John found himself yearning for that type of closeness. He'd assumed Eleanor would be like the rest of her family, but was he correct? How could he find out? The room seemed filled with music, but he could not give it his whole attention when he was so distracted by her. If they could have a future, what would it hold? Again, he watched her enjoy the music until the song concluded.

"That was so beautiful." She sighed. "I cannot wait to see the opera in which she is appearing."

He could make that happen for her. "If you would like, I shall ask my mother to form a party to attend a performance."

Eleanor's eyes widened. "How kind of you. But we have a box, and Grace has already set the date." Eleanor gazed at him for a long moment. "Would you like to join us?"

"Yes." The word was out before he had given it any thought at all. The invitation was as unexpected as it was welcome. "I would like to accompany you."

"I shall mention it to her." She rose, and John noticed other people were doing so as well.

He wasn't ready for the evening to end. "Is the entertainment over?"

"No." Footmen were strolling around with canapés. She took one with cheese. "There will be one more aria after this pause."

John was just about to bite into a chicken canapé and stopped. "What is an aria?"

She swallowed. "That is what the songs are called."

"Ah." Another footman approached. "Would you like a glass of champagne?"

"Yes, please, and another canapé. The one I had was delicious."

He agreed. "They are. Although, I think this is an odd way to serve food."

Her well-shaped brows drew together. "My understanding is that there used to be a supper room set up. Perhaps there was a problem with the arrangement."

John thought of what happened at balls. The guests who were not interested in dancing often lingered in the supper room. "I imagine it was more difficult to get them back in their chairs for the performance."

Her brow cleared. "You are probably correct. I cannot imagine Lady Brownly would be happy about having to chivy people back into the drawing room."

Lord and Lady Phinn joined John and Eleanor.

"Is she not wonderful?" Lady Phinn said. "We saw her in Milan."

"I didn't think I'd like the opera." Lord Phinn glanced at his wife with a soft smile on his face. "I was wrong. Indeed I have become a devotee."

John slid a look at Eleanor. "I can understand how that could happen."

Lord Phinn's smile broadened. "Have you a habit of coming to London during the Season?"

"No. This is the first time I've been here in years." The man was someone one did not see in the normal course of the day. He wasn't involved in politics, at least not that John knew of. "Do you come often?"

"One of the first and only times I was in Town for the Season I met Augusta. She didn't stay long and neither did I. We just returned for her sisters' come outs."

That was interesting. John knew Lady Phinn had wanted to attend university. "What do you do?"

"I study architecture and write articles about it." The man looked as if he wanted to burst out laughing. "Augusta studies dead and living languages. She also writes articles."

"I see." He wondered if Eleanor had any bluestocking tendencies. Not that he'd mind. It would just be interesting to know.

At that, Lord Phinn did bark a laugh. "We are the odd ones out in our families."

John remembered what Eleanor's brothers by marriage had said to him about the family being on the Radical side of the Whigs. "I'm not so sure about that. As far as I can see, the whole family does what it likes."

"You might be right." Lord Phinn appeared to think about that. "They did make it possible for Augusta to travel overseas."

Eleanor placed her hand on his sleeve. "The next aria will soon begin."

Lord Phinn and his wife left to take their seats, and it struck John that he had been able to remain with her the whole evening. He wanted to spend even more time with Eleanor and hoped to hell it didn't rain in the morning.

CHAPTER TWENTY-FOUR

Eleanor and her sisters rode out just as it was becoming light. The air was soft and warmer than it had been. The lilacs were now in full bloom and the trees had bright green leaves. Beneath her, Adela made it clear she was ready for a good gallop. "I think spring has finally arrived."

"It is about time," Alice grumbled.

Eleanor glanced at her twin. Alice was normally very good-natured in the morning. "What has you put out?"

"You might better ask *who* has her put out." Madeline raised a brow. "St. Albans, of course."

"He acted as if he could command my attention during the performance." Alice sniffed. "I trust he quickly learned he could not."

Madeline cast her gaze to the sky. "She refused to have anything to do with him and remained with me, Harry, Penelope, and Eloisa the entire time."

"Penelope and Eloisa were there?" Eleanor did not remember seeing them.

"It is not at all surprising you did not notice them," her twin said. "The only person you seemed to have eyes for was Lord Montagu."

"Did you find out anything helpful?" Madeline asked.

Last evening was one of the rare times they had not gathered in their parlor to discuss the entertainment. "He made me laugh." Eleanor smiled, remembering how hard it had been not to go into whoops. They rode through the gate into the Park. "To the oak tree?"

Her sisters nodded, and they quickly urged their horses to gallop. Eleanor gave Adela her head and reached the tree first.

When they reached her, she said, "He is coming to tea. We are going over the list of positions he needs to fill."

"Other than a wife." Alice really was frumpish today.

Madeline ignored Alice. "What positions?"

Eleanor realized she had told Matt about Montagu's needs but not her sisters. "After we talked about the mines, he told me of a difficulty he was having . . ."

"Hmm." Madeline started her horse at a walk. "You are correct. That would help both him and our family."

"I heard you laugh." Alice seemed to have shaken off her sour mood. "What did he say?"

"He told me about his sister's first Season and how she did not like it." They had met Lady Lytton, but had either of her sisters spoken with the lady? "Knowing her a little, it did not surprise me at all."

"What is she like?" Madeline asked.

As Eleanor told them about her ladyship, it occurred to her that for the first time in her life, they were not doing everything together. Usually that only happened when they were physically in different places for one reason or another. "I am going to make sure at least one of the Danes is with us at tea."

Alice smiled for the first time that morning. "What a good idea."

Madeline nodded. "If he likes them, that will be two more qualities he meets."

"If he listens to my recommendations, it will be three." Eleanor was growing more excited about the possibility that Montagu was the gentleman for her. "I also invited him to join us at the opera next week."

Her sisters' eyes widened.

"Is he coming with us?" Alice's astonishment was clear by her tone.

"He is." Eleanor could feel the smug smile on her face. "He seems quite interested in learning more about it."

"He is doing much better than any of the other peers we have met," Madeline said.

Eleanor was struck by the emphasis Madeline had put on peers thus not including Harry Stern in her assessment.

"Particularly St. Albans." Alice pulled a face.

Madeline gave a huff. "Why do you not simply tell him to go away?"

"I am not going to let him defeat me." Alice rode off, leaving them behind.

Madeline stared after their sister. "What on earth did she mean by that?"

"I have no idea at all." St. Albans and her sister seemed to have a very strange association. "I suppose we will just have to see how their . . . whatever it is, proceeds."

"I suppose you are right. Let us catch up to her."

Eleanor and Madeline cantered after Alice and caught up to her halfway to the gate. Eleanor was glad they had three grooms with them. Although one hardly knew they were there. She had never seen her twin act this way before.

She flanked her twin on one side while Madeline flanked Alice on the other. "You should have said you were ready to leave."

"I do not wish to remain long enough for anyone else to arrive."

In other words, St. Albans. Unfortunately, that meant

Eleanor would not see Montagu. There was always this afternoon. Perhaps they would go for a carriage ride after tea. "I must make a list of our dependents who might be willing to resettle to Lord Montagu's estate and town."

Alice leaned forward to look around Madeline. "How many people and what skills does he need?"

"I am not yet certain. From what he has said, a great many of his people died last winter." Thank God her family and their town had escaped the worst of the influenza. "I decided to first write down who we have and match them up with his needs."

They reached Worthington House and dismounted.

"You might also ask Charlie," Madeline ventured. "When I went to Stanwood with Grace in March, more than one mother was concerned about her older children."

"That is an excellent idea." Eleanor would send a note around this morning if he did not join them for breakfast.

"Would you like our help with the list?" Alice asked.

Eleanor smiled at her twin. "I would love your help, and Madeline's."

"Good." Alice nodded sharply. "We shall meet after breakfast."

"Do not forget we have fittings for our ball gowns," Madeline said. "Our come out ball is next week."

"It is." Eleanor had not forgotten about the ball, but it had not been foremost in her mind. "It should not take that long to decide who to suggest."

They strode into the house and up the main staircase to their chambers. She was looking forward to helping Montagu. It would give her an even better chance to see how he listened to her and took her suggestions. Oh, and she could not forget about the dogs. That would be two more things she would know by the end of the day.

* * *

John had seen Eleanor and her sisters riding away from the Park. He'd known he would be too late. Yet it hadn't been until he was dressed that he remembered she'd told him they went as soon as it was light enough to see. St. Albans hadn't shown up at all. John shouldn't be surprised. The man had probably gone back to his old habits. Fortunately, he had none to break. At least not in that respect.

He exercised Aramus and returned to the house. After he broke his fast, he went into his study. Eleanor wanted a list of his needs and he must have it completed by the time he joined her for tea. Looking at the letters on his desk, he really wished he'd hired a secretary. A younger man who had some experience would suit. Perhaps one of Eleanor's brothers knew someone.

The top letter on the stack was from his steward.

My lord,

As you might have supposed, planting has been proceeding more slowly than usual. Although I am happy to report that some of the farmers in the area have offered to assist us. Anything you can do to bring in new tenants would be greatly appreciated.
We have also had a bit of a problem with strangers—men—coming into the market town.
One of our new arrivals saw them and warned the others to remain out of their sight. Our old dependents gave the men a cold welcome and they soon left.

> *Yr. Servant,*
> *Pearsall*

Damn. Strangers looking to cause problems was a difficulty John did not need when he was stuck in Town. He hoped he wouldn't have to go home and then return. He raked his fingers through his hair.

The list.

He took out a cut sheet of foolscap, dipped his pen into the inkpot, and wrote the first position he had open.

Farmers

Other needs quickly followed.

Blacksmith

Tailor

He wondered how the woman who had experience in baking was coming along. Perhaps she needed help.

Baker

A childhood rhyme floated around in his head.

The butcher, the baker, and the candlestick maker.

He didn't need a butcher or a candlestick maker, but the butcher could use a wife. His had died.

Shopkeepers

At present, the whole area was reliant on traveling merchants. That reminded him of another position.

Innkeeper

How Eleanor could possibly have enough people available and willing to fill all those positions he had no idea. Setting the list aside, he started going through his other correspondence. He picked up one card. Eleanor's come out ball was next week. She hadn't even mentioned it. Then again, they had been talking about other things. While he was at her house today, he would ask for the opening set and a waltz. If she accepted two dances, he'd know a little more where he stood with her. John thought they were moving—

albeit slowly—on the same track, but it would be nice to be certain.

Several hours later, John arrived at Worthington House and was ushered into a bright, sunny room in the back of the house. Long windows covered two sides of the room, along with a pair of French windows leading out to the garden. The parlor was decorated more for comfort than fashion. Eleanor and Lady Worthington sat on one of the two large sofas standing opposite each other. Her sisters were seated on the other. A large, low, rectangular, solid oak table stood between them. Smaller tables of various sizes and woods were at the ends of the sofas and next to well-upholstered chairs. A small sofa stood before the fireplace. Colorful rugs covered the floor and lace curtains fluttered in the windows.

"The Marquis of Montagu," the butler intoned.

Eleanor glanced up and smiled, and two Great Danes lifted their heads. Their tails thumped on the floor before they rose. John had never seen dogs in the house before. Naturally he had heard of dogs like pugs allowed in the house, but not ones almost as large as a pony.

She came to him. "Good afternoon, my lord."

The dogs went to her, leaned forward, and started to sniff him. "Good afternoon, Lady Eleanor." He motioned to the dogs. "Will you introduce me?"

A mischievous sparkle was in her sky-blue eyes. "Posy, Zeus"—the dogs looked at her—"This is Lord Montagu. My lord, Posy and Zeus. They would like to be stroked."

This was obviously true, as Posy leaned up against John and stared at him longingly. He obliged, and soon he was also stroking Zeus. "Do they live in the house?"

Eleanor seemed a bit taken aback. "Of course; where else would they live?"

This seemed almost like a test. "You have a point."

She took his arm and led him to the sofa upon which she had been sitting. "Once Posy has puppies, I shall have a Great Dane of my own."

Ah, it *was* a test. If having her meant having a large dog in the house as well, that was an easy decision. "I've always admired Great Danes. Perhaps I can have one as well."

"I am sure we can accommodate you, my lord," Lady Worthington said, rising from the sofa. "Welcome. I understand you and Eleanor have some business to conduct after we have tea."

"We do. She is assisting me with an estate problem I am having." Lady Worthington probably knew all about it.

As if the butler and footmen had been waiting for a signal, the servants carried in three good-sized trays filled with teapots, small sandwiches, and sweets. They were followed by Lord Worthington, holding his son's and daughter's hands, Lord and Lady Phinn, and Lord Stanwood. John wondered if any of the other family members would join them as well.

They greeted one another and Ladies Alice and Madeline before finding places to sit.

"I live across the square," Stanwood said. "My sister and brother by marriage are staying with me for a while."

Eleanor settled back on the sofa and began to pour from a large teapot and, to John's amusement, little Elizabeth poured from a small pot. The tea she poured had already been fixed with lot of milk and, he supposed, some sugar.

Stanwood had taken a drink and put his cup down on a side table. "I understand you have need of people."

"I do. Ele—Lady Eleanor has offered to help me."

Stanwood leaned over and selected a jam tart from the tray nearest to him. "Yes. She has asked me if I have anyone available as well. I gave her a list of possibilities."

John glanced at Worthington, but he was in conversation with his son. John was struck by the confidence her family had in Eleanor to negotiate something this important.

Eleanor glanced at him. "Would you like me to make you a plate, or will you help yourself? As you see, we are informal at family teas."

He didn't know if this was yet another test or not. In for a penny, in for a pound. He reached out and took a biscuit. "I will help myself."

From the corner of his eye, he saw Lady Alice's look of approval. What else was going to happen today? Posy was suddenly next to him, and he assumed she wanted a biscuit. Instead, she inched forward, stretching her neck until she was just inches from his face, licked him lightly on his cheek, and stepped back.

John reached out and stroked her head. He really had not thought such a large dog could be so gentle. "Good girl."

"She likes you," Elizabeth explained.

Interestingly enough, no one else commented on the lick.

Lady Madeline, who had been quietly drinking her tea and eating a lemon tart, said, "Charlie, we will expect you at Worthington Place in July."

Her brother swallowed a biscuit he'd popped into his mouth. "I wouldn't miss it."

What was that about? The question must have been on his face, for Eleanor said, "We all get together every other summer at either Worthington Place or Stanwood Place. On the off years, the families gather at Christmas."

"That way"—Alice waved a biscuit around, reminding

him of her nephew Hugh—"we can all see one another and our brothers-in-law still have time with their families."

"I see." John had been right when he'd decided they were a close family.

"It is required," Elizabeth added.

"Elizabeth!" Eleanor's sharp tone brought a frown to the little girl's face.

"But it is," the child insisted. "That is what Rothwell told his mama."

Gideon nodded. "Dom said the same thing to his mama."

Eleanor turned to him. "And how do you know that?"

"They were talking about it." The lad shoved a whole biscuit into his mouth, ending the questioning.

John forced down the laughter rising in him. He'd never thought he wanted a large family, but to have been raised in this one must have been enjoyable. Then he remembered that the Carpenter members had lost their parents and Lady Worthington had fought to keep them together. And Worthington's father had died leaving him the guardianship of his sisters. No wonder they wanted to remain close. "Mandatory family gatherings sound like a great deal of fun."

"They are." Eleanor's eyes appeared misty; then she blinked and the look was gone. "Are you ready to review our respective lists?"

"Yes." He put down his cup. "Lead the way."

He had never expected tea to be yet another revelation about her, but it had been. Eleanor and her family were part of a set. Marry one, marry the rest of them. Even if he wanted to, which he did not, there would be no keeping her from them. He had an image of Worthington, Rothwell, Kenilworth, and Merton riding up to his house in armor, swords drawn, with their ladies demanding to see Eleanor. John wasn't sure which would scare him more, the ladies or the gentlemen. Or Eleanor. She would have to be kept under lock and key in a tower. Pity the idiot who tried to do such a thing.

She placed her fingers on his arm. "Are you well?"

"Perfectly. I merely had a flight of fancy. As if I'd been reading a medieval novel." Someday he'd tell her. After they wed.

CHAPTER TWENTY-FIVE

Eleanor could not believe how comfortable Montagu seemed to be even with the dogs, albeit she was pleased he was. She was glad Posy had licked him. It gave them all an opportunity to truly see how he was about the Danes. After she had realized just how important her family, including the dogs, was to her, she was more determined than ever to ensure any husband would fit in and want to be with her family too.

"If you will get another chair, I shall move this one over." The table had been made to seat several family members at one time and was more than large enough for two people to spread out papers as they worked. After the chairs had been moved, she took her list from her reticule and placed it on the desk. "Here are the names of people who might like to move to your town and estate. Once we have settled on what you require, I will have to ascertain that they are willing."

"Of course." He took his paper out of a pocket. "There is no point in raising expectations until we have made the decisions."

She spread out the foolscap next to his. "I think the easiest way to proceed is to go down your list of needs and match them with my list of people who might be interested." He nodded. "Well, then, let us start at the top. I assume by farmers you mean tenant farmers."

"Yes. The winter was particularly hard on them." He had a grim look on his face, as if he was again experiencing the deaths.

Eleanor wanted to cover his hand lying on the table with hers. "How many do you require?"

"Seven. Seven families died." Montagu's voice was choked with grief.

"I cannot bring them back." Eleanor softened her voice. "But I am able to give new life to those farms. I have at least that many young families and young men looking for their own places." That was especially true at Stanwood, where many of the families were large. "I will have to tell them exactly where they will be living and the state of the houses and land."

He cleared his throat. "The land is good, and it's been planted."

That was a relief. "The houses?"

"All in good repair." The corners of his lips rose slightly. "We had even added rooms to a few cottages. I can't remember if I told you, but I have taken in several widows with children. It would be helpful to have some single men who wish to wed."

"I believe that can be arranged. I took in a widow with young children, and she was married within two months." Eleanor made a point of sounding cheerful.

"A widow whose husband had been killed at Cinderloo?"

"Yes. I was visiting my sister Charlotte, and the children were huddled beside the road." She told him the rest of the story. "It has turned out well for all of them." Eleanor glanced at his list. "A blacksmith is next. I do have a well-qualified candidate for you. Interestingly enough, our blacksmith's elder son and his father are always at odds. The son has been on the verge of leaving several times already. I am certain he will be interested in taking over the smithy."

Montagu's brow furrowed. "What is the reason they do not get on?"

"From what I have seen, it is caused by the sameness in their personalities. They are both very nice and well-liked in the town. Let me ask Grace if she knows something to which I am not privy." Eleanor leaned back in her chair. "Grace, other than their personalities, is there any other reason Mr. Jones and his eldest son do not get along?"

"Yes. The son wants to marry one young woman and his father has selected another one for him."

No wonder Eleanor did not know about the problem. It was the type of thing kept from unmarried ladies. "Is there anything unsuitable about the woman the son wants to wed?"

"Nothing at all. Mr. Jones has been close friends with the father of the other girl since their childhood. Mrs. Jones believes the young woman her son wishes to marry is a better choice for him."

Montagu's brow cleared. "It seems I have found a new blacksmith." He smiled at Eleanor. "Please, carry on."

They quickly filled the remaining jobs. The innkeeper had a younger son in his late twenties who had been looking for an inn to purchase. He was still single. Eleanor tapped her pencil on the desk. "We cannot arrange a marriage, but we can see if one of your refugees would suit. Would you give his future wife a dowry?"

He gave her a curious look. "I can do. In fact, I should provide dowries for all the women."

"Excellent." Some ladies might find this boring, but she appeared to be having a good time. "Having a dowry will make marrying easier."

"I never would have thought of it." When he looked away

from the list and at her, she knew he was seeing her, all of her. "We've finished for the moment. I shall write to my brother-in-law's steward and ask him to approach the people we have chosen. I should probably write a short note to each of them as well."

"If you agree, I can add a message too."

"Yes, that will give the offer a finality I cannot provide. Perhaps you should write it at the end of each of my missives."

The clock struck the hour and he looked up. "Would you like to go for a carriage ride? We can write the letters when we return or tomorrow, if you have the time."

"I could use a bit of a break. We can continue after our ride." Montagu rose and held out his hand. Eleanor could imagine them working together like this, and afterward him kissing her, and telling her what a good match they were. She had seen Matt and Grace do that. Eleanor took Montagu's hand. "I must change my shoes and get my bonnet."

When he gazed down at her warmth lurked in his turquoise eyes. "There is no rush. I need to call around for my carriage. I walked here."

They were standing so close together. If her family had not been present, would he kiss her? Posy poked her head between them, and Montagu immediately stroked the Dane.

Eleanor grinned. He was fitting in very well. "I'll be back soon."

She reached her bedchamber, changed shoes, donned a spencer, then grabbed her gloves and bonnet. When she walked into the corridor, Alice and Madeline were there. Alice held their list of requirements. "I think he has met all the qualifications."

"All except one." He had not told Eleanor he loved her. Madeline nodded slowly. "Love."

"Yes. Although, I am hopeful that will come." At least Eleanor thought it would. That was how things were supposed to work. "I am going back down to the morning room. Are you coming?"

"I have a book I want to finish," Alice said.

"Harry is picking me up for a carriage ride," Madeline said. "I shall be down soon."

Montagu did tell Eleanor not to hurry. "I will wait for you."

"Very well." Madeline flashed a smile. "Give me a moment."

Alice stalked back to her room, and Eleanor wondered if her twin was upset because she and Madeline had been invited for rides and she had not. Madeline joined Eleanor in the corridor. "Do you think Alice is upset with us?"

"No. She refused St. Albans's offer of a carriage ride."

Alice was Eleanor's twin. How did she not know what was going on with her? "When did that happen?"

"When you were with Lord Montagu."

"Today?" It would have been rather insulting for him to have waited until the last minute.

"No, yesterday." They had reached the bottom of the stairs, and Madeline linked her arm with Eleanor's. "She will be fine."

"I suppose so." Her twin needed to find someone to love as well.

Love? Do I love Montagu?

Yet even if she did, that was only half of the equation. He had to love her too. And he had to say the words.

John was still petting Posy after Eleanor and her sisters had left the morning room. He'd been surprised when Posy licked his face. That hadn't happened since he was a child.

He remembered Eleanor saying she wanted one of the Dane's puppies. He glanced at Worthington and realized he was the only one left in the room with John. "Lady Eleanor said something about puppies."

"We plan to breed her during her next heat. That will be toward the end of June." The man's lips twitched. "Daisy, our last Dane, kept threatening to have the puppies during the latter part of the Season. A time or two it was a close call."

"Lady Eleanor was raised with large dogs in the house?" If that was the case, she would insist on having at least one.

"Yes. Her father was fond of them." Worthington glided his hand over Zeus's head. "They very much want to be around the family. I had them growing up as well."

Posy leaned against John, obviously settling in. His mother would probably throw a fit, but she would no longer be the mistress. "I would like to have a puppy, if they are not all spoken for."

Worthington eyed John with a steady gaze. "I think that can be arranged."

"Thorton just told me your curricle is here." Eleanor sailed into the room. "Shall we go?"

"Yes." John stepped around the dog and looked down at his trousers and attempted to brush them off.

"It was bound to happen. But there is no need to worry. We have a brush in the hall."

When he glanced at her again she was smiling. "I suppose it is all part of living with animals."

"It is." She took his arm and led him into the hall, where a footman was ready with a brush.

A few seconds later they were strolling to the carriage. "I asked Worthington if I could have a puppy."

"Did you?" The smile she gave him was so blinding, he had to blink.

John waved the footman off, placed his hands on her

waist and lifted her into the curricle. Eleanor sucked in a breath, and he had to fight off the urge to slide his thumbs over the undersides of her breasts. Ever since he'd first touched her, he'd wanted her. Eleanor was nothing like what he had thought he wanted in a wife, but he'd been wrong. The more he was with her, the more he knew he needed her in his life. The only thing he didn't know was if he was falling in love with her. Obviously, he had loved people and animals. He loved his sister even when she drove him mad. He loved his mother, but at more of a distance. He'd really loved his first pony. But he'd never been in love with a woman. How would he know?

While Eleanor settled her skirts, he climbed into the other side of the carriage. "Let them go." The groom stood aside, and John started the horses. "Thank you for assisting me. It would have taken so much longer to settle the problem without you."

"I enjoy helping others. Fortunately, Matt and Grace encouraged me." She glanced at him from beneath her golden-brown lashes. "I liked helping you."

It might have been John's imagination, but he could have sworn she had put an emphasis on "you." On its own, his chest puffed out. It was time to start claiming her. "Will you dance the opening dance of your come out ball with me, and the supper dance as well?"

She tilted her head as she gazed at him. After a long moment she nodded. "I will."

He let out the breath he'd been holding. "Thank you."

Her lips rose into a smile. "It was my pleasure. I enjoy dancing with you. However, I must warn you. The opening set is unlikely to be a waltz."

Why would she say—of course they had only danced the waltz together. He hadn't even thought of that. "It doesn't matter. I assume the supper set will be a waltz."

"Yes." Her eyes sparkled. "I am certain it is."

"Will you and your sisters be like Cinderella and disappear after supper, or will you remain until the ball ends?"

"Hmm. That is a good question. None of us have thought about when we will retire." Her lips pursed as she considered his question, but all he could think about was kissing her. "I suppose we will remain until it is over, or until we're too tired to stay."

"You and your family don't keep late hours. I can see Worthington running everyone off while other balls continue until the wee hours of the morning."

Eleanor let out a tinkling of laughter. "I can as well. The children will be able to remain up longer. There is a place to watch the dancing and see all the ladies in their gowns." She had a misty look, as if she was remembering it. "They will also be allowed to sample what will be served at supper."

John and his sister would never have been allowed such a treat. Aurelia would have loved it. "Will your brother be as interested?"

"I do not know." Eleanor had a thoughtful expression on her face. "I do remember Walter and Phillip liking the food. But Gideon and Elizabeth will not be alone. All the cousins will be there as well."

Of course they would. This was the only come out ball in the family. He suddenly had a vision of his and Eleanor's children watching with their cousins in the same circumstance. "It sounds like a great deal of fun."

"It was." She gave herself an almost imperceptible shake. "But this will be even more enjoyable."

They'd driven through the gate and were immediately accosted. "Lady Eleanor." Young Lord Brinkley smiled too widely at her. "Would you do me the honor of a set at Lady Fotherby's ball?"

Lady Fotherby's ball? When was that?

"Yes." She gave the puppy a polite smile. "The first country dance."

Before John could open his mouth to ask her for the supper set, Lord Holliwell was next to the carriage. "I say, Lady Eleanor, might you have a dance left for Lady Fotherby's ball?"

"You may have the second country dance."

"Jolly good, my lady." He tipped his hat before riding off.

"Supper dance?" John barely got the words out before Lord Athersuch was upon them.

"Lady Eleanor." He executed a credible bow from his gray gelding. "Are you free for the supper dance at Lady Fotherby's ball?"

Eleanor gave him a sympathetic look. "That set is taken. The only dance free is the opening set."

For the first time the man seemed to notice John. "Good day, my lord." Athersuch turned his attention back to her. "I would be honored to lead you out for the first set."

John would be honored to plant the bounder a facer. He had not liked seeing her stand up with other men, but it was now becoming intolerable. "Why has no one asked you to dance at your come out ball?"

"I have no sets left." She briefly placed her hand on his. "You always ask for the supper dance. Normally, I would be led out in the opening dance by one of my family, but no decisions had been made. Therefore, I gave it to you."

A great welling of an emotion he couldn't describe and had never felt before grew inside him. He'd had to stop the carriage because of traffic and took the opportunity to gaze into her magnificent blue eyes. He wanted to say something profound yet couldn't think of a thing. "Thank you for saving the supper set for me, and your opening dance."

"You are welcome." Her chin came up, pointed to the side. "We have more company."

John wanted to groan. Instead, he took out his quizzer and fixed it on Lord Folliot. The man almost turned away. Then he straightened his shoulders and approached. "My lord, my lady, good afternoon."

John was on the verge of telling Folliot she had no sets left when Eleanor put her hand on John's arm, staying him. "Good afternoon, my lord."

Folliot cleared his throat. "My lady, do you have any sets left for Lady Fotherby's ball?"

"I do not. Thank you for asking."

"I shall be earlier next time." He listed to the side as he bowed, and John tried to remember how old he was. Not past twenty. "Adieu."

Eleanor gave John a look and covered her lips with her hand. "Oh dear. My brother was right. He really should have been sent to school."

He was almost sorry he'd leveled his quizzing glass at Folliot. Almost. Right now, John had to work out how to go forward with Eleanor, and he needed advice, but who to ask? Yet this might be something he could do by himself. He just needed time to think. The problem was when he thought of her, she was almost always naked. Perhaps he should make a list.

CHAPTER TWENTY-SIX

Eleanor glanced at Montagu's lean, aristocratic profile. He seemed to be thinking about something. He had scowled at all the younger gentlemen who had approached them to ask her for a set. Did he even know what he was doing? She had surprised herself when she had touched him. Yet it felt right, like the natural thing to do. The feelings she experienced when he touched her were becoming deeper. It was still a jolt when he'd put his hands on her waist and lifted her. Would she ever stop feeling that way?

"Are you ready to leave or do you want to make another circuit?"

Eleanor looked around. The Park was packed. The only people who could move around at all were on horseback. "It is so busy here, I will miss dinner if we remain, and I still have letters to write."

He glanced at her, startled. "I do as well. How could I have forgotten so soon?"

Eleanor kept a straight face. Had the gentlemen bothered him even more than she had originally thought? "You probably were not thinking of it. You would have remembered." But she was correct. She would be rushed to make dinner on time. Madeline was out here in the mess as well. Eleanor looked around. She couldn't even see her sister. There certainly would not be time to write letters. "Would you like to join us for dinner? Grace always says it is easy to add another place setting."

"I would." A smile slowly grew on Montagu's lips, and she was fixated by them. Once again, she wanted to find out what it would feel like if he kissed her. "We could write the missives after dinner."

"Yes indeed. It would be the perfect time." He looked down at himself. "I will not be able to change."

"We do not dress in full evening gowns. I'm sure a footman can be sent to your house for your clothing. Remember, the children will be there." Sometimes Eleanor wished they would wear evening dress at dinner. On the other hand, when they were invited to someone's house she decided dressing in silk and jewels every evening would be tedious. If they dined later, it might be different.

"If you are sure?" Montagu still appeared concerned.

"I am. You will see."

They finally made it to the gate and drove back to Worthington House. He brought the carriage to a halt, jumped down, and before a footman could reach them, his hands were burning through her carriage gown. His hands slid a little higher as he lifted her to the ground, sending frissons coursing through her breasts. Did he know what an effect he had on her? She had been trying so hard to hide her reactions to him.

His hands left her body and there was a sudden chill. Eleanor drew an even breath and took his arm. He glanced at her, his hooded eyes capturing her gaze. "Are you all right?"

"Yes, of course." They strolled through the door. "Thorton, Lord Montagu will stay for dinner and will require a change of clothing."

"My lady, his lordship is not dressing for dinner."

Eleanor remembered Matt was wearing trousers at tea. They were gradually becoming acceptable dinner wear. Montagu was also wearing trousers and shoes. "You need not change."

"Very well. If you think what I am wearing is acceptable." She made a point of perusing his clothing. "I believe my brother will be wearing the same type of garments."

"My lord." Thorton motioned to the footman. "If you will follow George, he'll take you to a room where you can ready yourself."

Montagu inclined his head. "My thanks, Thorton."

Madeline entered as Montagu followed the footman up the stairs. "I have never seen the Park so busy."

"Neither have I. The Season is really underway now." She gave Eleanor a look. "I take it Montagu is staying for dinner?"

"Yes." Eleanor could not have stopped her broad smile if she tried. "I'll tell you the rest after we have changed."

She donned a muslin gown and joined her sisters in their parlor. The excitement she had been suppressing was bursting out. "We do not have much time, but I wanted to tell you, Montagu has asked for my opening set at our come out ball *and* the supper dance."

"Oh my!" Alice's eyes were as wide as saucers. "Eleanor, he must be getting ready to ask for your hand."

"I am so happy for you." Madeline hugged Eleanor. "After this afternoon, I was more certain than ever he was the right gentleman for you."

"Let us not get ahead of ourselves. He must still tell me he loves me." That was the most concerning part. Did he love her?

"It will happen," Alice said in a rallying tone.

Madeline clasped her hands together. "Would it not be wonderful if he proposed at our ball?"

"I do not want to even think about that." If only he *would* ask for her hand during their ball. Then again, it would take away from her sisters. She wanted to ask Madeline about her ride with Harry, but Alice did not seem to have any gentleman. "We must go to the drawing room."

When they entered Montagu was already there with Matt, Grace, Gideon, and Elizabeth. Matt immediately rose. "There you are. Your sister set dinner back a bit."

She was not surprised. Jacques used to complain, but he was used to it by now. "Do you want a glass of wine or sherry?"

"Yes, sherry please." Montagu tucked her hand in the crook of his arm, keeping his eyes on her as they ambled to the sideboard. "Montagu, would you like a glass of sherry?"

"I would."

Matt handed her a glass.

"Montagu"—Matt's tone was a mix of dryness and amusement—"if you do not watch where you are going in this house, you will eventually trip over a Great Dane."

Montagu shook his head and looked around. "They are not here."

"Not this time."

Eleanor glared at her brother-in-law. "They are never allowed in the dining room during dinner."

Matt shrugged. "It's always better to watch where one is walking. I have almost tripped over them before."

Eleanor could not argue with that. "With large dogs, it is amazingly easy to do."

"That is very true," Grace said with a cringe, and Eleanor knew her sister was remembering when she had been trying to hide from Matt and tripped over Duke's paws.

Poor Montagu appeared lost. "It is part of their courtship story," Eleanor explained. "I will tell you it later."

Thorton entered the drawing room and announced

dinner. Immediately someone plied the door knocker. "Who could that be?"

"Harry and Vivienne," Madeline said. "They are joining us for dinner." She told them about the twins being fussy.

After they dined, Eleanor and Montagu returned to the drawing room, and she went to a small desk in the corner of the room and took out a piece of foolscap large enough to enclose the other letters. Montagu followed her. First, she wrote to Matt's steward, then to Charlie's steward. After that, they began writing to the tenants and other people they had decided to approach with job proposals. She wrote the first part and Montagu added his firm offer at the end of each missive.

"Finished." She leaned back in her chair.

"I hope this bears the fruit we wish it to." He looked a bit worried, and once again she wanted to touch his hand.

"You must have faith in me."

Montagu searched her eyes. His own reflected his worry. "You're right. Everything will work out the way we planned."

This was exactly the partnership she wanted with a husband. "It will."

Eleanor was right. It would go the way they wanted it to because they had done it together. John had never believed a lady like this existed, or that he would find her. He'd heard other men—her brothers by marriage and their friends—comment that ladies ought to have more say in government, but he'd not taken them seriously. But Eleanor and ladies like her would be an asset to any political discussion or decision. "I wonder how long it will be before we hear from them."

"It should not be long. I'll have the packets sent by messenger."

Of course she would. For a few seconds, all he could do

was drink her in as they gazed at each other. "Yes, that would be best."

"Eleanor and Lord Montagu, come have some tea," Lady Worthington said.

Eleanor glanced up quickly, as if her sister's voice had startled her. She must have been as enthralled as he was. Or he hoped she was. "We are coming." She rose and he followed. "Matt, I need to have the packets sent by messenger."

"I'll include them with my estate business," Worthington said. "He can stop at Stanwood on the way."

John had never thought to ask or look up where the estates were. "Are they far from each other?"

"Not at all." Eleanor handed him a cup of tea. "Only a few hours." She took her own cup and sipped. "Thus far, we have been fortunate that everyone lives within a day's drive from either Worthington Place or Stanwood Place."

She had said she was traveling from Kenilworth's main estate when she came across the family she took in. That must mean that John's estate was also within a day's drive. At least now he knew she was far enough away from Birmingham not to be bothered by anyone running the mines. As his town and estate had been. A load of stone seemed to lift from his shoulders. Strange. He hadn't even realized it had been bothering him. "Where are the dogs?"

"With the children." Her eyes lit up from behind the teacup. "They have appointed themselves their guardians. You haven't met the twins yet. They are just turned nineteen months old."

Not for the first time, he pictured Eleanor carrying his child. "I would like to meet them someday."

She smiled, and he wondered if she was thinking the same thing. "They are very busy."

"Sorry to run you off, Montagu," Worthington said. "Tomorrow is a busy day for me."

"I understand." She and John rose together. "Until tomorrow."

"Until then." Her musical voice was soft and warm, making him want to take her into his arms.

"I'll see you out," Worthington said.

John bowed to Lady Worthington. "Thank you for dinner, my lady."

"I am glad you could come." She glanced at her husband. "Come back when you have seen Lord Montagu off."

John reached the pavement and started walking home. He would ask Eleanor to marry him. But first, he must tell his mother and sister. They could not hear of a proposal third hand. Although he was a bit concerned how they would take it. His mother had been cool to the idea of Eleanor as his wife. Not that it mattered. She was who he wanted and needed. And his mother would be at the dower house. If she was at home, there was no time like the present.

He strode through the door his butler opened. "Is her ladyship here?"

"In the drawing room, my lord. As are Lord and Lady Lytton."

"Very good." John could get this over with all at once.

They were probably getting ready to dine. He entered the family drawing room. His mother and sister were gowned in silk and wore the appropriate jewels. His brother-in-law was in knee breeches. He had enjoyed the informality of Worthington House much more. The children's chatter had been engaging, and everyone spoke with them as if they were as intelligent as the older members of the family. As they were. He had no doubt at all that Ladies Theo and Mary would set the *ton* on their collective on fire when it was their time to come out.

He cleared his throat to get his family's attention. "I am glad to find you all together." John went to the sideboard and poured a glass of wine.

His mother took in his attire and frowned slightly. "You are not dressed for dinner."

"I have already dined. I did send a message over."

"Dressed like that?" she replied in a shocked tone.

"Yes. Dressed like this." She opened her mouth again, and he held up a hand. "I do not want you to discuss what I am about to tell you until I have spoken with Lord Worthington." Aurelia's lips started to twitch, and she pressed them tightly together. She knew what he was going to say. He felt the connection he'd been afraid was lost. Lytton found something interesting to look at on the fireplace. "I am going to offer for Lady Eleanor."

"Are you certain she is the right lady for you?" Mama asked. "After all, you began the Season wanting someone entirely different."

"I am well aware I did. I was incorrect. She is exactly what I wish for in a wife." His sister and mother donned exactly the same broad smiles. He narrowed his eyes. "I thought you didn't like her."

"Oh no, my dear," Mama said. "From the first time we met her we thought she would be perfect for you."

He lowered himself onto his usual chair. "I don't understand."

"John," his sister said. "You have been so contrary over the past three years or more that we thought if we took a stand against her, you would look at her more closely and realize what you really wanted."

He speared his brother-in-law with a glare. "Were you in on this deception?"

"Not I." Lytton took a drink of wine. "I was merely an innocent bystander. It was not as if they were laying traps for the two of you."

"He is correct," Mama added. "You merely needed a little nudge."

"I was concerned you might lose her," Aurelia commented.

John couldn't believe this. Lytton was right; they did not do much, but it had clearly been enough. "Why?"

"Because you were acting as if you didn't have two intelligent thoughts to rub together."

She did have a point. What would have happened if Eleanor hadn't taken matters into her own capable hands? Was that the reason she mentioned the mines in the first place? "Yes, well, that has all been worked out."

His mother's face was still alight. "Have you told her you love her yet?"

"Er. Not yet."

"Why are you waiting?" Aurelia demanded.

Lytton took her free hand. "It might be that Montagu does not know he is in love. Remember, that was never a requirement for either of you."

Aurelia frowned. "Yes, yes, but you and I fell in love, and you told me."

"It took me a deuced long time to get up the courage, my love. I was afraid you did not love me in return."

This conversation was becoming very interesting. John wanted to know more. "How did you realize you were in love?"

His sister took a sip of wine, then frowned. "I do not know. Suddenly, it occurred to me that if anything was to happen to Marc, or if he were to find another woman, I would do everything I could to get him back."

Lytton raised her hand to his lips. "It struck me one day

that I did not want to live without Aurelia. That I would do whatever I could to make her happy."

John did not believe one person could be responsible for another person's happiness, but he did believe one could be responsible for great unhappiness. He would be very unhappy if Eleanor didn't care for him as he did for her. No, it was much more than that.

As if sensing what he was thinking, his twin said, "John, being in love doesn't always mean being silly about another. I would attribute that to puppy love. An immaturity that will not hold a marriage together. A gentleman must be attracted to a lady's mind as well as her body."

What Aurelia said made a great deal of sense. He was both fascinated by Eleanor's intellect and captivated by her body. "You have given me something about which to ponder."

"Where did you dine?" his mother asked again.

Mama was going to be shocked, and he felt a broad smile forming. "At Worthington House. They dine at six o'clock and do not dress. Lord and Lady Worthington's five-year-old son and four-year-old daughter, as well as their much younger sisters and brother join them." His mother's jaw had dropped, and he continued. "When I broke my fast with them, the married sisters and their families were there as well. I believe the number of five-year-olds were four. But I could be missing one of them." He ran through the names. "Four five-year-olds and one four-year-old. Oh, and two Great Danes have the run of the house. I have already asked Worthington if I may have a puppy from the next litter."

Mama shut her mouth with a snap. "Is there anything else?"

Shocking her was not worthy of him, but he was having entirely too much fun. "I mustn't forget. There are mandatory family gatherings every other Christmas and summer."

His mother still looked to be in a state of shock. "Why would you be told that? You have not asked for her yet?"

"Four- and five-year-olds do not recognize that sort of nicety."

"You do not think that Lady Eleanor would like to be a bit more, more . . . normal?" his mother asked weakly.

"I think Eleanor will run her household as she sees fit, and whatever she does is fine with me." He drank some of his wine. "Are you all right?"

"Yes." Mama straightened her drooping shoulders. "I suppose there is no need to dine formally among family. It merely never occurred to me."

Aurelia glanced at Lytton. "Our baby is still too young, but you have given me an idea to consider."

Now that surprised John. He thought she was set in her ways. "I find them delightful company. You never know what they will say." He tossed off his wine. "If you will excuse me, I have a proposal to plan."

John made his way to his study. He had to make sure Eleanor said yes.

CHAPTER TWENTY-SEVEN

"Did you tell them?" Madeline asked.

The day of their come out ball had finally arrived. Dressed in their ball gowns, Eleanor and her sisters were being allowed one glass of champagne before they went downstairs to take their places in the receiving line. "Yes. Neither Matt nor Grace seemed surprised."

"After yesterday, no one would," Alice added. "I am happy for you."

Eleanor was certain her twin was glad for her, but Alice did not look pleased on her own account. "How can we help you?"

"Unless you can conjure up a gentleman I like, there is nothing you can do." She took Eleanor's hands. "I will be fine. I promise."

A light tap sounded on the door. Madeline answered, "Come."

Theo, Mary, Gideon, Elizabeth, Constance, Hugh, Vivienne, and Alexandria crowded into the room.

Elizabeth stared up at them with wide lapis eyes. "Mama said we can see you dressed for the ball."

The rest of the children nodded.

"You all look very pretty," Gideon said.

"Beau-t-i-ful," Hugh agreed. "You look like my mama when she is dressed to go out."

Eleanor and her sisters had all taken a great deal of care in selecting their gowns for this evening, and she was very happy with hers. She curtseyed to them. "Thank you, sirs."

"I am going to curtsey like that one day," Mary said.

Eleanor remembered thinking the same thing about Charlotte, Louisa, and Dotty. "It just takes time and practice."

Thorton opened the door and bowed. "My ladies, his lordship said it is time."

Eleanor strolled beside her twin. "Will he be here this evening?"

"No. I asked Grace not to invite him."

"I see." It was time to change the subject. "Who is leading you out for the first set?"

"Rothwell." Alice smiled and shook her head. "He insisted."

"Madeline?"

"Harry Stern asked me, and I accepted."

"At least someone else asked you," Alice said.

Madeline exchanged a glance with Eleanor, and she looked at her twin. "No one asked for your opening set, or no one you wanted to dance with asked for the set?"

Alice's chin rose. "It is one and the same."

It was not, but there was no time to discuss it. "We must hurry."

Over the years, Eleanor and her sisters had picked up bits and pieces of information regarding the Season in general and the come out ball more particularly. One of the best pieces of advice had come from Charlotte, who told them not to wear tight slippers to a ball if they did not want blisters the next day. Eleanor was never so glad of that advice as she was standing in the receiving line.

"I've never smiled so much in my life," Alice grutched. "My face is going to freeze in this position."

She certainly had not smiled that much recently. "It will be over soon."

"The Marquis of Montagu, the Marchioness of Montagu, and the Earl and Countess of Lytton," Thorton announced.

Lady Montagu greeted them and smiled but seemed a little off balance. Eleanor wondered if something had happened to concern her ladyship.

"Good evening, my lady." Montagu took Eleanor's hands and squeezed them. "You are the most beautiful lady I have ever seen."

Eleanor curtseyed as he bowed. "Thank you, sir." She slid a look at his mother, who had wandered off to the side. "Is your mother all right?"

His lips tipped in a crooked smile. "I told her about dinner and the Danes. She is still in shock."

Behind him, his sister's voice was full of laughter as she said, "Mama likes to think she is very modern, but she really is not. Still, given a bit of time, I have no doubt she will decide it is a wonderful idea."

"We must move along," he whispered. "I'll see you in the ballroom."

"The Duke and Duchess of Cleveland," Thorton intoned.

"*He* had better not be here." Eleanor had never known her twin to be so agitated.

"Good evening, your grace." Madeline curtseyed.

"How good of you to come." Eleanor curtseyed as well.

She expected to hear her twin repeat the greeting; instead, the duchess said, "My son is not with us. I, however, am pleased to see the lady who has him tied in knots." Eleanor could feel her sister trying to think of a polite response when the duchess said, "I have no doubt he has done something stupid."

The duke merely bowed to them and strolled off after his wife.

"Well." Alice's gaze followed the older couple. "What do you think of that?"

"I think she is having a grand time watching her son hang in the wind." Charlie grinned at them. "The three of you will have all the gentlemen tripping over themselves."

Kenilworth strolled up behind their brother. "One of these days, Charlie Stanwood, you are going to have to court a lady, and when you find you've made a muddle of it, I'm going to take a great deal of pleasure laughing at you."

"I see we're all here," Matt said. "Let's repair to the ball-room."

Eleanor, Madeline, and Alice had all had a hand in the ballroom decorations, but they had not seen it completed. They had decided on a garden theme, with flowers that were currently in bloom. Swags of yellow and green silk interspersed with netting dotted with purple spangles hung from the ceiling above the windows and doors. The chandeliers were decorated with flowers and ribbons in the same colors. Along the walls, vases had been set on pedestals, holding branches of forsythia and lilacs. It was exactly as she had hoped it would be. "I never imagined it would turn out so well."

"I knew it would." Alice smiled. "We planned it."

Madeline grinned and pointed to one of the windows. "The birds and squirrels turned out well."

Placed on a few of the swags where they would catch an observant guest's eye, were papier-mâché birds and animals. Finches perched on some of the curtain rods, and squirrels peeped from behind a few of the vases.

Eleanor felt the now familiar warmth of Montagu's gaze on her neck. The next thing she knew, he was next to her, and her sisters had stepped away to speak with other guests.

He took her hand and placed it on his arm. It was a gesture she had seen her brothers-in-law do with her sisters.

Montagu waved his other arm to indicate the room. "I must say, this is the most interesting ballroom theme I have ever seen. It is fanciful and elegant at the same time."

A blush rose in her cheeks. "I am glad you like it. My sisters and I designed all of it."

His gaze captured hers, and it was as if they were the only two people in the room. "I am not surprised to hear it. You have excellent taste."

Before she could respond, Lady Lytton joined them. "Everyone is exclaiming over how cleverly the room is decorated. I have quite fallen in love with the squirrel next to the one vase of lilacs."

The strains of violins announcing the first set floated through the air. A smile hovered on Montagu's lips as he looked at her. "A waltz?"

"Yes." It had not taken much to convince Grace to have more waltzes after Matt threw his support behind the idea. "My sisters and I agreed that we should have the dances we wanted at our ball."

"I wholeheartedly support that idea." Montagu's smile grew wider. "Shall we?"

Eleanor had never enjoyed a waltz more. She was completely comfortable in Montagu's arms. It was like coming home. What would it be like to be able to dance with him for the rest of her life? Thinking about her life, where would it be lived? "Tell me about your home."

A sudden light appeared in his eyes. "My main estate, Montagu Hall, is an hour or so south of Birmingham. Legend has it the house was built on the ruins of an old Viking hall. My family has been there for several hundred years. Well before the marquisate was granted to my ancestor. The country is fairly hilly, with streams and a few small lakes."

The area sounded like a nice place to live. "Is the house very old?"

"No. My great-great-grandfather tore down the original house and built a more modern one. Unfortunately, no one bothered to do much to keep it up-to-date between then and now. Since I took the title, I have been renovating it a little at a time."

That sounded a bit like Stanwood House. Her father had only gone to Town when he absolutely had to. He much preferred to remain in the country. Mama remained home with the children. "Grace renovated Stanwood House before we came to Town for Charlotte's come out to make it more comfortable for all of us and fit our needs. After they married, Matt renovated Worthington House in much the same fashion. I found the process extremely interesting."

"Did you?" Montagu appeared surprised. "My mother detests the bother."

"I saw nothing to dislike about it. Of course one must relocate sleeping quarters for some changes. But in the end it is worth the trouble." Eleanor was excited about the possibility she might be able to renovate a whole house. It would be a dream come true. "My sister and I were allowed to choose the colors and furniture for our bedchamber when we were on the nursery floor in both Stanwood House and Worthington House, and then again when we moved to our own bedrooms on the main family floor." She smiled, thinking of drawings she, Alice, and Madeline painted on the walls of their first bedchamber so that she would feel included in the decoration. "Naturally, our tastes have matured since then."

"And that doesn't bother you?" She shook her head, and he grinned at her. "I suppose they must have. What colors do you prefer?"

She glanced around the ballroom. "As you might be able

to see, I like a light and airy feel to a home. Darker colors can be interesting to add dimension and interest, but I prefer walls and hangings to be in lighter colors."

"I agree. I do not like dark colors at all." He appeared to shudder.

He was so emphatic about his dislike, Eleanor wondered what his house looked like. If they decided to wed, she would find out soon.

The set ended, and they began strolling back to her family. She wished she could remain with him and continue their conversation. Perhaps he would discuss the other renovations he wished to make to his house. Unfortunately, she had partners for all her dances, and she would not be able to really talk with him again until the supper dance.

Still, there was a little more information to be discovered. "Do you have dark colors now?"

"Yes." His tone was filled with loathing. "I cannot wait to have it changed. The only problem is that I do not know which colors and patterns would be best for the various rooms."

"Do you mean to say that *all* the rooms are decorated in dark colors?" She could not imagine it could be true. Who would do something like that?

"Every single one of them."

"Oh dear. That must be dreadful." If they decided they suited, redecorating the house would be one of the first things she would do.

"You cannot imagine. It is as if I am living in a cave."

How horrible. Eleanor felt sorry for him to have to reside in a place that was not comfortable. She patted his arm. "I am sure something can be done."

He stopped walking and gazed down at her. "I certainly hope so, and soon."

Suddenly, she got the feeling he was not speaking only about his house. Was he preparing to propose? If so, she should give him some encouragement. After all, declarations of love typically accompanied proposals. "I hope so as well."

CHAPTER TWENTY-EIGHT

John couldn't have been happier, except that he had to watch another gentleman dance with Eleanor. The more they had talked during the dance, the more he wanted to drop to one knee and propose. Fortunately, he had managed to contain himself. Not only would it be a shocking thing to do, but he had not even spoken with Worthington yet. And it might ruin the ball for her sisters. No, the Exeter ball was a much better place to propose. He just had to decide what to say to make her agree to marry him.

John could barely keep a scowl off his face when she went off to dance with Bolingbroke. And that was knowing the man had attracted the attentions of a lady he seemed likely to wed. As quick as a flash of lightning, John knew he'd do anything to keep Eleanor with him. Life without her would be empty. This was the feeling his brother-in-law and his friends had felt for their wives. This was love.

I'm in love with Eleanor.

The realization was not earth-shattering. There were no bells ringing. His feet were still on the ground. His sister was probably correct when she said that was not the kind of love that lasted. What he was experiencing now went much deeper. Eleanor was his future and his home. Together they could build a life with love and laughter, children and house

animals—he smiled to himself, thinking of Posy's lick—
and helping others.

He had to speak with Worthington, but when? Tomorrow
there were early meetings at the Lords that threatened to
last all day. Somehow John would have to manage it. He
would not wait to propose to her. The sooner they were betrothed, the sooner they could be married. Damn, he needed
to write to his solicitor and have him ready his finances to
be reviewed.

"You're scowling," Aurelia murmured.

He glanced to his side. "I am not."

She raised a brow, giving him her I-know-better-than-
you look. "Shall I find you a mirror?"

"I don't like seeing her with other men." Too late; he
could have bitten his tongue. What the devil made him tell
his sister that?

"You do know that once you are betrothed, you may have
all of her dances? Providing she agrees, that is."

John dismissed the second part of his sister's sentence.
Of course Eleanor would agree. "I may?"

"Yes. It is one of the benefits of a betrothal."

If he could be the only one to stand up with her, what
else was he allowed? "Is there anything else I may do?"

"Hmmm. Ride with her in a closed carriage. She will of
course be allowed to come to your house and meet your
housekeeper. Although Mama or another female relative
must be in the house as well."

A closed carriage. A lot could be done in a closed carriage. He was getting hard just thinking about it. But he'd
rather show her his—their—bedchamber. Unfortunately,
that could hardly be accomplished with his mother in the
house. John glanced at Aurelia. Was she actually suggesting
she would turn a blind eye to what he and Eleanor decided
to do if she was there?

"But first you must speak to Worthington and propose to Lady Eleanor."

That ruined his growing erection. Just as well. He didn't want to advertise his intentions to the world. "I was just trying to work out a time Worthington would be available. I plan to ask Eleanor to marry me at the Exeter ball."

"Normally, I would suggest her house, but with the number of people living there, you might not have a chance to be alone with her."

Aurelia had no idea. John could imagine Elizabeth or one of the Danes popping into the parlor he was in with Eleanor to see what was going on. The garden would be worse. Lady Exeter's ball would be the place. He wondered how long they would have to wait to wed. From what he had heard, her sisters had not had long betrothals. Would Eleanor want a short engagement?

"Of course there are also the settlement agreements to be worked out." His sister blew out an exasperated breath. "Marc and I would have been married within a day or two of returning to Town if it had not been for them."

John had not been directly involved in his sister's marriage contract, but he did seem to recall their mother had dithered. "I don't understand why it took so long."

"Mama and the solicitor tried to keep me out of the negotiations. And the agreement they decided upon did not suit me at all. Finally Marc and I worked it out ourselves. I was amazed at how like-minded we were."

John couldn't see Worthington allowing John and Eleanor to draft their own agreements. She was a minor, where his sister had already reached her majority. Then again, the man had some experience. Four of his charges had already married. Worthington probably had a good idea of what he wanted in the contract.

"I do not think Worthington is one to shilly-shally."

Aurelia glanced at the man in question, who was standing just out of hearing range. "I agree. He will be quite firm."

Lytton strolled up and handed her a glass of champagne. "Thank you, my love."

"It was my pleasure." They gazed at each other for a long minute.

"Well, then." She took a sip of wine. "We are going to mingle. Please tell me if you require assistance with anything."

John watched them amble off, and his mind strayed back to Eleanor and closed coaches and beds.

The next thing he knew, a delicate hand touched his sleeve. *Eleanor*. "You look to be lost in thought."

Very pleasant thoughts. He smiled at her. "A bit. Are you enjoying your ball?"

"I am." She returned the smile. "Who are you standing up with other than me?"

"No one." He cleared his throat. It was time to let her know he was serious. "There is no one else with whom I wish to dance."

"No one?" Her voice was low and breathy. If only he could be alone with her.

"No." He caught her summer-blue gaze. "There is not another lady who interests me."

He didn't know how long they stood gazing at each other, but it was long enough for her sisters to join them.

"My lord, are you enjoying our ball?" Lady Alice said pointedly.

He dragged his eyes from Eleanor. "Immensely, my lady."

Lady Madeline turned her back to them and her shoulders began to shake. A few moments later, she turned back around. "Oh dear. This will be a ball to remember."

What did she mean by that?

Eleanor shook her head slightly. "It is our come out ball;

naturally we will remember it. Why would you think we would not?"

"It is not that. We joined you because some of the guests had noticed you and Lord Montagu staring at each other." Lady Alice raised an imperious brow. "You really must take care. Come along, Eleanor. You next dance partner will be here soon."

Her statement only strengthened his resolve to ask Eleanor to marry him. Otherwise they would become an *on-dit* for the curious. All he had to do was work out what to say to her.

Con watched Montagu and Eleanor staring at each other with rapt expressions. "That's a proposal waiting to happen."

"The Season will be over by the time he gets around to it," Rothwell said.

"No." Con shook his head. "It will be much sooner than that." Alice and Madeline had Eleanor's arms and were taking her away from Montagu.

Rothwell drew himself up in his dukely manner. "Take it from me. Nothing is going to happen in that direction any time in the near future. He hasn't even spoken with Worthington yet."

He might be a duke, but Con had been on the Town much longer than his brother-in-law, who had gone off to Canada for several years. "I'll wager you a pony he'll ask her within the next few days."

Rothwell had his superior I-am-a-duke-and-know-better look on his face. "I shall be happy to take your money from you."

"We shall see." Con smiled smugly. After hearing about Eleanor agreeing to help Montagu with his dependent problems, Con had been watching the man closely. Whether

Montagu asked Worthington first or not, it would be very
soon.

   The next evening, Eleanor entered the Exeter ballroom
more excited than she had ever been. Last night she knew
Montagu had met all the requirements on her list. The way
their eyes met and held, each searching the other's soul,
convinced her he loved her, and she loved him. Now that
that was decided, there was no reason to wait any longer.
Tonight she would encourage him. The only problem was
that she was not precisely certain how to proceed. Eleanor
gave herself a shake. There was nothing to worry about.
She would know what to do when the time came. It would
probably just come to her. Still, she wished she had spoken
with one of her older sisters or Dotty. They might have been
able to give her advice. As it was, Eleanor would simply
have to make it up as she went along.
   She was with her family's circle when the familiar prick-
ling started on her neck and raced down her spine to be followed by a warm sensation telling her that he was very close
to her.
   "Lady Eleanor." As it always did, Montagu's low voice
caused tiny fires to burn within her.
   She turned her head to him and smiled. "My lord. You
are here early this evening."
   "I trust Lady Exeter not to attempt to find me dance
partners with whom I do not wish to stand up."
   Happiness soared through Eleanor. He had said last
night he did not want to dance with anyone but her. "What
will you do until the supper dance?"
   "Begrudge the other gentlemen dancing with you."
He held out his arm. "Shall we stroll?" Unfortunately, the

violins started playing the prelude to the next dance. He let out a breath "That was poorly timed."

She wished they could have walked together as well. "We will be able to stroll later."

Her partner, one of the younger gentlemen, came up to her and bowed. "My lady."

Eleanor removed her hand from Montagu's arm and curtseyed. "Mr. Cornish."

The country dance gave her a chance to review how she had arranged her schedule this evening. For the first time she had the set before the supper dance open. Eleanor wished she had left some others open as well. Still, she would have an opportunity to stroll the room with Montagu.

The next two hours felt more like four. If she had had a watch or a clock nearby, she knew she would have been looking at it every minute or so. Eleanor had not dreamed dancing, even country dances, could go so slowly. Then again, all she had been able to think about was Montagu. Finally it was time to be with him.

True to his word, he had remained with her family, and Dorie Exeter had not attempted to introduce him to ladies in need of partners. Although she had been ruthless with the other single gentlemen. Was that it? Did she somehow know Montagu was no longer on the marriage mart?

Eleanor's partner escorted her back to her circle and left to find his next dance partner. She took out her fan and opened it. "It is warm in here."

Montagu placed her free hand on his arm. "Would you like a bit of fresh air before the next set?"

She glanced up at him and tried to open her eyes innocently wide, but seeing how he reacted was too much fun. She hoped he would play along. "I do not have a partner for this dance."

He started at her, seemingly in shock. "Indeed?"

"Indeed. Shall we?" Eleanor tightened her fingers on his arm as flames shot through her. If that kept up, her legs would crumble. She could not have planned this better if she had tried.

Montagu led her toward the French windows at the other end of the ballroom. "I hope the terrace is cooler than in here."

"As do I." All the windows were open, but it really was warm. They stepped onto the flagstone, and she was happy to find it was cooler outside.

Small lanterns hung from the trees and torches lined the paths. It was almost as crowded out here as it was in the ballroom.

"We aren't the only ones to seek relief from the heat." His breath caressed her cheek, and suddenly her breasts felt fuller. She was glad Charlotte had spoken to her about what happened between a man and a woman. If only she had given Eleanor hints on encouraging a gentleman. She glanced at Montagu and her gaze landed on his lips. How would they feel? They looked firm. Would she like to be kissed as much as her older sisters did? Some of it had sounded a bit odd. They turned down a path at the edge of the garden that, while still lighted, did not have anyone else on it.

They approached a rose arbor, and Montagu stopped and turned her to him. "Eleanor, I want to kiss you." He took both her hands in his. "I have wanted to kiss you for weeks. A lifetime."

She peeked at his eyes, but his lips drew her gaze back to them. "I want to kiss you as well."

Her words were a mere whisper on the breeze, but John had heard them. He bent his head and brushed his lips softly across hers. She raised her head and leaned into him. He had to remember this was her first time kissing. Yet the urge to gather her into his arms and carry her off to his bed was getting harder to resist. He pressed his lips to her puckered ones.

Definitely her first kiss.

Slowly, he moved his mouth on hers, until she began to match his movements. He licked the seam of her lips and she moaned, allowing him to deepen the kiss. Soon her tongue was tangling with his. Pulling her against him, he caressed her breast, wishing she wasn't wearing stays. Still, she moaned.

He didn't want to go too fast or scare her. "Did you like that?"

"Yes. Do that again."

He brushed his thumb over where he thought her nipple was. If only he could feel it harden beneath his touch. Damn stays. "Like that?"

"Ummm. I feel so strange. Everything is on fire."

John stifled a groan. If only he could make her hotter. Lift her skirts and feel how tight and wet she was. But before he could do that, he had to get permission to wed her. He raised his head, breaking the kiss. "Eleanor, I still need to speak with your brother-in-law, but will you marry me? You are the only lady I want as my wife. The only one I have ever wanted to be in my life forever."

"Yes, Montagu." She drew his head down and kissed him. "Yes, I will marry you."

"John. Please call me John. No one else does."

She smiled up at him. "John."

He sent a prayer to the deity. *Please let it be soon.*

Off to the side, leaves rustled. "We must go in. I must talk to Worthington." But John couldn't seem to let her go. He kissed her again, stroking his hand over her bottom. And as he'd hoped, she pressed herself fully against him. He had to have her soon. Reluctantly, he raised his head. He must take her back inside before anyone saw them. "We really do have to go. Anyone seeing us would only upset your family."

Eleanor sighed and her shoulders slumped. "I suppose you are right."

The path was still empty as they slowly made their way back. "I think we missed the supper dance."

She glanced up at him with a sly look. "I did not miss anything, my lord."

"Minx." Her light laughter filled the air. John hoped he could convince her to a short betrothal.

CHAPTER TWENTY-NINE

Kenilworth strode through the French doors from the terrace and came directly to Matt. "Well?"

"You will receive a request for her hand before the night is out." Kenilworth had a smug look on his face. "They are well matched. And Rothwell owes me a monkey."

Matt stared at his old friend and brother by marriage. "How the deuce did that come about?"

Kenilworth shrugged. "You know how he can be. He went on and on about Montagu being a slow-top. I got tired of it and finely wagered five hundred quid."

"That will teach him." In general, Rothwell did not display the pomposity of most dukes, but every time he did, someone in the family got the better of him.

"Until the next time." Kenilworth grinned.

Charlotte and Grace came up to them, taking their arms. Grace glanced at the French windows. "Well?"

"He proposed." Matt glanced at his friend and raised a brow.

"He did," Kenilworth confirmed. "Although, to do him credit, he did say he had to talk to you."

"Very proper." Charlotte nodded. "I thought he would be perfect for her."

"I agree," Grace said. "It was just something about the

way he was willing to listen to her. I noticed it when she helped him with his dependents."

"Not to mention putting up with us," Kenilworth added. "I warned him he'd better accept her as she was, and he didn't run away."

Matt was proud of the way everyone in the family worked together and helped one another.

Grace appeared thoughtful. "He does seem to like the children and the Danes."

"Excellent." He grinned. "One down and two to go."

His darling wife scowled at him. "You should not think about them as tasks."

"My love, I will not rest well until they are all safely wed." He drew her closer to him. "We will have four years until the next come out. Then Mary will be the last for a long while."

"Don't get so excited." Kenilworth's dry tone drew Matt's attention. "In no time at all we have four girls coming out."

Matt mentally counted them. "Three."

"Four." Kenilworth looked at Matt. "Do you really think Elizabeth will not insist on coming out with the others?"

Hell and damnation. He was right.

"I have Theo and Mary to deal with first." At least the boys wouldn't be any trouble.

Grace nudged him. "Here they come."

"Worthington." Montagu bowed. "I need to have a word with you."

Matt was glad to see Eleanor's face alight with happiness. He would give the same answer to Montagu he always did. "My study no later than nine o'clock tomorrow morning."

Montagu grinned at Eleanor. "I'll be there."

Eleanor had never been so happy in her life. She was marrying not only a gentleman who met all her requirements but they were in love! Her sisters hugged her while her brothers and brothers-in-law slapped Montagu on his back and congratulated him.

The prelude to a dance began. "We did not miss the supper dance."

Alice gave her a look. "If you had been gone that long, Matt would have had our brothers looking for you."

"He would have, wouldn't he?" Eleanor said. "But now I can waltz with my betrothed."

John slid his hand down her back to her waist and frissons of pleasure raced through her. "Shall we, my love?"

Her eyes met his, and she could see how much he loved her. "We shall."

They took their places, and she put her hand on his waist, but this time, she knew what it was like to be held and kissed by him. The memory brought a slight warmth to her cheeks.

He leaned his head down so that his lips were close to her ear. "I love your blushes." His words only caused more heat to rush into her face. "If only I could kiss you now."

"You are going to have me as red as a beet if you do not stop." She was going to get him back for this. Unfortunately, she could not respond in kind. "When would you like to wed?"

"The day after tomorrow?" John had a hopeful look on his handsome face.

That would be very nice, but it took time to arrange the church, write the invitations, and have new clothing made. "I think two or three weeks is the best we will be able to manage."

He uttered a low groan. "I'm never going to make it that long."

"You poor man." She chuckled softly. "Perhaps Grace will take pity on you."

"Your sister?" John seemed shocked. "What does she have to do with it?"

"My dear, Matt might negotiate the settlement agreements, but Grace plans the weddings. We need her approval for the date."

John stared at Eleanor for a few seconds until they had to change positions and twirl. "Of course we do. I have been so focused on Worthington, I completely forgot Lady Worthington would play a large part. She has stood in lieu of a mother to you."

"Yes." Tears pricked Eleanor's eyes and she blinked them back. "She has."

"Very well, then," John said in a rallying tone. "May we ask her at supper?"

She almost burst out laughing. "Oh, I have no doubt that will be a major part of the conversation this evening."

His forehead wrinkled as if in thought. "Naturally with all your sisters here, and mine, and my mother, I'll be surprised if anything else is discussed. I feel like a laggard, not immediately understanding."

John reminded her of her brothers-in-law. None of them seemed to understand there was more to getting married than the actual wedding. She was proud of his quick acceptance of the fact. "I think you have been more focused on the actual time of the ceremony rather than the planning."

"You're right. I was." They ended the set with a twirl. "If it was up to me, I'd carry you off tonight."

"Like a knight of old carrying a lady off on his horse?" Eleanor tried to remember who had said only a man could think that was at all comfortable but could not.

"I suppose most gentlemen would like to do that." He tucked her hand in his arm and headed slowly toward her family. "I have read family accounts of elaborate wedding celebrations going on for days."

It was time to change the conversation to another aspect of the wedding. "Shall we take a honeymoon or go directly to your estate?"

"Hmm." John's countenance became serious. "I want a wedding trip. Once we arrive home, we will have much to do with our new dependents arriving."

She loved how he said "our home" and "our dependents." He was already thinking of her as his partner. "We will have to plan their arrival." Eleanor was glad he agreed with her about the honeymoon. "Where shall we go? I have been told Paris is beautiful in the spring."

"Yes. I have heard that as well." He grinned at her. "Let's travel there for a few weeks. We have friends who can give us advice about the journey and the city."

"Perfect." She felt like skipping. "Our wedding trip is the one thing over which we do have complete control."

"That will be nice." His tone was so dry she had to stifle a laugh.

"It will be." Her mind was already recalling the bits and pieces of information about Paris and the journey there and back. It would be much more interesting to plan the trip than a wedding breakfast.

When they arrived back at her family's circle, John's mother, sister, and brother-in-law were there. Lady Montagu was in a close conversation with Grace and Lady Lytton. Her husband was speaking with Matt. It appeared that everyone else had been dancing. Strange. Eleanor had not even seen them.

Once Alice and her partner, Lord Athersuch, arrived, they went down to supper.

John drew Eleanor closer to him as they walked down the stairs. "The usual?"

"Yes." From the beginning, he had remembered the foods she liked best. "I wonder if they will have ices."

"We will soon find out."

A footman led them to a group of tables that had already been put together and bowed. "Compliments of Lady Exeter."

"Where is she?" Eleanor had not seen Dorie since the receiving line.

"I am not sure, my lady," the servant said. "If I see her, should I say you were asking about her?"

"No. I suspect she is very busy this evening." Most hostesses were. Giving a ball required making sure everything went well during the entertainment.

But a few minutes later, she, Georgie Turley, Henrietta Fotherby, and Adeline Littleton swooped down on their table.

Dorie looked at Eleanor. "I saw what appeared to be congratulations being given to Montagu."

"We are betrothed." What a heady feeling it was to tell someone not of her family.

"I am very happy for you and Montagu." Dorie beamed.

"I hope he knows what a treasure he is getting," Henrietta said as she embraced Eleanor.

"I wish you both happy," Adeline said.

"I as well." Georgie smiled at Eleanor. "When is the wedding?"

"In two or three weeks, I think." She glanced at Grace. "Two or three weeks?"

"It is still fairly early in the Season, but I believe we can manage it in two weeks."

Eleanor let out the breath she had been holding. John was going to be happy about not having to wait long. "That is perfect."

* * *

John was not surprised to find Kenilworth behind him as they approached the table where supper had been laid. "What can I expect from Worthington concerning the settlement discussions?"

"That there will be no discussion." Kenilworth picked up two plates. "He knows exactly what he wants for his sisters and will accept nothing less."

That didn't sound fair. "What if one has less wealth?"

"It doesn't matter. His contract is all about percentages." He looked at John. "Believe me when I tell you he knows almost to the penny what your assets are."

This discussion was starting to put John's back up. The only person who had ever dictated to him was his father. "What if I disagree?"

"Then you will not wed Eleanor."

Hell if he wouldn't marry her. "That is unacceptable."

They had reached the end of the table, where he found ices. "I know you aren't happy to hear this, but you must. I've known Worthington since we were in school together, and it made no difference to him. There are two other things you must know. Eleanor will be there as well, and the agreement will state that she keeps her property, both personal and real."

"Bloody hell-hounds," John muttered under his breath.

"Precisely." Kenilworth asked a footman to assist them, and they started back to the table. "If it makes you feel any better, Grace kept all her property."

That was surprising. But perhaps it was the reason Worthington insisted on doing the same for their sisters. "Did she?"

Kenilworth nodded. "She did. If you want Eleanor . . ."

"All of you have agreed? Even Merton?"

"Merton was the first. He was not at all happy about it, but he wanted Dotty."

"Phinn?" John didn't know why he had to make sure there was not a way for him to take control of the negotiations, but he did.

"Worthington sent the contract to Phinn's brother and the agreement was made. He then sent it to the cousins with whom Augusta was traveling."

"Damn." It appeared there was nothing to do but agree. John did not want to give Eleanor the impression he didn't want to marry her. "Why are the ladies present?"

"It is their life." Kenilworth shrugged. "He believes they should know what the financial terms are."

"Thank you for warning me." John didn't know what he would have done if Kenilworth had not prepared him. Probably made a pickle of things.

"Welcome to the family." The man grinned. "Believe me when I tell you the benefits outweigh any perceived initial drawbacks."

When John returned to the table Eleanor gave him a magnificent smile. "Two weeks."

That was the best he could have hoped. He almost yelled *huzzah*. "Two weeks?"

"Yes." She was still smiling. "In two weeks we will be married."

Two weeks, then a honeymoon in Paris. Everything was going superbly. He had never in his life been happier. It was as if everything was finally the way it should be.

He gave Eleanor a glass of champagne and resisted kissing her shell-like ear. "White wine ices."

"They sound delightful."

"No." Down the table, Lady Alice was giving his mother

a stern look. For her part, Mama appeared shocked. "Eleanor would not like that at all."

It seemed as if he was not the only one who would have to get used to her family. "I wonder what they are discussing."

Eleanor swallowed a bite of asparagus. "I have no idea. Nor do I wish to know. I trust my sisters to do what I would wish."

John cut a piece of a lobster patty with his fork. It made sense for the bride not to be involved in the wedding breakfast plans, and thus avoid any conflict with her future mother-in-law. "I believe we are well out of it."

A sly smile graced her lips. "I agree. Now, shall we discuss our honeymoon, or is there another subject you would like better?"

That gave him an idea. "What will you be doing during the next weeks?"

She lifted one shoulder and dropped it. "Selecting new gowns and fittings. Why?"

He remembered how much she seemed to enjoy the idea of remodeling and decorating. "How long does it take to redecorate a house?"

Her eyes widened with interest. "That depends on how much there is to do. By house, do you mean everything?"

He held her gaze. "Every single room."

"To decide on the colors and patterns, about a week, I would think." The look in her eyes changed from interest to thoughtfulness. "Yes, that would do it. The decorationist who did both my family's homes could make the changes while we are gone."

John wanted to take her in his arms. "Will you need me to assist you?"

"Of course." Her hand brushed against his. "You must be happy with the results."

"Do you think we could begin tomorrow? After I speak with your brother?"

"I do not see why not." She frowned slightly. "As long as your mother is at home. You should join us for breakfast."

"Thank you. The sooner I am able to speak with Worthington, the sooner we can be off. I will see to it that either my mother or sister is present." Thank the Lord he would not have to wait until their wedding to make love to her.

CHAPTER THIRTY

It was drizzling when Eleanor woke the next morning and padded to the window. The clouds were so dark, she was certain it would rain all day. That was just as well. There was much to accomplish. Before the Season began, Matt had reviewed the marriage contract with her and her sisters. He had made it very clear that any gentleman wishing to marry them had to agree to it. It had not occurred to her, until now, that John might not like the contract. Granted, all her brothers-in-law had signed the same agreement. Ergo, she probably did not have anything about which to be concerned. Still, what would she do if he refused? Part of her thought she would wed him despite his not agreeing, but Matt and Grace would not allow it. Fortunately, everyone would be at breakfast. Eleanor would just ask her sisters if they had had any difficulties.

She went to her desk and wrote four short notes to them and Dotty, requesting they arrive in enough time to meet with her about the settlement agreements in the Young Ladies' Parlor. By the time she had finished, Jobert was in the dressing room.

Eleanor strode into the small room. "I have some letters that need to be sent immediately."

Her maid held out her hand. "I shall give them to Turner. The yellow or cream today?"

"The yellow twill. I am going out after the meeting."

Jobert nodded. "I'll be back by the time you have washed."

"Thank you." Eleanor's worries seemed to bury themselves under the excitement that was starting to grow. Today she would see her new home for the first time. From what John had said, it desperately needed to be refurbished. She had never taken on such a large task, but neither had Grace before she had remodeled Stanwood House and Worthington House. The prospect made Eleanor a little nervous, but if her sister could do it, so could she. After all, she had trained her whole life to be the mistress of large estates.

She went behind the screen and began her ablutions. True to her word, by the time Eleanor was finished, Jobert had returned and laid out her clothing. She had also brought a cup of tea and a piece of toast.

"It seems everyone is up before times this morning. Mrs. Thorton said it must be because of your betrothal."

"She is probably right." When they had returned home last evening, Matt made the announcement to Thorton and his wife, who told the rest of the staff. Naturally, Eleanor went immediately to her chambers to notify Jobert.

She held Eleanor's gown up to be donned. "I am looking forward to meeting the staff at Montagu House."

"I do hope you like them. Please tell me if there is any difficulty at all." Eleanor wanted the transition to their new home to be easy for her servants and the old staff.

"Thank you, my lady. I will."

Less than an hour later, Eleanor was pacing the parlor when Alice and Madeline entered.

"Good morning." Alice took a seat on the small sofa. "You should be happy, not agitated."

"I am merely a little concerned. I know what is in the agreements, but I do not know what I will do if Montagu balks."

Charlotte strolled in through the open door. "Is that what this is about?" She hugged Eleanor, then leaned back and looked at her. "I do not think you have to worry. It is clear he loves you, and the contract is part of being able to wed you."

"What are we discussing?" Dotty asked from the doorway.

"Eleanor is concerned Montagu might have a problem with the settlement agreements," Charlotte replied.

"Dom did." Dotty shrugged. "Not that I knew about it until later. Matt is extremely firm about the agreement. Dom wanted to marry me, so he signed it."

"You see?" Alice said. "I told you that would happen."

Louisa must have been lingering in the corridor for she strolled in and said, "Gideon insisted on increasing what the contract gave me."

Dotty's eyes widened. "Could he afford it?"

"I have no idea." Louisa shook her head. "And I never asked. A man has his pride."

"Especially a duke." Madeline chuckled. "If this is settled, may we break our fast? I am starving."

"We may. I am hungry as well." Eleanor took Charlotte's arm. "Is there anything else I should know about the meeting?"

"Let Matt do the talking. This is his way of protecting your future."

"And your children's future," Louisa added as they walked up the corridor to the main staircase. "Really, Eleanor, you have nothing about which to be concerned."

Then why was she still nervous? "You are right. There is nothing to worry about at all."

Con came to Charlotte when they entered the breakfast room. "Is anything wrong?"

"No." She shook her head and smiled. "Eleanor was just a bit anxious about the settlement contracts."

He glanced at John, who had been talking with Hugh and Gideon and had just noticed Eleanor and her sisters entering the room. "Everything will be fine."

"Good morning." John took Eleanor's hands and raised them to his lips. "I was just assuring the boys I would take good care of you."

She took in Gideon's solemn mien. "Ever since he found out Alice, Madeline, and I would most likely wed this year he has been concerned."

John squeezed her fingers. "He made that quite clear."

"He would have. He takes his future role seriously." He had always been the serious one of the cousins.

Madeline gave John her usual seat, allowing him to sit next to Eleanor. It was odd not sitting next to her sister. But after they wed, they would sit next to their husbands. Yet there was no time to consider the changes further. Footmen were carrying around trays, and a pot of tea appeared next to her plate.

"How do you take your morning tea?"

"One lump of sugar and a little milk." He gave his head an imperceptible shake. "How did you know I might like my morning tea differently?"

"Many people do. In our house, our morning tea is much stronger than what we serve in the afternoon."

He took a sip. "I hadn't even noticed how the tea tasted the last time I broke my fast with you."

That was not surprising. He probably was not thinking about the food at all. "It was your first time with the family."

"True." He took two pieces of ham from a plate a footman offered him.

Eleanor dug into a coddled egg. For a short period of time the table was relatively quiet. A very short period of time.

"Have you decided if you will take a wedding trip?" Dotty asked.

John had just taken a bite of toast and Eleanor swallowed her piece of egg. "Yes. We will go to Paris for a few weeks."

As it had at supper last evening, the talk turned to the wedding, with the children adding their ideas.

"I think we should have the ceremony in the garden. Like we did with Duke and Daisy," Augusta said. "It was the most beautiful wedding I have been to."

Mary nodded her head in agreement. "I think so too."

"Duke and Daisy?" John whispered.

"Our old dogs. Daisy was expecting puppies, and we decided they needed to marry."

Across from them, Con started coughing, and Charlotte's eyes sparkled with laughter.

"Con, do you need a glass of water?" Eleanor asked.

"He will be fine." Charlotte patted her husband's back. "You do not know that he thought I was marrying someone else and ran out to the garden only to find it was the dogs."

"Papa." Elizabeth's brows drew together. "You said Posy would have puppies this autumn. She will need to be married first."

"We can help plan the wedding," Constance said.

Soon all the younger members of the family were planning Posy and Zeus's wedding.

"It's almost a relief the focus is no longer on us," John murmured.

If Eleanor could be certain it would not rain, she would

like a garden service. Unfortunately, one could not depend upon the weather. "For the moment."

Soon everyone was finishing their repast, and Matt stood. "Montagu, Eleanor, please come with me."

This was the moment John had been dreading. They rose and followed his future brother-in-law out of the room. He'd sent a note to his solicitor about his financial information but did not know if it had been delivered to Worthington. Although from what Kenilworth had said, it wouldn't matter.

They entered the study, and John was struck by how light the room looked even with the dreary sky. Ash wood bookshelves lined three walls, while a bank of windows covered the fourth wall. Unlike the parlor, where he'd met with the other gentlemen, there was no door to the garden.

Eleanor gracefully lowered herself onto one of two dark leather chairs before a large mahogany desk. He could see now what she had meant when she mentioned dark pieces in a light-colored room. He took the chair next to her and wished they were close enough together that he could hold her hand. He shouldn't be so damn nervous.

Worthington took his place behind the desk, and John noticed three small stacks of paper.

"Now, then." Worthington placed a hand on one of the stacks. "I received your financial information this morning Fortunately, my solicitor is used to being called upon to draft settlement agreements without much notice." He moved the hand to the top of the next set of documents. "These are Eleanor's assets. They will be put in trust for her use and the use of any children after the heir is born."

John's jaw clenched. "I am well able to provide for our children."

"Very well." Worthington inclined his head and glanced

at her. "Eleanor, if you have no objections, I will be your trustee."

She sat with her hands demurely in her lap, but John could tell she was paying close attention. "I have no objections."

Her brother-in-law must have appointed himself trustee for all his sisters.

The man looked at him. "It is your right to review her property."

What did it matter what she had? It would never be his. "It does not matter. It is hers."

"The last issue I will mention before you read the agreements is that of custody of the children in the event you die while the children are still minors. Eleanor will be granted custody of them." Worthington's gaze on John was steady. "My wife fought tooth and nail to keep her brothers and sisters together. I will not have any of my sisters suffer the same hardship."

For a moment, John couldn't speak. He had never even thought of what would happen if he died and left her with minor children. The demand was fairly unusual, but knowing what he did of Eleanor and hearing the story about how Lady Worthington had fought for her family, he would agree. If anything were to happen to him, Eleanor would be surrounded by a family who loved and helped her.

He cleared his throat. "It is something I had not considered, but I agree. Eleanor would be the best person to care for them." Next to him, he thought he heard her let out a breath of air. "There is one other item. My mother will move to the dower house. In the event of my demise, I would not want Eleanor to be forced to have to live with her. She will have the pick of my properties on which to reside."

Worthington raised a brow at her. "Eleanor?"

"Yes." She smiled at John. "I appreciate and will accept the offer."

Her brother divided the last pile of papers in half and slid them across the desk to him. "One contract was in the event you agreed Eleanor's dowry should be used for the children and one was if you did not. The contact it is not overly long, but I believe it is sufficient."

As was his habit, he read the agreements carefully and found them extremely reasonable. Of course that could very well be because she had charge of her own property. Now he understood why Kenilworth was not concerned about the rest of the financial settlement. Still, John thought he might raise her pin money. She would be his wife, and he did wish to provide for her.

"I agree." He reached for the pen and standish that had been placed on the corner of the desk, dipped the pen in the ink, and signed the documents.

Worthington did the same, then sanded the contract, and smiled. "Welcome to the family."

"Thank you." John grinned at Eleanor. "I am glad to be a part of it."

"Matt, I shall see you later." She took John's hand and led him out of the study. Once they were in the corridor, she told a footman to call for his coach. "Shall we see what needs to be done to our home?"

He had to force himself not to take her in his arms. "I think that's a brilliant idea."

They passed the breakfast room, and female voices filtered out from behind the door.

Eleanor grinned. "They must be planning at least one wedding."

"I do hope we are here to attend Posy and Zeus's wedding." The idea of what the children would plan fascinated him.

"It will be this summer, when we are all together." Eleanor's hat—a stiff, wide-brimmed hat with a medium-height crown of oilcloth that one would wear in the country—and a pair of leather gloves were already by the door. The butler held up a long Spanish, brown-colored coat also made of oil-cloth. John took it from him and assisted Eleanor. He then donned his great coat, hat, and gloves. A footman stood on the small, covered porch, holding an umbrella. The rain was coming down much harder than it was earlier.

He took her arm as the footman with the umbrella held it over them. "At least we won't arrive soaked."

"There is that. I should bring my maid. She will wish to meet the senior staff."

That was not at all what he had planned for today. "Can you do it another time?"

"I suppose I could. I will just take a look at the house today."

He opened the door and assisted her into the carriage. Thank the Lord they could be in a closed carriage now, but his plan to keep her distracted until they reached his house was at an end. Their rain kit would have to remain on for the short ride.

"Is there a reason your coachman does not have a cover to keep him dry?"

"Not that I know of." The larger, traveling coach had one. "I'll have to see about having one added."

A few minutes later, they arrived at Montagu House, but there was no footman waiting to cover them with an umbrella. He jumped out of the carriage. "We will have to make a dash for the door."

Eleanor nodded and he grabbed her hand. Fortunately, the door opened just as they got to it.

"Lumner, do we not have an umbrella?"

"I believe we might have an older one," the butler said slowly. "I shall see about procuring one immediately."

"Good man." He was about to take Eleanor upstairs when he remembered to introduce his butler. "My love, I would like to introduce Lumner, our butler. Lumner, Lady Eleanor."

He bowed. "It will be my great pleasure to serve you, my lady."

She smiled and inclined her head. "Thank you, Lumner."

"There you are." The sound of his mother's voice made John want to groan. Aurelia was to have kept Mama out of the way. "Lady Eleanor, that is a most unusual coat and bonnet."

"My sister, Lady Phinn, brought them back with her. I believe it is her own design."

"Very practical." Aurelia strolled into the hall, glanced pointedly at their mother, and rolled her eyes. He would obviously have to come up with a better plan.

"They are." Eleanor waited while he removed her coat, then turned to him. "Where shall we begin?"

"My dears, would you not like a cup of tea before meeting with the housekeeper?" Mama asked.

Meeting with the housekeeper? "Eleanor?"

"No, thank you. We have much to accomplish." She smiled at his mother. "Perhaps later?"

"Yes, of course," Mama said in a weak voice.

"My lord, my lady." Rennie curtseyed.

"Lady Eleanor, allow me to present our housekeeper, Mrs. Rennie. Rennie, Lady Eleanor, who, as you know, will soon be my wife."

The older woman smiled. "My lady, I am very happy to meet you. Shall we start at in the attics?"

"Of course." Eleanor placed her hand on his arm. "Lead on, Mrs. Rennie."

"Oh, please, my lady. To the family I am Rennie."

John gave up. This situation was obviously out of his control. He should have known his staff would be thrilled to meet her. The only thing he could do now was go along with whatever had been arranged. So much for introducing her to his bedchamber.

CHAPTER THIRTY-ONE

Montagu House had been built on a double lot, meaning it must have been one of the earlier residences in Mayfair. Unlike Worthington House, which had a walk, albeit a very short one, from the pavement to the door, Montagu House's front door was just up two steps from the pavement. That was something Eleanor would have to become used to. Nevertheless, there was enough room for two tall, narrow planters on either side of the door. She took out her pocketbook and pencil and started making notes. As she followed Rennie up the stairs, she agreed with John. The house was much too dark. Even the hall, which boasted a fan window over the door and had yellow-colored marble, was made dimmer by the wallpaper. By the time they reached the servants' quarters, she had a good idea what must be done to make the house more comfortable. But first, she must contact the architect and decorationist Grace had hired. Or perhaps she should consult with John about everything first.

They had entered the nursery area. He was right. The whole house was like a dungeon.

John stroked her back, and small fires licked her skin. "What do you think?"

That her knees were going to turn to jelly if he continued. "You were correct. The colors are much too dark and drab."

The next level held the bedrooms, and although they were all a good size, the furniture and hangings made them appear smaller. The housekeeper opened the door to a chamber with a lovely cherry bed, but the dark red hangings distracted from it. Doors leading to what must be a dressing room and parlor and access to the master's chamber were on either side of the room.

"This is the mistress's apartment, my lady," Rennie said.

A maid came running in. "Mrs. Rennie, I've been looking everywhere for you. Sally broke a vase . . ." The maid must have just noticed Eleanor and John. She quickly bobbed a curtsey before turning back to the housekeeper. "Please come."

Rennie glanced at Eleanor. "Will you excuse me, my lady?"

"Yes, of course."

"I'll be back as soon as I can." The housekeeper followed the maid out of the room.

John took Eleanor's hand. "I'll show you the rest of these apartments."

They looked into the parlor and dressing room. "My mother vacated these rooms after my father died." She could understand that. It was what widows did. They crossed the bedroom, and he opened the door. The arrangement was identical to the other rooms. Facing her, he took Eleanor into his arms. "Where do you plan to begin?"

But before she could answer, his lips touched hers, and the fires that had been simmering since his first touch sprang back to life. John's hand caressed her derrière, causing the spot between her legs to throb with want. Thankfully she had been told what to expect, but would he make love to her now?

One hand covered her breast and her nipples furled into

hard buds. "I never gave much thought to stays before. I can't say I like them very much."

"At least they are short stays." He deepened the kiss and she moaned. Everywhere he had touched, and some places he had not, tingled and became hot. She speared her fingers through his hair and rubbed her body against his, wanting relief from the tension building within her. His lips feathered kisses down her neck and over her décolleté. "Do something."

Never stopping his kisses, he backed her against a wall. "If I take you to my bed, someone will catch us."

Eleanor cupped his face in her hands and kissed him, tangling her tongue with his. "You can do something else. I know you can."

"Yes." Slowly, he lifted her skirt, trailing his fingers against her thigh, and the throbbing got harder. Her hips pushed forward to meet his hand reaching the apex of her thighs. "You are so wet." His fingers brushed past the sensitive nubbin. "You are so hot." He slipped a finger into her sheath, and she thought she would die from the pleasure. His palm pressed on her pearl, and for a moment she lost her breath. "Come for me, my love."

Suddenly, she convulsed around his finger and blissful relief coursed through her. She and her sisters had gone into whoops when Louisa had very seriously called it "a pearl of pleasure." Eleanor would never laugh again. She rocked her hips forward, trying to capture every last wave.

The loud footsteps coming from the corridor was akin to having a bucket of cold water thrown over her head. "Someone is coming."

John removed his hand and helped straighten her skirts. "Nothing is mussed. Take a few breaths." He kept one hand on her as he dipped the other in a nearby bowl, then rubbed it against a towel. "Are you all right?"

Eleanor touched her lips. Her breathing was still too quick. "I am wonderful. It was even more magnificent than I was told."

He didn't have to ask, but he couldn't help himself. "Your older sisters?"

She took in a deep breath and nodded. "Yes. They wanted us to know. That was how I was able to recognize the feeling I had whenever you touched me."

Thank God he hadn't been the only one having "feelings," as she put it. "You are going to be the death of me. All I can think of now is how to get you into my bed to make love to you."

She looked at the bed. "I am sure if we give it some thought we can find a way."

"My lord, my lady?" Rennie called.

Eleanor pushed herself away from the wall. "We are in here." Just before the door opened, she said, "What do you think of taking one of the dressing rooms and turning it into a bathing chamber?"

Her lips were still rosy from his attentions, but she was a cool as a cucumber. "I think that is an excellent idea."

She flashed him a smile that almost brought him to his knees. "Excellent. We can also see about having water piped in. That way no one is wasting time carrying buckets from the kitchen." She glanced at Rennie. "Speaking of the kitchen, will it require new fittings?"

"Cook has grumbled about it," Rennie said, giving the bed a good look. "Let me show you the main parlors and other rooms before we go downstairs."

Eleanor took out her pocketbook again. "An excellent idea."

John followed along behind, watching the sway of her hips and considering ways to get her alone for longer than a few minutes. He wanted her hair down so he could run his fingers through it. He'd had a small taste of how soft her skin was and he wanted more. Soon. He'd find a way soon.

"Do you have any secret passageways in this house?" Eleanor asked. "Merton has one in his, and we found one in Worthington House when my sister renovated it." Her lips formed a pout. "Unfortunately, they removed it."

The question took John aback. The house was certainly old enough to have a secret passage. "I don't know. We should ask one of the servants."

Rennie coughed. "There is one, but it's not been used in well over half a century. The previous housekeeper told me it was boarded up when your father got stuck in it. Everyone's forgotten about it. I don't think her ladyship even knows the passage exists."

That was interesting and helpful. "What rooms does it connect?"

They reached the hall, and Rennie turned into the corridor off the breakfast room, his study, and the library. "It goes from the library, my lord, up to your apartments, and down to the cellars. I think it was meant as a way to escape if trouble ever came."

Eleanor looked as if she was hanging on the housekeeper's every word. "May we see it?"

"If I can remember how to open the door, my lady." They walked into the library and Rennie led them to the fireplace.

"All the best passages are next to the fireplace," Eleanor assured him. "It was easier to build them there."

That made sense. A builder could easily conceal the space behind a fireplace or off to the side of one. He watched as his housekeeper touched a few places on the ornamental mantel. Finally, a bookshelf swung open. "Amazing. I never would have found it." Unfortunately, it had indeed been blocked. "It could be worse. They could have bricked it closed. The wood shouldn't take too long to remove."

Eleanor inspected the wood. "You father must have been a very obedient child. Those boards would not have kept any of my brothers or sisters out of it."

He suddenly had a vision of their children playing in the damn thing and finding their way to his chamber at a most awkward time. "We will have to keep it a secret."

"His lordship didn't know how to open it. He was very young. The cousin who put him in there was sent away quick enough."

John tried to think of a cousin he had that was no longer around and couldn't come up with one. "Who was that?"

"He's dead now, my lord. They sent him to the navy."

It couldn't be . . . "Uncle Crispin?"

Rennie scowled. "That's the name. Always getting into trouble, he was. According to the old housekeeper."

Eleanor tilted her head. "Did you know him?"

"Lord yes." John barked a laugh. "He made admiral. He'd visit when we were children and tell us all sorts of stories about fighting pirates."

"I'm glad to hear he redeemed himself." His housekeeper gave an emphatic nod. "He sounded like a ne'er-do-well to me."

John remembered one of his uncles talking about Crispin as a boy. "Apparently, he was a great deal of trouble until he was sent off. He took to the navy like a duck to water." John glanced at Eleanor. "Do you still want to open it?"

"Absolutely." Her eyes shone. "I have always wanted a secret passage."

"In that case we will make it happen." He could think of

uses for it as well. "Let's keep it among the three of us. I do not want it widely known."

"No, my lord," Rennie agreed. "My lady, shall I show you the rest of the rooms?"

"If you would, please." Eleanor scribbled something in her pocketbook. "After which I shall be ready for a cup of tea."

"I'll be ready for more than tea." He had not eaten much at breakfast and was famished.

"Do you usually serve luncheon?" Eleanor asked Rennie.

His housekeeper shook her head. "It depends what time everyone breaks their fast. Will that be something you'll want to change?"

"Yes." Again, Eleanor made a note. "I will speak to the cook about it."

By the time they finished the tour of his—their—house, he was sure his beloved had filled her pocketbook with ideas and other notes. In fact, he had not been in many of the rooms. Some were still covered in dust-cloths. "Why are so many of the parlors not open?"

"Her ladyship didn't order them to be," Rennie said.

"Hmm." As Eleanor's lips pressed together, he could feel her dissatisfaction. "That cannot be good for the house. Even if a room is not used very much, it should still be cleaned on a regular basis and ready for use." She glanced at the housekeeper. "Do you have sufficient staff?"

Rennie looked away and grimaced. "Not to keep up the whole house, my lady."

"That will have to change." Eleanor gave the housekeeper a reassuring smile. "Please decide which positions must be filled and have the list ready the day after tomorrow."

"Why not tomorrow?" He wanted her here every day. This was her home now.

She waved her hand. "I have a modiste appointment and

some other meetings that will take up the morning. Grace's at home is in the afternoon." She tilted her head. "Do you not have something you must do?"

He couldn't think of anything. John shook his head.

"Something you must procure before the wedding?" He could imagine her using the same tone with one of their children.

Worthington was going to visit the rector at St George's. Her sisters were planning the wedding breakfast. He had to ask Turley to stand up with him. Eleanor had folded her arms across her chest, causing her breasts to plump. Then she raised a brow. Witness, church, ceremony . . . license! "Er, yes. I shall fetch the special license."

She grinned at him as if he'd won a prize. "I knew you would not forget." Eleanor tucked her hand in the crook of his arm. "Let us finish the tour. Rennie, please lead us to the kitchen."

The housekeeper's jaw dropped. "Are you sure you want to do that without any warning, my lady?"

What the devil was wrong? Their cook had been with them as long as he could remember. The kitchen was always orderly and spotless. As he knew from the many times he'd been threatened with a spoon for trying to enter it with muddy shoes. Or sneaked down to try to get biscuits straight out of the oven. "Is Beasley not feeling well?"

"Oh no, my lord." Rennie wrung her hands. "I mean, I don't know how she's feeling. Her ladyship said she retired when you came to Town, and we have a new one. Cook that is. She doesn't like to be bothered."

"Indeed." John took a breath and let it out. "Shall we see what we have, my love?"

"I think we had better." He led her toward the servants' stairs. "Whatever you do, do not dismiss her on the spot. We must find a new one." Eleanor frowned. "Did you not notice the food tasted differently?"

"The only meal I've had with any consistency was breakfast. Many times I was out." They arrived at the entrance to the kitchen, and he stopped short. It was an utter mess. Dirty pots and dishes covered almost every surface, and a woman with gray hair escaping from her mobcap was drinking a clear liquid from a glass. It could be water, but he was almost certain it was gin.

"What's this?" The cook stood, and John could see the stains on her apron. Mrs. Beasley would have wept. The woman pointed at him. "And who 're you?"

Rennie bustled forward. "You'd better keep a civil tongue in your head." She indicated the cook. "My lord, my lady, this is Goater." The housekeeper looked around. "Where is Sissy?"

"Sent her out shopp'n," the cook mumbled, then swayed.

The woman was drunk. "This Sissy, can she cook?"

Rennie closed her eyes for a moment. "She's been making breakfast and the biscuits, my lord."

Eleanor's jaw had firmed and her normally plump lips formed a thin line. She scanned the kitchen. Her survey stopped when she got to Goater. "I want the kitchen cleaned immediately. Rennie"—his beloved's gaze didn't waver from the cook—"Get every maid and footman down here and put to work. I have never seen such a disgrace."

"Here now," Goater said. "I don't want people in me kitchen."

Despite Eleanor's warning not to fire the servant immediately, he couldn't stand having Goater in poor Beasley's kitchen. Not that he would ever have his old cook back, but he wasn't going to allow this slovenly slattern to stay for one day more. With any luck, Sissy could hold things together until they had a new cook. "It is no longer your kitchen. You may collect your possessions and leave."

The woman stood slack-jawed for several seconds, as if she couldn't believe she'd just been sacked.

"I'll have Lumner call you a hack." Rennie took the former cook's arm. "We'll get your things."

The women walked out, leaving John and Eleanor alone. "I'm sorry I didn't follow your advice."

"No. I would have done the same thing. This is far worse than I imagined." She touched her lips to his. "I shall find a new cook."

He folded her into his arms and rested his chin on the crown of her head. "I have no words for how happy I am that you are in my life. I love you."

"I love you too." Stepping back, she cupped his face in her hands, feathering her thumbs over his cheeks. "Kiss me."

She didn't have to ask him twice. He covered her mouth with his, and she opened to him. John thought he was experienced, but her innocent kisses undid him. He didn't know what he'd do if anything ever happened to her.

CHAPTER THIRTY-TWO

Eleanor and John broke apart at the sound of people coming down the steps, and she put her arm through his as they waited. Fortunately, the maids and footmen arrived at the same time the cook was leaving. Soon, Rennie had everyone in hand. Eleanor really had not thought there would be much more to do than refurbish the house. Yet this morning had made clear that the house needed much more.

"We won't get any tea until this mess is cleaned up." One maid filled a sink with water, while another got out buckets and mops. The servants here seemed willing to do what they must. "Shall I take you home?"

"Yes." She glanced at her brooch watch. It was much later than she had thought. "It is almost time for luncheon. That will also give me an opportunity to ask Jacques if he has any recommendations for a new cook."

"Jacques?" John looked confused. "Who is he? Wouldn't the housekeeper be the one to help find a cook?"

"Jacques is our chef de cuisine. He assisted one of my sisters when she required a new cook. Apparently, he is still involved with the servants in the émigré community. That is how I found my maid. She is of French descent on her mother's side and trained with one of the French dressers."

"In that case, please speak to him straightaway." They

started up the stairs that she supposed went to the hall, where sunlight poured though the fan window over the door.

"The rain has stopped. Do you mind walking to Berkeley Square?" Her hat might look strange, but Eleanor wanted the exercise.

"Not at all. If it is warm, I'll have your coat brought over."

"Thank you." She had not really thought about how considerate he was.

Lumner opened the door and bowed. "Shall I have a footman follow you with your coat, my lady?"

"That would be perfect, Lumner." It seemed everyone in the house was conscious. "We are very glad you will soon be here, my lady."

"As am I." She smiled at the butler as she and John strolled out the door. She would have liked to hold his hand but constrained herself, taking his arm instead. The rain seemed to have made the air cleaner. "I will ask Jacques to attend us during luncheon."

"Thank you." He slid her a smile. "It occurred to me that if you had not agreed to come today, I would not have known about the problems in my own house."

Eleanor was surprised Lady Montagu had not taken more of a role. "Does your mother not like the town house?"

"I have no idea." John shrugged. "She has seemed rather distracted lately. Perhaps she has been too busy to be bothered."

She would give her ladyship the benefit of the doubt. On the other hand, Grace was busy this Season as well, and she had not allowed the household standards to slip. It did not matter. Eleanor would soon have control over Montagu House. "Yes, that must be it."

He guided her around a puddle. "When will you be able to visit the house again?"

"The day after tomorrow. I will also bring my footman and maid so they can meet the staff. It is important they all get along." They would also tell her if there was anything she needed to know about the senior staff especially. "I take it Rennie does not travel from the country and back again."

"No. She and Lumner remain here with a skeleton staff." And for whatever reason, Lady Montagu did not increase the staff.

They turned the corner on to South Audley Street. "If you allow me a free hand, I shall make the changes I believe should be made."

John glanced at her, the warmth in his eyes making her want to walk closer to him. "Of course you may do as you see fit." They made the turn onto Mount Street. "I forgot all about a betrothal ring for you." He pulled her to a stop. "We have several family rings if you would be interested."

"I would love to see them." Many of the older rings were so much more beautiful than the modern ones. They also served to act as a thread to the history of a lady's new family.

"Excellent." He began walking again. "I will have them ready the next time you come."

This was going even better than she had thought it would. Thus far, they had been completely in accord. And the passion she felt for him exceeded even her wildest hopes. Her sisters and Dotty had been right. Passion was almost impossible to describe, but so very enjoyable. Perhaps the next time she was at Montagu House, they would make love. After all, none of her sisters had waited until their wedding day. But right now, Eleanor needed to find a cook. "We have Dotty's ball tomorrow evening."

John's eyes dropped to Eleanor's lips. "I want all your waltzes."

Just his look made her lips tingle. Fortunately, although

she had received several notes asking for dances, she had not had time to answer them. "Then you shall have them. Would you like to join us for dinner?"

"Thank you." He grinned. "May I bring my mother if she is free? After all, we have no cook."

"You may." She wished she knew what Lady Montagu would make of their family dinner.

After luncheon, John went off in search of Turley and Eleanor to attend to her correspondence. Later that afternoon, a knock sounded on her door. "Come."

Grace strolled in. "I received a message from Lady Montagu that she already had dinner plans. And Matt wants you to know that around nine tomorrow morning you will interview a man to manage your mine."

"That is famous!" Things were finally happening.

John returned home through the mews and entered the house through the servants' door. He looked in the kitchen and was pleased to see it was almost back to Beasley's standards. Sissy had returned as well and was busy making tarts. She couldn't be more than twenty years old, with sandy hair and freckles.

"Oh my lord." She bobbed a curtsey. "I want to thank you for letting that Goater go. Mrs. Beasley woulda never let her in the house."

It had not occurred to either Eleanor or him, but Sissy might be the solution to their problems "You were not here to ask, but would you like the cook's position?"

"Me? Oh no, my lord. I've a dab hand with pastries and bread, but I never got the knack of joints, and fish, and alike."

So much for that idea. He hoped Eleanor found someone soon. "In that case, I will continue looking for a new cook."

"Thank you, my lord." Sissy curtseyed again.

"I'll leave you to it." He made his way up the stairs to the hall.

"My lord." Lumner bowed. "As you were not here, I took it upon myself to inform her ladyship that we are temporarily lacking a cook. She decided to spend a few days with Lady Lytton."

"Thank you, Lumner." John had not been looking forward to telling his mother about the cook she'd hired. "It is my great hope Lady Eleanor will soon find a replacement."

"Yes, my lord. We are all quite impressed with Lady Eleanor."

So was he. Kenilworth had not been exaggerating when he said all the Worthington females were highly skilled. But there was one area where he had the experience. The only problem was how to get her alone. "She is an extraordinary lady." John was glad the household liked her. It would make the transition much easier. "Please bring me a tea tray. I'll be on my terrace."

"Yes, my lord."

He scanned the correspondence on his desk, reminding himself again that he must find a secretary. Taking the papers with him, he lowered himself into the large leather chair. A few minutes later, his butler brought tea and biscuits. He had just finished reading the last letter when Turley was announced.

John rose and waved his friend to the other chair. "Welcome. I'm glad you are here. There is something I wish to ask you."

Lumner brought more tea and biscuits, and John poured Turley a cup.

"Thank you." He took a sip. "What can I do for you?"

"Will you stand up with me at my wedding?"

Turley grinned. "I would be honored. I understand it will

be in two weeks." He munched on a biscuit. "I must say, of all of us, you seem to have had the easiest time finding and securing your lady."

"I can't say I thought it was easy." It wasn't as if she fell right into his arms.

"I didn't mean you had no challenges. But it wasn't nearly as difficult as with Littleton, Exeter, and me."

"I will take your word for it." John wondered if they'd had difficulties spending time alone with their ladies before the wedding. "We have decided to take a wedding trip to Paris. Can you give me some ideas of where to stay and what to do?"

"I'd be happy to." Turley smiled. "I'll send some recommendations over. If you would like, I can write to the hotel where Georgie and I stayed. They were very accommodating."

"Thank you. I'd appreciate the help. I've asked Eleanor to help me renovate the town house. I have a feeling I'll be very busy with that."

Turley nodded. "I set Georgie loose on my houses. They are much more comfortable now."

John remembered that his friend's mother had died when he was still young. "It's always good to redecorate and renovate every so often."

"It's very nice to be able to have water piped directly to the bathtub."

"Eleanor mentioned that as well." Although he imagined such work would be done while they were in the country. The fireplace mantel clock chimed. "I hate to run you off, but I am dining at Worthington House."

"Ah, yes." Turley stood. "The early dinners. I suspect we will begin that custom when our children are a bit older."

John rose as well. "Perhaps we will start a fashion."

"Only among those who are more forward-thinking."
Turley held out his hand to John. "Congratulations again."

"Thank you." He shook his friend's hand. "I have a feeling this is going to be a long two weeks. I'll walk you to the hall."

"Don't bother." Turley pointed to the garden. "I'll go through the mews. It's faster."

John watched his friend stroll to the gate, then looked up at the neighbor's town house. Both gardens had tall trees planted along the wall. For the first time he realized that there was no view from that house to his garden gate. Would Eleanor mind coming though the mews? It would ensure them privacy, especially with his mother away for a few days. He'd ask her after dinner.

He arrived at Worthington House to find the whole family had gathered once again.

Worthington pressed a glass of sherry into John's hand. "We all dine together when there are no evening entertainments we wish to attend."

He searched for Eleanor but couldn't find her. "I imagine it allows the children to spend more time together as well."

"Yes. It's important to all of us that they have close ties."

Eleanor appeared by his side. "I was running a bit late. Grace wrote to the architect and the decorationist. The decorationist's letter came while I was dressing. I wrote her back asking if we could meet tomorrow afternoon."

"That was quick." She was giving up her sister's at home for him. "Do you not have morning visits?"

She placed her hand on his arm. "I do, but there will be plenty of time. She arrives at four o'clock. It is slow for her with the Season in full swing."

He hadn't thought of that. "This is the perfect time to start making the changes we discussed."

"It is." Eleanor's smile was different somehow. It was more comfortable and warmer. "Here come Theo and Mary."

Theo was a replica of her older sisters the duchess and Lady Phinn, and Mary looked strongly like Eleanor and her other sisters.

"We realized we had not had a chance to speak with you," Mary said. He had a feeling she meant "interrogate him."

"Indeed." Theo nodded. "You are shortly to be a member of our family and we would like to know you better."

He spent the next several minutes explaining the size of all his estates and where they were located. He was surprised they had not asked what he grew.

"You like dogs,." Mary commented. "Posy licked you and you did not mind." She narrowed her eyes. "Did you?"

"No, not at all." Beside him, Eleanor seemed hard-pressed not to burst out laughing.

"Will Eleanor have her own carriage?" Theo asked. "All my other sisters have their own carriages."

John supposed Eleanor would like at least a landau or a barouche, and maybe a sporting carriage. "That is her decision. If she would like a carriage or two, she may have them."

"And horses as well?" Mary asked.

"That is quite enough." Eleanor gave them "the look."

"Very well." Mary raised her chin as if she had been insulted.

"In any event, Thorton is here." Eleanor tucked her arm in the crook of his elbow. "I would have stopped them before, but they would only have got you alone for their questioning."

They joined the line moving toward the dining room. "Do they do this with everyone?"

"Phinn was not around, but they did it with Con and Rothwell. Madeline, Alice, and I were Theo's age, and we joined in too."

"I knew you had an early start."

Eleanor grinned. "We were all precocious."

John did not doubt that at all. He had already noticed it with the younger children. "It must be a family trait."

He wanted children with her, and the sooner he could get started, the sooner they would come. Tomorrow seemed like a fine time to begin.

CHAPTER THIRTY-THREE

Eleanor woke the next day excited, but apprehensive as well. She was over thirty minutes early when she got to Matt's office, and she started to pace.

"Eleanor, sit." Matt motioned to the second chair behind his desk, which had been placed there for her.

She glanced at the clock. The man she was interviewing for the position of mine manager was due to arrive any time. "I am nervous."

"I don't know why you should be." Her brother by marriage stared at her. "You have been responsible for hiring servants and letting them go for well over two years now."

She stopped pacing but started playing with the fringe on her shawl. "Yes, but not alone."

He raised a brow. "Have we ever disagreed with your decisions?"

"No." No, they had not. "It does not feel the same. The mine is such a different sort of thing."

Matt leaned back against his chair. "May I remind you that you will soon be the mistress of several estates and two market towns?"

That had not seemed as daunting as this. Eleanor took

a breath, went behind the desk, and sank into the chair. "You are right. I have no good reason to be nervous." Yet she was. "I have arranged for tea to arrive when Mr. Russon and Edman are shown in."

Matt nodded. "I think that is a good decision."

"I am hoping it will put Mr. Russon at ease. I suppose he might never have visited the metropolis before."

A light tapping sounded on the door, and Matt slid his chair back as she moved her chair to the desk. They had decided that although he should be present, she must be seen to be in control. "Come."

Edman, Matt's steward from one of his secondary estates, who had agreed to work as her steward, entered first and bowed. He was followed by a man of about medium height, with dark brown hair and brown eyes. The man was younger than she had thought he would be. Mr. Russon could not have reached the age of forty. He bowed as well.

"Lady Eleanor, may I introduce Mr. Russon. Russon, Lady Eleanor Carpenter. She is the new owner of the mine."

"Mr. Russon, I am pleased to meet you." She pointed to the chair directly in front of the desk. "Please have a seat."

Mr. Russon bowed again. "Thank you, me lady."

Thorton brought the tea tray and set it down. "Gentlemen, how do you take your tea?"

"One sugar and milk, please," Edman said.

"The same, please." Mr. Russon appeared a bit unsettled but not that nervous. Eleanor was glad of that.

Once everyone had their cups of tea, she moved the employment contract from the side of the desk to the middle. "I chose to interview you for the position of mine manager because of your experience in mining, but also because of your interest in the welfare of the miners and their families." His eyes widened as if he was surprised. "I would like to develop the mine as a model. Much like Holkham Hall has been made into an experimental or model farm." He nodded. "Therefore, I wish to work with you in developing the best procedures for operating a mine and the best ways to support the families." She waited for him to speak, but he only nodded. Eleanor hoped he agreed with her. "I have some ideas, such as no child labor. They should attend school. And different working conditions for women." She smiled at him. "Please tell me your ideas."

He set his untouched teacup on the desk. "Me lady, you have good ideas. Safety is also important. There are shafts that need to be framed so the dirt don't bury the folks workin' below. We need pay that can't be taken away. And we need that our daughters and wives aren't . . . aren't"—he was clearly uncomfortable—"well, they just need to be left alone."

Eleanor bit the inside of her lip. Someone was molesting the females. That could not stand. "If you will tell me who has been harming the girls and women, I will have them removed immediately."

Mr. Russon's jaw dropped, but he quickly recovered. "It's Dobbins and his guards."

Dobbins? The blackguard is working at my mine?

Her jaw clenched as she glanced at Edman. "Immediately, Mr. Russon."

"Yes, me lady."

Looking back at Mr. Russon, she gave him an encouraging smile. "Please continue."

For the next hour they discussed living conditions and mine safety, as well as the futures of the children. Edman took notes as they spoke.

Finally, it appeared they had exhausted the subject, at least for now. "Is there anything else you would like to say?"

"Expect trouble, me lady." The lines around Mr. Russon's

mouth deepened. "Once it gets out, other operators aren't going to like it. They make a lot of money the way they are."

She inclined her head. "I am aware of the risk and have hired several former soldiers to guard the mine. You need not be afraid they will threaten you, your miners, or the women and children." Eleanor paused for a moment. "If any of them misbehave, send word directly to Mr. Edman. We will take care of the problem." She looked at the men. "Is there anything else we must discuss?"

Edman cleared his throat. "Might I suggest that we do not allow the current manager to linger in the area? I can arrange for the house he was provided to be packed and his personal belongings to be conveyed to a larger market town in the area. I would suggest replacing the furniture as well."

"An excellent idea." She had no idea of the dimensions of the house and its rooms, but she trusted he did. "I will leave it to you." There was one thing she had not asked. "Mr. Russon, are you married?"

To her surprise, he flushed. "Not yet, me lady. I'd talked to a woman's father, but then got let go."

"Your new position should settle that problem." She glanced at Edman. "Arrange for Mr. Russon to have tempo-rary lodgings while the house is being refurbished." She looked back at him. "Perhaps your betrothed will like to have a say in the furnishings."

"You don't have to do that, me lady."

"Mr. Russon, I am well aware that I do not. I, however, choose to do so." Edman put away his notebook. "If there is nothing else, I look forward to hearing about your progress."

The two men rose and bowed. Edman had a slight smile on his face. "Good day, my lady. It was a pleasure."

"A real pleasure, me lady." Mr. Russon grinned. "It's like you gave me my dream."

A feeling of accomplishment infused her. Still, she must remember this was an experiment. "I want this scheme to work, Mr. Russon. Make that happen and we will all be happy."

The door closed behind the men and Matt pulled his chair up to the desk. "Well done, Eleanor. I couldn't be prouder. You did a better job than most gentlemen would have done."

She appreciated his praise. "I daresay most gentlemen would not have interviewed a mine manager themselves."

"Even if they had, they wouldn't have offered the future Mrs. Russon the opportunity to select what she wanted for the house." He tugged the bell-pull. "What occupation do you have in mind for her?"

"I thought she could keep her ears open, as it were, for the families, and make sure their needs are met. Much as we do at Worthington Place." She glanced at the clock on the fireplace mantel. John would be here soon. She considered telling him about her mine but decided to wait until she had everything in place. It would be a much bigger surprise. He would be thrilled to discover they owned a model mine. Everything should be in place by the end of the Season. They could visit the Cornflower Hill Mine on their way to his—their—main estate after their honeymoon.

John fetched Eleanor thirty minutes before their appointment with the decorationist. She was coming down the stairs as he entered the hall. The pale yellow of her carriage gown showed off her creamy complexion, and the small chip bonnet did nothing to hide her golden hair. "You look enchanting."

Smiling, she took his arm, and they walked out of the house. "You look quite handsome. Are you excited to meet the decorationist?"

He was excited for a chance to get her in his bed. "I am happy to meet anyone who can help us change the colors in our house."

"Mrs. Rollins will do that. We meet with the architect tomorrow. Did I mention they are a married couple?"

"No." He was surprised the person doing the work was a woman. "Did they meet while working on a house?"

"I have no idea." He assisted Eleanor into his curricle. Once he was settled, he started the horses. "The only thing I know about her personal life is that her father is a merchant. Mr. Rollins's father is a vicar. The fourth or fifth son of a baron, and he is the third son of his parents."

Therefore, Rollins must make his own way. John wondered what the man's family had thought of him marrying into the merchant class. Then again, what did it matter? The world was changing. There would come a day when bloodlines would not mean as much. "How does this process work?"

"I know what I want for the general color scheme and have an idea of the patterns I like. She will make sketches, giving us a picture of what my ideas will look like when a room is finished. I think it's very helpful that she and her husband work closely together."

He drove into the mews behind Montagu House. "I thought you might like to see the garden. You can also take a look at the stables, if you wish."

"I would." She waited for him to lift her from the carriage. "I only got a glimpse of the garden yesterday."

Mindful of the stable servants, he resisted the urge to skim his hands under her breasts. "You will like our stable master."

The older servant appeared immediately. "I would have been happy to send a groom round to fetch the pair, my lord."

"I know you would have." He turned to Eleanor. "May I introduce Fitch, the stable master? Fitch, my betrothed, Lady Eleanor Carpenter."

"My lady"—Fitch bowed—"thank you for coming to see the stables." John didn't think he'd ever seen Fitch bow before. "I'll get the rest of the grooms and coachmen."

Getting the rest of the servants consisted of walking to the stable doors and shouting for them.

Chuckling softly, Eleanor glanced at John. "And that is the difference between indoor servants and outdoor servants."

It only took a matter of a few minutes for the rest of the stable staff to be made known to her. Afterward, they toured the stable and attached carriage house. "As you see, there is enough room for more horses and carriages."

"It is quite large." She looked at Fitch. "And very well maintained. I am confident my horse and groom will be very happy here."

He nodded. "We'll be happy to meet them both, my lady."

"Tomorrow, I had planned to bring my dresser and footman to meet the household staff. If you do not mind, I will bring my groom as well."

"We'll make him feel right at home," Fitch said.

"My love." John took her hand. "We must be going if you are going to see the garden before Mrs. Rollins arrives."

"Yes, of course." She smiled at Fitch, who appeared almost

starstruck. "It was delightful meeting you. I am not a stranger to the stables."

"You're welcome anytime, my lady." Fitch beamed.

They strolled across the alley and John opened the gate. "You have a devoted follower."

"I am just someone new." The corners of her lips rose. "In no time at all he will be treating me as if he taught me to ride my first pony."

"That is certainly how he treats my sister and me. Of course, he did teach us how to ride."

"It does form a special bond." She laughed. "And an ingrained feeling they can treat one like a child anytime they please." Eleanor stopped and surveyed the garden. "This is beautiful. I love how natural the flower beds are, and how the trees on the shared wall give one privacy." She turned around. "That path looks like it is part of a woodland walk. Where does it lead?"

"A rose arbor and a small fountain." He hadn't been there in years, but John had a feeling that would soon change. "There is a bench as well. Is there anything you would like to change?"

"No." She took his hand again. "I like it a great deal."

A few minutes later they met with Mrs. Rollins. She was a cheery woman with light brown hair pulled into a low knot. "Lady Eleanor, I have not seen you since you were much younger."

"It is good to see you again." They shook hands. "I am so glad you were able to see the house so quickly."

She immediately set about making notes and sketches of the rooms he and Eleanor showed her. They entered the morning room and she cringed. "All new wall coverings and hangings, I take it."

Eleanor nodded. "Some of the furniture may remain, but most of it will need to be recovered."

"I quite agree." Mrs. Rollins glanced at him. "I'm sorry, my lord, but it looks as if the whole house was done up for mourning."

He only nodded. It had seemed like that to him as well. "I trust between the two of you, our home will be a much nicer place to live."

"To be sure it will be." She followed Eleanor into the music room. "How long will you be away after your wedding?"

"Three weeks." Eleanor had been gazing out the window, where climbing rosebushes were just starting to show their buds. "I would like to bring the colors of the flowers into this room."

Mrs. Rollins made some notes. "I will ask the head gardener what flowers were used for the bed under the roses."

They finally ended up in John's bedroom. He could already see how much brighter the house would feel when it was finished.

"Where do you want the bathing chamber?" Mrs. Rollins asked.

His betrothed frowned. "We forgot to discuss that part."

"We will need to know by tomorrow." She put her pads in a large satchel. "I shall leave you now to work it out. Ideally, it should be near the servants' stairs for the access to the kitchen or cellar." He must have looked confused because she added, "Pipes."

"Of course. Shall I walk you out?" John asked

"Thank you, my lord, but that is not necessary." She picked up her bag. "I will be in and out of here a great deal.

It would be a nuisance for both of us if I had to be escorted around."

"I see what you mean." She left the room, closing the door behind her and leaving him alone with Eleanor. "What shall we do now?"

She smiled slowly. "I think I might have an idea or two."

Good Lord. Was she really thinking what he was?

CHAPTER THIRTY-FOUR

So far, things were working out better than she had expected. Eleanor had had her dresser put her hair up in a simple knot and worn a gown with buttons down the back. She took off the light spencer, laying it across the back of a wooden chair. John stared at her and swallowed. "Where is your valet?"

"I gave him a half day off. He won't be back until it's time for me to dress for the ball." He sauntered over to her as she reached up to take the pins out of her hair. "Allow me. I've been wanting to touch your hair since the first time I saw you."

This was the thing that kept drawing her to him. The passion that sizzled between them. "Do not lose the hairpins."

Bending his head, he pressed his firm lips to hers, and she opened her mouth. Their tongues tangled as he walked her back toward the bed. Tress by tress, her hair fell over her shoulders and down her back.

He threaded his fingers through her hair. "Beautiful and so soft. I want to see the rest of you."

"I have the same thoughts about you." Eleanor untied his cravat and pulled it off. At the same time her bodice started to gape.

John shrugged out of his jacket as she unbuttoned his waistcoat. Her gown dropped to her hips. He cupped her cheeks in his hands, and fissions of pleasure shot through her body as he kissed her.

"Stays," he grumbled.

She grinned against his strong, lean neck. "Short stays."

They dropped to her hips, bunching her gown. It made a soft, swishing sound as it traveled over her legs. His fingers skimmed over her breasts, and her nipples turned into tight buds. "That is much better."

Eleanor's breath caught when her chemise floated to the floor, and his bare hands touched her. She tugged his shirt out of his trousers and pushed it up. His torso was much more muscular than she had expected it to be. Soft, auburn hair covered his chest, and she ran her fingers through it. John groaned and lifted her into his arms, gently placing her on the bed. "Shoes."

John took his off before removing hers. When she reached for her garter, he stayed her. "Leave them on." Fire lurked in his eyes as he gazed at her. "I love you."

"I love you too." His trousers dropped to the floor and the only thing Eleanor could see was his appendage. Thankfully she had been warned. Dragging her gaze back to his face, she held out her arms. "Come to me."

He crawled onto the bed gracefully and covered her. Her body thrummed with desire and need. Soon he was kissing her again, and fires lit every time and every place their bodies touched. She had thought she was hot the last time, but it had been nothing like this. His lips moved from hers to her breasts, laving her tight buds. She squirmed beneath him, wanted more, wanting the relief she had the last time. Then his tongue touched her thighs, and lightning shot through her. "John, please."

"Soon my love." His mouth moved higher until it covered her pearl.

Of their own volition, her hips rose. His fingers entered her sheath and the tension she'd been feeling broke, shattering into a million pieces. She was still convulsing when he broke through her maiden head. She bit back a scream.

"Did it hurt badly?" His voice was full of concern.

"I will be fine. Just give me a moment." Gradually the pain and burning eased, and she moved against him.

He took the cue and moved as well. Soon the heat began to build again. He pulled back and thrust forward. "Wrap your legs around me."

She did as he said and immediately felt the difference. The fires built again, and soon waves of pleasure swept over her. His mouth covered hers as she started to call out.

Thank God she had come.

John thrust twice more, spilling his seed into her. She was his as much as he was hers. Rolling off her, he gathered Eleanor into his arms and nuzzled her hair. If only they could stay here the rest of the day and night. Her arm crossed his chest as her head lay on his shoulder. She fit perfectly.

Rousing herself, she kissed his chest. "It did not hurt that badly, and the end was very fine. Like a Catherine wheel. I suppose we must move soon."

"Not yet." He kissed the top of her head, breathing in the scent of lemons. "We still have to decide where to put our bathing chamber."

She rearranged herself and looked up at him. "We can rearrange the rooms. I would like to keep the parlor and the dressing room, but there is no reason why we should sleep apart."

Her words struck him. His mother had always had her own bedchamber. He didn't know, quite frankly didn't want to know, how often his parents slept together. "No reason at all. We will have to move some walls."

"That is not much of a problem. I will choose one of the parlors for my study."

He remembered Lady Worthington's study was used for family meetings. John liked that idea. It wasn't nearly as intimidating as his father's or Worthington's study. "That's a good idea." He turned his head to see the mantel clock. Damn. "We must dress if we are not to be late to dinner."

Pushing against him, she sat up. "Leave a note for your valet to bring your clothing to Worthington House. You may change there."

He pulled her down to him and kissed her. "Don't forget. Tonight I get every waltz."

Eleanor leaned back against the pillows. Her hair curled around her and she had a soft smile on her rosy lips. "Every one of them. I am glad we found each other."

He traced her lips, then kissed her again. "I am too."

She started to rise. "I must clean myself."

"Allow me." He climbed out of the bed and went to the washstand and dipped the linen cloth in the water. At least his dark counterpane wouldn't show the blood. Going back to Eleanor, he cleaned her, then helped her to her feet. "Shall I play lady's maid?"

"If you wouldn't mind."

They dressed quickly, then hurried down the servants' stairs to the morning room and through the garden to the mews. John listened as she chatted with his stable master about her mare while the curricle was being readied. He didn't know how he'd got so lucky to have her, but nothing was going to separate them now.

Cornflower Hill Mine

"Dobbins."

Fred Dobbins turned to look at the man who'd called his name. Kitching was Dobbins's contact with the company that operated the mine. He liked that the man left him alone to run the operation as he saw fit. "Mr. Kitching, what can I do fer you?" There was a scowl on his face as he walked past Dobbins into the office. "Is something wrong?"

"I received a letter the other day from the company that there would be some changes."

Dobbins didn't like changes. "I thought the company was happy with the way I ran the mine." Sure, he managed to make a little extra and made sure the women he wanted knew their jobs depended on pleasing him. But everyone did that. "What happened?"

"The property was in trust. It's now been turned over to the owner."

"Why would that matter? Don't the contract say the owner don't have nothing to do with what we do?"

Kitching nodded. "Normally that would be the case. However, because the property was in trust, the lease on this mine was always a shorter period of time than most."

Dobbins scratched his head. "Are they closing it?"

"No. Worse." The man's scowl deepened. "They're making it into a so-called 'model mine.'"

"A what?" He'd never heard of such a thing.

"They're going to change how the mine's run based on the ideas of the people who want to reform the mines."

"Reformers?" Dobbins almost spat on the floor. "What do we do to stop it?"

"There's nothing to be done. The arrangements have been made."

"I won't do it. We do just fine here without anyone's

interference." The door opened and Russon, a miner Dobbins had fired, strolled in like he owned the place. A tall man followed him. "What the hell are you doing here? Get out before I have my men help you leave." He turned to look at the other man. "Who are you?"

"Dobbins." There was a warning in Kitching's voice. "This is Mr. Edman. He represents the new owner."

An ill feeling settled in Dobbin's stomach and he glanced at Russon. "You ain't gone yet?"

Russon just stood there, arms crossed over his chest. For as mouthy as the rabble-rouser usually was, that was more than passing strange.

"Mr. Russon will not be leaving," the new man said. "Kitching, have you not told him yet?"

Kitching almost pulled his forelock. Dobbins had never seen him act that way. "I was just getting to it." Kitching looked at Dobbins. "The thing is, you're being let go. The company will pay you one month's wages because it's been so sudden. But you have to leave today."

Edman inclined his head. "I have made arrangements for you to travel to the market town and paid for a room for you there. You will have a few days to decide where you want to go."

Anger overcame Dobbins's sick stomach. "Who's taking over?"

"I am," Russon said.

Dobbins fisted his hands.

"I would not do that if I were you," Edman drawled like some nob. "Not unless you would like to spend the next month or so in gaol."

It was clear to Dobbins the man meant it. He needed more time to think, to work things out. To find a way to keep his job. "I can't get packed up in a day."

Edman took out a pocket watch and flipped open the lid. "You won't have to worry about that. By the time you arrive at the inn, your personal items will be there. You will be allowed to take the furniture as well. That's being moved and will be kept in storage for you."

"It's a good deal," Kitching said. "Just do what he's telling you to do. It won't go well if you make trouble."

Dobbins knew the man was right. It just riled him that he didn't have a say. He gave a sharp nod. "I'll go." He glared at Russon. "But you won't do better with him in charge."

"Be that as it may, the decision's been made." Edman walked to the door and opened it. "Good luck to you."

He walked out of the office and looked around. None of his lads were there. Instead, there were strangers. "Where are my men?"

"Gone," a tall man who looked like a soldier said. "They've been reassigned."

Shite! They still got jobs and he didn't. Someone was going to pay for that. He'd teach the reformer not to mess with his business. First Dobbins had to find him. And he'd have to be careful. Wouldn't do for word to get back to that steward he was lookin' for the owner. But someone who knew one of the servants at the manor house, or maybe one of the townspeople might know the name of the owner. Once he found the man, he'd make sure things went back to the way they were.

The next week was so busy, Eleanor did not know in which direction she was going most of the time. When she was not at fittings, or choosing luggage, or doing other shopping, she was at Montagu House consulting with the Rollinses. She had been pleased that Jobert, Turner, and

Jemmy, her groom, seemed to be getting on well with the Montagu staff.

She was frowning over the nursery and schoolroom floor plans when John was announced.

He strolled over to her. "What are you doing?"

"Trying to decide how to arrange the schoolroom and nursery." She rolled up the plans and grabbed his hand. "Come with me."

He let her drag him up to the nursery. "This is nice." John walked around, looking at everything. "It's much nicer than ours was." He flashed her a grin. "But you know that. It's why we're here."

"I am considering using the design Grace used for this house and Stanwood House." She took his hand again. "Take a look at the schoolroom."

Once again he walked around, looking into the various rooms. "There is even a bathing chamber and a music room."

"She planned for everything. At the time the renovations were done, Charlotte was making her come out. It would have been mad for her to practice and to find time for Mary, Alice, and me to practice as well. Then, when she married Matt, we added Augusta, Madeline, and Louisa."

He nodded distractedly. "It is amazing how light these rooms are." Once he had finished his tour, he glanced at her. "If you wish to do the same thing at Montagu House, tell Rollins that's what you want."

"The only problem is that this is a great deal of room, and we have no idea how many children we'll have."

"That's true." He surveyed the area again. "But it is better to have the space and not use it. or make some small changes, than not have the room." John drew Eleanor into his arms. "Aside from that, any children of ours will have cousins who will visit."

"I suppose." She pressed kisses on his jaw.

He lifted her chin and kissed her. "Speaking of children, where is everyone?"

"The babies are outside. I am not certain where the others are. But neither Mr. Winters nor Mrs. Winters are here. There must be an outing."

John slid his hand down her back to the top of her buttock. "It's a shame we are not at Montagu House."

Embers were already starting to come to life as he continued his caresses. But she did not dare suggest they make love here. "I am sure there is something I must do over there."

"Some wallpaper samples arrived. You really should take a look at them." His teeth gently scraped her ear.

"I must. I'll call for your carriage to be brought around."

"No need. I came to fetch you so that you can make a decision about them and speak to the chef Jacques is sending over."

That was like a splash of cold water. "Why was I not told before now?"

"I got word he was available to see us and came straightaway."

"Let us be off." She did not want their potential cook to leave before they arrived.

They entered through the French windows in the morning room and found Lumner in the hall. "The man for the cook's position is here in the kitchen. Would you like to have him sent to you?"

"No, thank you." Eleanor had already decided she wanted to speak with him in the kitchen. It was important to see how he got along with the staff. "Is Sissy there as well?"

"Yes, my lady."

"Excellent." John held open the green baize door. She went through it and down the stairs.

When they arrived Sissy was showing the man around. "My lady." She curtseyed. "This is Guillaume"—she stumbled over the name, and Eleanor was pleased to see he took it good-naturedly—"Martin for the chef position."

He bowed. "It is a pleasure, my lady, my lord. My uncle Jacques said you required a chef de cuisine. I have been working under . . ."

By the time he had finished telling them his qualifications, Eleanor had decided to hire him. For a week now, poor Rennie had been responsible for seeing the household was fed. As good as Sissy's baked goods were, one could only eat so many of them.

She had had the forethought to have a copy of Jacques's contract delivered to Montagu House so it could work as the basis for the new cook's contract. She discussed the terms with Guillaume, as he preferred to be called, and he agreed. "When can you start?"

"If you like, my lady, I will bring my belongings here today and I will begin tomorrow morning. I would ask that additional kitchen workers be hired."

She was glad he had not seen the kitchen as it had looked before. "I agree. The contract will be ready to be signed."

She and John used the servants' stairs to reach his study. The second they entered, he picked her up and twirled her around. "We have a cook! The only problem is that I will no longer have an excuse to dine at Worthington House."

"Perhaps your mother can invite my family to dine here."

John laughed. "That is a wonderful idea." He pressed his lips to hers. "Now, decide on the coverings and we can find something else to occupy our time."

The best part of her day was when she and John could sneak off to what would be their bedchamber and make love.

CHAPTER THIRTY-FIVE

Three days before the wedding, Eleanor went to look in on her twin. Alice had been in bed with a head cold for the past five days. "Are you feeling any better?"

"A little." She sneezed into her handkerchief. "Grace says seven days."

"She would know." She had taken care of all of them for years. "You must be well by my wedding. I need you with me."

"I will be. If you are going shopping, will you stop by Hatchards and pick up the books I ordered? They should be in."

"Of course." Eleanor could also find something to cheer her sister up. "You drink your barley water."

"I will." Alice picked up the glass and took a sip. "At least this tastes good. Much better than the gruel Nurse insisted I have."

Eleanor shuddered at the thought of having to consume gruel. "It would be worth it never to be ill just to avoid that."

A knock sounded on the door and Walter poked his head in the room. "There you are." He glanced at Alice. "Feeling any better?"

"A little." She nodded.

"That's good." Walter glanced at Eleanor. "I have something for you."

"What is it?"

"You'll see." Taking her hand, he pulled her out of the room and down the corridor. "Charlie mentioned that he and Matt had warned you to take extra care because of the mine. So I thought if men can have sword sticks, why can't a lady have a sword parasol? I went to Wilkinson's, and it turns out he's made them before. I think it works well." He went into his chambers and brought out a parasol covered with a heavy cotton in Pomona Green. "You can always change the fabric. Let me show you how it works." He held up the handle that had a button on it. "Press this, like so." A lethal blade poked out of the tip of the parasol. "The ribs are a bit sturdier than a normal parasol."

Eleanor took it from him. "How do I get the sword back inside?"

"This lever. Most of them have to be taken out of the parasol, but I thought it might take too long, so we came up with this design."

"This is ingenious." She threw her arms around him. "Thank you! You picked a lovely color as well." She and her sisters had all had fencing lessons and were familiar with the proper method of thrusting. The parasol could not be used in an actual sword fight, but it could be used to gain enough time to get out of a bad situation. Not that she thought one would occur. She was sure the parasol would be more of an interesting item to have. "I am going shopping soon, but I think I shall practice before I leave."

After telling Turner they would depart in about a half hour, she spent the time working with her sword parasol until she was finally comfortable using the controls and quickly thrusting with it. Donning her bonnet, Eleanor went to the hall, where her footman was waiting.

"The town coach is waiting, my lady."

"Thank you. I do not have much to buy, but I told my sister I would stop at Hatchards." It was a lovely day. There was no real reason to take the coach. "We should walk."

Turner stared down at the floor and mumbled something.

"I did not hear you."

"His lordship said if you were going alone you had to take the coach."

She did not know if Matt was simply being cautious and the rule applied to all of them, or if there really might be a threat of some sort. Either way, there was no point arguing with her footman. He could not countermand Matt's orders and neither could she. "Very well. The coach it is."

London was every bit as dirty and smelly as Dobbins had heard, but this was where Lady Eleanor Carpenter was. She'd took away his woman, and now his job. This time he'd stop her. He found a room over a pub not far from a place called Covent Garden. Finding men to scare her enough to change the mine back to the way it'd been wasn't as hard as finding who owned it in the first place. There were lots of people here lookin' for work. He'd hired a boy to watch the house she lived in and see where she went. It'd be easier and safer to get her on a busy street than near her house. The next time she went to Bond Street he'd nab her. Once she was gone everything'd go back to normal.

"Sir." The boy he'd hired to watch Lady Eleanor came running up. "She's on her way to shopp'en." It was good fortune the woman went to the same places all the time, and in the same order.

"Good lad." Dobbins flipped him a coin. "Keep an eye

out." He waited for the boy to leave and sent one of the other lads hangin' around the inn to get his men. Dobbins had taken the one called Mickey with him to look for a likely place and they found an alley between two of the shops she went to. "Won't be long now."

Eleanor's town coach drove out of Berkley Square onto Bruton Street, where she stopped at Madame Lisette's for a fitting. From there, as Eleanor would normally do with her sisters, she walked on to Bond Street, with Turner behind her and the coach traveling as close to them as possible given the busy street. She glanced over her shoulder at Turner. "One more stop before Hatchards."

"Very well, my lady."

Eleanor turned onto Old Bond Street and went into a toyshop the family frequented. She found wooden ducks on wheels her younger niece and nephew would like. "Could you send these to Worthington House in Berkeley Square?"

"Of course, my lady." The clerk began wrapping the toys.

"Thank you." She left the store and suddenly had a feeling something was not right. She had always been told to listen to her inner voice. Tightening her grip on her parasol, she continued toward Piccadilly.

"My lady, on the left!" Turner shouted, and a pistol shot went off.

A burly man rushed out of a narrow alley between the buildings. Eleanor had just enough time as he reached for her to shove the parasol between them, press the button, and thrust. His scream filled the air.

"Good Lord!" A constable ran up. "What's going on here?"

"Clearly, an attack on this lady." Lady Bellamny rushed to Eleanor. "Are you all right, my girl?"

"I cannot believe a lady could be attacked in the middle

of the day!" A woman Eleanor had never seen before glared at the constable. "Your people must do a better job!"

A crowd was forming as she glanced at one ruffian on the ground with a bullet hole in him and the other man bleeding from her sword parasol. Her hands trembled slightly. "I will be fine."

Her ladyship looked down her nose at the blackguards before turning back to Eleanor. "You did well. Is that a new style of sword parasol?"

She dragged her gaze away from the criminals and all the blood. "It is. My brother Walter had it made for me."

"It is very effective." Lady Bellamny nodded approvingly.

Another constable had joined them and dashed off again to get a conveyance for the wounded criminals. "I will need a statement."

"What the de-deuce is going on?" John reached for her. "Thank God I came this way. Eleanor, are you hurt?"

"I will be fine." The number of people suddenly there was making it hard to breathe.

He took her arm, tucking it in his.

Lady Bellamny poked the constable with her cane. "You need to find out what they were after. I saw the whole thing and will give you a statement. Bellamny House on Upper Brook Street. You may wait upon me there." She turned to Eleanor and John. "Come along, you two. There is no need to be the subject of the curious. Where were you going?"

Eleanor was suddenly sluggish. As if she was underwater and couldn't seem to see or hear well, but her ladyship's brisk, no-nonsense tone brought her about. "To Hatchards."

"Be on your way."

John glared at her ladyship. "I should take her home."

Lady Bellamny narrowed her eyes. "You will do exactly what I am telling you to do. I shall come by later."

Eleanor tugged John's arm. "Let us go."

"What happened?"

"I was attacked. Turner saw them come out of the alley and shouted. He shot the first blackguard and I turned just in time to use my sword parasol on the other. Matt was right when he warned there might be repercussions because of the mine."

"What mine?" John's tone was low but had become more of a growl.

"My mine. I was going to tell you, but I wanted to wait until everything was in place." This was one piece of good news. "I discovered I had inherited an estate with a mine operating on part of it. I decided to make it into a model mine. We finished the arrangements not quite two weeks ago."

His jaw hardened and he stared at her with a stern look. "Eleanor, no. I won't have it. You will give the operation back to the mining concern immediately. I will not have your life in danger for an experiment."

He would not what?

A surge of anger rushed through her. She stopped walking and stared up at him. She had to have heard him incorrectly. "I beg your pardon. Surely you did not just say what I thought I heard. '*You* won't have it?' Let me tell you, my lord, that it is my property, and under the settlement agreements it will remain my property, and I will run it the way I see fit."

His face flushed and his eyes bore into her. "You will be my wife and will do what I say."

If he'd slapped her, she could not have been more shocked. How could she have been so wrong about him? If he changed his mind at the first sign of a little trouble, she could not trust him. "In that case, perhaps we should not be wed. You clearly want a wife who is more malleable than I." Eleanor glanced over her shoulder. "Turner."

"Right here, my lady."

The footman gave John a sympathetic look as he hurried after her.

Bloody hellhounds!

He raked his finger through his hair, knocking off his hat.

Hell and damnation!

She was stubborn and willful—the sight of the ruffian bleeding from her sword had scared him to death—and too damn brave. She had to understand that he could not allow her to—to do what? Protect herself? Still, if she hadn't decided to interfere with a mining operation, she would not have been in danger. Noticing he was still walking toward Hatchards, he turned around. It was one thing for a group of gentlemen to change how a mine operated. But a lady? And a young lady at that? Yet that was not how she had been raised. How was he going to keep her safe? Then part of what she said finally sank in. Had Eleanor just called off the wedding? She could not. She might be carrying his child.

This couldn't be happening. He needed her. He needed to think. John headed home but found his mother and sister in the hall when he arrived. That reminded him that Aurelia had given Eleanor the mining information. "Well, well, look who we have here. My sister. The person who just got my betrothed"—if she was still his betrothed—"attacked."

Rather than beg his pardon, she turned on him and poked a finger in his chest. "Have you gone mad? What happened to Eleanor, and why would you think I had anything to do with it?"

This was too much. "You were the one who gave her the information on the mines, and she decided to take one and make it a model based on those damned pamphlets you gave her. Now two criminals just tried to attack her."

Aurelia's chin rose. "I gave her the information because

she asked for it. What I want to know is how she came by a mine."

"She inherited one." This conversation was not going at all the way it should. "What do you mean, she asked for the information?"

"Dear," his mother said. "Let us go to the morning room and you can explain everything to us in a calm manner."

"I don't want to go to the morning room and I am anything but calm. If she hadn't stabbed one of them, she would have been killed!"

"Oh, good Lord," Aurelia huffed. "We will get nothing from him. I'm going to see Eleanor. If she had the presence of mind to wound a criminal, she will be able to explain the situation better than he is doing."

His sister strode out the door and Mama donned her hat. "Your sister is right. You need to compose yourself. I will see you later."

He needed a brandy. A whole bottle of brandy.

CHAPTER THIRTY-SIX

Eleanor lingered at Hatchards, collecting her sister's books and searching for some of her own. She had to think about her future. There was no point in remaining in Town. Grace would agree Eleanor could return home within the next few days.

Turner helped her into the coach. By the time she arrived at Worthington House, Lady Bellamny, Lady Montagu, and Lady Lytton were there with Grace, Matt, Kenilworth, Rothwell, and Merton.

Her sister quickly rose from the sofa and came to her. "Eleanor, are you well?"

"Yes." Eleanor nodded. At least she thought she was. "I was a bit shaky at first, but Lady Bellamny was so matter-of-fact, I felt myself again." Eleanor looked around her sister. "Thank you, my lady."

"You are welcome, my dear. No one died, and as far as I could see, there was no reason to go into hysterics about the matter. The blackguards have been arrested and taken in. If they are smart, which I will depend upon, they will confess who hired them."

"There are ways to provide inducements," Matt said in a grim tone.

Lady Lytton pressed her lips together for a moment. "Was all this caused by the pamphlets I gave you?"

"No, of course not. Whatever"—Eleanor studied her ladyship's face for a second—"or should I say, whoever gave you that thought? I would have acquired them myself, eventually."

Her ladyship rose. "That is all I wanted to know. I am glad you were not injured, and I am really very interested in your sword parasol, but perhaps not today." She turned to her mother. "Mama, are you ready to leave?"

"Yes, dear." She rose from the sofa. "I have some choice words for a certain male child of mine."

At the mention of Montagu, tears pricked Eleanor's eyes. She was not going to cry. Yet she must tell her family she now knew he was not the man she thought he was. "I have decided Lord Montagu and I do not suit. I am going to my chamber."

"I will go with her," Grace said, and Eleanor was glad. She needed to talk with someone.

Matt stared at the door as it closed behind his wife and sister. Lady Bellamny had informed them of what had occurred. Then Lady Montagu and Lady Lytton told them Montagu had been in a towering rage and blamed his sister for the attack on Eleanor. The question they must deal with now was what to do about the idiot's behavior and Eleanor's refusal to marry him because of it. Matt had no doubt his sister and Montagu had been intimate. Unfortunately, in this family that became a minor event when a gentleman became a tyrant. Left to the ladies, Eleanor would be sent abroad to travel or some other such thing. It was up to Matt to try to get the couple back together again in time for the wedding.

He turned to his cousin and brothers-in-law. "Does anyone want to take a wild guess at what Montagu said to her?"

Kenilworth's elbows were on the chair arms and he pressed the tip of one finger to his mouth. "I think it will have been along the lines of telling her she can no longer have anything to do with the mine. And she will do as he says."

"At least I wasn't that stupid," Rothwell mused.

Of course he almost lost Louisa by *not* telling her what she needed to know.

Kenilworth strolled over to the sideboard and held up a decanter of wine. "One of us has to talk to him."

Matt nodded, and his old friend handed him a glass of his own wine. "It must be someone who behaved in the same fashion and understands what Montagu is suffering."

Rothwell took a glass of claret as well. "That would not be me."

"No." Matt took a sip of wine. "Nor me, nor Kenilworth. Merton."

He took a glass from Kenilworth. "Yes, I'll do it.

Rothwell saluted Merton with his glass. "Groveling will be required."

"You're still not over that?" Kenilworth quipped. "I'm certain the rest of us have recovered from our groveling."

Rothwell looked into his wineglass, then twirled it. "I may never be over it. Dukes aren't supposed to grovel."

"They are when they want to keep their duchesses." Matt saluted their family duke with the wine, then took a drink. "This had better work."

"What do we do if it doesn't?" Rothwell asked.

Matt had no idea. "One problem at a time."

Merton tossed off his glass and stood. "There is no time like the present. He should be in his remorseful stage about now."

* * *

John was in his study, staring at the decanter of brandy he'd had his butler bring him. The wedding was only a few days away and he was going to lose Eleanor. She was not the type of lady who would wed him if she thought he'd make her miserable. Worst of all, he didn't know what to do to make things better. After his initial rage had subsided, he realized he had acted out of fear. What he'd said was bound to drive her away, and it *had* been inexcusable. If only he'd stopped to think before he'd spoken.

Lumner opened the door. "The Marquis of Merton to see you, my lord. I shall bring a tea tray."

This was it. His lordship had most likely come to tell John his betrothal was over. "Merton, what brings you here?"

The man strolled into the room and fixed a stern look on John. "I am here to help. It was decided that I was the one with an experience closest to your own."

What the hell did that mean? "Please have a seat. Brandy?"

"No, thank you. And I suggest you would be much better drinking tea."

They waited in uncomfortable silence until the tray arrived. Once the door closed, Merton began, "I am going to assume that Eleanor was threatened and you panicked and said things you should not have said. Am I correct?"

"I saw the blood on her parasol and on the man lying on the ground." John raked his fingers through his hair. "All I could think of was that she could have died."

"Let me tell you a story. Thea—Dotty, as you have no doubt heard her called—and I were betrothed when I discovered she was involved in trying to rescue a young boy from a very, shall we say, unsavory group of criminals. I was firmly against her involvement. She made clear to me that she was going to do what she thought right no matter what I said. I might have responded with something like she was my wife and would do what I said. She took the opportunity to remind me we were not yet wed." He took a sip of tea John had poured. "Needless to say, it caused a rather serious rift."

That sounded exactly like what had happened between Eleanor and him. "What was the resolution?"

"I ceased trying to stop her and helped her instead." Merton picked up his cup. "Ultimately, I found her work most rewarding. Of course I also had to admit I was wrong and beg her to forgive me for being an idiot." He took a few sips of tea. "That was the hardest part. It was quite lowering to discover I was not always right."

"I don't understand why Worthington would allow her to involve herself in something dangerous."

"My dear man. Has no one told you that she is followed by an armed footman, or that she and her sisters have been trained with pistols, swords, and knives?"

John shook his head. Now he really did feel like an idiot. "Will she speak with me?" John wasn't sure he'd speak with himself under the circumstances.

"I think she will." Merton lifted a brow. "There is only one way to find out."

"I'll go now." His guest looked pointedly at the carafe of brandy. "I didn't drink any of it."

Merton nodded. "Be prepared to grovel."

"I understand." John left the room. He decided walking would give him time to plan what he'd say to her to convince her to marry him. Unfortunately, he had no idea what to do if she refused to see him or rejected his apology. After Kenilworth told John how the family had stood with Charlotte after he'd inadvertently compromised her, he didn't think telling Worthington Eleanor might be with child would help matters. He straightened his shoulders. One of the things he'd have to do was promise never to act the tyrant with her again. He just hoped she'd believe him.

He arrived at Worthington House and handed the butler

his hat. For a second, he thought the man was going to hand it back. "I am here to see Lady Eleanor."

The butler looked at a spot over John's left shoulder. "I shall inquire as to whether she is in." Thorton pointed to a footman. "Please show his lordship into the blue parlor."

John followed the footman down the corridor to a room that had only one piece of furniture that was blue. At least he wasn't being put in the front parlor. That would have meant they did not expect him to stay long. A few minutes later, tea and some tarts were brought to him, but his stomach roiled and he couldn't make himself eat or drink anything. Instead, he stared out the window.

Sometime later—there was no clock in the room, and he'd forgotten to look at his pocket watch—the door opened. He touched the ring he'd brought with him and turned, hoping to see Eleanor, but it was Worthington.

John's heart dropped to his stomach. It was as if a part of him was withering away. "She has refused to see me."

"No. She has been with Grace, and I believe she will allow you to apologize." He raised one dark brow. "There are only two days before the wedding. You had better succeed. I know what happens when a couple in love are renovating a house."

Despite the veiled threat, John had never been so happy in his life. Eleanor was giving him another chance. "Thank you."

"I knew this had been too easy." With that cryptic remark, Worthington left the parlor.

Despite telling herself Montagu was not worth crying over, Eleanor, for some reason, wept anyway while trying to tell Grace what he had said.

"I understand why you are upset enough to break the

betrothal, but have you thought he might have been frightened as well?"

Eleanor was not going to forgive him that easily. "In that case, he should have said that instead of telling me I had to give up what I have been working to achieve."

Her sister sighed. "I seem to recall having this very same discussion with Dotty when Merton overreacted to her being threatened. Montagu will come to see you. Do you think you can listen to what he has to say?"

A vague memory of Dotty being furious with Merton rose in Eleanor's mind. "I wonder what he said to change her mind."

"Will you speak with him?" Grace repeated.

"Assuming he does promise not to behave like a tyrant, I do not know if I can believe him."

She put her arm around Eleanor's shoulders. "Has he done anything like this previously?"

"No. But nothing like this has happened before."

"From what I have seen, men—and women as well—who are prone to this type of behavior do so without being prodded. It is their personality. Do you remember why no one on the Vivers side liked Merton?"

Eleanor nodded. "Because he tried to tell everyone what to do."

"Precisely." Grace gave her a sympathetic look. "But he was never actually a tyrant because as much as his uncle tried to make him into one, he was not made that way."

"You are saying that Montagu might not actually be a tyrant."

"Well, you have seen how his sister and mother react to him. They are not at all afraid of what he might do."

That was true. "He still must apologize to me."

"Not only that, he must not try to blame you," Grace

said. "He must take responsibility for his own regrettable behavior."

Eleanor blew her nose. When he came she did not want him to know she had been crying. "I should put a cold cloth on my eyes."

A few minutes later a knock came on the door, and Matt strolled in. "Are you feeling better?"

"I am." She was not sure how much the compress had helped. Cucumbers would have been better.

"Montagu is here. He would like to speak with you." Matt took her hand and squeezed it. "Are you ready to listen to him?"

She rose from her bed and tried to shake out her skirts, but they were so creased it did not do any good. "I shall have to change."

"I'll let him know you will be a little while." He kissed Grace on the cheek before he walked out the door.

She rang the bellpull, and before long Jobert came into the room carrying a Pomona green gown. One of Eleanor's new ones. Once she was dressed, her maid insisted on re-pining her hair. Finally Jobert stepped back. "That should do it."

Eleanor glanced in the mirror. She appeared older. It must be the gown. It was designed for a young matron. There was nothing she could do about her puffy eyes, but she pinched her cheeks to get some color into them. She would listen to what he had to say before she decided. "I am ready."

Jobert held the door open. "The blue parlor, my lady."

It appeared the household knew what was going on. "Thank you, Jobert."

Eleanor made her way to the room that was halfway between the breakfast room and Matt's study. When she reached the door she paused and took a deep breath. The next few minutes would decide the rest of her life. Slowly, she reached out and lifted the latch, opening the door. Montagu stood with his back to the room staring out the window.

He turned around when she stepped into the room. "Thank God you have come." He strode forward, stopping just a foot or so away from her. He searched her face, his eyes pleading. It was all she could do not to run into his arms. But what he said now would define their lives. "Please forgive me." His arms came up, as if he would reach out to her, then he dropped them. "I was terrified you could have been hurt or worse, but that is no excuse for the way I spoke to you. I was wrong." His strong neck worked as he swallowed hard. "I promise you I will never attempt to forbid you anything. All I ask is that you tell me when you are doing something dangerous. Let me be a part of your schemes." John took another step closer to her. "Please be my partner and allow me to be yours."

Eleanor wanted to trust him. "Do you mean everything you said? Because if you do not, tell me now."

"I mean every word from the bottom of my soul."

This time she searched his face, his eyes, but all she could see was his love for her. "Yes. I will be your partner."

He drew her into his arms and tears flooded her eyes. "I was so angry and so sad at the same time."

Holding her tight, John nuzzled her hair. "Thank you for taking me back."

She pressed her body against him and felt something hard digging into her. "What do you have in your waistcoat pocket?"

"I have something for you. If you don't like it, we'll find another one." Still holding her close, he took out a gold ring set with a square ruby. Two diamonds flanked each side. "With everything going on, we forgot the ring."

She held out her right hand and he slipped it on. "It is beautiful."

"But not as beautiful as you are, both in your manner and your face." He wrapped his arms around her again. "I love you."

"I love you too." She leaned into him, feeling his warmth and love. Her sister was right. John had been afraid.

The door opened and Matt, accompanied by Grace, strolled into the room.

"Do I need to remind you we are attending the opera this evening?" Grace said.

Eleanor had completely forgotten. She glanced around the room before remembering there was no clock in there. "What time is it?"

"Almost time for dinner," Matt said. He looked at John. "I have sent for your valet. There is no point in you going home to change."

"Thank you." John smiled down at her.

"How is Alice feeling?" Eleanor asked. "Will she be able to come?"

"No." Grace shook her head. "But we will attend again. I know how much Montagu wanted to see his first opera and I could not put it off any longer if we were to go before your wedding."

That was now only two days away. Eleanor held John's hand. She knew he would find he loved the opera as much as she did.

"We will make a family showing," Grace said. "I had a visit from Aunt Herndon. Apparently, several people saw you two arguing and Eleanor walking away."

That was just what they did not need. Gossip. It would not last long, but it was still aggravating. She shrugged one shoulder. "Once they see us happily together the talk will die."

CHAPTER THIRTY-SEVEN

Ever since the men Dobbins had hired to kill Lady Eleanor had failed and been taken up by the police, he'd been hiding in different squalid rooms. This was all that bitch's fault. He hated this city. He hated that he didn't have any status, that there was no one who looked up to him or at least obeyed him. And if he wanted a woman, he had to pay for her. He peered in the small, poorly made mirror at his hair. He had to use blacking to make his hair darker and change how he looked. He stopped staring in the looking glass. The men he'd hired must have told the police everything they knew. The constables had gone to the pub where he'd met the scabs and then started searching the area. He'd got out of the place he was staying just in time but lost the money he'd paid for the week. The newssheet Dobbins had read said her wedding would be in two days. He just wasn't sure of the time. Marrying some lord, she was. He'd make sure she never saw her wedding night. Dobbins wished he had a pop. It'd be easier than a knife. But pops cost a lot. A knife would have to do. Besides, no one would expect him to be at the church.

John really had enjoyed the opera, but he would have liked it better if he knew Italian. The gossip had turned out to be more humorous than not. Several gentlemen who had not, apparently, seen him enter with Eleanor and her family, visited the box only to be disappointed when he greeted them.

The following day Worthington, Charlie Stanwood, his other future brothers-in-law, Turley, and Exeter all came to see John. "To what do I owe the honor?"

"We need to make a plan for tomorrow," Stanwood said. "There have not been any more attempts on Eleanor, but the blackguard is still out there. He knows who she is, and news of your wedding has been in the gossip columns."

He was right. There had been no further attacks on her yet. The criminals had given up the man who hired them, but he'd not been found. John knew another attempt would be made and he'd just as soon have it over with.

"We do know who the scoundrel might be," Stanwood said. "Worthington received a letter from the steward at the estate where the mine is located. He wrote that a man by the name of Dobbins had been extremely angry about being dismissed. He gave a description, but I have to assume the man has disguised himself."

That was something, John supposed. "How do you suggest we proceed?"

"Eleanor will come in the side door," Worthington said. "That is quite common, and what we had planned to do in any event. However, the carriage will be moved to the steps outside the front door. Naturally you and she will be expected to walk out that way. You cannot carry anything but your bride's arm, but we have all agreed to bring our sword sticks. Additionally, the footmen and coachman will be armed."

"Random people often sit in the back of the church to watch the weddings," Rothwell said. "We will have our men there as well."

"There is one ceremony before yours," Kenilworth said. "We'll start keeping watch as that service is getting started."

They were correct, of course. John could not carry a

cane to the wedding, but he could keep it in the town coach. It was comforting that many of the footmen and grooms were former military men. "It sounds like everything is covered. I shall keep an eye on the people around us."

"You will be lucky if you see anyone but Eleanor," Exeter said.

Turley rose. "And now a toast." He glanced at John. "I hope you don't mind, but I had Lumner fetch some champagne." His friend went to the door and opened it. "Please bring it in."

John lifted a brow. "My champagne."

"Of course yours." Turley started filling the glasses.

"Does he do this often?" Stanwood asked.

"Every time he visits." John took his glass. "Fortunately, it's not often."

After dinner that evening, his mother had surprised him by remembering a ruby parure was among the Montagu jewels. He'd give them to Eleanor when they arrived in Paris. For her wedding gift, he had bought a ruby pendant and earrings of a more modern design she could wear whenever she wished.

As he was getting ready to seek his couch, he glanced around his bedchamber. This was the last night he'd sleep in a room that reminded him of a dungeon and the last night he'd sleep alone.

John yawned as his valet helped him out of his jacket. Turley and Exeter would be here no later than eight to join John for breakfast and accompany him to the church. He and Eleanor would use his traveling coach to depart from Worthington House. It was all going just as they had planned.

He woke up the next morning and swung his legs over the side of the bed. Today was the day he took Eleanor as his own. He'd even bought a new jacket, trousers, and waistcoat. His shoes had been shined even more highly than they usually were. He finished tying his cravat, and his valet handed him a sapphire tiepin that he nestled in his cravat. Then he joined his friends for breakfast.

The clock chimed the hour and he rose. "We'd better get to the church."

"You have an hour," Exeter said. "There is another wedding going on now."

"Aside from that," Turley swallowed the last of his tea, "if you arrive too early, you are only going to become nervous and look at your watch every second or so."

"I am not nervous. I am excited. I want to be there when she arrives."

The ticking from the fireplace mantel seemed too slow. "Has anyone wound that clock?"

"It is wound every day, my lord," Lumner said.

"You see." Turley poured a cup from a fresh pot of tea. "It is happening already."

Finally, at eight thirty, they agreed to travel to the church. They arrived just as the first ceremony was ending. Shortly afterward, his future brothers-in-law arrived with their ladies.

"You are much too early," Kenilworth said.

John almost rolled his eyes. "Not you too. That's what Turley and Exeter told me."

His mother, sister, and Lytton arrived, and John opened his pocket watch. Damn, he still had almost ten minutes before Eleanor would get there.

"There he goes," Rothwell commented. "Pacing. It's all a man can do."

Lady Merton sighed. "You do realize this happens at every wedding? Rothwell, you were no better. By the time Louisa arrived you had convinced yourself she had jilted you."

"Why are all of you here so early?" John asked.

"To keep you company," Lady Kenilworth said. "Once the children and Grace arrive, Eleanor will come shortly thereafter."

He glanced at the growing number of what Rothwell rightly termed "random" people taking their places at the back of the church, and his neck started to prick him. When he looked again, he recognized one of the Worthington footmen dressed in regular clothing and knew there were more. He took out his pocket watch again, then put it away. Eleanor would arrive soon. Worthington and Stanwood were with her and her sisters. Until the service was over, there was nothing to worry about.

Finally, it was time to kill the bitch. Dobbins had gone by the massive church they called St. George's a few times during the past two days. It seemed like it was always busy with weddings. One after another, all morning long. Fancy carriages came and let people out, then waited until the same people were ready to leave. It was nothin' at all like a village wedding, where everyone showed up and stayed outside, talking for a bit. These people got in and got out in a rush. But like a village wedding, anyone could walk in and watch the couple get married. He sat through a couple of the ceremonies to see how it worked. Unfortunately, it looked like he'd have to kill her in the church. He wasn't a religious man, but he knew he'd probably go to hell for that. But he couldn't see how hell could be any worse than his life now. He'd gone down to the docks and almost hired on as a seaman to America. But this was his home and he didn't want to leave. He just wanted his life back. He finished his piece of bread and set out early, walking to the church near Hanover Square. As he expected, there were a lot of folks around for a nob's wedding.

"I'll wager we'll see a duke today," one old woman said.

"How do ye know that?" another woman asked.

"Been to a lot of these Worthington weddings, I have." The old woman's grin showed her missing teeth. "All the brothers and sisters come to the church."

"Lud! That'll be a show, won't it?"

"Always is." The old woman nodded. "Be close to get the vails they give out. Right generous they are."

"When'll they be here?" the other woman asked.

"Can't say, but you'll see all the carriages."

The fools always brought money to give to the people hanging around. Dobbins found a place against the building. When she got there he'd go to the church door and wait. If he killed her outside the door, it wouldn't be as much of a sin. Once she was dead, everything'd go back to the way it should be. An hour later he watched a couple go off and another coach arrive, but there was no one in it. A few minutes later some nobs came out of the church, followed by a couple. Other people joined them when the couple got in the carriage. So much for thinking he'd be able to do it outside the door. He'd never get to Lady Eleanor standing here. He had to get into the church.

Eleanor stood still as her dresser lifted a cream-colored gown with red, gold, and green embroidery over her head. A wide red sash tied just under her bosom. Her bonnet was made of silk the same color as her gown, decorated with flowers and a red ribbon.

A knock came on the door and Jobert opened it. "My lady, a box for you from Lord Montagu."

She wondered what it could be. He had already given her a ring. Of course that would be handed to Alice to give to Turley for the wedding ring. Eleanor opened the square box.

"Oh my. Look at these." A large ruby set in gold hung from a gold chain. Earrings made to match the necklace were nestled in the middle. "Put the pearls away. I'll wear the rubies and switch to the pearls for our journey."

A few seconds later another knock sounded. "Come."

Mary, Theo, Alice, Madeline, Elizabeth, Constance, and Vivienne piled into the room.

"I am to give you this bracelet." Alice handed Eleanor a slim bracelet of rubies set in gold. "It is quite old and belonged to our mother, and her mother before her. We thought it would go well with your ring."

"Thank you." She hugged her sister. "It is just the right choice."

"This is something blue," Elizabeth gave her embroidered handkerchiefs with three blue flowers embroidered on them.

They were a little lopsided and lumpy, but they were the most beautiful handkerchiefs Eleanor had ever seen. "These are lovely, thank you."

The girls filed past, giving Eleanor hugs.

Mary and Theo were next. "This is new." Theo handed Eleanor a cream silk reticule with red drawstrings. "We designed it ourselves."

"And made it," Mary added.

"Thank you both so much." Eleanor embraced them.

"And last but not least." Madeline held out the garnet combs she had bought. "Something borrowed. I want them back when you change after the wedding."

Eleanor grinned. "These are one of your most treasured possessions. Thank you."

"Girls, it's time to go," Grace said. "You will see Eleanor at the church."

"Mama, Aunt Grace." Gideon and Hugh dashed into the bedchamber. "The coach is ready."

They were both dressed in their best skeleton suits, with wide white colors trimmed with a thin band of lace. The boys also had top hats made especially for them and carried short canes. "You are both very dapper."

Hugh gave Eleanor a suspicious look. "What does that mean?"

"Well dressed and handsome."

"Oh." He stood up straighter. "Thank you, Aunt Eleanor."

"Mama." Gideon took Grace's hand.

"We are going." With her other hand she waved the girls forward. "Matt and Charlie will be waiting."

Eleanor and her sisters waited until the children left. "It's time."

"No crying." Alice took out one of the handkerchiefs Eleanor had put in her new reticule. "You will set us all off, and you do not want puffy eyes for your wedding."

"I am just so happy."

"Grace's coach has gone," Charlie said from the doorway. "Eleanor, you look radiant."

"Are you giving me away?" Eleanor had not been able to make up her mind. Matt had acted in lieu of a father for the past six years, but Charlie was her brother and the head of the Carpenter family. She loved them both. Someone had suggested they draw straws, but she was still not certain of the resolution.

"We both are." Her brother grinned. "It only seemed fair."

"It is a good decision." Now neither of them would feel slighted.

Charlie held out his arm to Eleanor. "Ladies, your coach awaits."

"My bouquet." She glanced around.

"I have it," Madeline said.

Matt and two footmen stood by the coach and assisted her sisters into the carriage while Charlie helped her. The footmen stepped onto the back platform of the carriage. Once they were settled, Matt gave the order to depart.

"How long will you stay at the wedding breakfast?" Madeline asked.

"An hour or so, I imagine. Turley gave John the name of a hotel on the way to Dover. We will spend the night there."

"Have you decided how long you will be gone?" Alice said.

"It will take several days to travel from Calais to Paris, and we would like to have two weeks there. Therefore, it will be close to a month. I will write to you, and we will stop in Town on our way to Montagu Hall." It occurred to Eleanor a great deal could happen in a month. "If either of you decide to wed, write to me immediately and we will return."

"I do not think you need to worry about that," Alice commented. "At least not on my behalf."

The coach drew to a halt in front of the side door of the church. Eleanor and her family entered the transept via a recessed wooden door. Turley said something to John. He turned to face her. His Prussian blue jacket and trousers set off his auburn hair, making him more handsome than ever. But she was almost stopped by the joy on his face. He was as happy about this day as she was.

John could only stare at Eleanor as she made her way to him. She had worn his rubies. They glowed, setting off her flawless skin. He held out his arm. "Exquisite."

"Not yet," Worthington said to the soft laughter of his soon-to-be family.

Stanwood stood on Eleanor's other side, smiling.

"This family is certainly growing," the vicar said. "If everyone is ready, we shall begin."

John was not really surprised that both Worthington and Stanwood gave Eleanor away. All that mattered to John was that he had her now. They repeated their vows in strong voices, although they both blushed when he promised to worship her body. He'd been working on perfecting that for almost two weeks.

"With this ring, I thee wed." He slipped the ruby ring on her left hand this time. When the vicar proclaimed them man and wife, the only thing he wanted to do was protect her, and he almost carried her off out the side door. They had to end the threat as soon as possible.

"You must sign the register," the vicar whispered.

Once that was done, Eleanor placed her hand on his arm. "Shall we go?"

"Yes." John scanned the growing number of people who had decided to come to watch the weddings taking place that day.

They were almost to the door when a grimy man not far from Eleanor jumped up and shouted. It had to be Dobbins. John pushed her back behind him. His brothers-in-law ran in front of them, but the people abandoning the pews around the criminal kept them from getting to the man himself. From the corner of his eye, Hugh and Gideon were waving their canes, one on the pew behind the blackguard and the other on the same pew as the scoundrel. They rushed Dobbins and hit him on the head with the metal knobs of their canes. The man cowered for a second, but it was enough time for Turner to bash Dobbins on the head with the grip of his pistol, knocking the blackguard out.

"What the deuce were you thinking?" Kenilworth grabbed Hugh.

The boy's chin firmed. "We had to protect Aunt Eleanor."

"Papa." Gideon looked up at Worthington, who had a

firm hand on the child's collar. "He had a knife. No one was looking at us."

"We can't very well punish them," Kenilworth muttered.

"No. We can't." Worthington picked up his son. "But we can get them back to the house."

From behind John, Lady Alice drawled, "This is an interesting way of concluding a wedding ceremony."

"Interesting indeed," Lady Madeline said, "however, I do not think it should become the fashion."

John's jaw dropped. He had expected them to be at least a little frightened. Then he saw the parasols. They looked very much like Eleanor's.

Three constables ran in through the front door, the first one demanding to know what had happened.

"Montagu." Stanwood touched John's shoulder. "Leave others to speak with the constables. You and Eleanor should depart. Go out the side door. I'll send the coach around."

Less than forty minutes later, Turley and Merton were shown into the drawing room.

Merton accepted a glass of champagne. "We gave statements and agreed to testify. I told them both Stanwood and Worthington would press charges."

"I am glad it is over," Eleanor said.

Grace rose. "Our guests will be here soon."

Just over an hour after that, John and Eleanor were in his large traveling coach on their way to Canterbury for the night.

Eleanor had removed her bonnet and he placed it on the shelf above. "How long is the trip today?"

"About six hours. We'll arrive in time for dinner."

A slow smile dawned on her face. "I suppose we could talk about the weather or look at the view, but I can think of a better way to spend our time." She reached out and pulled the shade closest to her shut. "You?"

He pulled down his shade as well. "A much better way."

EPILOGUE

Eleanor and John had arrived that morning to discover Augusta was already in labor.

Not long afterward, Phinn strolled into the morning room holding a swaddled babe. "I would like you all to meet Mr. Anthony Hector Carter-Woods. We can't stay long. He's going to want to eat."

Everyone took turns either taking a small hand or looking at the newest member of the family.

Grace stroked the infant's head. "You must write to your brother. He will be delighted."

"He will," Phinn agreed, but he did not appear happy about it. "Augusta and I will not raise our son with all the pomp my brother had to endure."

"At least now the succession is secured." Matt gazed at the infant.

"There is that." Phinn juggled his son as Anthony started to fuss. "I must get him back to Augusta."

Eleanor stroked her swelling stomach that was still hidden by her gown. "I suppose it is time to tell you that John and I will have a baby this winter."

Rothwell grimaced. "I am never gambling with Kenilworth again."

"How much this time?" Matt grinned.

"A monkey."

Montagu Hall, February 1822

Eleanor cried out, and John downed the brandy he'd poured hours before. "I can't take this."

Kenilworth groaned. "Then go up to her and make sure they're using the birthing chair Charlotte brought. Don't let a doctor tell you what to do. She is your wife and those babies are your children."

"You're right. We should have called the midwife first."

"I'll see what's happened to her; you go to Eleanor."

John set down the glass and took the stairs two at a time. What he found was a deadlock in the birthing room. "What is going on?"

Charlotte pointed at the doctor. "I do not know why anyone could have thought he was the right person to attend Eleanor. This man has never used a birthing chair before."

Grace was sitting on the bed, speaking in a low voice with Eleanor.

"That's old-fashioned thinking, my lord." The doctor had apparently decided John could be there, but not to help Eleanor.

He decided to listen to his sisters-in-law. "Old-fashioned or not, these ladies have six children between them, including two sets of twins." He looked at Charlotte. "Are you able to manage until the midwife arrives? Kenilworth is finding out what is keeping her."

"We are. Your housekeeper has some experience of birthing as well." She put her hands on her hips. "She still has a ways to go. We must get her up and moving. It will make the process easier." She glared at the doctor. "She has been in that bed much too long."

John went to his wife. "Eleanor?"

"Yes, get me up. I do not think I can manage it by myself."

"If you won't listen to me, there is no point in my staying." The doctor closed his bag and huffed as he left the room.

"Good riddance," Eleanor muttered.

Now that she was on her feet, she seemed to be doing better. "I am starving."

"Something little," Grace said. "Too much might make you sick."

A maid slipped out of the chamber. "Refreshments will be here soon."

Eleanor walked around the room and then up and down the hall. She was getting ready to start on the other wing of the house when the midwife arrived.

"I'm sorry it took so long." The woman removed her bonnet as she entered the hall. "We had a bit of a problem with another birth, but mother and baby are well." His butler took her cloak. "How is her ladyship?"

John told her what had occurred with the doctor and what they were doing now.

"Excellent." The midwife smiled at him. He wished he could recall her name, but he'd only met her once. "I'll go to her now."

"She is walking around upstairs. One of her sisters is with her."

"Have either of the ladies had twins?"

"Both of them have." John wondered how Eleanor was doing. "I'll take you up to her." He found her doubled over in the west wing. "Is she all right?"

Charlotte continued rubbing Eleanor's back. "I think it's time to go back to the birthing room."

"You must be Lady Kenilworth," the midwife said. "I'm

Mrs. Fallows, the midwife. If you do not mind, I'd like to take a look at her ladyship."

Mrs. Fallows pressed on Eleanor's stomach as she went through another contraction. It was so strong, John could see it ripple under her gown. "You are correct. It is almost time."

Three stools stood around the birthing chair. One on each side and a lower one in front of the chair. He took the one on Eleanor's right and held her hand. The next thing he knew, she was crushing his fingers. He'd had no idea how strong she was.

"Push." The midwife reached beneath the chair. "Again, my lady. It won't be long now. I can see the first one's head." John tried to bend down and look, but Eleanor's grip got stronger. "There we are." Mrs. Fallows passed the baby covered in white stuff to Grace.

"Is it all right? What is it?"

"*He* is fine," Grace said with a smile. "We just need to get this little fellow cleaned."

A son. I have a son!

John wondered if a daughter would be next. That seemed to be the trend in the family.

"Push once more, my lady." The midwife held out her hands. "Another little boy."

Two sons! "How are we going to tell them apart?"

"For the moment at least," Grace said as she took the second child, "they have different color hair. The first has blond hair, and the second one has reddish hair.

"That will make it easier."

"You will have to watch them. The hair might fall out or change color," she advised.

"This is the last time, my lady. Push."

His jaw dropped. "Is there another one?"

Mrs. Fallows shook her head. "She must deliver the afterbirth."

He watched in horror as two bloody bags slid out of his wife. "That's the afterbirth?"

"It is, my lord."

Grace handed him the first baby. John had never held a person so little in his life. A rush of love so strong it almost brought tears to his eyes overcame him as he gazed down at his firstborn. "How did we make such a perfect being?"

Eleanor was being helped from the chair. "I do not know. He is beautiful."

While she was being cleaned and the bed readied, Charlotte handed him the second baby. This one was just as perfect as the first. The love he felt for this baby was just as strong as for the first. What would they be like as they grew?

"John." Charlotte held out her hands. "I want to hold at least one of them."

"Yes. Of course. They are perfect." He handed her the first one. "I can't keep thinking of them as the first and second. We were so sure we'd have a boy and a girl. We don't have two boys' names."

"What is the first name?" Charlotte asked.

"Adam, after John's father, Timothy after our grand-uncle, and Charles after Charlie," Eleanor said. "The Earl of Fauconberg."

"We already have two Gideons, so you do not want to select that name," Charlotte mused.

"Why not pick our maternal grandfather's name, John's maternal grandfather's name, and the name of someone he admires?" Grace suggested.

All three of them, looked at him and waited. "What is the first name?"

"Bertin," Eleanor said.

"Very well. The second name is Oliver and the third name will be Fredrick, after my grand-uncle on my father's side."

The babies began to fuss.

"They must be hungry." Eleanor unbuttoned her nightgown, and Grace showed her how to nurse the baby.

"I'll get the wet nurse, my lady." Jobert hurried out of the room and returned a few seconds later with a young woman, who took the child from him.

"I suppose I should tell Kenilworth he is an uncle to two boys."

"Hugh will be thrilled that there are more boy cousins." The man strolled into the room and glanced around. "I see I am a bit de trop. I shall go down and announce the news."

"I'll go with you. We must have a meal served up here and in the family dining room."

Eleanor grinned at John. "Congratulations, my lord. You have sons."

He kissed her lightly on the lips. "Congratulations, my lady, you have sons."

AUTHOR'S NOTES

In 1821, Almack's was still a necessary venue for marriage-minded ladies. The Patronesses, more properly called the Lady Patronesses, did indeed run it like a fiefdom. Money played no part in being able to procure a voucher. Rank and bloodlines were what was important. But even some in the highest ranks were not allowed to attend if they led dissolute lives or had insulted one or more of the Patronesses. The dress code was strictly enforced, and it is true that Wellington was denied permission to enter. Some accounts say it was because he wore trousers and some say because he had arrived after eleven, the cut-off time to enter.

There are some words that might have sounded strange to you. I used "gigglish" instead of "giggly" because the latter was not used until after the middle of the century.

Interestingly, ladies' fashions were not changing much at this time. The high waist was still fashionable, although the skirts were fuller. However, gentlemen's fashions were changing. Trousers, a narrower cut than used for day wear, were beginning to be accepted for evening wear. The exceptions were at Court and at Almack's.

A chapeau bras—which really did fold—had been de rigueur for evening wear. But by 1821, collapsible top hats were more common and the chapeau bras was only required at court and at Almack's. Truthfully, I have no idea what gentlemen did with their hats. I do know that they could not dance with them. Ergo they must have gone in the cloakroom.

Eleanor and John were twenty years ahead of their time

trying to write bills concerning mine reform. The first bill to pass was the Mines Act of 1842. It restricted working underground in mines to men and boys ten and older. Before then, children as young as four were found working underground. The act also allowed miners to select inspectors from their ranks. English miners do not seem to have been treated as badly as in the United States, where they were paid in company paper and not real currency, but there was plenty of mistreatment of the workers by the companies and the overseers.

Giuditta Pasta was a famous opera singer who was performing in London during 1821. She has been described as a nineteenth-century Maria Callas. In 1821, she performed in the opera *Norma*, which Bellini wrote for her.

Marriage settlement agreements set out a lady's financial future, both during the marriage and after her husband's death. They also provided funds for children other than the heir, such as dowries for any girls born of the union and younger sons. Some of you might ask why Matt would have negotiated with Phinn's brother. The reason is that an heir or a younger son who did not have his own money was dependent on the title holder for funds. Phinn did have independent means, but he also received money from the marquisate. Those of you who read *Desiring Lady Caro* might remember that Huntley and Caro's fathers argued over the agreements.

"Grutch" means "grouse," a word that was not used until the twentieth century.

Horripilation—I fell in love with this word. It is the proper term for gooseflesh, the latter being a vulgar term at this time.

Sword parasols did exist. In most of them, the sword had to be removed from the parasol, which I think is awkward. However, the technology did exist for blades to be thrust out and retracted. Therefore, Walter's idea could have been used at the time.

Regency weddings were nothing like modern ones. In larger cities, the wedding was attended only by close family. There was no kissing after the bride and groom were pronounced man and wife. There is some evidence that in villages the whole population would attend. But in cities, especially London, strangers were known to just go to watch the wedding ceremony.

Doctors for childbirth were problematic. It is now believed, and might have been believed at the time, that Princess Charlotte's death and that of her baby's was due to the doctor attending her. He committed suicide afterward. Unfortunately, in London midwives were almost frozen out of work because of extremely onerous requirements. However, in the countryside they were frequently used. Birthing chairs allowed gravity to help the baby arrive.

I hope you enjoyed Eleanor and John's story, and a return to the Worthingtons. Please visit my website, www.ellaquinnauthor.com for the latest news and books, to follow me on social media, or sign up for my newsletter.

Ella

Visit our website at
KensingtonBooks.com
to sign up for our newsletters, read
more from your favorite authors, see
books by series, view reading group
guides, and more!

Become a Part of Our
Between the Chapters Book Club
Community and Join the Conversation